CORRIGAN

CORRIGAN

Caroline Blackwood

HEINEMANN : LONDON

William Heinemann Ltd
10 Upper Grosvenor Street, London W1X 9PA
LONDON   MELBOURNE   TORONTO
JOHANNESBURG   AUCKLAND

First published in Great Britain 1984
Copyright © Caroline Blackwood 1984
SBN 434 07467 5

Phototypeset by Wyvern Typesetting Limited, Bristol
Printed and bound in Great Britain by
Biddles Ltd, Guildford and King's Lynn

To Evgenia, Ivana and Sheridan

I

'There's a crippled gentleman at the door. And he wants to see you!'

Mrs Murphy came slamming into her employer's bedroom with this excited announcement and Mrs Blunt gave a little shiver of astonishment. She was sitting up in bed reading *The Times*. Since her husband had died three years ago she saw very few people. Living alone in her pretty little period house on the edge of a remote village in Wiltshire she felt that she should try to keep abreast of current events.

Very little happened in Mrs Blunt's life and sometimes it frightened her that she now lived so much in the past. She grieved continually for her husband but her grief was discreet and subdued. Mrs Blunt dressed in pearl-grey rather than black, for she saw black as too violent and final. Almost every afternoon she took a walk to the village churchyard where the Colonel was buried. She liked to put fresh flowers in front of his gravestone. This was easy for her in the summer for she obtained them from a market garden in the neighbourhood. In winter she had an arrangement with an expensive florist in Salisbury who delivered them to her in a van. After she had taken her bouquet to the cemetery, she would go back home and make tea.

When Mrs Murphy came into her bedroom and told Mrs Blunt about the arrival of the cripple, Mrs Blunt gave a shiver not only because it was so seldom that anyone rang her bell, but because the rowdiness of Mrs Murphy's behaviour still continued to shock and surprise her.

Mrs Murphy was an astonishingly noisy woman. Mrs Blunt had never got used to the way she seemed incapable of knocking gently and waiting before entering a room. She always only ever banged on the door with her huge and ham-coloured fist, then without waiting for any reply she would come barging in.

Mrs Murphy never climbed Mrs Blunt's stairs, she always stormed them like a military unit making a headlong charge to gain some useful vantage-point. She was very short and her squat body carried enormous weight. Yet she still moved around the house with a pointless but frenetic speed. When she charged up Mrs Blunt's staircase, she always managed to make the carpet slippers that she wore, since shoes hurt her swollen feet, sound just as menacing as the running tread of regimental boots.

Mrs Blunt had no real need to employ Mrs Murphy to come in to clean her house. She ate almost nothing now she was alone and she was very tidy by nature. Mrs Murphy was always offering to make her nourishing soups and stews, because she was very troubled that her employer had become so thin. Mrs Blunt would refuse these offers with as much politeness as she could muster, for Mrs Murphy's gastronomic skills were scanty. She was reckless in her use of fat which she poured over her food, straight from the pan, treating it as a sauce.

But although Mrs Blunt saw Mrs Murphy as a rather barbaric figure and attributed her ability to create needless and violent commotion to her Irish origins, she was often very grateful for her talent for extracting the maximum amount of noise from the dullest of everyday routines.

Lying in bed in the morning with the lilac wall-paper of her bedroom enclosing the grey mist of loss and nostalgia that seemed to seep out of her brain and then re-enter it, Mrs Blunt was quite glad to hear the sound of Mrs Murphy crashing about downstairs in the kitchen. She rather liked to hear her slamming the frying-pan against the steel of the sink with such savage gusto that she might have been beating a gong. It created the illusion that her house was still the centre of some kind of important activity.

Mrs Murphy was very uncoordinated, and as a result she continually dropped things. She was frank about her breakages and never tried to conceal them from Mrs Blunt. She would come careening into the soft-hued bedroom carrying the jagged pieces of some cup or plate she had just smashed. She would then become histrionic and the explanations that she made to excuse her elephantine clumsiness were so raucous and emotional that Mrs Blunt sometimes wondered if she was drunk. Mrs Blunt didn't really mind if Mrs Murphy was drunk any more than she minded about the damage that she kept inflicting on her china. She had ceased to care what happened to her possessions. Since her husband had died, she no longer felt that she needed them. She would gaze blankly at the broken pieces of the object that Mrs Murphy kept waving at her. She would register with melancholy that she had suffered yet another loss. But it was a loss that she saw as small.

Mrs Murphy stopped working and went home at lunch-time and when Mrs Blunt heard the disagreeable fading splutter of the exhaust of her motor bike as she went roaring away, she always regretted her departure. Mrs Murphy liked to talk to her incessantly and with great ebullience. Most of her talk tended to revolve around the activities of her teenage sons, Seamus and Patrick. Mrs Blunt had been rather careful never to allow this unruly couple to come to her house, but as their mother spoke with such explosive emotion as she described their exploits, they had become very vivid to her and were almost like companions, for she often had the impression that they were rampaging round it.

According to Mrs Murphy, Seamus and Patrick were the unhappy victims of the Salisbury police. Mrs Blunt had a conventional respect for the law and Mrs Murphy was always trying to open her eyes to its corruption.

'Those pigs in uniform,' she would say. 'They go for the Irish and they go for the fatherless . . .'

Mrs Blunt certainly felt this to be the case as she listened to the various corrupt and trumped-up charges they were always issuing against Mrs Murphy's sons.

The Salisbury police seemed to her indefatigable in their role of oppressors as she heard how they continually planted Seamus and Patrick with stolen motor bikes and hi-fi equipment and hauls of marijuana. Mrs Blunt never quite knew which of these two boys was currently serving a sentence in a remand home for delinquents, which was making an appeal, which had recently been released. Convinced of their innocence, and with her belief in British justice rudely damaged, Mrs Blunt put up bail for them whenever she was told that they needed her support. They were real to her to the extent that they appeared to have inherited all the vigour of their mother. They were unreal to her in so far as the turbulence of their illicit activities extended beyond the perimeters of consciousness that were permitted by her grief.

When Mrs Murphy got off the subject of the persecution of her two boys, she would regale Mrs Blunt with various inconsequential scraps of news to which she gave such importance she could have been issuing international war bulletins.

'You'd never believe it! It's a terrible thing. Do you know that storm last night – it brought down a tree right there in Coombe Lane. Someone could have been under it . . .'

'Yes, I heard the storm last night,' Mrs Blunt would say. 'How awful about the tree.'

'Those new people that bought the pub in Main Street, they're painting it up, you know. They've got all these ladders up the front of it. It's going to be a beautiful place when they finish with it. You ought to take a look at it.'

As Mrs Murphy prattled, Mrs Blunt's replies would have less and less animation. 'Oh really,' she'd say with her blue eyes looking more and more distant.

She knew Mrs Murphy was trying to nurse her. She suspected that Mrs Murphy saw her as an invalid and that when she brought her these pointless pieces of local news, she was offering them like the broth with which she so often attempted to nurture her. And although she occasionally wished Mrs Murphy would give up trying to cheer her by keeping her informed of every small local happening, once Mrs Murphy had gone zooming off she always started to feel the panic of a small child who has been left alone in the dark. It was as if all energy had left her house. She had nothing to distract her except the sounds from the garden, the tweet of the birds, the patter of the rain, the rustling branches of a tree.

Mrs Blunt would turn on her radio, and try to write a letter to her married daughter who lived in London. But she felt her letters were so dull that she almost invariably tore them up. Mrs Blunt found she had nothing to tell Nadine that would fill a page. She would end up by writing her daughter a postcard.

'I am very well. Life is very quiet. Long to hear your news. I know you must be very busy with the children. Is there a hope that one of these days you might all come down . . .?'

When Mrs Blunt heard about the arrival of the crippled gentleman, for a moment her reaction was totally irrational. She thought that her husband had come back and was outside her door asking to see her. It was as if in some buried part of her mind, she had always been expecting this to happen. All his tweed suits were still hanging in the cupboards, and his beautifully polished shoes were in a rack. His well-laundered shirts still lay in his chest of drawers. It had never occurred to her to throw them out.

In the grey limbo in which she had existed since his death, she still retained the feeling that she was endlessly waiting for something miraculous to happen. She hardly dared to admit what she kept waiting for. She dreaded that good sense might destroy the only fantasy which enabled her to endure her aimless existence. But now, hearing that a cripple was outside her door, she felt a surge of joy, believing that her husband had returned. She didn't stop to ask herself how he had managed to accomplish this. She just accepted that he had come home. She didn't even find it all that amazing. Nor was Mrs Blunt surprised by the idea that he had come back crippled. If death had somehow maimed him – that was to be expected – it could all be woven into the fabric of her wishful thinking.

'Shall I carry the gentleman's invalid chair up the steps and put him in the drawing-room?'

This question immediately shattered Mrs Blunt's little

moment of happiness. All her old feelings of loss and sadness returned. She found the mention of the invalid chair extremely cruel. The chair was such a concrete object that it was impossible for Mrs Blunt to incorporate it within her pipe-dream. She could vault away from reality and let herself believe that her husband had made a supernatural return, but the mention of the chair forced her to ask disturbing and painful questions. Where – and how – could her husband have obtained it?

'Yes, I suppose you'd better put the gentleman in the drawing-room,' she told Mrs Murphy. She realised she was giving dangerous instructions. If Mrs Murphy tried to carry the wheelchair up the front steps, being such a rough and clumsy woman she would very probably drop it and then the poor wretch would tip out on his head. But now she knew she had to face the fact that the crippled visitor was not her husband, she felt so cheated and depressed that she didn't really care what happened to him.

'Tell him he'll have to wait until I get dressed. I really can't see a stranger in my night clothes. And why does he want to see me anyway?' Mrs Blunt suddenly sounded peevish.

Mrs Murphy shrugged and went clumping off downstairs. Mrs Blunt could hear the sound of her crashing round as she lifted the wheelchair into the hall. Mrs Murphy kept shouting encouragements to the visitor in the way that grooms sometimes shout at a horse. 'Easy! Easy! Hold it! You're nearly there! That's a boy!'

Mrs Blunt got out of bed and slowly got herself dressed. Her mood was now one of self-disgust. It frightened her to think that she could have been insane enough to imagine even for one moment that the visiting gentleman could be her husband. She wondered if her mind was going. She had read an article in some magazine which claimed that people who lived alone for long periods started to become deranged. They conversed with the dead. They saw things that weren't there . . .

She felt angry with herself, angry with her crippled visitor. She had no desire to go down and speak to him. She loathed him. She saw him as an impostor. But she combed her pale silvery curls and put on a little pale pink lipstick. Dressed as

6

usual in pearl-grey, Mrs Blunt went down the stairs and entered the drawing-room.

She found her visitor seated in his wheelchair in front of her little marble fireplace. He introduced himself as Corrigan. She found it slightly peculiar that he told her only his surname, but she very soon accepted it because she thought that this single name somehow suited him. Corrigan had dark hair and a thin gaunt face. His eyes were bluish-green with long black lashes. He looked about thirty-five. He was a large man with very broad shoulders. He was wearing a tweed jacket, a white shirt, and a red tie. His bent knees were wrapped in a heavy brown tartan rug.

He apologised for disturbing Mrs Blunt. She noticed that his accent was Irish and she found his manner pleasant.

'Your good lady has the strength of a female Hercules,' Corrigan said to her with a smile. 'While she was lifting me up into your house she made me feel like Icarus. I felt I was soaring towards the sun!'

Mrs Blunt thought this quite a curious way to describe his entrance and the aid that he had received from Mrs Murphy. However, she agreed with him that Mrs Murphy was a very powerful woman.

Corrigan was holding a box of white paper flags in his lap. He explained that he was selling them to raise money for the disabled. He was making an appeal for a fund that would go to an institution called St Crispins which was a home for the handicapped in London. Apparently this hospital was run almost entirely on private donations and it received very little state support. Corrigan had spent three years being cared for in this nursing home. He would always be eternally grateful for the loving care and the superb medical attention that he had received there from the staff.

'They helped to lighten "the heavy and the weary weight of this unintelligible world",' Corrigan said.

He went on to explain that although the level of nursing was extremely high at St Crispins, the institution lacked the money to provide the various recreational facilities which were so vital for those who had to spend their life in a chair. There was only

7

one television set in the whole building and it was an extremely old one and it gave a very bad and fuzzy picture. The library at St Crispins was also inadequate.

'In fact, it's a holy abomination,' he said.

He wanted to see it equipped with interesting reading matter rather than the trashy old second-hand thrillers and love stories which was all it had at the moment. If he could raise the funds, he would like to see that the library contained educational and foreign books, as well as all the English classics. He would also like to provide it with various serious games that would stimulate the mind and the imagination.

'If you have lost the use of your body, at least you ought to get the chance to use your brain,' he said.

Mrs Blunt shifted nervously. She was embarrassed by Corrigan's mention of his infirmity. She found it very upsetting that such a big well-built man should be condemned to life in a wheelchair.

'It has been said that excessive studying is nothing more than a form of sloth,' he said. 'I've never been able to believe that. When I first became a patient at St Crispins, I studied so excessively that I think it would be harsh to say that I was slothful. My mother was a librarian, so I was extremely fortunate. She used to smuggle me out great loads of books in huge paper carriers. I'd finish them all by the morning, and then she'd slip them back to the library and no one would be any the wiser.'

'I used to enjoy reading very much,' Mrs Blunt said. 'But recently I have hardly been reading at all. I keep telling myself I should read much more.'

'Yes, you *certainly* should read much more.' Corrigan stared at her accusingly. 'Mark Twain said that the man who refuses to read good books has very little advantage over the man who is unable to read them.'

'Oh, dear, did he say that? I'm afraid it's probably true.'

'Of course it's true. You can tell a man's character from the books you see on his shelves. But if you applied that same test to all the patients who know they've got to stay until they die in St Crispins it would be a very cruel way to judge them.'

8

'You're right. You're making me feel quite ashamed.'

'If I made you feel ashamed – I must profoundly apologise. This whole subject of books and reading is a dangerous one for me. I should try to avoid it. I feel too violently about it. Now I'm the one who feels the shame. You must think me very ill-mannered and presumptuous. And that's the last thing I want when you've been so kind as to ask me into your beautiful house.'

'Oh, I didn't find you in the least ill-mannered.' Mrs Blunt was lying. She had not enjoyed the conversation – any criticism made her very nervous. She was certain that he had intended to criticise her when he'd mentioned the plight of the patients in St Crispins. And now that he seemed so ashamed of himself and had started to apologise to her, he was making her feel worse.

'Everything you said was very interesting,' she murmured. 'Everything you said was very true.'

'Even if it was true – I'd no right to start haranguing you in such an inexcusable fashion. And nothing that I said was intended as a criticism – you must believe that.'

Mrs Blunt still didn't believe that for one moment, but she nodded uneasily, finding it easier to pretend that she accepted his statement.

'When you told me that you'd given up reading it really distressed me,' Corrigan said. 'I felt you'd shut out the only world where you can find infinity within the finite. I don't think anyone can shut that out with complete inpunity.'

Mrs Blunt, who only ever glanced at *The Times* in the morning and sometimes even restricted her reading to the obituary column because she found its contents in keeping with her general mood, wished that Corrigan would change the subject. She knew that the world he had just referred to was certainly not to be found in the only reading matter that could nowadays keep her interest.

'If I could tell you a little about myself,' Corrigan said, 'perhaps you'll understand why I'm such a fanatic about reading and maybe you'll forgive me for having tried to convert you to my particular way of thinking.'

Mrs Blunt was certainly curious to learn more about this dark, intense man who'd come bursting into the uneventful langour of her morning and had instantly started chiding her in a manner to which she was not at all accustomed.

'In the period when I first entered St Crispins,' Corrigan said, 'reading was not just an enjoyable hobby for me. It was obviously far, far more than that – it was the only thing that could cut the chain that grinds into the flesh of the prisoner . . .'

'I can understand that,' Mrs Blunt murmured. She then felt that her response had been most inept.

'I'd always had a passion for Irish poetry,' Corrigan continued, 'but when I was in hospital, thanks to my mother, I was able to start reading much more widely. At that point in my life, my days had a hideous and unforgettable monotony which was only broken by bouts of fearful pain, so it was very necessary that I find something outside all that – if I was to make any bid for survival. I had to breathe some air that was not saturated with anaesthetic. I made poetry my air hole. It could bring me the lily and the lotus. I made it my wine, I made it my wine and my walnuts. You look a little confused when I say all this. I know that I am getting carried away by my images. But I'm sure you can grasp what I mean . . .'

'Yes, I really do think I can understand,' Mrs Blunt said with sudden fervour. 'And would you perhaps care for a glass of wine?' She then looked nervously at her watch. She didn't want him to think she was a debauchee, making this impetuous offer at such an early hour of the morning.

Corrigan said he would prefer to have coffee and Mrs Blunt felt faintly rebuffed. She only had one bottle of wine in the house. It was a bottle of claret that she had bought for the Colonel on the same day that he had suffered his heart attack. Because her husband had never been able to drink it, she saw it as sacred and had kept it as if it was a relic. She'd often seen Mrs Murphy looking at it with an expression of scorn. She obviously thought it very stupid that it should be preserved as a holy memento.

Corrigan had no idea of the symbolic importance of the wine he'd just refused.

'As I've told you – reading was my only life-line when I was in hospital. That's why I started to have this dream of building a really superb library at St Crispins,' he said.

'I think your project sounds extremely worthwhile.' Mrs Blunt nodded approvingly. 'Have you been fund-raising long?'

'Ever since I left the home. They helped me so much there. At the beginning, just after I had my accident, all I really craved were the poppies of oblivion. But they made me realise that I shouldn't see myself as ashes where I'd once been fire. The psychological help they gave me was invaluable. They also taught me to manage physically so that I can now live alone and not feel the humiliation of being anyone's dependant.'

Mrs Murphy arrived with some coffee – Mrs Blunt watched with apprehension as she poured Corrigan a cup. Mrs Murphy was such a desperately rough and careless woman that Mrs Blunt was terrified that she would spill the boiling coffee all over him. The last thing the unfortunate man needed was a really nasty scald from Mrs Murphy. Corrigan looked such a vulnerable figure sitting there trapped in his invalid chair.

As it turned out, Mrs Murphy was uncharacteristically careful as she poured out coffee for Corrigan, but she irritated Mrs Blunt because she kept saying 'That's a boy!' as he took the cup from her hand. Just because he was disabled, Mrs Blunt saw no good reason why Mrs Murphy should continue to speak to him as if she were addressing a horse.

After he'd drunk his coffee Corrigan told Mrs Blunt that once he had been discharged from St Crispins, he had felt that it was his mission to do something to repay the doctors and the staff for all they had done for him. He had also seen it as his duty to do all in his power to help those less fortunate than he was.

Corrigan lifted up his muscular arms. 'I can get around with these,' he said. 'Many people aren't blessed with my good luck.'

Mrs Blunt asked Corrigan if he lived in the neighbourhood. He shook his head. He had a flat in London. It was just a little pad. But it suited him very well. It was on the ground floor so he had no trouble with the stairs. The staff at St Crispins had helped him furnish it and they had installed certain important equipment for the disabled; as a result he could manage there quite well by himself.

'But I'm not in London very much,' Corrigan said. 'I'm always touring the countryside. The doctors and the patients at St Crispins love to tease me. They call me the Rolling Stone.'

He clapped one of the wheels of his invalid chair with a hearty gesture. 'I certainly keep rolling!' he said.

He then explained that he much preferred to fund-raise in the country. 'I find the attitude of people who live out of the towns much more sympathetic. Urban people have so many pressures, it's as if their souls become poisoned by all the fret and the fumes of the city. They tend to develop some kind of traffic jam of the mind, it makes them very selfish.'

'Have you had an encouraging response to your appeal here in Coombe Abbot?' Mrs Blunt asked him.

Corrigan explained that he had just arrived this morning, but had been thrilled by the reactions of the people he had visited.

'I've only had the time to call on a couple of houses, but I found the enthusiasm with which I was greeted rather astonishing. They invited me into their homes and they listened to what I am trying to accomplish. I think they really saw the point of my project. In the city, I rarely meet with that kind of intelligence.'

Mrs Blunt asked Corrigan if he returned to London every night after he'd spent the day fund-raising in the country.

'I tend to return to the city,' he said. 'You see, my little London flat is very well equipped. And for me, equipment is all. Just once in a while I've been the guest of strangers who have treated me exactly as if I was a member of their family. They've put me up in the ground floor of their house and they've helped me with my various needs. When I've encountered these very special people, I have been able to avail myself of their kindness without feeling that I'm eating the sour crust of humiliation. But I don't find such people very often . . . That's why I tend to return every night to London.'

He said that he was constantly astounded by the generosity

of the strangers whom he met within the course of his work. They often offered him a free bed.

'I find these offers very beautiful – even if my pride will not often allow me to accept them. You see, I've got a horror of being seen as an inconvenience.'

'I'm quite sure that no one ever sees you as that,' Mrs Blunt said quickly.

'Well, I hope to God they don't. Obviously I have a lot of problems with my old throne of a chair. Stairs, kerbs, hills, they can all become giant hurdles for me. But someone always gives me a hand and I never have to worry. Somehow I seem to manage.'

Mrs Blunt said that she would very much like to make a contribution to his appeal. She had lost all her feelings of irrational resentment because he was not her dead husband. The gallantry of this man impressed her. She admired the happy-go-lucky attitude with which he seemed able to deal with his crushing disability.

He made her feel ashamed of her own aimless life. Corrigan, despite his handicap, was doing something worthwhile. He made her realise that she now did nothing that was of any use to the world.

When her daughter, Nadine, tried to make her see this, Mrs Blunt had always become silent and aggrieved. Nadine was a very different character from her mother. She was energetic and lively and she was irritated and distressed by her mother's apathetic acceptance that her life was over. She couldn't understand why Mrs Blunt seemed to want to wrap herself up in her sadness as if it was a heavy grey knitted shawl. She felt that Mrs Blunt, having lived for so many years for her father, should now be living her own life. She kept urging her to sell the house in the country and move to London. Nadine thought she should try to find herself new interests and make new friends. She felt Mrs Blunt should involve herself in some charity. She kept telling her mother that she was still an attractive and intelligent woman. In the past, Nadine had sometimes also suggested it might be good for her morale if she got herself a job.

Mrs Blunt had always listened to her daughter with a

mournful apathy. She was quite unable to express how much it appalled her that her only child cared so little for the memory of her dead father. Mrs Blunt could also never say how much it upset her that Nadine had turned out to be so insensitive and unable to understand her feelings. When she heard her daughter's advice she made no protest, but in her mute fashion she remained stubborn. She was never going to sell her house. Her house contained all that she valued from her past. As she felt she had no future and she experienced the present only as pain, her past was all she wanted to cling to.

Nadine's attempts to galvanise her mother always failed because Mrs Blunt saw them as cruel and disloyal and therefore they made her become even more entrenched in her quiet and sorrowing position. Corrigan was the first person who had ever managed to make her feel that there was something shameful in the way she had become so defeated and reclusive.

When he said that he was immensely touched and grateful for her offer to make a contribution, a pale pink blush spread across the whiteness of Mrs Blunt's cheeks.

He then insisted that she must on no account give more than she could afford. He never wanted anyone to make any financial sacrifice. Quite often he'd knocked on the doors of the little tumble-down cottages and farms and been met with such a generous response that he'd had to refuse what they offered him. If he was given ten pence here, ten pence there, he was absolutely delighted. It all mounted up in the end. He felt it was much better to raise the money slowly.

Before he accepted any donation from Mrs Blunt, he would also like to make certain that her husband approved of it. In the past he had found that if a wife or husband made a contribution without informing their partner, it could lead to domestic disputes, recriminations, the very last thing that he wanted.

'I'm afraid I lost my husband a few years ago,' said Mrs Blunt softly.

'I'm very sorry,' Corrigan murmured. 'I hope I haven't been tactless.'

'You couldn't have known,' Mrs Blunt shrugged and she gave a little sigh.

Her sense of desolation was returning. A feeling of depriva-
tion hurt her once again like a tangible object. She experienced
it as if it was a small piece of jagged rock that had got lodged in
her chest. When her husband was still alive she used to discuss
everything with him. She had fused her personality with his to
the point that, like a chameleon, she had taken on every tint and
shadow of his thoughts and feelings. When he died she had
been left bereft, only able to identify with a nothingness that
she saw as a gaping tunnel of grey.

'My mother died last year,' Corrigan said. 'I think I understand what you're going through.'

'Oh, I'm really sorry.' It was then Mrs Blunt's turn to
apologise.

'I still haven't got over it. I doubt that I ever will. "Winter
has come and gone but grief returns." I am sure you must
know what I am saying.'

'Yes, I'm afraid that I do,' Mrs Blunt said. 'I always used to
know that something dreadful could happen to Tom. Even in
our happiest times I deliberately reminded myself of that every
day. It may sound silly, but I was trying to protect myself. I
thought that if I was prepared enough, I wouldn't mind so
much when it happened. But all that preparing hasn't been any
use at all. I don't know if you have found the same?'

'I've found it exactly the same,' Corrigan said. 'I was
particularly close to my mother. After I got smashed up it was
her love and concern that kept me going. She was a wonderful
person but I'm afraid that her life was not a happy one. She
never really recovered from the shock of my accident. It
annihilated her. I think she tried to take my suffering on to
herself, and if I'm to face the truth – the poor creature may well
have suffered more than I did. But there's no point in thinking
about that too much, although I sometimes find myself trying
to relive the suffering that she experienced on my behalf. But
one should never allow one's grief to become tortuous and self-
flagellating, for then it becomes indulgent and it's of little use
to anyone . . .'

'It's so difficult not to keep on minding,' Mrs Blunt said.

'It's difficult indeed,' Corrigan spoke with an impassioned

emphasis. 'I was furiously angry, of course, when I was first told the news. I had that wild, almost insane anger that just wants to scream and shake its fists at the heavens. But that was egotistical. And now I keep reminding myself that she is out of all her misery . . . She has left me all her strengths, so I have not been stripped completely. I know I must use these strengths as she would have wanted me to, otherwise I make a mockery of everything she accomplished. I've now learnt to take the view that man cannot remake himself without suffering. He has to become both the marble and the sculptor. And when I think of the life my mother led – I should be grateful that she has gone. For there is one thing that I'm certain of – she is better off where she is . . .' Corrigan faltered. His hands gripped both wheels of his chair as if he was making an attempt to control himself.

'I have many friends all over the country,' he continued. 'If one had no friends, surely one would perish. I agree with Santayana that one's friends are the only part of the human race with whom one can be human. Some of my friends are disabled, some of them have become my friends because of their generosity towards the handicapped, but obviously I will never be able to form a really close relationship with another human being. I have to accept that. My tragedy is the tragedy of all severely injured people. When I lost my mother it was no ordinary loss. For many months after her death, I was very close to giving up. I loathed days – I loathed hours – they both wearied and disgusted me. That was part of my great anger. I loathed everything except sleep. At that time such a lethal death-wish came over me that it was like a great black hood. It enveloped me completely and I was near to suffocating in its destructive smothering folds. But you look as if I am embarrassing you. I can only apologise. I should not have been so personal. I see I should never have talked like this.'

Mrs Blunt was trembling. She felt exposed and inadequate sitting in her neat little drawing-room with the cold autumn sunshine dappling the restrained beige of her drawing-room carpet. She had never had such an emotional conversation with a stranger. She herself was inhibited and found it very difficult to speak about her feelings. But she suddenly wanted to tell Corrigan that when he had first arrived at her door she had thought he was her dead husband. She didn't feel that he would think she was demented, but finding it wiser not to test him, she merely repeated that she was sorry to hear about his mother and that she would be delighted to make a contribution to his charity.

Corrigan made a negative gesture. He didn't want to ask her for money. As a widow living on her own, she probably had her own troubles. If she was interested in helping the disabled there were other things she could do which would be just as valuable as any donation. Did Mrs Blunt have any idea how much many handicapped people longed to receive a letter?

'You *can* lead a perfectly normal healthy life,' Corrigan said. 'You probably can't imagine the terrible sense of isolation that disabled people experience. Some of them have the feeling they have been thrown away by the world and completely forgotten. They start to lose all sense of their own identity and worth. That's why they have this desperate need to receive letters. They long to see their own name written out on an envelope because it represents proof that someone recognises they are still human beings. Even if it's only their surname that's written on the letter – they just die to see it there. I lost my first name very soon after I entered the institution. If someone addressed me by it now, I doubt that I'd recognise it. Anyone who has to pass their life in an institution knows that the quickest thing to go is your first name.'

Mrs Blunt was a little bewildered. She did not find this true in her personal experience. She'd only spent a few days in hospital when she'd given birth to Nadine, and when she'd had her appendix removed. But she had got the impression that when one was ill one was addressed only by one's first name. 'Come on Harry, take your pain-killer!' 'We must get you cleaned up before the doctor pops in, Devina.' She remembered it all being like that. She'd even found all this boisterous over-familiar use of first names annoying. It had seemed condescending, as if it was generally considered that people who are ill had to be treated as children. But Corrigan had a different complaint and as his experience of institutions was so much more extensive than hers, she was very interested to hear it.

'It's quite a loss to lose your first name,' Corrigan said. 'It's a bigger loss than you'd imagine. I've always seen it as a major amputation of identity. You can still learn to live with the loss, but the sense that one has lost all contact with one's fellow beings, that's a much harder thing to bear. When I was a patient in St Crispins I used to dread the arrival of the mail every morning. That was always the moment of the day when I suffered most. I never used to bother to look and see if I had a letter. I knew all too well that no one was ever going to write to me. That was after my mother died, of course.'

Corrigan's voice started to shake. He seemed unable to continue. But then he recovered himself. He went on to tell Mrs Blunt that there was a very attractive and intelligent man who was currently a patient in St Crispins. His name was Rupert Sinclair. He was in his sixties and he had been very severely injured in the last war. If Mrs Blunt would agree to become this man's pen-friend, to write to him weekly, send him the odd postcard, it would be a far more valuable act than if she made a donation. If Mrs Blunt would be kind enough to write to Mr Sinclair and explain that his old friend Corrigan had suggested she get in touch, he would be deeply grateful. She couldn't believe how much it would mean to a very charming and courageous person. If Mrs Blunt was to write to Mr Sinclair, he would almost certainly reply. Corrigan hoped that there could then be the start of a correspondence which would be of immeasurable psychological comfort to Rupert Sinclair – also intensely rewarding to Mrs Blunt herself.

Mrs Blunt looked flustered. She murmured nervously that she would be delighted to become Mr Sinclair's pen-friend. But unfortunately she was a very poor letter writer. She would never be able to think what to say to him.

Corrigan waved aside her objections with a sweeping movement of his huge muscular arm. It hardly mattered what she said in her letter. That was not the point.

He asked for a pencil and pad. He wrote out the address of St Crispins and told her to address her letter to Mr Rupert

Sinclair, c/o the Secretary. He then announced that he had to be on his way. He planned to call on several other houses in the neighbourhood. He thanked Mrs Blunt for her great hospitality and her understanding. Mrs Blunt summoned Mrs Murphy and asked her to help the gentleman down the front steps. Mrs Murphy managed to get him down without causing him any overt injury although she made the helpless man's neck jerk with a violence Mrs Blunt found very worrying and unnecessary. Once he was safe on Mrs Blunt's gravel patio, Corrigan thanked her for her kindness, he apologised for having been over-emotional, and then, turning the wheels of his chair with a graceful and powerful movement of his arms, he went swirling off down the drive and on to the main road.

Mrs Blunt stood on her doorstep looking so fragile that, like a dandelion in full fluff, she seemed ready for any wind to blow her away. She felt very moved by the sight of the lonely crippled man as he vanished down the road. She went back into her house, deciding she would try and write to Mr Sinclair.

Mrs Murphy was hanging around in the hallway. Mrs Blunt wished she wouldn't stand about. Even if there was very little to do in the house, there was surely some furniture that she could polish. When Mrs Murphy was idle Mrs Blunt felt she was like some formidable over-charged engine attached to a vehicle that was far too light for it.

'He was quite a heavy fellow,' Mrs Murphy said.

Mrs Blunt sniffed. She found this remark most inappropriate. She didn't feel that that was all that should be said about her visitor.

'Yes, I'm afraid those chairs are dreadfully heavy,' she said coldly. 'Can you imagine how tiring it must be for him having to wheel himself around like that? It's awful to think how much his arms must ache.'

She went into her drawing-room and sat down at her little Queen-Anne walnut desk. She found some mauve writing-paper that her son-in-law had given her for Christmas.

'I wonder why Justin chose such a vulgar colour?' she thought. 'How could he think that I'd like it? It's really quite horribly genteel.'

It worried her that Rupert Sinclair would get a very bad and false impression of her taste when he saw her unpleasant stationery. But as she'd more or less given up writing letters to anyone and only used postcards when she corresponded with Nadine, she had no other paper in the house and she could only hope that the invalid soldier to whom she was writing would not judge her too harshly.

'Dear Mr Sinclair,' Mrs Blunt wrote. She then tore the page up. It seemed too formal a beginning. She took another page. 'Dear Rupert Sinclair.' But that seemed too intimate a way to address a stranger.

She kept thinking of Corrigan wheeling along through the countryside all alone. She now felt she should have asked him to lunch. She wondered where the poor man was planning to spend the night. If he hoped to find a comfortable room in Coombe Abbot, she certainly pitied him. She only knew of one boarding house which provided bed and breakfast and she had been told that the rooms were icy-cold and the sheets not clean. She wondered how he would manage to get up the stairs to his room. Maybe he would find a couple of men to lift him. The whole thing seemed extremely problematic and disquieting. She felt she had been inhumanly callous to have let him go off like that.

She went to find Mrs Murphy and asked her if she would set off on her motor bike and catch up with Corrigan – he couldn't have gone very far. She wanted Mrs Murphy to tell him that if he had not yet found other accommodation she would be delighted if he would be her guest for the night.

Mrs Murphy stood with her short stout legs planted far apart, looking thoughtfully at her employer. She had very red-veined and bulbous eyes. She was smoking and as she had lost all her teeth and had not bothered to wear her dentures, she was holding the filter of her Marlboro cigarette between her lumpy, maroon-coloured gums.

'You want me to chase that cripple and ask him to come and spend the night with you?'

Mrs Blunt quivered with distaste. She loathed the way Mrs Murphy phrased things. 'It looks as if it's going to rain.' Her voice was acid. 'That unfortunate man does such a lot of good in the world – while he is in the neighbourhood I'd really like him to know he always has a roof.'

Mrs Murphy went off on her motor bike and Mrs Blunt waited in a state of nervous excitement for her return. She saw that it was indeed starting to rain. This made her feel very upset. She hated the idea of Corrigan getting wet. It was a long time since she had felt she wanted anything, and the feeling astonished her. Now she found she really hoped Mrs Murphy would persuade him to come back and stay the night.

In about half an hour she heard the sound of Mrs Murphy's bike as it roared back down the drive churning up the stones on the gravel. She had finally found Corrigan wheeling himself down the main street of Coombe Abbot. He had thanked Mrs Blunt for her kind offer. He was going round some more houses and then he planned to return to London later that evening. When he was next in the neighbourhood he would try to come and see her.

'I hope he wasn't getting soaked in this awful rain,' Mrs Blunt said wistfully. She felt very disappointed.

'He had a big black umbrella hooked on to the side of his chair,' Mrs Murphy said. 'He was bowling along, eating a ham sandwich. He didn't seem to mind the rain at all.'

'What a courageous man he is.' Mrs Blunt shook her head and gave a sigh.

She felt peculiar and restless. She couldn't settle down to anything. She wondered if she would ever hear from Corrigan again. Mrs Murphy collected his coffee cup from the drawing-room and took it off to the kitchen to wash it.

> 'And the cow kicked
> Nelly, in the belly,
> In the barn,'

chanted Mrs Murphy in booming, tuneless tones and her voice came floating into Mrs Blunt's peaceful panelled drawing-room.

Mrs Blunt wondered if these horrid words came from some pop song. She rarely watched television and disliked pop music, and was therefore not very up to date with the current hits.

> 'And the cow kicked
> Nelly, in the belly,
> In the barn,'

crooned Mrs Murphy.

> 'Second verse,
> Same as the first,
> And the cow kicked
> Nelly, in the belly,
> In the barn.'

Mrs Blunt always detested it when Mrs Murphy started to sing. Recently she had done this all too frequently. Usually Mrs Blunt was stoical and made no protest, but today, since Corrigan had arrived and she had allowed him to leave, her nerves felt very frayed and the sound of Mrs Murphy's loud singing seemed insufferable. She felt she had never heard anything quite as ugly and irritating as this song with its stupid repeating verse. And something about the lyrics sounded oddly menacing, although Mrs Blunt could not have explained why.

She decided she really had to put a stop to the singing even if it hurt Mrs Murphy's feelings. She went into the kitchen where she found her by the sink, with her rotund, purple-skinned arms plunged up to the elbow in a snowy foam of detergent.

'What is that song?' asked Mrs Blunt.

'It's something my mother used to sing way, way back.' Mrs Murphy answered her with such a cheerful and simple pride that Mrs Blunt realised with despondency that it would be an act of inexcusable cruelty to beg her never to sing it again. Mrs Blunt wondered whether the fact that Mrs Murphy's mother had sung this atrocious song throughout her infancy could in any sense explain why Mrs Murphy had turned out the way she had. However, she kept this thought to herself and asked if Corrigan had given any indication of when he would be returning to the neighbourhood. If she managed to keep Mrs

Murphy talking, at least it prevented her from singing. But she also did it for a more important reason. She longed to talk about Corrigan, and Mrs Murphy was the only human being with whom she could do this.

'He didn't say when he'd be back,' Mrs Murphy said. 'But I think it won't be long. I have that feeling.'

Mrs Blunt wished she could feel the same. She had little faith that Corrigan would soon come back. There were so many other parts of the English countryside that he might see as preferable for fund-raising. She feared that he might decide that her part of Wiltshire had been exhausted. She wished she had asked him for the address of his London flat.

'What part of Ireland would you say that Corrigan came from?' she asked.

'I'd say he was a Dublin man,' surmised Mrs Murphy.

'How do you think he gets himself on and off the train?' Mrs Blunt asked.

Apparently he had told Mrs Murphy that he only used the big main-line stations. The small ones were not very suitable for him because the train only stopped there for such a short time. At the big stations he always found people to lift his chair into the luggage van, and when he arrived at his destination he got the same kind of help and was lifted out.

'He's such a sympathetic character, I'm sure he always finds people who are delighted to give him a hand,' Mrs Blunt said. She then told Mrs Murphy that she could go home. She suddenly wanted to be all alone so that she could give her full attention to the letter she planned to write to Rupert Sinclair. She felt it was urgent that she should write to him, for he was now her only link with Corrigan.

'Dear Rupert,' she scribbled, once she had got out her flimsy mauve writing-paper. If this was an over-familiar way to address him – she didn't care. Since she had met Corrigan she felt braver about everything. She decided his courage was infectious.

    'Dear Rupert,
        'I am writing to you at the suggestion of your friend,

Corrigan,' she began in her delicate and ornate hand-writing. 'He paid me a visit recently when he was down in this part of the world. What an unusual and fascinating character he is! He spoke of you with great warmth. He seems to be one of your greatest admirers. He made me feel I had known you all my life, so I hope you will not find it impertinent when you get this letter from a stranger.

'I will tell you a little about myself – although there is not all that much to say. In the last few years my life has not been a happy one. I have had my blows. I lost the husband I adored. But you and Corrigan have also had very great trials to bear, and when I think of your bravery you make me feel ashamed I have sometimes let myself feel despair. The church is right to see it as a sin. In the future, it is a sin I do not intend to be guilty of.

'I have one child – a daughter who lives in London. She is very attractive. Nadine is a brunette. I don't know why I tell you that. Except it still always surprises me. I, myself, was always so fair and Nadine's father was also very blond. He went grey when he got old, but as a young man my husband had the colouring of a prince in a fairy tale. He really had golden hair.

'I don't see Nadine all that often. She is married to a successful, charming young journalist called Justin Conroy. You may have seen his articles in the papers. Nadine has twins. She has two lovely little boys called Felix and Roland.

'My husband was a military man – a Colonel. We did service in India for many years and our life was very interesting. I still miss India. I miss the obvious things, the smells, the flowers, the mountains. My husband and I used to love sitting out together on our veranda when the evenings were cool. In a way, I'd love to go back there, but I think I'd find it sad, and without my husband I know I never really will.

'We found it quite a difficult adjustment when we

first returned to England. It seemed to have changed so much, the whole world that we'd known seemed to have vanished. Maybe we had changed. Those things are hard to say.

'We missed our old friends very much. They were scattered all over the place and we'd lost touch with them. Somehow we never really made new ones. We didn't seem to fit in any more. Something was wrong. Maybe it was our fault. Maybe we were too old to make ourselves a new set of friends. I don't really know. But we had each other. In fact, all the upset of leaving India made us get closer than we'd ever been before.

'When my husband retired we were extremely fortunate. He inherited some trust funds from his mother and we were able to buy a really lovely little period house down here in Wiltshire and were able to do it up nicely and we could furnish it with antiques and various pretty things.

'We kept ourselves very much to ourselves and we never got to know our neighbours in the village. But our last years together were the happiest ones of our whole lives.

'My husband was a great country lover. He had a passion for wild flowers. He was writing a book about the English hedgerows when he died. I used to love wild flowers myself. In fact, I used to love all flowers. I once adored gardening. My husband adored it too. I haven't done anything to our garden since he died. It's really wicked the way I have let it revert and become a wilderness. Our garden used to be really very beautiful. I can say that without boasting, because it certainly isn't beautiful any more.

'Nadine was shocked when she saw what had become of my garden. She didn't say anything, but I could tell that it horrified her. I hated seeing her get so distressed about it, but I still haven't been able to bring myself to do anything to improve it, and it's still in the most terrible state and overrun by nettles and briars.

'When my husband was writing his book, I did some illustrations of wild flowers which he planned to use. It was lovely having a project that we both shared. I used to draw rather well when I was a girl and then I gave it up. When we got back from India, my husband persuaded me to take it up again. I don't know if my wild flower illustrations were much good. He admired them very much, but then he admired everything I did. He was always so encouraging. He was a very kind man. The whole time we were married I never knew him to have a 'mood'. He was always sunny. He was always pleased with everything. He was extraordinary.

'I am going to leave my flower illustrations to Nadine, not because I think they are great works of art, but because her father liked them and I think she will treasure them for that reason.

'I do hope you are well. I was wondering if there was anything you would like in the way of books or magazines. I would be delighted to send you anything you feel like reading. Corrigan tells me that the library at St Crispins is not its strongest point. I assume the food is also not very good. I'm afraid the food in all institutions tends to be pretty inedible. So if there is anything you would like in the way of fruit or drinks or delicacies, I would be all too pleased to see they are sent to you. I hope we will have a valuable pen-friendship. If you see Corrigan, please give him my regards.

Yours sincerely,
Devina Blunt.'

When Mrs Blunt reread her own letter she found it rather eerie. As it was addressed to an unknown man it seemed to say nothing of any importance at all – yet rather more than she ever disclosed to anyone else.

She was afraid it made her appear very self-obsessed. It hardly asked anything about Rupert Sinclair. But that was deliberate for she was starting to understand the problems of writing to someone in a wheelchair. She couldn't even ask him what he had been doing lately in case the question might be tactless. She had written that she hoped he was well – he might even find that in poor taste. But she decided she was going to take a risk and leave it in because she really had to wish him something nice.

She felt she was taking a very important step when she wrote to Sinclair, and she was anxious to get it right. As she once again went through her letter sentence by sentence, it struck her that she was reading the outpourings of a woman who was so lonely that she hardly cared if poor Sinclair was interested in receiving her self-indulgent and rambling account of a life that probably seemed very dull once it was put down on paper. She decided she had no right to bore him with such a lot of information about herself and she took out quite a few paragraphs before rewriting the whole thing. She still found herself burdened with the problem that if she didn't write in a personal tone she had no material for a letter of any kind. She felt it would be really pointless to tell him her political views – that seemed almost worse than telling him about her husband, and Nadine, and her veranda in India.

Although she was still dissatisfied with its contents, she found she got a lot of pleasure from writing out the words 'Rupert Sinclair' on an envelope. She wrote them very large and she painstakingly decorated every letter with various bold flourishes and swirls. When she'd finished writing out his name and address, she felt quite proud of her handiwork. She wished she could show it to Corrigan. He had laid such stress on the vital importance of the name on the envelope. As she sealed it, she had the feeling that Corrigan would be very pleased with her – very pleased on behalf of his crippled friend.

2

The same day that Mrs Blunt wrote her letter to Rupert Sinclair, Justin Conroy made her daughter cry because he was unable to understand why she so rarely visited her mother.

It was a Sunday and Nadine was tired. Usually she had so much nervous energy that she seemed tireless. She hated to show any weakness. In the restricted domestic arena in which she operated, she always drove herself to do everything as well as possible. She was extremely organised and efficient and her home was beautifully run. She dressed very smartly. Her pretty little figure had a very tiny waist and she wore big shiny belts to emphasise it and her belts perfectly matched her shining black patent-leather shoes.

After she had left school she had taken a cookery course, and the food she served was always delicious. She was very proud of her house in Chelsea and had furnished it with a lot of stripped pine and old-fashioned curtains made of flowered chintz. Her kitchen was so well laid out that it was like a model kitchen in a showroom.

But the day that Mrs Blunt wrote her letter had been an exhausting one for Nadine. She had a sore throat and she had a headache. As it was a Sunday, the twins had not gone to school and they had been up since six in the morning racing round the house fighting and giggling and crying and strewing the floor of every room with a litter of electronic toys and plastic soldiers and guns. All day Nadine had trailed after them trying to preserve the order they seemed wantonly keen on destroying. But by the evening she felt drained and when she had finally persuaded them to settle down to play electronic tennis on the television in their playroom she went to the drawing-room to light the fire for Justin. He stopped working at six and he then liked to relax in front of the fire and he would ask her to bring him a whisky and soda.

Justin was a tall young man, and Nadine, who was very small, felt that he towered above her. He had supercilious grey eyes and his nose and his chin curved towards each other in his thin, bony face and from certain side angles he looked a little like Punch.

Justin was writing an article on the care of the elderly in modern Britain, and that morning he had driven down to visit an old persons' home in Kent and been shocked by what he had seen. After Nadine brought him his whisky he told her that when he had first arrived there, the sister in charge of the place had come out to his car and warned him that she was afraid that he was going to be horrified by the smell.

'And oh God, darling!' he said, 'the sister was right to warn me. The stench was indescribable!'

'It's dreadful they should be allowed to smell,' Nadine shivered. 'It's degrading. And old people have to put up with so many humiliations anyway.'

'That's the whole problem,' Justin said. 'A lot of nurses refuse to work with the elderly. Most of the work is pretty repulsive. You need a very strong stomach to do it. The sister I saw this morning told me they were always appealing for local voluntary workers. They usually get a good response and a lot of well-intentioned applicants turn up. But they hardly ever stick it. They usually only work for about one day and then they discover that they've had it. They find the things they're required to do too sickening.'

Nadine said that when the twins were a bit older she felt she would like to do voluntary work for the aged. She was lucky – she had never been squeamish and she didn't feel she would be upset by the aspects of the work that most people found so daunting.

Justin was often irritated by his wife's need to feel she could cope with things that most people found very difficult. He liked to needle her – to puncture her confidence.

He said that he didn't believe she would enjoy rubbing ointment on the bottom of some rotting old man with a ghastly rash. It was nonsense to say she would. Nadine said she didn't pretend she would enjoy it. She still felt quite prepared to do it.

Justin found her attitude smug and he told her that he couldn't see why she chose to see herself as a Florence Nightingale for the elderly. He thought she was unkind to her own mother. He reminded Nadine that she hadn't bothered to go down to see Mrs Blunt for several months. He also had the suspicion she didn't even telephone the poor woman very often.

He had no idea that Nadine was going to have such a violent reaction to these accusations. She gave a jump as if he had stabbed her and her neat-featured little face went scarlet. He saw that he had upset her, but he didn't understand to what degree. He was still keen to make his wife realise that she was not perfect and he continued to reproach her for neglecting her mother and although his tone was light and bantering he managed to make Nadine feel she was being impaled.

'We've only gone down to see the poor creature twice since your father died,' he said. 'She's hardly been allowed to meet the twins.'

Justin went on to tell his wife that he would have understood the heartless way that Nadine treated Mrs Blunt if she'd been an awful old witch of a mother.

'But I find her utterly charming,' he said. 'I think she's still rather beautiful. She has such a gentle expression, and she obviously adores you. Her excitement when you last went down to see her was a pathetic thing to see. If you can't make the effort to go down to see her in the country I really think you ought to invite her to come and stay with us here in London. She knows we have a spare bedroom. She must be feeling terribly hurt that we never suggest she comes to see us . . .'

Having first blushed when Justin had started his accusations, Nadine had now suddenly gone very pale.

'I *have* invited her to stay.' Her voice sounded choked and peculiar and bitter. 'I've invited her lots of times. But she always refuses to come . . .'

Justin frowned and his Punch-like face took on a censorious expression. He said that he suspected that Nadine had not sounded sufficiently enthusiastic when she had asked her mother to visit them. If Mrs Blunt had been made to feel she was really wanted he was certain she would have accepted the invitation.

'Oh no, she wouldn't!' Nadine gave an hysterical shake of her head. Justin's obtuseness made her feel frantic. 'You don't understand my mother at all,' she said. 'She's never going to come up to London. It doesn't matter how many times I beg her to come. It doesn't matter how enthusiastic I make my invitations sound. Oh, don't you see, Justin? She doesn't ever want to leave that house because Daddy died there. She feels she must never leave the spot where she lost him, she thinks that would be an act of criminal desertion.'

'All the more reason for us to go down and see her,' Justin said. 'I think it's touching the way she clings to your father's memory. I know you think she's overdoing it. But I think that kind of loyalty is very moving.'

It was at this point that Nadine ran out of the room in tears and Justin became faintly agitated because he had never seen her behave in such a histrionic manner. He followed her as she ran up the stairs into their bedroom and found her lying face down on their modern pine four-poster with its pink chintz flowered hangings. She was using her white organdie night-dress as if it was a great handkerchief and her whole face was buried in it. She was crying pitifully. Justin sat down on the bed beside her and impatiently stroked Nadine's dark hair.

'I'm sorry darling,' he said. 'I shouldn't have bullied you. It's none of my business how badly you treat your mother.'

'Oh please don't say that! I can't bear you saying that,' Nadine kept her face in her nightdress and her sobbing continued.

'Your mother is perfectly all right,' Justin said. He hated it when women showed any signs of weakness and he longed to stop her crying. 'Look darling, I was exaggerating the whole thing. I can only say that I'm sorry I upset you. I don't think your mother feels nearly as lonely as I was making out. I'm certain you needn't worry about her. You must remember she's not completely on her own. After all, she has that Irish woman who seems very attached to her. I'm sure Mrs Murphy looks after her beautifully. And I bet your mother has made lots of friends in the neighbourhood. She's probably got quite a few admirers. I wouldn't be surprised if she has a large following of love-sick curates and widowers. Those sort of suitors abound in the country, or they certainly do in novels. Your mother is such an attractive person. I'm certain she's very popular. And don't forget that if she really wanted to see us all that badly there's nothing to stop her getting on a train and whipping up to London.'

Nadine went on silently crying. He could make her feel so desperately lonely. She had never been able to make Justin understand her feelings on anything she considered important. She knew it was useless to make any protest as Justin distorted the reality and tried to comfort her by pretending that Mrs Blunt was leading a dashing social life in the country, that her mother was happy and busy and beautifully cared for by Mrs Murphy.

Nadine realised it would be utterly pointless to tell him that the last time she had been to see her mother she had been truly appalled by Mrs Murphy. She had felt that the fact that Mrs Blunt, who in the past had always been extremely fastidious, was now prepared to employ such an uncouth and pre-posterous figure cast a very disquieting light on her mother's state of mind. Not only had Nadine found Mrs Murphy's physical presence extremely uncongenial, but she suspected that she might well be rather dishonest. She feared that Mrs Murphy was taking advantage of Mrs Blunt's vagueness and ordering herself large quantities of meat and groceries and charging them to her mother's account. Nadine lacked any definite proof that Mrs Murphy was not to be trusted, but the possibility was still very distressing to her, as she saw her mother as a total innocent. It also exasperated her to realise that even if she was to open her mother's eyes to some piece of grossly unscrupulous behaviour on the part of Mrs Murphy, she would never be able to make her care.

It was her mother's new inability to care about anything that terrified Nadine, and as it frightened her it made her very angry. It had given her a horror of going down to the country to see her. Every day for the last few months Nadine had resolved that she would ring up her mother and make a plan to bring the twins down to visit her. She knew her mother must be puzzled and wounded that she so rarely heard from her only child at such an unhappy period in her life. Her mother's sad little postcards would arrive and Nadine would go to the telephone with the intention of speaking to her, but then she would be overcome by a feeling of neurotic panic. Her stomach muscles would go into spasm and she would start trembling and feel she was going to be sick. She dreaded the idea of going down to stay with her mother, for she had developed a loathing of the charming house which Mrs Blunt had turned into such a house of death.

The last time that Nadine had gone down to Wiltshire she had found the whole experience insufferable. Her mother had made a great effort to make the occasion pleasant and festive. She had served champagne and although she had given up cooking for herself since her husband's death, she had taken a lot of trouble and prepared a delicious lunch with smoked salmon, and wild duck, and chocolate mousse for the twins.

Justin had enjoyed it all very much. Nadine had found him insensitive to the point of cruelty as she'd watched him swigging down her mother's excellent wine and becoming increasingly jocular and fatuous. He had treated Mrs Blunt with a heavily flirtatious courtesy and had become fulsome in his praise of her pretty house with its exquisite panelling and lovely furniture.

The more Justin had enjoyed the visit, the more Nadine had loathed it. Her mother made her feel that her father's absence filled every room in the house. Mrs Blunt had clearly been glad to see her daughter, but she had made her feel extremely inadequate and depressed. Nadine always wanted to believe that she could improve things, and make people happier. She felt totally defeated and frustrated by her inability to alleviate her mother's suffering.

She had been chilled by the way that her mother's fragile will to live seemed to be getting more and more feeble as every day went by. Although Mrs Blunt had provided such a delicious lunch for her family, her daughter noticed that, very unobtrusively, she'd left all her own food untouched. When she had lifted her glass of champagne in a toast, Nadine felt her mother was drinking to her own impending extinction.

Mrs Blunt had been agreeable and gracious as Justin showered her with compliments and tried to regale her with his heavy-handed jokes, but Nadine could see she was smiling as a courtesy, for her eyes continued to express only pain.

Mrs Blunt had bought two extremely expensive model aeroplanes as presents for Felix and Roland. Her mother had always been a very generous character and it embarrassed Nadine to realise how much she must have spent on these toys. Yet she wished that Mrs Blunt could have shown more excitement about the twins. 'I see they have your nice dark colouring,' Mrs Blunt had said to her. Her remark was an affectionate one. Everything she said to her daughter had been affectionate. Yet Nadine longed for her to have said something more enthusiastic. She wondered if she was being paranoid when she suspected that in an oblique way, Mrs Blunt was expressing a secret disappointment. Nadine had the feeling that she would have preferred the twins to have been blond, for then she might have been able to like them a little better. She could have seen them as resembling her late husband.

Felix and Roland had been particularly rowdy and obstreperous during the visit and that had added to the tension in the atmosphere. Their squeals and their giggles had been jarring. They had seemed almost sacrilegious in this little house with its sinister hush of the morgue.

Mrs Murphy had made the twins behave much more badly than they need have done, and had put Nadine in the mortifying position of being unable to control them. The arrival of visitors and numerous glasses of champagne had over-excited Mrs Murphy and she had seemed to regress to some infantile state where all adult good sense deserted her. She'd started to chase the twins round the house, roaring and whooping and clapping her hand over her mouth as she let out Red Indian war-cries. When she caught up with them she tickled them in the ribs with such violence that they went scarlet in the face and let out frenzied howls of pain and over-stimulation.

The whole house shook as Mrs Murphy went tearing round in her uproarious pursuit of the twins, and hearing them all thundering about upstairs Nadine was terrified that her mother's ancient, fragile floor-boards would be unable to stand the strain and the ceilings would collapse.

Nadine had kept praying that her mother would tell the woman to put a stop to her dangerous game, which she could predict was bound to end in some kind of disaster.

'Aren't the twins getting much too wild, darling? Don't you think you should do something to calm them down?' Justin asked her. Nadine had quivered with annoyance, for although her husband always got extremely angry whenever the twins started to run riot, it never occurred to him to exert any discipline himself. He always stood on the sidelines of the situation, an ill-tempered martyr who felt he was being forced to put up with an insufferable display of childish anarchy because his wife was too incompetent and feeble to crack the whip and call the twins to order.

Nadine found it typical that Justin was unable to see that only a squad of armed police could have quietened the little boys as long as Mrs Murphy continued to work them into a state verging on mania by all her chasing and her tickling.

She noticed that her mother had winced as she heard the terrible thumps and crashes that were coming from the upstairs landing. But she clearly had no intention of intervening. It was obvious that she had not enjoyed what was going on. However, she had been quite resigned to letting it continue. Nadine felt disgusted by her mother's attitude, seeing it as just one more frightening example of the way Mrs Blunt no longer wanted to make things pleasant for herself. Whether her life was made more agreeable or less so, it simply made no difference to her. She couldn't be made to care.

Finally Felix had come hurtling into the drawing-room with Mrs Murphy pounding at his heels. He had knocked over a little ornamental table and sent it flying and a pair of binoculars crashed on the floor. Nadine picked them up and she saw to her horror that one of the lenses had been slightly damaged. She had suddenly scolded Felix so violently that he had started to cry. She very rarely lost her temper with either of the twins. Her son was not accustomed to such an unexpected display of nervous fury and it terrified him.

Mrs Blunt had sat very still throughout this unfortunate little incident. She made no reproaches, but the expression in her eyes grew just a little sadder. The binoculars had belonged to the Colonel. He had been a passionate bird-watcher.

While Felix bawled and Nadine did her best to comfort him, Mrs Blunt withdrew her attention and hardly seemed to hear all the commotion. It was as if, temporarily, she had ceased to inhabit her house, and her mind had flown back into the lovely woods of her past and she was trampling through golden bracken under the branches of elms and copper beeches, and the song of birds sounded in her ears, and she was once again studying wildlife with her husband.

At no point during the whole visit had Mrs Blunt made any direct mention of the Colonel. Justin had seen this as an encouraging sign that she was recovering from the shock of his loss. But Nadine felt it was a very bad sign indeed, and she resented her mother's unwillingness to discuss him. It hurt her that her mother refused to allow her to share her grief. Nadine had adored her father and she felt that Mrs Blunt, by her inability to recognise that she also mourned him, was seizing him away from her and appropriating his memory all to herself.

She felt that her mother was depriving her of her father in death, just as she had seemed to deprive her of her father in life. The Colonel had always been very kind to Nadine. She couldn't remember a single occasion when he'd ever been angry with her. But although he had treated her with courtesy and gentleness, he had given her a sense of defeat. All through her childhood she had endlessly striven to become the centre of his affections, and she had always failed.

Her mother had been the sun that dominated his universe and, as if blinded by her rays, he hardly seemed able to see anyone else.

Nadine's relationship with her mother had been much the same. Mrs Blunt had brought her up very conscientiously and she had always treated her lovingly, but Nadine had never had the feeling that she was the central figure in her mother's emotional galaxy. Mrs Blunt had been so totally devoted to her husband that she'd given Nadine the sense she was receiving only the crumbs of her mother's love.

Nadine's contemporaries often complained about the marriages of their parents. They claimed they had been scarred by all the rows and the cruelty, the drunkenness and the infidelities they had been forced to witness. When she listened to these complaints she sympathised with her friends for the painful childhoods they had endured, yet secretly she felt a little jealous. Perversely, she often thought that she would have preferred to have been the child of a couple who were always at each others' throats, rather than have been brought up by the Blunts who were so blissfully contented in each other's company that their mutual absorption had created a wall that had separated her from them, and made her feel the permanent odd man out.

In certain moods Nadine wished she could have accused her parents of neglecting her, for then she would have felt less ungrateful and guilty when she experienced strong feelings of resentment and hostility towards both of them. It troubled her that she could never honestly claim that she had been neglected. However, she was certain that she had suffered from the fact that the relationship of her parents was so self-sufficient that it had often given her the impression that she was not really needed. As a child, her confidence and sense of her own worth had been affected by finding herself always in a role as the spectator of a happiness to which she contributed little.

Mrs Blunt had a framed photograph which she treasured

very much and kept on a little table by her bed. Nadine disliked it, hating the way the camera seemed to have made a cold recording of her childhood predicament. In the photograph her parents were standing, holding hands. Her father looked very handsome and blond and he was wearing an army uniform. Mrs Blunt was wearing a white muslin dress and her fair hair was loose and fell streaming over her shoulders. Her mother looked so young she seemed like a radiant child bride. It always startled Nadine to see how beautiful she had been in her youth. It made her feel both envious and awed.

In the photograph, Nadine was sitting in front of her parents on a chair. Her skinny little legs with their spotless white socks looked vulnerable as they dangled helplessly down. Whenever she examined her child image as it appeared in that picture, she was disturbed by the impression that she'd been much too clean and well-cared for. It was as if she had been put there for show. Her dark hair was perfectly neat and glossy. Her frock was very pretty with frills and a scarlet sash.

Behind this small, dolled-up figure stood her father and her mother gazing at each other with an expression of mutual rapture and admiration. Nadine found something troubling and forlorn in the expression of the tiny, tidy child in the photograph. She occupied so little of her parents' attention. It was as if once she'd been put on display, she'd somehow slipped their notice. There was a desperation in the way her eyes were focused with such intensity on the camera as if she hoped even a machine could give her a little approbation.

Nadine had found that many painful and unresolved feelings from her past had been revived during her last visit to her mother. As she'd watched Mrs Blunt wafting round the house with her gentle smile, playing the gracious hostess, she had felt very threatened by the way her mother's despair seemed to be trailing behind her like an invisible bridal train.

Nadine was much too sensitive to Mrs Blunt's moods not to realise that despite all her attempts to make their visit an enjoyable one, she was only longing for the moment when her guests would be packed into the family car and she could stand in her doorway blowing kisses and waving loving goodbyes as they set off for London, leaving her to the isolation that she craved.

Mrs Blunt had made her choice, and her choice was very wounding to her daughter. Nadine had offered to help her mother build up a new life, but her offer had not been accepted and she took the rejection personally. Mrs Blunt seemed to prefer the death-in-life existence that she now led with her lost husband to anything that her daughter could give her. This seemed to confirm her old childish suspicion that her mother saw her as a figure of little consequence as compared to the Colonel.

Even though she knew she ought to excuse her mother on the grounds of her ill-health, Nadine found herself taking the derelict state of Mrs Blunt's garden as a subtle personal insult. She didn't expect her to do heavy manual work herself, but she was still in a position in which she could easily employ a gardener. This, however, she was clearly not prepared to do.

Nadine saw this refusal as an aggressive display of her mother's current attitude. Mrs Blunt was content to allow nature to wreak its havoc and destroy something which had once been very lovely. To her daughter this seemed like a brutal statement that in the absence of the Colonel, she considered she had no one in the world for whom she felt it worth her while to preserve its beauty.

At one point during that tense and long-drawn-out visit, Nadine's general exasperation with her mother had finally culminated in a little act of rebellion, a small cruelty that she later forever regretted.

At four o'clock Mrs Blunt had suddenly looked at her delicate diamond wrist-watch. In her unassuming fashion she had made it clear that she had an important appointment. She had slipped off into the kitchen and got a bunch of chrysanthemums which were lying ready in the sink. She had then put on her pale cream raincoat and had come back into the drawing-room. Without saying a word she had made a little gesture to Nadine which indicated that she was going outside and she expected her daughter to accompany her.

Nadine's face had gone very red as if all the resentment she had repressed during this mockery of a pleasant family reunion was now seeking expression in her blazing cheeks.

She had ignored Mrs Blunt's mute plea that she should come with her on her ritual afternoon mission to pay tribute to her late husband. Nadine, in her irritation, had not been able to see it as a plea. Instead she had taken it as an inexcusable and insensitive command.

She had suddenly realised that nothing was going to induce her to make a reverential trip to the graveyard with her mother. If she was to make a pilgrimage to the resting-place of her father, she would do so only when she had the personal inclination. Mrs Blunt had decided that four o'clock was an appropriate time to perform her daily act of symbolic obeisance. But Nadine was maddened by the way that it never occurred to Mrs Blunt to find out whether she too felt like setting off on this morbid, distressing little mission at the precise time that her mother had dictated.

She felt that Mrs Blunt was being far too high-handed in trying to impose her will in a matter which should have been treated with much more tact and delicacy. Nadine had her own response to the loss of her father and she resented her mother's refusal to concede that she might have any individual feelings on this subject. She had hoped this visit could be a happy one and was shaken by the way that Mrs Blunt seemed all too keen to darken it by introducing her melancholy note of death. Very probably she thought she was inviting her daughter to share the most precious and sacred experience she could offer. But Nadine didn't see it like that at all. If her mother wanted to hang around her father's grave, Nadine felt she should have waited until her family had gone back to London.

'Get the Monopoly board out of the car,' she had told the twins. 'If you run and get it, I'll play a game with you.'

Felix and Roland had gone rushing off to get the board and when they came back with it, Nadine had spread it out on the floor and dropped down on the carpet putting on an over-hearty act of throwing herself into the game. Mrs Blunt had looked at her daughter with an expression of mild surprise, but she had seemed relieved rather than distressed by the snub.

Nadine had not expected such a reaction and she found it very insulting indeed. It was suddenly driven home to her that when her mother went off to commune with her lost husband, she found the experience so intense and fulfilling that she had little desire for anyone to share it with her. To Mrs Blunt it was a mystical act, and she saw the presence of any other human being, even that of her own child, as totally superfluous. She was only prepared to tolerate it because her whole nature was considerate.

'Aren't you coming, Nadine?' Mrs Blunt's question was extremely casual. Her daughter felt it should have had very much more urgency.

'Can't you see I'm in the middle of a game with the children?' Nadine had said irritably. As she bought up a valuable paper property she wondered if the most odious and acquisitive of real-life urban developers could have displayed more ferocity and greed. She'd found herself maniacally keen to seize property at the expense of the twins because if she let them pick up the plums from the Monopoly board, she knew she'd end up having to pay them rent. She felt that her mother, by asking her to come to the churchyard, and then showing her that she didn't care at all if she remained behind, had already extracted some kind of emotional rent. She was, therefore, determined not to get into a position where any more payments could be demanded of her, either in genuine or symbolic form.

When Nadine had refused to accompany her mother to her father's grave, it had been the most extreme act of defiance that she had ever committed in her life. Justin had been quite unaware of the painful mother-daughter confrontation that was taking place in Mrs Blunt's drawing-room. He was stretched out in a chintz-covered chair enjoying his mother-in-law's brandy and he was becoming affably tipsy.

'Goodness, it's lovely to be here,' he said to Nadine, 'When one comes down to the country one sees that it's much nicer than London. I'm sure you feel the same, darling. It makes me wonder if we shouldn't look for some week-end cottage in the neighbourhood. Then you could see all that you want of your mother. I think there would be a lot to be said for it all round . . .'

Nadine had refused to answer him. She had tried to seem to be concentrating on the game of Monopoly. When she'd won the little battle and Mrs Blunt had gone swaying out of the house without a word of protest she felt her mother was carrying the hurt she'd just inflicted on her as bravely as she was carrying her bunch of flowers.

Nadine had been unable to resist going to the window to watch her mother walking off forlornly down the drive alone. Her mother's tiny vanishing figure in the creamy raincoat had such a pathos that she'd been overcome by remorse and she saw her own behaviour as fiendish. The fact that Mrs Blunt didn't seem to mind what had been done to her made her feel worse rather than better. She felt she had tried to kick her on the head when she was already down on the ground. She knew her mother could overlook her cruelty because it hadn't touched her, but she still found it difficult to forgive herself.

Nadine's mood of self-recrimination had not been improved by Mrs Murphy, who had come bumbling into the drawing-room carrying a great wooden tray holding the various scones and cakes and pots of jam that were to be served for tea.

Her bulbous eye rolled towards Nadine as she saw her playing Monopoly on the floor. 'I didn't think to find you here,' she said accusingly.

Nadine was determined not to let her know that she understood what she was referring to.

'Oh, yes, this was quite an impromptu visit.' She'd tried to sound casual and detached.

Mrs Murphy gave her a canny look. It had been obvious that she could not be easily fobbed off. 'I didn't expect to find you here right at this minute. I'd have thought that at least you'd have had the heart to go with her. You know, Nadine, she goes down there to see him all by herself every day of the year. It seems a terrible pity that the one time she has her daughter with her, she's still forced to go off with her flowers all on her own.'

'She wanted to go on her own.' Nadine hoped that her manner seemed crushingly off-hand. As she made this statement she longed for it to be more of a lie than it was. She thought her own voice sounded like cracking ice.

When Mrs Blunt had come back from the graveyard, Nadine was still engaged in the seemingly endless and boring game on which she'd stupidly embarked. She had put hotels on all her expensive properties and, in order to try and conquer the guilt she felt about her recent treatment of her mother, she was getting a savage pleasure from extracting cruel rents from the twins who were starting to hate the game and becoming increasingly sulky and petulant since they only enjoyed playing with her when she let them cheat.

Mrs Blunt had never made any mention of Nadine's refusal to come to the grave, and Nadine was irrationally annoyed by this. Within the game, she went to jail and then drew a card that got her out. Later she won a beauty competition which awarded her twenty-five pounds and all the time she kept wondering if it was her imagination that her mother looked much iller and more miserable than when her family had all arrived that morning. She prayed that she was not seeing signs of a deterioration in her mother's general condition, simply because on some unworthy level, she felt that she deserved it.

'Your mother seems in very good form,' Justin cheerfully announced when they were all in the car on their way back to the city. As he was driving, Nadine had restrained herself. But if he'd been in the back seat, she'd have behaved the same, for she always felt imprisoned by her own compulsion to show restraint.

Justin had a theory that all Americans suffered from a national inferiority complex. Something on the car radio got him on to this subject and he affably propounded it the whole way back to London. He felt that proof of this complex was to be found in every Hollywood movie, that it was also tellingly evidenced in the American choice of presidential candidates. Nadine kept grunting her agreement as she tried to prevent the twins getting bored by feeding them chocolate bars and making them play noughts and crosses. As Justin droned on and instructed his family, it never seemed to cross his mind that his wife could gladly have wrung his neck.

Now, as Nadine wept, lying on the four-poster bed, she remembered every detail of that disastrous last visit to her mother. She cried because she felt uncertain that she would ever be able to bring herself to repeat it, and because she knew Justin didn't really care if she neglected her mother. He simply enjoyed putting himself in a position where he could become censorious and apportion blame. In the interviews he wrote for the newspapers, he always took a very moral tone. He liked laying traps for the people he talked to. He encouraged them to make contradictory statements and then took pleasure in raising horrified hands as he pointed out their inconsistencies.

When Nadine's tearful outburst finally subsided, she got up and went to the bathroom and washed her face. She tidied her dark hair and when she looked in the mirror she could see no sign that she'd recently been very upset. She disliked the veneer of composure with which she felt obliged to meet the world. She couldn't respect it and find it stoical. Instead she found it false.

3

The day after Justin made Nadine cry with his accusations of her ill-treatment of her mother, she lunched with her friend Sabrina in a small Italian restaurant near her house. The two girls had once been at the same English boarding school. In that period, Nadine had been very unhappy and had suffered from homesickness. Her parents were still in India and although the Blunts had thought that it was in their daughter's interests that she be given a British education, Nadine had felt they had banished her and had been convinced that they had arranged for thousands of miles to separate her from them because they found their life much more pleasant in her absence.

Sabrina had done her best to comfort the unpopular and miserable little girl when she heard her sobbing at night under the brown school blankets. In those days, even in high summer, Nadine had always felt painfully cold. Accustomed to the tropics, her thin little body had been unable to adjust to the English climate, and she'd become prone to bronchitis and developed a hacking cough. Sabrina had insisted she borrow her woolly vests and her cardigan for she'd sometimes worried that Nadine was going to die – her face looked so pinched and blue. Although Nadine often used to wear her friend's clothes on top of her own, she'd found that the cold still seemed able to penetrate all the layers, although they made her look fat and bunched and the other children laughed at the cumbersome way in which she moved.

When Sabrina's father and mother had come to take her out to lunch in the local village restaurant at the week-ends, she had always insisted they invite Nadine as well. Sabrina had been a very good student, whereas Nadine had found the work hard. Feeling miserable and lost and frozen, she had difficulty concentrating. Sabrina used to let her copy out the answers to her sums and helped her with her spelling; as a result her marks had improved.

Nadine, who had been so vulnerable at that time, had become very dependent on Sabrina, loving her for her protectiveness and her generosity, and their friendship had continued after they left school. The two young women still liked to meet every week and eat spaghetti and drink red wine and tell each other about their lives.

Sabrina had become very good-looking and flamboyant. She was a tall girl with sleek blonde hair and green eyes. She had a beautiful figure and was a successful fashion model, dressing with great elegance and moving with such poise that she could appear supercilious and haughty. Her proud demeanour and the flawless chic of her appearance were deceptive, concealing the chaotic streak in her nature. She had many lovers, but her affairs usually ended disastrously, and Nadine was mystified by the way she so often chose men who turned out to be alcoholics, or to have similar neurotic problems.

When Nadine visited her friend's flat, she was always astonished by the squalor in which she lived. Sabrina's floor was constantly cluttered with clothes, records, cassettes, magazines, jewellery and make-up. Old bottles of wine and whisky and milk would also be lying around together with various cans which had once contained Coca-Cola or beer.

Sabrina used the floor of her flat as if it was a table to suit all purposes. As if she had picnicked on it, it was invariably littered with dirty plates and glasses. Nadine was shocked to see the remnants of uneaten food lying in dishes that had somehow got perched on top of a pile of underwear or valuable furs. She would shiver when she caught sight of a slice of ham or Camembert into which someone had stubbed their cigarette.

Sabrina's bed never seemed to be made and there was rarely a clean towel in her bathroom, where the basin was usually caked with spilt face-powder and foundation cream. But although the disorder of her friend's living conditions often dismayed Nadine, she was impressed by the way that, like a phoenix, Sabrina had the ability to rise from her own sordid debris. When she left her slovenly flat she was so faultlessly well-groomed that no one could have suspected from what chaos she had emerged.

Nadine could never understand why Sabrina's clothes always looked impeccably unsoiled and uncrumpled since she treated them with contempt and threw them down with all the other refuse on her floor. Like many fashion models, she had developed a hatred of clothes and if Sabrina owned an iron, Nadine had certainly never seen her use it. Yet she had a natural talent for dressing and Nadine always felt she could have taken an old grubby sheet and slung a belt round it, thereby managing to create the illusion she was wearing an exotic evening-gown.

'I had the most awful night last night,' Nadine said as she joined her friend in the restaurant. 'I didn't sleep one wink.'

'What on earth's happened?' Sabrina had rarely seen her friend look so tense and unhappy. Usually it was Sabrina who had the bad nights for she often spent them drinking very heavily and quarrelling with her current lover. She was always asking Nadine 'Do I have bags?', worrying that traces of the dissolute way that she lived would start to show on her face and damage her professional career.

'Oh, God, if you knew how much I loathe those cameras,' she often complained to Nadine. 'What could be more nightmarish on some early awful morning than sitting in a studio with the disgusting lens of a camera panning in on your hangover?'

It impressed Nadine that although Sabrina spoke so dismissively of her own appearance, she never seemed to get 'bags'. She had such a beautiful, healthy skin that her excesses appeared unable to flaw it. She gave the impression that she led the monastic existence of a health freak, worshipping sleep,

47

exercise, and unrefined foods. Whereas, in fact, Sabrina had never done an exercise in her life and ate entirely according to her immediate whim, ignoring the content of her food. She had no fear of fats and carbohydrates and by her lack of interest in their possible ill-effects she seemed to have deprived them of all power to injure her physique.

'Quick, let's order you some wine,' Sabrina said. She knew Nadine found it difficult to admit that anything in her life had gone awry. She realised that her friend had a dream of being in total control of her circumstances and though she respected this aspiration she still saw it as doomed. Order and control were foreign to Sabrina. She knew she could conceal the fact that her own life was devoid of them, but she was also aware that she could only retain this pretence for very short periods. She had learnt that she was able to present the world with a façade that could sometimes be mistaken for physical perfection, but knowing she was creating an illusion, she despised her own ability to do so. In the past, she'd had lovers who seemed to be much more in love with the exotic fashion photographs in the portfolio that she'd prepared for her modelling agency than they could ever be with her.

Her profession had placed her in the ambiguous position where she often felt that she was in competition with her own concocted and romanticised image. This had made her cynical for she was often defeated by it and she regarded all beautiful images as lies.

Seeing Nadine looking so tearful and distraught she was sorry that her friend was in distress, but also glad that, for once, she seemed to want to abandon the pretence that she was the permanently happy wife and mother, and discuss her feelings on a more intimate level than she was usually prepared to do.

'What happened last night?' Sabrina asked.

'Well, nothing – well, everything. I just lay awake all night. And as the hours went by, I just kept thinking and thinking. Then I suddenly realised something terrible. I don't love Justin at all.'

'But did you ever love him?' Sabrina had always found him rather selfish and smug, although she had thought it tactful to hide this from her friend. Secretly, she had often felt angered by the way he seemed to treat Nadine as an unpaid servant.

'Maybe I never really did love him. I started to wonder that last night. You see, when I left school, I was wildly in love with the idea of marriage. Do you remember how I used to read magazines called *Bride* and *Homemaker*? I even used to cut out brides with lovely white lace veils and I'd stick them up on the wall.'

'I remember you doing that,' said Sabrina.

'I think my whole dream of marriage came from my parents. You see, Mummy was an oddity. I think she really had a perfectly happy marriage. But maybe I'm seeing it all through rose-coloured spectacles?'

'No, I really feel you're right,' Sabrina said. 'When I came to visit your parents, I used to envy them. They certainly struck me as perfectly happy.'

'But all that happiness has ended in a downfall for my mother, so one wonders if it was really worth it.' Nadine's manner was still extremely agitated and she spoke with bitterness. 'My mother's life is pathetic now and she refuses to make any effort to improve it. The last time I went down to see her – I can't tell you how much she depressed me. I really have the horrible feeling she's going to die – and I don't mean in the far future – I think she's going to die very soon. I find it all so pointless. I can't believe there's nothing in life for her besides my father.'

'Yes, there must be something else.' Sabrina was trying to cheer her friend, but as she remembered staying with the Blunts after they returned from India, and recalled the way Nadine's mother had appeared to rely entirely on the Colonel, she was not as certain as she tried to sound.

'It must be quite a nightmare for your mother,' she said. 'She's got to readjust her whole life. I remember that I was shocked when you told me that until your father died, she'd never even owned her own cheque book.'

'I'm afraid that's perfectly true,' Nadine said. 'She didn't even know how one wrote out a cheque. It was ridiculous. I had to give her lessons.'

'I find that kind of helplessness rather moving. I can't help envying her. I wish I didn't know how to write a cheque. I think it would be so good for curbing my extravagance. I'd find it really very pleasant.'

'Oh, no, you wouldn't, Sabrina. It was awful for my mother. When Daddy died, it left her terrified and confused. She was pitiful. She hadn't taken in that my father received income from his family trusts. She went into a panic. She thought she would have to sleep out like a tramp on the streets. She'd never had a clue as to what money she had. My father had always paid all her household bills. He'd always taken complete control of all her affairs. He left her a huge life insurance policy, but even that frightened her. She didn't have any idea how to collect it. She didn't know the name of his solicitor. She didn't even know what a solicitor was. I did my best to teach her how to deal with all the boring things of life. But it was agony for her at first. She was like a baby.'

'I think that's rather sad,' Sabrina said. 'I still don't really understand why it seems to make you so cross with her.'

'I really can't bear that kind of helplessness!' Nadine spoke with sudden violence. 'I really resent my mother for having passed it on to me.'

'But you've never struck me as being in the least like your mother. You seem to be the very soul of capability. Just look at your life compared to mine. You've got your marriage, your children, your household. You know how to run all that beautifully. I don't even know how to cook. You've tasted my food. It always turns out foul. I seem to burn everything. I loathe domesticity. It really doesn't suit me. But I can't pretend I've found a very brilliant alternative. I go floating round London like a piece of seaweed washed along by the tide. I'm nothing but a clothes-peg – and soon I'll be a clothes-peg that's too old to be used. The fashion world is very cruel. They'll soon find a bunch of new and stunning girls of fifteen and one of these days when I go rolling along to the studios the photographers will say to me, "Oh, forget it darling! Get thee to an old persons' home!"'

Sabrina was deliberately presenting her own situation as

bleakly as possible in order to make Nadine feel that her own was cheerful by contrast. It worried her to see that she had the same pinched, miserable look that she used to have at school. Sabrina started to eat a plate of spaghetti, twirling the pasta round her fork with a deft and elegant gesture. Nadine drank some wine, but she left her food untouched. Sabrina couldn't understand if it was anxiety about her mother's unhappy predicament or her relationship with Justin that was making her friend so distraught.

'I'm afraid we've both ended up in much the same boat,' Nadine said. 'And in some ways it's all our own fault. We were cowardly and lazy when we settled for marriage and modelling. But at least you're free, Sabrina. At least you're not tied down in a rut.' Nadine, now, in her turn, was trying to cheer her friend. She was disturbed by the harsh terms in which she'd just described her life. Secretly, it worried her to think about Sabrina's future. She couldn't imagine what she was going to do when she was no longer able to earn her living as a model.

'You can't really get very much bird-like freedom from a profession which has inbuilt obsolescence,' Sabrina said. 'My career will be about as lasting as that of an American domestic appliance.'

'But surely there are other things you could do,' Nadine said. 'You could go on to the stage, you could go into television or the movies.'

Sabrina shook her head. 'I don't have the talent for any of that. I can only expose myself for very short periods – that's why my character is suited to photographic modelling. You create an image. The camera goes click and it's all over. The whole thing is very fraudulent – but it's also mercifully brief. I could never sustain any form of public performance. I wouldn't want to. At heart, I'm not sufficiently exhibitionistic. The whole enterprise wouldn't seem worth the necessary effort. It would bore me.'

'You should probably never have gone into modelling. You should probably have done something else,' Nadine said.

'Oh, I know that now. You remember that I signed my first modelling contract when I was only fifteen. It seemed such a

51

brilliant move at the time. I wanted only two things when I was that age. I wanted to find a way to be independent of my parents and I wanted to drop out of school. Now I've got much less than you have, Nadine. Your marriage may not be perfect, but at least you've got the twins. All I'll be left with is a bunch of old photographs and they'll be very poor company in the declining years. Who wants to pore over documents that are only faithful records of how very much better you once looked than you do now?'

Sabrina was again trying to console her friend. She couldn't really see that Felix and Roland were very desirable assets, but knowing that her friend saw them quite differently, she thought it a good thing to mention them while she was trying to make her take a more positive view of her present life.

'I adore the twins,' Nadine said. 'But it's really only my terror that Justin might take them away from me that stops me from leaving him. Justin would turn very nasty if I left him. He holds all the cards. I couldn't send the twins to an expensive school like he can.'

'Do they have to go to such an expensive school?' Sabrina asked. 'If their mother's miserable, I can't believe that it's very good for them.'

'I don't think they know what I feel. I put on such a cheerful front. I'm not exactly miserable. It's less dramatic than that and much more dreary. When I couldn't sleep last night, I started thinking about my marriage. I felt it was rather like those awful old chipped caravans you see sitting in fields stuck deep in the mud. You can live in them – at least you can cook and sleep in them. They give you a roof so you're protected from the rain. But if you don't have any vehicle to pull them, they aren't going to take you anywhere at all. And that's the trouble with my marriage to Justin. We have nothing to pull us. We're completely static. I used to think that marriages should go somewhere interesting. I felt that every couple ought to have a goal – something serious and interesting that was outside the marriage – something they felt was just as important as the children. But Justin and I don't have that at all. It's awful to admit it, but I think we have even less of a purpose than an old-fashioned pair like my parents. You see, Daddy believed in serving his country – he really believed in the Empire. And then Mummy believed she was doing something fantastically worthwhile when she helped him serve it.'

'You're being unfair on Justin. At this point in history, I really think it's unfair for you to expect him to start serving the Empire,' Sabrina interrupted.

Nadine's fervent and idealistic attitude to marriage always baffled her. It was so different from her own that it shocked her, yet she was always intrigued to be allowed to peep at it. She felt she was viewing a relic of historical interest that had been put on display in a glass case. Nadine also confused her when at times she could be so critical of her mother, while at others showing a perverse desire to present her as a model.

'I'm not being unfair. Of course I don't expect Justin to wave Union Jacks and start serving the Empire,' Nadine said. 'But I still feel he ought to aspire to something more interesting than he does. Oh yes, Sabrina, I know you'll say that he's got his journalism – but I can never get myself very involved with that. I try and pretend that I admire his articles, but I never really see they have much point. He just churns them out for the money . . . Now I may have to confess that if we had to live on his earnings as a writer, I might very well have more respect for them than I do. But you know we've never lived on Justin's writing. So that question doesn't arise. We've always lived on the capital he inherited from his father. If you want the truth, I really feel that Justin only writes for his own vanity. He always takes a vaguely liberal position. He deplores this, he deplores that. He's always trying to improve society. But I don't believe he cares about the things that he pretends to. I think he likes to see his name splashed about the newspapers. He is very childish about his articles. He always makes me cut them out and paste them in an album. You know that he often gets fan letters from various readers. I have to paste all those silly letters in his album too. Often they seem to have been written by raving lunatics. Justin never seems to grasp that. He's always thrilled by them.'

'I never knew you hated him so much.'

'I don't hate him . . . But you may be right. Maybe I do hate him and I don't want to admit it because I can't see how I'll ever be able to leave him.'

'You could always move in with me,' Sabrina said.

'No, I couldn't do that,' Nadine's eyes had filled with tears. 'But, oh goodness, Sabrina, you are incredibly nice to suggest it. You must know I couldn't really move in with you. The twins would soon send you mad.'

Sabrina knew there was a lot of truth in Nadine's statement. She therefore tried to think of an alternative solution.

'Couldn't you leave Justin – take the children – and go off to the country and stay there for a while with your mother?'

'You must be joking!' Nadine's voice sounded shrill. The suggestion clearly appalled her. 'I can put up with semi-hell Sabrina – but I really can't manage total hell. Can you imagine what my life would be like if I went to live in that depressing house in Wiltshire? I don't think I'd survive for more than a week. I can't think of anything much worse than living – day in, day out – with my mother's grief and Mrs Murphy!'

'But there must be other arrangements you could make, Nadine. Your mother is really very well off. I can understand you might find it difficult to live with her. But I know she adores you. If she knew you were unhappy with Justin, I'm sure she'd get you a flat so that you could be independent.'

'But I wouldn't be independent if I started taking money from my mother. I don't think you understand, Sabrina . . . I can't even bring myself to make a telephone call to her. I'm horrible to her. I know she must be desperately lonely – especially in the evenings. I know she'd love to have someone she could chat to. But somehow I can't face the idea of speaking to her. At the moment, there's something about her voice that makes me want to shake her. It sounds so weak, so quavering, so hopeless. I find it maddening. I can see that you think I'm disgusting . . .'

'Does your mother keep telephoning you?' Sabrina asked.

'Oh, no. My mother certainly never telephones me.' Nadine spoke with a bitterness that her friend found inconsistent. 'She always says she's worried that I might be busy. She claims she doesn't want to disturb me . . . You'll probably find my reaction to that quite petty and unreasonable, but I often resent her for making me feel so guilty that I don't keep in touch with her. Why should she expect me to be the one to make the first move?'

'Maybe your mother isn't as lonely as you think. Maybe there's no need for you to feel so guilty about her. I think she's quite a resilient character. It's quite possible that she's starting to get her life in order.'

'My mother is every bit as lonely as I think. You know that she's never learnt to drive – so she's just sitting there in that house, totally marooned. Oh, Sabrina, please don't spin me the line that you think she's fine and happy and thriving. Justin always does that. It really makes me hate him. I promise you, my mother is getting worse and worse. She's just wasting away. She's lost so much weight, she's like a wafer. She doesn't show one little sign that she's trying to get her life in order. Every time I see her, she looks more ill and miserable. I don't seem to be able to do a thing to cheer her up – that's why I feel there's no point in having much contact with her.'

Sabrina found Nadine's ambivalent attitude towards her mother slightly exasperating, but as her friend was obviously in such distress, she didn't want to let her know this.

'Do you really want to break up your marriage?' she asked.

'Oh, yes, Sabrina. I do . . . I most certainly do. I decided that last night. But I feel I've put myself in a trap. I can't just pack a suitcase and leave Justin in the night, taking the twins. I don't know where I could take them. We'd all have to sleep out on a bench in the park.'

'It really seems quite absurd that you won't accept any help from your mother. As we know, she's loaded with all this money and from what you tell me, she's not putting it to any good purpose.'

'I'm not taking any money from my mother!'

Sabrina thought that Nadine's announcement was childish in its determination and its defiance. As the whole tapestry of Sabrina's life was woven with threads of compromise, she could never understand why her friend had such a horror of it.

'If you can't bear to speak to someone on the telephone,' Nadine said, 'I don't really see that you can start asking them for money.'

Sabrina shrugged. Her beautiful face looked pitying. Her eyebrows had been plucked so that her expression was unchangingly quizzical. They were shaped like the tops of two triangles.

'Why is it better to take money from Justin? From what you've told me, you don't seem over-fond of him?'

'I'm horribly ashamed to be living on Justin's money,' Nadine said. 'I loathe what I'm doing. But I can't see any alternative. I'm not trained for anything except marriage. If I left Justin, I don't know how I could support the twins.'

Sabrina wished that her friend had never had the twins. Nadine had made her their godmother, but she still saw them as two stones tied round their mother's neck.

'How long have you been unhappy with Justin?' she asked. 'You fooled me completely. I always thought your marriage was a great success.'

'Yes, I know I've never complained about Justin. I felt it would be disloyal. Remember that I was brought up to believe you had to be loyal to your husband. And in a sense I've got nothing to complain of. He isn't cruel. He isn't unfaithful. Or if he is, it has certainly never come to my notice.'

'But something must be wrong,' Sabrina said. 'Otherwise you wouldn't be thinking of leaving him.'

'Oh, yes, something is very wrong indeed. You see, I think I married the idea of marriage when I got engaged to Justin. At the beginning it wasn't so bad. I was grateful to him for giving me the role I'd always wanted. Then I got pregnant almost immediately and I became completely involved with my own pregnancy. It may sound silly – but I hardly noticed Justin. He was just there. He was rather like our furniture.'

'But Justin doesn't seem to me like furniture. He's always struck me as rather selfish and demanding.'

'Oh, yes, he's selfish all right. Everything in our household revolves round Justin's wishes. But once the twins were born I was so busy bringing them up that I wasn't very affected by

Justin. Oh, I know that I scurried round obeying his orders. I cooked for him, I entertained his friends. I made our house as nice as I could. But somehow I never felt I was doing it all for Justin. I always thought that I was doing it for the twins.'

'But what has changed?' Sabrina asked. 'You've still got the twins.'

'*I've* changed,' Nadine said. 'My whole attitude towards my marriage has changed. Remember that the twins are much older now. They go to school most of the day. They take up much less of my time. Now I'm finding it pointless to put so much energy into running the household. You see, I feel I'm only doing it for Justin. And now I've faced the fact that I don't love him, I can't see it's very sensible to devote my life to his well-being.'

Sabrina couldn't argue with this. She found the idea of anyone devoting their life to Justin a most unrewarding prospect. Her friend's predicament depressed her. She wished she could do something practical to help her as she'd once lent her woolly vests and cardigans at school.

'Does Justin have any idea how you feel?' she inquired.

'Oh, good gracious, no! Justin never notices how people feel. It doesn't interest him. When we last went down to see my mother she looked so wretched I thought she was going to drop down dead in front of my very eyes, but Justin never registered that anything was the matter with her.'

'That doesn't surprise me,' Sabrina said. 'Do you remember that awful time when I came round to see you after I'd been bashed on the eye by that maniac American? Justin immediately suggested that we all go out to dinner in a restaurant. I couldn't open my eye at all. The whole thing had vanished under a repulsive black and purple mountain of swelling. Justin simply couldn't understand why I wasn't very keen to go out in public. "Don't be so stupid. You look perfectly all right," he kept telling me. I deeply resented him for saying that. After all, I am a fashion model and my whole career depends on appearance. I really looked like hell that night. But I don't think he noticed I looked any different from usual.'

'No, I'm afraid that Justin probably didn't notice,' Nadine

said. 'Or if he did notice, it didn't interest him. That's what I'm complaining about. He's got this knack of never being at all interested in anyone else's feelings – and you've no idea how lonely that can make you. Of course, I'm a bit to blame because I never let him know what I'm really thinking. I never lose my temper and I never stand up to him. You see, my mother never stood up to my father. But then he doted on her so much, there wasn't really anything for her to stand up to. My situation is different and it's stupid that I'm so obedient to Justin. "Darling," he says, "why do we have to have these bloody steel ice-containers? Why don't we have the rubber ones?" And I go rushing off to the shops and I get him the rubber ice-containers. My whole life's like that and I'm really starting to find it so pointless. The rubber ice-containers don't make either of us very happy.'

'Is Justin unhappy with you?'

Nadine hesitated. 'You may find this silly,' she said, 'but I don't really know. It's impossible to tell if Justin is happy or unhappy. It's as if he doesn't notice his own feelings any more than he notices anyone else's. Justin's like a telegraph-pole, Sabrina. Do you see what I mean? You know how tall he is, you know how wooden he is. But I can't believe that Justin can really be very happy with me even though I still come on like those awful wives in the television commercials – you know, those wives who are always wearing spotless aprons, and beaming pearly smiles as they carry sizzling dishes to the family table.'

'Why do you put on such an act?' Sabrina asked.

'I don't know. I feel I have to. It's as if the act is ingrained in me. I'll tell you something that you'll really find pathetic. I couldn't bear my mother to know that my marriage has turned out to be a failure.'

'Yes, I do find that rather insane, Nadine. Surely you don't think she'd blame you. Obviously she'd be sorry that your marriage hadn't worked out for you. But I see no good reason why it should all be hidden from her. She's a very sympathetic woman and as I said before if she realised you were in trouble, she'd do everything to help you.'

Nadine's face had reddened because she could see that her friend thought she was being neurotic.

'Oh, I know that my mother would do everything to help me. But she's never going to be allowed to find out that I need any help. I can't explain how strongly I feel about that.'

'But Nadine, this is ridiculous. If you eventually leave Justin, your mother is bound to find out about it. I don't see how you can hide it from her . . . Surely you're not telling me that you'd be prepared to stay in an unhappy marriage rather than let your mother find out that you've made a mess of it.'

Sabrina found her friend's position incomprehensible. She'd always liked Mrs Blunt, and she couldn't understand why Nadine sometimes spoke of her with dread as if she saw her as an ogress. Sabrina had not seen Nadine's mother since the day that she had gone down to the country with her friend to give her support at her father's funeral. She had never forgotten the sight of Mrs Blunt standing by her husband's graveside. She had rarely seen a human being in such a state of shock and misery. As Nadine claimed that her mother had never really recovered from the death of the Colonel, Sabrina felt that her friend was being unrealistic when she believed that someone as emotionally shattered as Mrs Blunt would be able to get very concerned by the failure or success of her daughter's marriage.

'No, Sabrina, I'll never be so insane as to stay endlessly married to Justin just in order to hide the real truth from my mother,' Nadine said. 'But as I can't see any way that I can leave him at the moment, I really don't want her to find out that my whole set-up isn't nearly as perfect as she thinks it is. I'd find it humiliating . . .'

Sabrina thought her logic spurious. She saw no good reason why Nadine should feel humiliated. She was puzzled by the way that Nadine seemed to see marriage as a competition in which she had been defeated by her mother. She was certain that Mrs Blunt would be astonished if she knew that her daughter had a horror of letting her know that she was unhappily married because she had the distorted idea that the knowledge would make her mother feel triumphant.

'I find your happy housewife act so odd,' Sabrina said. 'I

couldn't put on such an act for a moment. I'm very quick to voice my discontents. As a result, as you well know, my relationships are of very brief duration. That's usually quite fortunate. At least I find it so . . . I'm always relieved to have a quick turnover.'

'Have you got anyone new in your life?' Nadine asked. She felt she had been egocentric speaking only of her own problems.

'Oh, yes, I have. I met him in a cocktail bar a few nights ago and somehow he has ended up in my flat. If you have complaints to make about Justin, it might cheer you to hear the virtues of my newest acquisition. He's called Coco. He says he's Italian, but I think he's probably really Algerian. He's homosexual with very faint leanings towards "bi". His actual sexual orientation hardly matters very much because he's a speed freak and he's so stoned out of his head because he mixes amphetamines with such vast quantities of alcohol, that most of the time he hardly knows where he is.'

'What does this attractive creature do?' Nadine asked.

'He doesn't . . . Well, he claims to be a male model. He's quite handsome in rather a decadent way. But he never seems to get round to doing any modelling. As a result, he's already proving quite a severe financial drain on me. I don't think I can afford to support such a languid lily . . . Coco's really got to go. Surely you agree with me . . . When he comes round tonight I don't think I'm going to let him in.'

Nadine listened to her friend's description of Coco with the same bafflement that Sabrina had listened to her reasons for refusing to ask her mother to help extricate herself from her loveless marriage. She looked at her beautiful friend and she found it incomprehensible that she could be so unselective.

Sabrina's lackadaisical and frivolous approach to her love affairs sometimes chilled Nadine. She found it difficult to understand her horror of personal commitment – she could therefore never grasp that her genius for finding unsatisfactory figures was self-protective. Sabrina always knew from the start that her relationship with disreputable figures like Coco was doomed to be transitory. This was what she wanted.

As Sabrina never had any expectation that her liaisons would be conducive to long-term happiness, when they ended she emerged emotionally unscathed for she was never plagued by any sense of disillusionment. She stepped out of her unrewarding love affairs with detachment and dignity, just as she stepped with cool elegance from the self-created messiness of her flat.

'Yes, it sounds as if Coco should go,' Nadine said.

'And Justin should go, too.'

Nadine winced when she heard her husband linked with an unsavoury character such as Coco.

'I sometimes feel quite guilty about Justin,' she said. 'It's an awful thing to share a house with someone you don't love. If I go to the lavatory and I find that Justin's in there, I feel really annoyed and I then have to remind myself that the poor man is entitled to use his own lavatory. I'm afraid that it's the silly little things that are getting on my nerves more and more. When I go into the bathroom and I see his toothbrush and his razor on the basin, I want to sweep them away because I feel they've got no right to be there. Justin is very untidy. I don't expect you've realised that. You see, I have this need to make everything very neat. I've always run round after him. I've always mopped up all the mess he leaves behind him. But now I've reached a point where I can hardly bear to do it. He leaves his clothes and his papers strewn all over the house, and although I put them in tidy piles for him, I see them as rubbish and I'd really like to throw them in the rubbish-bin. And I mind his shoes almost the worst of all. He likes to slip them off in the drawing-room and he leaves them lying there on the carpet. And I hate to have to pick them up. They look so huge and black and I find them so smelly . . .'

Sabrina listened to her friend with the despondency of someone who has to listen to the dissatisfactions of a person who seems more interested in recounting every miserable detail of her situation than in taking steps to improve it.

'And then I can't bear sleeping with Justin any more,' Nadine continued. 'I don't like to tell him that, so I make every sort of excuse to get out of it. I tell him I've got a cold, that I've got a headache. I get quite inventive with all my ailments. I say that I've got stomach pains, that I've got the curse. Oh, you can imagine all the things I tell him. Poor Justin must really think he's married to a chronic invalid. I've moved into our guest room because I dread sharing the same bed as him.'

As Sabrina felt frustrated by her inability to help Nadine extricate herself from a marriage that sounded gruesome, she decided she would try and do something to relieve the guilt Nadine seemed to feel about her grieving mother.

She told her that she had some cousins who lived in Wiltshire and she would soon be going down to stay with them. She'd then arrange to drive over and visit Mrs Blunt and see if there was anything to be done to make her life less forlorn and aimless. Nadine was very grateful to hear this, although it made her ashamed that she was so eager to shift her obligations on to her friend. When their lunch ended, Nadine felt closer to Sabrina than she had ever felt before.

4

Mrs Blunt stood on the top of the beautiful old stone steps that led up to her front door. She was wearing a pale quilted dressing-gown. She shivered for there had been a frost in the night and her over-grown garden looked white and hard. She had heard the postman arrive on his bicycle and had rushed down to see if there was a letter from Rupert Sinclair. But there was only one dismal-looking bill in a dull brown envelope.

The milkman had left a bottle of milk on her steps and she saw that a bird had pecked a hole through its silver top in order to drink off the cream. Mrs Blunt felt slightly outraged by this impudent and brazen act. It seemed human rather than bird-like. She decided she'd better get some kind of box to protect her milk from the attack of greedy thrushes and crows. This was a sensible decision. However, having made it she wondered if she would ever carry it out. She minded that Rupert Sinclair had not answered her letter, but she found she could not care for more than a moment about the theft of her cream.

She looked at her watch and saw it was only half past eight and she realised that it would be nearly two hours until Mrs Murphy arrived. This thought was accompanied by a mood of panic. For the last three years the pain of her grief had been so ever-present that it had prevented her from feeling lonely. It had been always with her like an unpleasant but faithful companion. On this cold fresh morning it no longer staved off her sense of loneliness. Nor did she feel as she'd felt for a very long time, that mourning was sufficient as an occupation. It shocked her to realise that her existence was now so boring and empty she was prepared to count the minutes until the arrival of Mrs Murphy.

'What shall I do with my life?' Mrs Blunt wondered. And having no one to put this question to, she suddenly thought she would write and ask Rupert Sinclair. But as he hadn't bothered to answer her last letter, she was too proud to do something so undignified.

Mrs Blunt then asked herself why she found herself hoping that an unknown cripple could give her any valuable answer. She decided it was because she believed that wisdom came out of suffering. Rupert Sinclair must have suffered horribly. She couldn't bear to think about it. Nor did she like to think what Corrigan must have gone through. She felt that he had certainly acquired wisdom. He'd placed his ruined life at the service of others and by so doing he seemed to have succeeded in saving his soul from the wreckage.

When she thought of all the things that Sinclair and Corrigan had been forced to endure, Mrs Blunt was ashamed to admit that she felt quite piqued that she had not received any reply to her letter. She realised that it was outrageous to blame a disabled man, but she still couldn't help feeling that Corrigan had let her down. He had persuaded her to write to a stranger and he'd assured her that if she did this it would be the start of an interesting and valuable correspondence. Nothing that Corrigan had promised her had happened and she found her own disappointment puzzling. She wondered what on earth she'd hoped that Rupert Sinclair would say to her in the answer she'd hoped to get from him. It was as if she'd believed that his reply might contain something that could change her whole life. Standing on the front steps of her house in the early morning with the cold turning her breath to steam like that of a fairy-tale dragon, Mrs Blunt wondered what that could possibly be.

She went back inside her house and made a cup of tea. She tried to imagine Rupert Sinclair. She visualised him as classically handsome. She remembered that Corrigan had described him as extremely attractive and charming. She saw Sinclair as having the very English and conventional good looks of the male models who advertised cigars and port in glossy magazines. She saw Rupert Sinclair's hair as dark brown. She felt that everything about him – his eyes, his hair, his tweed jackets, his invalid's rug, would all be brown. She was certain that he smelled of tobacco. The Colonel used to smell of cigar smoke. Rupert Sinclair might very well be a little bit like him. Corrigan was, however, different – she didn't feel that he was like the Colonel at all.

It suddenly occurred to her with a nasty tingle of shock that there was no earthly reason why she need ever hear from Corrigan again. He had come into her house and made her aware of the tragedies of his life, his terrible accident, the death of his mother, and just when she'd started to have a longing to help him, he had vanished. He obviously had no idea how much his account of his vicissitudes now haunted her. When she thought of London, she had the image of a vast, cruel monster that had swallowed him up alive. She remembered the expression in Corrigan's intense blue-green eyes as he had talked of his love for poetry, and she felt another unworthy pang of annoyance that Rupert Sinclair had not answered her letter. If the man had only replied, it would have made it possible for her to write to him again. She could then have asked him if he had any news of Corrigan.

She wondered if she dared to write to Rupert Sinclair once more. Would he find it unseemly if she wrote to him again before he had given her any sign that he was at all keen to hear from her? It suddenly occurred to her that Corrigan could have been mistaken when he insisted that this mysterious man would be enchanted to get a letter from a woman whom she had never set eyes on. Perhaps he had not replied because he already saw her as a crackpot, the sort of pathetic nut-case who tries to correspond with the Queen. It was also possible that instead of being thrilled, Sinclair had in fact been insulted by her assumption that his existence was now so lonely and loveless that he had a frantic need to receive a charity letter from a total stranger. Mrs Blunt reminded herself that she knew nothing about him. Even if the unlucky fellow was condemned to live out his days in an institution, he could still have many loving relatives and friends who wrote to him daily. For all she knew, Sinclair might very well be married and therefore feel even less desire to get letters from an unknown person when he was carrying on a precious correspondence with his wife.

However, when Mrs Blunt thought about it a little more, she decided that it was unlikely that Sinclair had a wife. She couldn't believe that Corrigan would have been so tactless and insensitive as to ask her to write to a married man without first informing her of his circumstances. She'd not received the impression that he was in the least insensitive. She'd admired the way he was always so careful not to create any marital friction in the households that he approached for donations. She had also admired him for refusing to allow his fervour for his excellent cause to permit him to take more money than certain families could afford.

She was touched that he had not allowed her to make a donation because he feared that as a widow she might be financially distressed. Although she applauded the delicacy with which he had treated her, it made her feel a little fraudulent when she thought of the trusts that had come to her from her late husband's family. However, she realised that Corrigan could not possibly have known her real position. In fact, there was every reason for him to assume that her economic situation was abysmal. She felt deeply ashamed when it occurred to her that Corrigan must have noticed the catastrophic condition of her garden. She suddenly decided that in the next few days she would get hold of a couple of gardeners and get them to plough it up and replant it.

When Mrs Murphy arrived she told her about this decision. Mrs Murphy gave her one of her shrewd looks. 'Ach, so we're having flowers again, are we?'

Mrs Blunt fidgeted as if she sensed there was something derisory in this question.

'Well, I was thinking that it was really time that I restored it to some kind of order,' she said defensively. Mrs Murphy had a way of saying things that seemed to insinuate something very different from what she actually expressed and Mrs Blunt had never found this trait at all appealing.

'There's no time like the right time!' Mrs Murphy said cheerfully, and because Mrs Blunt had not taken the address of Corrigan's flat in London and therefore felt she would never again be able to get in touch with him, she found this comment extremely aggravating. She had suddenly made up her mind that she very much wanted to send him a donation. Since he had paid her his visit, she had started to accuse herself of being disgustingly selfish in the way that she spent her money. She always gave Nadine very large cheques on her birthday, and also at Christmas, and she spent a lot on toys for she enjoyed sending presents to the twins, but otherwise, she had to admit with shame, she only spent her money on herself. Since the arrival of Corrigan, she had been wondering why it had never occurred to her before, that because she had been lucky, and had inherited a little jewel of a house and received unearned income far in excess of her needs, that she was under any moral obligation to see that her money benefited those who were less privileged. Nadine had always urged her to do some charitable work and she had rejected her suggestion because she resented her daughter's refusal to recognise that she was totally prostrated by her loss. But since Corrigan's visit, she felt sorry that she had been too blind to see that her daughter's suggestions had always been valuable ones. She felt that, like someone in the Bible, her eyes had been opened by Corrigan. She suddenly understood that grief had made her cruel and she thought that at last she knew why her relationship with her daughter had become so distant and strained. She found it very distressing that just when she felt she was starting to come out of the unhappy torpor in which she had slept through life ever since the death of her husband, she had no way of informing Corrigan that she had made the decision to put her money and energies to better use.

She wondered if he had a telephone in his little flat. It was always possible that he was listed in the London telephone directory. She was just about to look him up when she remembered that she didn't know his first name. There were bound to be many Corrigans in the book and without knowing his first initial she realised that it would be hopeless to try to trace his number.

'Have you heard anything from the cripple?' Mrs Murphy asked her when she next went into the kitchen. Mrs Blunt wished she wouldn't describe Corrigan like that. She somehow managed to make the word sound offensively pejorative. She also hated to be asked if she had heard from him just when she was feeling so upset because she'd no way of letting him know that she was longing to make him a donation. She wondered how often he went to St Crispins. He had made it sound as if he dropped in there quite frequently. If she wrote him a letter c/o the Secretary, there was therefore a hope he might get it. She decided to do this although she knew there was a danger he might have gone off on some great tour of the countryside and then he would very probably never receive it. She still felt it was worth trying.

'Dear Corrigan,' she wrote and she kept rereading his name. It looked so bold and forceful written out on her flimsy writing-paper. The letters seemed to grow as she looked at them. They had a largeness that had so little to do with her restricted existence that she could hardly believe she herself had actually formed them. She had the curious feeling that the two words that started her letter had somehow written themselves, that they had always been there as if inscribed in invisible ink, only waiting for her to read them.

After she had read and reread Corrigan's name countless times, she was seized by a bout of paralysis and she realised she could not continue to write to him. She felt it would be crass if she simply offered him a donation without adding something else, and although she longed to write him something he would find interesting, she found herself unable to do it.

When she had written to Rupert Sinclair she had scribbled a lot of trivial information about herself. She had realised that her letter was not very inspired, but as she'd never met him, she'd still been prepared to finish it and seal the envelope and send it off. But when she tried to write to Corrigan she found the task very much more challenging. Since he'd come to her house and let her know deeply he cared about literature, she was frightened that her letter might display her illiteracy and ignorance.

He had given her the impression that he was an extremely kind man. As he was Irish, she assumed he was a Catholic and most probably a very devout one. She sensed that he was a person who had profound spiritual resources. She felt that something must have given him the strength to conquer his disability and maintain his largeness of soul and intellect.

Even if the letter she wrote him struck him as the outpourings of a mindless, limited woman, she didn't feel that his attitude towards her would be a harsh one. It was her own attitude towards herself that had become so intensely critical. Corrigan had made her realise that she had no excuse for being so ill-read. All those years she'd spent with the Colonel in India she had enjoyed enormous leisure. She had seen the suffering all round her and done very little to try to alleviate it. When Nadine was a small child she had been looked after by an ayah, so Mrs Blunt realised she had not even taken on the full burden of her daughter's upbringing. Later when Nadine had been sent off to boarding-school in England, Mrs Blunt now had to admit she'd had even less to occupy her. She had devoted herself to the needs of the Colonel and even in her new self-lacerating frame of mind, she thought she could claim that she had been a good wife to him.

However, in her new mood, this no longer seemed to have been enough. When she thought about her life as compared to that of Corrigan, she felt that whereas he had found a way to escape from the prison of his infirmity by the use of his mind and imagination, she, who had never suffered from any physical disability, had crippled and imprisoned herself by her refusal to use her brain. Such was her feeling of inferiority that she abandoned her attempt to write to him.

On that same afternoon when she took some flowers down to her late husband's grave, she stood in front of it and like someone consulting an oracle, without using words, she asked him what she ought to do. She told him how much she still missed him and asked him if he could understand that she felt her life had reached a point of crisis, and she now thought she ought to try and cast off the grey weeds of her bereavement and try and do some good in a world on which she had turned her back since his death.

The churchyard which lay on the outskirts of Coombe Abbot was a peaceful little spot. As the village was underpopulated, it was not overcrowded like many modern cemeteries. It had a smooth and springy turf that reminded Mrs Blunt of a very still green lake, and she'd often wished she could dive into its emerald depths and submerge herself in its stillness.

In the early spring, snowdrops, celandines and crocuses dotted its smooth grass like little fairy lights of hope and the sight of them always saddened her for they mocked her sense of hopelessness and yet she was also glad that her late husband was surrounded by the wild flowers that had meant so much to him. She therefore always regarded their beauty with ambivalence.

Today, as she stood looking at the Colonel's grey flat stone, she felt she could hear his voice whispering in the wind that was blowing through the yew trees that encircled the cemetery. At first she couldn't make out what he was trying to tell her, but as she listened more intently, she thought she could hear him saying that he would not regard it as disloyal if she now started to re-engage herself in life. He seemed to be telling her that he approved her desire to support Corrigan and his charitable cause, and he advised her to pluck up her courage, to write once again to Rupert Sinclair and find out from him how he could be traced. Feeling a joy that the Colonel approved of her enterprise, Mrs Blunt returned to her house and once again got out her writing-paper.

The second letter she wrote to Sinclair was very short and to the point. She asked him if he knew how she could get hold of Corrigan. She told him she was anxious to make him a donation because she had found his goals admirable. Once again she told Sinclair that she hoped he was well, although she had the same old doubts as to whether he would find this greeting an appropriate one. She then took the letter to Mrs Murphy and asked her to post it on her way home.

Mrs Murphy looked at the envelope with great curiosity. 'This Mr Sinclair – he seems to be getting quite a few letters from you. Does he have anything to do with that cripple?' she asked.

'Mr Sinclair also has the misfortune to be disabled.' Mrs Blunt's voice crackled with acidity. She didn't feel it was Mrs Murphy's business to take such a keen interest in whom she wrote to.

'So we are suddenly surrounded by cripples!' Mrs Murphy's announcement had a satisfaction that Mrs Blunt found most offensive.

'I must say that I don't really see that to be the case.' Mrs Blunt's remark had the same sharp tone. But as she spoke she had a feeling of regret and she longed for Mrs Murphy's statement to be true.

After Mrs Blunt wrote her second letter to Rupert Sinclair a whole week went by and she received no reply from him. She felt humiliated and irritable and she found Mrs Murphy's general noisiness and the boom of her singing increasingly painful.

When Mrs Murphy mopped the kitchen floor, she performed this simple task with such unnecessary panache that even if Mrs Blunt retired to her bedroom she was still disagreeably aware of it. Mrs Murphy approached this chore as if she was some over-hearty sailor swabbing down a deck. She would fill up a bucket of water and then hurl its contents on to the linoleum, hitting it with such a resounding smack that the whole house shook from the violence of the impact. She would then take off her carpet slippers and her woolly socks and paddle around in all the water, swishing and splashing, as she made childish whirlpools with her mop.

Mrs Blunt always thought there was something dangerously unhygienic about Mrs Murphy's purple, bunion-ridden feet, and she often secretly worried that they were going to spread germs that would contaminate her food. She also found it tiresome that her kitchen took so long to dry out after it had

71

been pointlessly flooded. But she still never complained. Some kind of profound inertia came over her whenever she thought of trying to correct any of Mrs Murphy's energetic habits, and although since Corrigan had made her question the very premises on which her whole life was now constructed, Mrs Murphy's ability to make her constantly aware of her presence in the house no longer seemed as desirable as it used to, she never once thought of dismissing her. She was very fond of Mrs Murphy, although she found she sometimes clashed with her temperamentally. She therefore continued to bow to the force of her impetuous personality as a poplar silently bows before the force of a violent gale.

5

A letter arrived from Rupert Sinclair just when Mrs Blunt had given up hope of ever receiving an answer from him. He apologised for taking so long to reply. Apparently he had not been at all well, and she thought there was great tact in the way he refrained from explaining what had been the matter with him. Corrigan had told her that he had been severely injured in the last war and she was deeply ashamed that she'd felt so angry and rebuffed that he'd not answered her letter immediately. She knew that Sinclair had lost the use of his legs, but she now hardly dared to imagine what other physical injuries he had sustained. For all she knew, the poor man was in constant pain. She was appalled that she had written to him like some silly effusive schoolgirl, saying she hoped he was well.

Mrs Blunt read his letter in her bedroom. Mrs Murphy had been the one to find it lying on the floor of her hall, for as the days had gone by she had no longer felt there was any point in rushing downstairs every time she heard the sound of the postman arriving with her mail.

When she had handed her Sinclair's letter, Mrs Murphy had behaved in such an over-excited manner that Mrs Blunt feared she was going to rip it open and read its contents aloud. Her own excitement about its arrival was not only mirrored, but in some way mocked, by Mrs Murphy's attitude towards it. Mrs Blunt had irritably snatched the envelope from her purple hand and taken it off to her bedroom feeling rather like a dog going off to hide with its bone.

Rupert Sinclair's reply was written in a firm and legible handwriting. It said that Corrigan had told him that he would be hearing from her. It went on to say that he hoped she wouldn't find it fanciful and impertinent, but Corrigan had given him such a delightful description of her that when he'd received her letter he had felt it came from an old and treasured friend rather than a stranger.

Mrs Blunt was very relieved to hear that she had made such a good impression on Corrigan. But she still wondered what on earth he could have told Sinclair about her. She couldn't believe that she had cut a particularly impressive figure during his visit. He had been extremely frank and open with her and in retrospect she felt she had been unpleasantly bottled up and stiff in return. When he'd confided how much he'd suffered after the death of his mother, she now feared that he must have seen her response as deeply inadequate. It distressed her to think that he had probably found her cold and unfeeling. She also still felt guilty that she had let him go off in the rain without finding out if he had a decent place to stay, and she was mortified that she'd been so ungenerous as to fail to insist that he accept some money for his charity.

As she went on reading Rupert Sinclair's letter, she was embarrassed by the pleasure that her letter seemed to have given him. He repeatedly thanked her for writing to him. He said that although he had heard from her at a very grim moment in his life, she had managed to cheer him up, that her letter had helped him get through a very unpleasant period.

His gratitude made Mrs Blunt feel more and more uneasy. She couldn't see that it had been a very praiseworthy act when she'd written to him. However, it struck her that Corrigan was obviously right when he insisted that people who were forced to spend their lives in institutions had a desperate need to feel that they retained some communication with the outside world.

Rupert Sinclair also told her that he had been extremely interested by everything she'd told him about herself. He was very sorry to hear that she had lost her husband and he prayed that she had religious beliefs which would help her to endure her loss. He described himself as a very religious man and told her that it had been his faith that had enabled him to endure the 'slings and arrows of outrageous fortune'.

Mrs Blunt did not feel she was really religious although she believed in God. When she tried to imagine him she saw him like the painted golden sun with the benign and smiling human face and the bright rays encircling his head that had decorated the face of her parents' grandfather clock. However, she now only attended the local church on Christmas Day for she could never manage to feel that God was very near her when she was kneeling on a dusty hassock in a cold stone interior or chanting a psalm to a wheezing organ that was painfully out of tune.

In the old days, she'd felt she could sense His presence when she worked in the garden with her husband and the sun was shining on all the roses they had planted together. But now that she had let her garden fall into such a horrible disarray and the beauties of nature no longer gave her much pleasure, God seemed increasingly distant from her. She felt less and less eager to attend church services on Sundays because when she was praying alone amongst the village congregation she was always stricken by a terrible feeling of isolation, and she hated it when she left the church and had to walk back to her house by herself. She felt that leaving a church was something one should only do with someone one loved, and although the other people from the village who attended the service always greeted her after it finished and seemed prepared to be friendly, she always got the feeling that had once plagued her at dances when she was a young girl, the same terror of being considered a wallflower, and she would hurry off saying hardly a word to anyone. She had acquired a local reputation for being stand-offish and weird.

When the Colonel was still alive she used to go to church quite often. He enjoyed singing hymns and he liked to attend morning services in order to have the chance to belt them out, rather than because he was a very devout believer. She had enjoyed accompanying him for she had liked to stand beside him while he got such childish pleasure from his loud and rather militaristic renderings. But now her only reason for going to church on Christmas Day was because she thought it would be insulting to the Vicar if she never put in an appearance at all. As her husband was lying in his parish graveyard she felt she ought to show the Vicar a little politeness.

When she read how Sinclair felt himself to have been sustained by his religion she realised he must have a very much more real and passionate faith than she had, and she envied him for possessing it. If she was to carry on a correspondence with him, she wondered whether he could teach her how to share it.

'I have been seeing a lot of Corrigan.' Mrs Blunt found herself feeling strangely agitated as she read this line in Sinclair's letter. He went on to tell her that in the last weeks when he'd been so ill, Corrigan had come to see him at St Crispins every single day. He had been planning a fund-raising trip to the north of England, but he had put it off when he heard his friend was unwell. In the last weeks, Sinclair described himself as having been in 'extreme discomfort'. Apparently Corrigan had stayed for hours by his bed, and he had read to him and helped to distract him and he felt that it was really only the incredible kindness of his friend that had helped him to pull through. 'Corrigan is the most extraordinary human being,' Rupert Sinclair wrote.

He told Mrs Blunt that although he had been beautifully cared for by the doctors and the nurses at St Crispins, they were naturally very overworked, and for that reason had little time to attend to the psychological needs of their patients. Whereas Corrigan, who had suffered so much pain himself, knew that when people were in severe physical distress, it was often the little gestures of human concern that gave them the strength to fight their disease.

Corrigan had appeared every day at Sinclair's bedside bringing little treats and surprises. He had turned up with flowers and muscat grapes and marshmallows because he knew his friend was very fond of them. During his illness Sinclair for many weeks had completely lost his appetite, but he had still enjoyed the delicious things that Corrigan had brought him. While he was so unwell he had found he developed the eccentric gastronomic cravings of a pregnant woman and he'd only had to express a desire for some kind of special food and Corrigan had instantly gone wheeling off to the shops and brought it back to him. He had also smuggled him in a daily quota of champagne. Sinclair was not allowed any alcohol, but Corrigan had realised that while his days were so bleak, the symbolic and emotional value of this expensive festive drink outweighed its physical dangers, and as Corrigan slipped him glasses of champagne when the nurses were not looking he had found himself feeling quite tipsy and elated. Hope had started to come back to him and he was certain this had aided his recovery. Sinclair told her that Corrigan had developed a canny technique for bringing champagne to the patients at St Crispins. He would open the bottle before he arrived so that no one heard the pop of the cork. He would then place the bottle under his rug and when he came spinning along in his chair, he only appeared to be bringing some innocent drink such as orangeade.

Rupert Sinclair ended his letter by once again thanking Mrs Blunt for having been so extremely kind as to have written to him. He said that he would love to hear from her again if she had the time. He found it wonderful to hear about all the things that were going on in the outside world. He was thrilled to be told that she was anxious to make Corrigan a donation. In his opinion, she couldn't be giving her money to a better cause. 'I find it a miracle what that man accomplishes,' he wrote. 'And everything that he does is always for others.'

Mrs Blunt felt more and more guilty that Sinclair appeared to have been so grateful for her letter. She suddenly felt she wanted to do much more than write uninspired letters. She wanted to imitate Corrigan and bring champagne and muscat grapes to those whose lives were deprived of all hope and luxury and glamour.

'How was your letter?' Mrs Murphy asked Mrs Blunt when they next met in the kitchen.

'It was a very nice letter.'

'It took him a fair time to write it.'

'Mr Sinclair has not been at all well.' Mrs Blunt hated the

way Mrs Murphy always made her feel on the defensive. She would have liked to show Sinclair's letter to someone because she had found it very moving, but Mrs Murphy's attitude was much too prying for her to bear to satisfy her curiosity. She decided to hide it very carefully for she suspected that if she went out Mrs Murphy would ransack her bedroom and go through all her drawers and cupboards in the hope of finding it.

'And you've heard nothing from the other cripple?' Mrs Murphy asked her.

'No, I haven't heard from him. But I expect to do so in the near future.'

'It's a pity all these men are crippled,' Mrs Murphy said. 'We could do with a healthy man around here.'

'She's really impossible,' Mrs Blunt thought. She went back to her bedroom in order to reread Rupert Sinclair's letter.

6

Two days later Mrs Blunt heard the sound she had been waiting for, the scrunch of Corrigan's chair as it came wheeling up her gravel drive.

She remained in her bedroom and let Mrs Murphy answer the door when he rang. She wanted to appear to be surprised when she saw him. But when she had heard the sound of his wheels it had not astonished her at all. All the anxiety that she had experienced in the last weeks, all her fears that she might never see him again seemed totally unreal and ludicrous. All at once she had the feeling she had known all along that it was inevitable that she would eventually hear the sound of his approaching chair. She was very cool when Mrs Murphy came crashing upstairs to announce his arrival, and she was very calm as she got herself dressed while her employee created a typical and tedious commotion as she got him up the steps.

'I should have telephoned to say I was planning to call on you,' Corrigan said. 'It's very rude of me to arrive unannounced. But I didn't know your telephone number. I happened to be in the neighbourhood, so I decided that I'd just drop in.'

She thought he looked a little thinner. She assumed that Rupert Sinclair's illness had been a great strain on him. She saw that he was wearing a bright red shirt, that a huge bunch of roses was lying across the tartan rug that covered his knees. She then suddenly noticed with dismay that both his hands were bandaged.

'I brought you these as an expression of thanks for the marvellous thing you did for my friend Sinclair.' Corrigan reached forward and with a clumsy gesture he held out the flowers.

'But I didn't really do anything,' Mrs Blunt said nervously. 'I only wrote him a letter. It was a pleasure to do it. I'm afraid I don't feel I did very much for the poor man at all.'

'Ah, but there you fail to understand the mentality of the disabled human being,' Corrigan said. 'Maybe you could say all happiness is a question of expectations and a man like Sinclair has learnt to expect very little from life, but at the same time he knows how to get the most from the small petals that are thrown his way, and your charming letter came like a flower into his desert. It brought him great joy. I was a witness. I was sitting by his bedside when he received it.'

'What would you like to drink?' Mrs Blunt asked him. It made her very nervous when he kept praising her for all the joy her letter had brought to Rupert Sinclair. She wanted to turn the conversation and let Corrigan know how much she admired the loyalty that had helped to give his friend the will, and the fight, to recover from his recent bout of illness.

She also wanted to know how he had hurt his hands, but she thought he might find it rude if she inquired.

'Would you like a cup of coffee like last time? Mrs Blunt asked him.

'Well, it's certainly very kind of you to suggest it,' Corrigan answered. 'But if I remember correctly, the last time I visited, you were generous enough to offer me a glass of wine. And today I think I'll avail myself of that lovely offer. I had a nasty thing happen to me yesterday. And to be truthful I still haven't quite recovered from the shock.'

'Oh dear, I'm so sorry to hear that something unpleasant happened to you. I see that you've hurt your hands. Did you have an accident? Or perhaps you don't want to talk about it. I hope I'm not being too personal.'

'You are not being too personal at all,' Corrigan's eyes looked very intense as they stared at her through his long black eyelashes.

'I don't feel that anyone can ever be too personal,' he said. 'Impersonality is surely one of mankind's most pernicious enemies. It's like a great stone wall that human beings place between one and the other. It's a wall that creates the most horrible compounds of loneliness. I hate that wall. I always try to smash it down. I hope you feel the same way as me.'

'Let me get you a glass of wine. I would very much like one myself,' Mrs Blunt said quickly. Corrigan made her feel flustered, and she couldn't always find the right way to answer the things that he said to her. She went off to her dining-room and out of an ivory-inlaid cabinet she got the bottle of claret she had once bought for the Colonel. When she came back to the drawing-room, she uncorked it and poured out a glass for Corrigan.

'Can you hold it all right?' she asked. 'I'm afraid you may have a bit of trouble with your bandages.'

'I think I'll be able to manage very well even with bandages. I can always find a way to get my hands round a glass of wine! I wish I had more difficulty. If the truth be told, I would have liked to have used my injuries as an excuse to ask you to hold the wine to my lips. That would have been a splendid and decadent way to drink!'

Mrs Blunt was quite relieved that Corrigan seemed to be able to hold his own glass. As she poured out some claret for herself, she had a feeling of guilt which was tinged with defiance. 'This wine is no good to him now,' she thought. But as she looked down at the claret she'd just poured, for a moment it didn't seem like wine to her. It reminded her of blood.

'I was going to tell you the disagreeable thing that happened to me yesterday,' Corrigan said.

'Oh, yes, indeed. I long to hear. I just hope it wasn't too serious.' Mrs Blunt took a little hectic sip of the claret and as she tasted it she ceased to feel she was committing a treacherous act when she drank the Colonel's wine with Corrigan.

'I was on a hilly road – just to the north of Salisbury. It was a deserted narrow road and it was very steep. Something happened to me that has never happened to me before in my life. I can hardly bear to speak about it because it makes me relive the nightmare. My chair went out of control! Oh, my God – you will never know the terror I experienced! I tried to brake, but the more I braked, the more I gained momentum. To the left of me there was a sheer drop. There was no fence. There was just this horrible drop that went down into a pit. I think it must have been some old deserted slate pit. The road kept twisting and twisting. I don't know if you understand, but the steering devices on these chairs are not sophisticated. They are not designed for navigating treacherous roads. I gave myself up for lost. Oh Jesus! My chair was soon careening. I'll confess to you now with much shame – I let out a fearful scream. And yet even at the time I knew that my scream was useless. There was no one around to save me. It was as if my scream was going up to the sky and I felt only the vultures could hear it.'

Corrigan seemed to be getting increasingly agitated as he spoke and his distress infected Mrs Blunt and she started coughing because she found herself drinking the Colonel's claret much too quickly. The image of a wheelchair going out of control was horrifying to her, and she could never have explained why she found it so threatening and sinister.

'I really thought my last moment had come,' Corrigan said. 'Several times my chair went right up on to the edge of the ravine. Yet somehow I managed to twist it back so that I still held the road. But never in my life have I had such a degrading feeling of helplessness. I promise you that the speed at which I was going was truly ghastly. An invalid chair is an extremely heavy object as your herculean lady, the magnificent Mrs Murphy, knows all too well. And once something of that weight really gets going, there's no stopping it.'

'Oh, what an awful thing to happen! You're lucky to be here today.'

'Yes. It's a miracle to be sure. And I'm lucky in two senses. I'm lucky to be alive, and I'm lucky to be drinking this excellent wine with you.' Corrigan lifted his glass and he made her a toast.

Mrs Blunt had now become more agitated than Corrigan. 'I find this all so upsetting that I hardly know what to say to you!' she said. 'For goodness sake, tell me how it all ended.'

'Well, in a way, the whole thing had a happy ending. As my chair hurtled down the hill, I saw a hairpin bend approaching. I really started praying then. I knew I wasn't going to make it . . . I realised there was only one thing to be done and I gathered up all my force and I hurled myself out of my chair. That was how I hurt my hands. You see, I wanted to save my face from the road and I used my two hands to break my fall.'

'Oh, how brave of you to have done that!'

'Well, I don't think I'd call it all that brave . . . But it was the only sensible thing I could have done. For my chair continued down the hill and when it came to the bend, the old chariot didn't make the turn and it went speeding over the edge and it went crashing over and over, and it ended up at the bottom of the pit.'

'But this is really the most terrible story,' Mrs Blunt said. 'What on earth did you do next?'

'I just lay there in the road, and I said a fervent prayer of thanks for my escape. Then I dragged myself to the side. I was frightened a car might come speeding by and run right over me before the driver had the chance to see I was there. After that I went on lying in the dust and I waited for someone to drive past and rescue me. It was curious. I felt very happy as I lay there. I had the sense of euphoria that comes after the narrow escape. I felt that as God had chosen to save my life, He must have done it for some purpose. Lying there in a humiliating position like some dying Indian beggar in the gutter, I had a feeling of exaltation. It was as if this near-accident was God's way of telling me that my existence was still valuable to Him, that even with my useless body, He didn't see me as useless since there were still important missions in this world that He wanted me to fulfill.'

'I admire you for seeing it like that,' Mrs Blunt said. 'But who rescued you? It's dreadful to think of it. You say the road was a deserted one – you could have been lying there all night.'

'I could indeed. But for once the untrustworthy dogs of destiny seemed to be on my side. I only lay there about four hours. Then a couple appeared in an estate car, and a very extraordinary couple they were. They were not angels – not in the conventional haloed and feather-winged garb, but they were part of the host none the less, although they were too ultra-English for my normal taste and very pearled and tweeded. They lifted me into their car and they took me to the emergency ward in the hospital in Salisbury. I was treated there for a few cuts and bruises. I soon felt fine, although of course I was still very shaken. I have to tell you my main anxiety was the fate of my chair. But the couple were extremely helpful about that. They arranged for some men to get it out of the pit, and then they saw that it was taken into the town where I hoped I could get it repaired. But apparently the damage that had been done to it was much too extensive. I'm afraid it's now a mangled wreck. I know that I shouldn't burden you with this – but it seems it can never be put in use again.'

'But what's that chair that you are using now?' Mrs Blunt asked.

'This one is only on loan from the Salisbury hospital. I've been told I can't use it indefinitely. They have a shortage of chairs and they need them for their regular patients. The couple that rescued me from the road were quite astonishing. Do you know, they offered to buy me a brand-new chair. Obviously I couldn't accept it from them. I am much too proud to accept such a gift from total strangers. But I was certainly very moved by their generosity.'

'But what are you going to do? What will you do when you have to return this chair to the hospital in Salisbury?'

Corrigan shrugged. 'I'll have to deal with that hurdle when it becomes immediate. I am planning to go back to London. Obviously it's urgent that I inform the doctors at St Crispins of my predicament. They treat me as if I was their son. The physicians in any institution of that kind start to see their patients as their children. The process of rehabilitation is such a long-drawn-out and emotional one that it gives birth to a very subtle and rewarding symbiosis. But I'll tell you something that you may find ridiculous. I dread the idea of admitting to my doctors that I've let that chair get destroyed. I feel that I committed a stupid, wicked act when I let it go crashing into that pit and I can only curse myself for my imbecility.'

'But you shouldn't feel like that,' Mrs Blunt said. 'It's terrible that you blame yourself for something that was not your fault at all.'

'It was my fault that I chose to travel on that steep and dangerous road. Certain roads are not meant to be taken – to be more precise they are not meant to be used by those who are ill-equipped to take them. There is great arrogance underlying certain acts of recklessness. Superficially such acts can seem courageous, but on a deeper level I now realise they are criminal.'

Mrs Blunt noticed that Corrigan's gaunt cheeks were twitching. She could see that the loss of his chair had been a very humiliating experience for him. It pointed up his helplessness. She hated to think of him yesterday, out of control and screaming on that dangerous hill. It also frightened her to think he could easily have been killed.

'I *am* glad you came to visit me today,' she said. 'I was trying to get in touch with you, but I didn't know your address. I wanted to tell you that I would very much like to make you a donation. I think the work you are doing is really incredibly worthwhile. And now you have told me about this awful thing that's just happened, I was wondering if I could make a contribution that would help you to get yourself a new chair. All the valuable things you are doing must depend on your ability to get around. I hope you won't feel embarrassed by my offer as you felt with the couple yesterday. If you could see it as a tribute to your work rather than a personal gift . . .'

Corrigan bent over and held his head in his bandaged hands. He took a long time to answer her. Mrs Blunt started sipping her claret in nervous gulps and her gentle blue eyes gazed at him with apprehension. He looked incredibly forlorn, incredibly defeated and she was very worried that by her offer, she had added a further injury to his self-esteem.

When he finally looked up, his eyes had a frenzied and glittering expression. 'I am a very proud man,' he said. 'You must understand that it's not easy for me to roll in the dust in front of you. Yesterday when I was lying like a dying beggar in the road, I probably had more dignity than I do at this moment. But I must try to remember that pride is only vanity and therefore it is something to be conquered rather than revered. You are obviously a very exceptional person. I can't tell you how grateful I am that you've offered me a new chair as a tribute to my work. It would destroy me if I thought you were taking pity on me as a benighted cripple.'

Corrigan sat up very straight and he clenched one of his injured fists and he held it up in the air. 'I accept!' he said. 'Yes, I accept, although it's very painful for me to do so! If I refuse your offer, I am really saying that my work is of no value, and once I say that, I might as well curl up and die. You see, I know that the doctors at St Crispins will immediately arrange to get me a new chair. But if I let them procure me one, I will accept it only with shame. I'll know that I am depriving some other person of his mobility. There is a horrifying shortage of chairs. Most probably you don't know that. The disabled have to go on a waiting-list and many people have to wait months, sometimes even years, before they are able to get themselves mobilised. I'm quite aware that I could jump to the top of the list because I have so many medical friends and contacts, but I could only do that with a very murky conscience. The chair that I wrecked through my irresponsibility when I stupidly took that over-steep road would continue to haunt me. Whereas if I accept your offer, at least I don't have to feel any of the crushing guilt that I'm depriving another human being of their only source of comparative freedom.'

Mrs Blunt could see by his agonised expression that he was finding it very difficult to allow her to help him and she pitied him for the way he still insisted on blaming himself for yesterday's unlucky incident.

'It's quite curious,' he said. 'I can raise funds for others – I can do it with an exuberant confidence and I never feel a pang of embarrassment – but the idea of accepting any financial aid for myself is a very unwelcome prospect indeed. However, I've decided to stamp on my pride – I am going to treat it like the ugly little insect it is. So I will now drink to your amazing generosity!' He lifted his wine glass in a toast.

'It's really a pleasure to do something to help your work,'

Mrs Blunt said. 'Now, tell me exactly what I should do. What is the next move? How can we get you a new chair?'

Corrigan hesitated. He then said he felt that the best thing would be that she send a cheque to a Mr Robinson, who was the current Secretary at St Crispins. He thought it would work out cheaper than if she made it out to him direct. If she bought the chair through St Crispins she would be able to get it at a wholesale price which would involve a considerable saving. All institutions and hospitals had special arrangements with the makers of medical equipment.

'I am so ignorant,' Mrs Blunt said. 'I've no idea of the cost of a wheelchair. If you could just give me some idea of their general price range, I'd be delighted to go and find my cheque book right now.'

'Now this is going to be the most mortifying part for me. I know the price is really going to shock you, so if you want to reconsider your offer for God's sake do so immediately! I'm afraid that the price – even wholesale – is something abominable! I assure you, I will completely understand if you decide to change your mind.'

'What is the price?' Mrs Blunt asked him. She suddenly looked a little anxious.

'I feel so ashamed,' he said. 'You'll find me foolish, but when you ask me the price, I can't bring myself to tell you.'

'But you have really got to tell me. Otherwise I can't write you out the cheque.' Mrs Blunt's voice was starting to have just a hint of hysteria.

'You are right,' he said. 'Obviously I've got to tell you. But I want you to know that the sum appals me just as much as it will appal you. A wheelchair, nowadays, costs just about a thousand pounds.'

'Good gracious!' Mrs Blunt exclaimed. She then immediately hated herself for having said that. She saw that her dismayed exclamation had made him wince. For a moment all his dignity and confidence seemed to have deserted him. Never before had his vulnerability seemed so exposed. It was the first time she had seen Corrigan look crushed and almost abject.

'A lot of workmanship goes into these chairs,' he said. 'As

you know, the costs of labour are fearful at this moment. I'm afraid that's our current evil. That's the reason why these things are so disgustingly expensive to produce. It's because I'm all too horribly aware of their value that I curse myself for the idiotic and destructive thing that I allowed to happen yesterday. And there is something else I want to say to you – when I accept your gift – I want to make it quite clear that I will only accept it as a loan.'

Mrs Blunt started fidgeting as she always did when Corrigan addressed her with too much intensity. She got out a handkerchief from her handbag and squeezed it until it felt like an ice-hard snowball in her hand.

'Oh, don't worry about that,' she murmured. She noticed that once again Corrigan's gaunt cheeks were twitching.

'But I do worry,' he said. 'Yesterday's accident has made me aware of something that I've been trying to conceal from myself – something I've been trying to keep hidden away in the back roads of my mind. Ever since I left the hospital I have been doing all this fund-raising as you know. The results have certainly been valuable to many people. I can truthfully say that without too much preening. But now I think I have to question the role in which I have placed myself. When I raised my bright banner for the disabled, was I not making myself into a knight and lifting myself on to such a big white charger that I felt too elevated to have to examine my own true situation?'

'My act of knighthood was a device. I now admit it,' Corrigan continued. 'Like all our pretensions it was a pathetic device to protect the ego and avoid facing reality. But now all that has got to stop . . . I shall continue to fund-raise, of course. But I shall do it in a much braver way. I will do it with much more real courage because I'll do it with much more honesty and humility. When I go round the houses collecting I will no longer pretend that I am only asking for charity for the great anonymous army of the disabled. I will hold out my cap like a supplicant and I'll admit that the bold knight is in need of help himself. I'll not only ask for money for others, but I'll eat the pig's swill and I'll say that I desperately need aid myself. In that way, I hope I'll eventually repay you for the fantastic gift of the new chair.'

Mrs Blunt hated hearing him talk like this. She felt he was, indeed, rolling in the dust in front of her and yet his situation was so dire she could understand why he felt obliged to debase himself. As he was such a proud man she could see that he would find it insufferable to allow her to pay for the chair without consoling himself with the dream that he would one day be able to repay her. And it would take him so long to do so. If, as he'd told her, he often only raised ten pence here, ten pence there, she felt it might very well take him years to get the sum he needed. It horrified her to think of this unfortunate man forcing himself to spend the next part of his life struggling painfully round the countryside knocking on doors in order to repay his debt to her. She dreaded to think of the slights and rebuffs he would probably receive as he embarked on this enterprise. She was certain that if he begged for charity for himself rather than for others, any rejection that he met with on his travels would sting him like acid thrown in his face. Corrigan didn't really have to tell the people he approached for donations that he was in need of money himself. But she feared that he would feel obliged to be truthful with them out of his personal sense of honour. She sensed there was something stubborn about Corrigan. He seemed very impetuous. She didn't think he was a man whom it would be possible to persuade to take any course that he saw as dishonest and easy. He seemed to rush at life in much the same headlong fashion that his chair had gone crashing down that hill. But when he made mistakes he seemed to have the bravery to face their consequences, and she felt it was this reckless buoyant energy that gave Corrigan his strengths and his resilience, that it was this same force that had helped save his friend Sinclair's life when he'd come wheeling into the hospital bringing a gift of illicit champagne.

Mrs Blunt suddenly felt rather faint. She often started to feel a physical giddiness when she found herself in any serious dilemma. She now realised it was impossible for her to give Corrigan the chair as an outright present, for if she did so she would only be grinding his pride in the dirt. Yet realising that it would be such a small sacrifice for her to provide him with this essential object, she felt it would be obnoxious if she let him leave her house feeling that he had to devote his future life to reimbursing her.

Her mind felt as if it was whirling like a windmill as various impractical solutions went racing through it. She wondered if, in some tactful fashion, she could get out of giving him the chair and thereby salvage his dignity.

Maybe she could pretend that when she had originally made her offer she had not quite appreciated what a large sum would be involved. She could hint that her current financial circumstances were a little precarious, but assure him that in the future she would do her best to help him. Even if he went off to London feeling very discouraged this might be the best thing for his morale for she could then send off an anonymous cheque for a thousand pounds to the Secretary at his hospital. Mrs Blunt was pleased by the idea of this ruse but only for a second. It occurred to her that cheques could not be signed anonymously. She realised she could always get someone else to write the cheque for her – but Nadine was really the only person of whom she would dare to make this strange demand, and somehow she didn't feel like allowing Nadine to get mixed up with this whole delicate business of Corrigan's chair. Her daughter rather frightened her recently. She had become so reserved and something in her manner was always accusatory. Nadine made her feel that she had committed some crime and sometimes she wished that she'd bring it out into the open and tell her what it was. She could now admit that in the last years her grief about her husband had made her self-absorbed and unforthcoming. But although she regretted this, she sensed that Nadine's current hostility towards her had some deeper cause, and she was unable to fathom what it was.

Although it hurt her that her daughter made very few attempts to communicate with her, she was perversely relieved that she heard from her so seldom. If Nadine was to telephone her and sound annoyed, without proper explanation, she felt that this would be even more upsetting.

She had the nagging sense that she had unintentionally offended her daughter when she'd last come down to the country bringing Justin and the twins. She had made every effort to provide them all with nice food and she had cooked it herself although Mrs Murphy had offered to prepare the lunch for her. But although she'd done her best, she knew that something had still gone sadly amiss. She would have really preferred Nadine to have come to see her without bringing the twins, but she'd been frightened to offend her by telling her this. Felix and Roland were lovely little boys, but her nerves had felt very raw that day, and their hyperactivity and their ill-manners had jarred on her so profoundly that she had found their presence in her house almost unendurable.

Ever since that family visit she had been wondering if she'd somehow conveyed to Nadine that she had found the twins a strain. Maybe her daughter had expected her to romp around with them and kick footballs on the lawn and make their visit more fun. She could only pray that this wasn't the case, for if Nadine was ever to bring Felix and Roland down to see her again, she didn't feel she would be able to cope with their turbulence and muster the force to behave in a more satisfactory fashion than she had on the last occasion.

All these thoughts went through her head as Mrs Blunt deliberated whether she dared to approach Nadine about the cheque and she finally came to the decision that while her relationship with her daughter remained riddled with unexplained tensions, it was better not to take any risk of asking her for favours.

Another factor made her decide that it would be unwise to send the money anonymously to Corrigan's hospital. He seemed to be a very intelligent man and she felt that he would instantly suspect the source of her secret gift. She was certain he would find it too great a coincidence if a large sum was to arrive with such startling promptitude from an unknown benefactor.

While Mrs Blunt was working herself into a state of nervous anguish as she tried to solve her dilemma as to how she could present Corrigan with a new chair without causing him severe emotional offence, he seemed to sense that he had put her in an awkward position. His sensitivity astonished her for he immediately tried to alleviate the embarrassment he had just created.

'You will see me as a weather-vane,' Corrigan said. 'But having accepted your dazzling gift, I now formally withdraw my acceptance. Do you believe I would ever really dream of taking a huge sum like that from someone in your unhappy situation? Do you think my accident has removed all my sense of chivalry? Oh, my God! If that was true I might as well seize the nearest razor and carve a slice in my own jugular!'

'Oh, you really mustn't think like that,' Mrs Blunt said. The impassioned manner in which Corrigan expressed himself was foreign to her. His utterances also often had a violence that she found very unfamiliar. She noticed that occasionally his eyes scrutinised her with such intensity that they seemed to be trying to see through the wan and lady-like image that she was presenting him. They appeared to be attempting to recover something much more vital in her personality – something that had been lost so long ago that she herself could no longer recapture it.

At other times when Corrigan became a little hysterical, his eyes no longer seemed to look out at the world at all. It was as if their pupils had reversed their normal process of seeing and were intent on examining some dark distressing landscape of experience that lay recorded in the cells of his own brain.

His eyes had this strange and agonised blind look when he accused her of seeing him as lacking in chivalry.

He suddenly started moving his chair towards her. She was sitting there by the fire that had been lit by Mrs Murphy. Her knees were crossed and she was looking very nervous.

'May I offer you my profound apologies,' he said. 'It was cruel of me to burden you with my current fiasco. My particular problem is purely technical and therefore trivial and temporary. I've always had a healthy contempt for all technicalities. I believe they can be quite easily surmounted. Man has invented science for that very purpose. Now would you not agree with me?'

Mrs Blunt was frightened by Corrigan's eyes and by his outstretched hand which loomed at her like some huge white shapeless bundle. It embarrassed her to shake it and in her shyness she looked down and she noticed that as Corrigan had come sliding towards her, the wheels of his chair had left dark muddy lines on the beige of her carpet. The sight of these marks made her recoil. She then felt immediately disgusted with herself. She very much disliked having to admit that her emotions in regard to her soiled carpet were instinctive. She would not excuse herself and pretend that this made them any the less unworthy.

In order to compensate for her own secret and despicable distress at the messy traces that Corrigan had left behind him as he crossed her drawing-room, Mrs Blunt forced herself to take his hand. She was uneasily aware of the roughness of the texture of its bandages, and as she gingerly held it in her own, she felt that under its inanimate surface there was something that was throbbing like a wounded animal.

'God bless you!' Corrigan said. 'God bless you for accepting my apology.' His eyes had lost their unfocused look and they were now staring into her face as she sat primly upright in her silk striped Regency armchair.

She once again had the dizzy sensation that always came over her when she was in any situation in which she felt confused. In the brief dealings that she'd had with Corrigan, she'd noticed that their conversations seemed to go circling round and round. He always ended up apologising to her, just at the very point where she felt that it was she who should be offering him some apology. Dialogues with Corrigan turned as quickly as the wheels of his chair. Mrs Blunt found that her mind was sometimes too slow to keep up with their swift rotations.

Still holding Corrigan's hand over-gently in her own, she was not happy to be the recipient of his overcharged apologies. They were very daunting to her. They were like Rupert Sinclair's gratitude – she saw them as a burden rather than a welcome bouquet.

'Do you understand why I'm asking you to pardon me,' Corrigan asked her.

'Well, no,' Mrs Blunt said. 'I must say I don't.'

'I was testing you when I brought up my confounded problem with the chair. I had no right to do that. You passed my wicked test with flying colours. Your generosity of spirit shone bright as a diamond. But when I tried to test you the shame was mine. I should have had faith in my own intuitions. I should have trusted the feeling I had about you the very first time I set eyes on you. Do you remember that I told you that I felt I was soaring like Icarus when I first entered your house? You may have found the metaphor exaggerated, but it was true to my feelings none the less.'

Mrs Blunt quickly let go of his hand. She didn't care to have any physical contact with him while he was delivering this bewildering address.

'Did you know that a disabled man develops sensibilities that are far keener than those of the average able-bodied person?' Corrigan said to her.

Mrs Blunt could think of nothing to reply to this. She could only give a soft and agitated cough.

'My sense of the true character of the people that I encounter is as refined as any radar system,' Corrigan said. 'I pick up all the waves and currents of their inner evil and their beauty. Sometimes I wish my radar system was less highly developed. I often receive a feedback of so much cruelty, greed, and envy, that it makes me pessimistic. But in your case, I am grateful that I possess this overdeveloped capacity to discern the hidden workings of the hearts and the souls of other human beings. Why do you think I've returned to your house? I've certainly not come back to ask you for a donation. I've already explained that I always refuse to accept any help from those who are themselves in very grave trouble. I can tell you that I picked up the terrifying force of your grief the very moment I entered this sublime drawing-room. It hit me like a blast in the face. I experienced it as a hurricane. I felt that it was raging round this lovely peaceful house. I had the sense that you had released a force so powerful and elemental that you yourself were no longer completely in control of it. Do you think anything I've just said is true?'

Mrs Blunt sat by her marble fireplace and she felt stunned. Corrigan's interpretation of her condition was not at all as she saw it herself. The numbness that she'd experienced since the Colonel's death had none of the force that she associated with that of the hurricane.

'I have psychic powers,' Corrigan said. 'They are my curse and they are also my blessing. You will never be able to deceive me. I am quite aware that the energies you are releasing spring from very valid sources. I respect them as such. I also know that they are bound to become destructive unless you soon start to harness them to something greater than your own personal despair. Despair is like the pelican. It takes blood from its own breast. I know what I'm talking about. I've been through all this myself.'

Mrs Blunt had started shaking. Her gentle blue eyes suddenly filled with tears. She had cried when she had attended the Colonel's funeral, but after that she'd never cried about his death again. Tears had seemed useless to her. She felt that tears should accomplish something – produce some desired result. Once she had accepted they were unable to do this, she'd seen little point in shedding them. She knew that at any given moment she could bring them into her eyes, just as she could bring saliva into her mouth. But she saw saliva and tears as equally contemptible. Neither of them seemed to have the power to do anything that could relieve her pain.

But now Mrs Blunt was astonished to find herself crying in front of Corrigan. He reached out from his wheelchair and he awkwardly stroked her pale curls with his injured hand. It amazed her that she was not in the least dismayed by the intimacy of his gesture. The Colonel had loved to play with her hair. She had forgotten the comfort it used to give her. Corrigan's tender gesture soothed her. She cried harder. As she sobbed like a child she wondered if the stone that she had felt like a permanent fixture in her chest had really always been a small rock of unshed tears.

'I didn't mean to make you cry,' Corrigan said. 'When I said that I experienced your grief like a hurricane, I hope to God I didn't hurt you. I can promise you that I never intended the comparison to sound derogatory.'

He had withdrawn his hand and Mrs Blunt felt that his sympathy had been withdrawn. She instantly straightened herself and made an attempt to reassert her self-control. She tried to wipe her eyes with the ineffective little hard ball of a handkerchief she had been squeezing in her fist.

Corrigan still kept his chair very close to hers, although he no longer touched her.

'Will you allow me to pursue my analogy, for I think you may then find it somewhat less offensive,' he said. 'You must remember that there is an eye to every hurricane. And thanks to God there is always a non-destructive little area existing at the heart of all the tumultuous raging emotions that afflict us poor human creatures. It is that benign little pocket of serenity that we should try to find in each other. I can feel that eye of the hurricane in you. I can feel its peace, its goodness, its beauty. I'm not sure you can find it in yourself. Just at this moment, I think you have lost all contact with it. I have the sense that your life is being blown helter-skelter. I don't believe you can separate your best self from the whirlwind that is consuming you.'

Mrs Blunt felt that Corrigan was attempting to say something important about her situation although she was bemused by his rapid images and she was puzzled as to why he seemed to see her as such a fiery and tempestuous figure when she often accused herself of being over-placid. Yet when she thought more seriously about the things that he'd said to her, she suspected that he might well be correct when he claimed that she'd allowed herself to become controlled by forces that were destructive within her character. She had to admit there was an enormous anger in her grief and she was trying to repress it. As she allowed it no expression she wondered if she was turning it in on herself – if it was manifesting itself in her constant wish to die.

'Tell me more about Rupert Sinclair,' she said. 'How is the poor fellow?' Corrigan's chair was still drawn up very close to hers and she wanted to distance the conversation.

'He is much improved. But he had a truly terrible time in these last weeks. It was an abominable thing to be the witness to so much physical suffering. Oh, Jesus Christ, I'm afraid I had to watch the poor man struggle through the pits of hell and back.'

'He wrote to me that you were like an angel to him. I think he was particularly thrilled when you brought him the champagne!'

Corrigan laughed and Mrs Blunt found it very attractive that he so obviously enjoyed having cheered his friend with his generous present.

'Oh, yes, Rupert Sinclair certainly savoured the champagne,' he said. 'It had the glorious appeal of the illicit. I think that every golden bubble represented pleasure to him. In the course of my work I've learnt that pleasure is the best medicine for people in his situation. They feel that all the pleasures of life have been made forever taboo to them. Can you see that's a fearful feeling? I'm afraid that feeling is the long dark freezing beach where true despair lies.'

'It must be the most dreadful feeling. I'd never thought of it that way,' Mrs Blunt said. 'I'd really like to send Rupert Sinclair some champagne myself. I wonder if Mrs Murphy could pick up a bottle from the pub in Coombe Abbot.'

'Sinclair would most certainly be overjoyed to receive such a pleasant gift. It would be the blackest lie if I was to tell you that he'd find it abhorrent.'

'I'll go and have a word with her,' Mrs Blunt said.

As she went out of the door of her drawing-room she nearly knocked Mrs Murphy over.

'Were you listening?' she asked her crossly.

'I was just coming to ask you if you wanted lunch for the cripple,' Mrs Murphy's bulbous eyes looked shifty. 'Then I heard you wanted champagne,' she added quickly.

'Yes, I do. But I don't want it for Mr Corrigan. I want to get some champagne for his friend. Well, come to think of it, maybe Mr Corrigan would also like a little champagne before he goes back to London. He had a horrible accident yesterday.'

'So I saw . . .' Mrs Murphy said. 'Sure, he's in terrible shape, that man. He doesn't have his legs and now he doesn't even have his hands.'

'Yes, I know all that. It's very sad for him. But he's still managing very well . . .' As usual Mrs Blunt was dismayed by the crudity of Mrs Murphy's description.

'All the more reason for us to offer him a glass of champagne,' she added briskly. 'Perhaps you could pick us up three bottles. I think they must have some champagne in the pub. Otherwise what on earth do they do when their clients have birthdays.'

'Ah, I'm certain they'll be bound to sell champagne,' Mrs Murphy said. 'It's a beautiful place, that pub, now it's all painted up. I'm always telling you that you ought to go and take a look at it.'

'Well, I don't want to take a look at the pub right now. But I'm sure it looks very pretty. So get me the three bottles of champagne. And I'd also like you to get something nice for Corrigan's lunch. Could you pick me up some good french bread from the bakery. And you know that little shop that sells delicacies. They used to make a very nice pâté.'

'Now, what's pâté?' Mrs Murphy asked.

'You don't have to know what it is. Just ask them for their best goose-liver pâté. Why don't you write down the word if you can't remember it?'

Mrs Murphy went and got a piece of paper. Mrs Blunt noticed that she was writing the word as if it was divided – 'Pat A'.

'Ask them for goose-liver pâté for two,' Mrs Blunt said. 'No, I've changed my mind. Ask them to give you enough for three. I think it would be nice to send something tasty to Mr Corrigan's friend in London.'

'Is that the Mr Sinclair you wrote the letter to? He'll be doing quite well for himself.'

'Mr Sinclair is *disabled*, Mrs Murphy,' Mrs Blunt murmured reproachfully.

She went and fetched her purse from her bedroom. She always kept a lot of cash in the house because she disliked making trips to the bank. Such excursions still frightened her even though Nadine had been very patient after the Colonel's death and accompanied her there many times in order to explain all the procedures.

She was quite aware that Nadine would be horrified if she was to find out that she liked to keep hundreds of pound notes lying loose in her handbag. She knew her daughter would think it dangerous and warn her that someone could very easily break into her house and take it. However, Mrs Blunt was convinced that if anyone took the trouble to break in to rob her house, they would probably knock her viciously on the head. If they also took her cash, she couldn't see that she would then care all that much.

'Could you pick up two excellent fillet steaks from the butcher?' She handed Mrs Murphy the money. 'Do you remember the steaks that the Colonel used to enjoy?'

'Ach, I do. But you know that I could bake up some kidneys for Corrigan's lunch if you'd like. That would come out quite a bit cheaper.'

'Oh, that's very kind of you. But I don't want you to go to any trouble. I can do his lunch myself. I think Corrigan would prefer steak.'

Mrs Murphy had once prepared some kidneys for Mrs Blunt when she was feeling particularly sickly and depressed. She had cooked them in the most extraordinary manner using a recipe that had made Mrs Blunt feel so queasy she'd had to slip away and put them down the lavatory. Mrs Murphy had not removed any of the fat from the kidneys, nor had she taken out their cores. Instead she had put them straight in the oven to bake using their coating of white congealed grease as if it was a pastry shell.

When Mrs Murphy went off on her errands, Mrs Blunt returned to her drawing-room. She saw that Corrigan had finished the bottle of claret and she was glad that he had enjoyed it and she looked forward to surprising him with some champagne.

'I hope you will stay for lunch,' she said.

'It would be a very great pleasure. But I most certainly don't want to inconvenience you. I didn't come here to burden you in any way. I came to bring you something that I find very beautiful – something that I thought you would be pleased to read.'

Mrs Blunt couldn't imagine what Corrigan could have brought her. She found it astounding that he'd travelled down from London in order to bring her anything at all.

He reached under the rug that covered his knees and, fumbling because of his bandages, he brought out some sheets of paper.

'I typed this out for you the day before I had my perfidious débâcle on the hill. It was just as well I got it over with, and managed to finish it for you. Until my hands heal up I won't be typing for some time yet.'

'How very kind of you to have typed it for me,' Mrs Blunt said. She was eager to know what he had chosen to bring her.

'I've brought you "The Lament for Art O'Leary". I don't know if you are familiar with it.'

'No, I'm not.' Mrs Blunt looked disconcerted.

'He was murdered by the English, like many others. His widow wrote this lament for him. It's in simple language, but I find it very lovely. This is a translation, of course. The original was in the Gaelic.'

Corrigan started reading in his deep voice.

'My love and my delight,
The day I saw you first
Beside the market-house
I had eyes for nothing else
And love for none but you.
I left my father's house
And ran away with you,
And that was no bad choice;
You gave me everything.

'There were parlours whitened for me,
Bedrooms painted for me,
Ovens reddened for me,

Loaves baked for me,
Joints spitted for me,
Beds made for me
To take my ease on flock
Until the milking time
And later if I pleased.'

Mrs Blunt sat still and rigid listening to Corrigan. She liked the verses, but she was too shy to tell him.

'I won't read the whole poem. You should do that on your own. I'll just read a little more so you get the feeling and the rhythm.'

'My love and my mate
That I never thought dead
Till your horse came to me
With bridle trailing,
All blood from forehead
To polished saddle
Where you should be,
Either sitting or standing;
I gave one leap to the threshold,
A second to the gate,
A third upon its back.

'I clapped my hands,
And off at a gallop;
I never lingered
Till I found you lying
By a little furze-bush
Without pope or bishop
Or priest or cleric
One prayer to whisper
But an old, old woman,
And her cloak about you,
And your blood in torrents –
Art O'Leary –
I did not wipe it off,
I drank it from my palms.'

Mrs Blunt's eyes had filled with tears. It was the second time that morning that Corrigan had made her cry.

This time he pretended that he hadn't noticed and she was grateful for his tact. She was embarrassed that she kept breaking down and being so emotional in front of him. He handed her the pages he had typed for her.

'I'll read the poem tonight when I'm alone,' she said. 'I find it exquisite – but also quite upsetting. I'm still very grateful that you thought of bringing it to me.'

She suddenly wished that Corrigan would go back to London rather than stay for lunch. All at once she longed to be alone so that she could read the poem in the peace of her bedroom. At that moment she would have preferred to be with Corrigan's gift rather than with him. She still found him an unsettling presence although she couldn't precisely analyse why. It was something to do with his wheelchair and the glittery expression in his eyes when he scrutinised her. The 'Lament' had stirred up painful memories. She kept seeing the Colonel lying in the hall where she had found him. There had been no blood, but his face had been bruised where he'd hit the floor as he'd fallen and she'd found the sight of that bruise unbearable because it made him seem so defenceless. As she remembered the Colonel lying there in the hall, she lost all desire to drink champagne with Corrigan.

However, she could hear Mrs Murphy roaring back with her provisions and as usual she put on her brakes with such violence that her motor bike gave the most horrible screech as if it was protesting against the agony she had caused it.

Mrs Blunt asked Corrigan to excuse her and she left him alone in the drawing-room while she went off to prepare his lunch.

She was keen to get to the kitchen because she knew there was a grave danger that Mrs Murphy, in her excitement about the strange guest and her zealous eagerness to please, would start cooking the steaks without having been asked to do so. She would then almost certainly ruin them by using one of her eccentric procedures. Mrs Blunt could not bear the idea of the shame she would feel if she had to offer such disgusting food to Corrigan.

'I picked up three bottles of the most expensive champagne in the pub. Now was that right?' Mrs Murphy asked. 'There was some cheap stuff, but I hardly thought that was what you'd be wanting.'

'Oh no, you were quite right,' Mrs Blunt said.

'The pub's looking beautiful as a church inside. It looks great since they fixed it up. It's got all these gold glittering mirrors. The new bar they've put in – it's a lovely thing too. You can see your face in it, it's so steely and polished.'

Mrs Blunt was making a salad for Corrigan and she wished Mrs Murphy wouldn't talk to her while she was cooking. It made it so difficult for her to concentrate.

She was still also desperately worried about what she ought to do about Corrigan's lack of a chair. She'd suddenly had the idea that she could get her solicitor to send a personal cheque to the hospital and then she'd arrange to pay him back. Even if Corrigan suspected that the cheque had arrived at her instigation, she couldn't see that it would really matter. It would be difficult for him to prove that she'd been his benefactor. He wouldn't recognise her solicitor's name. She now felt it was urgent that she get him the chair as soon as possible.

'Did you know there was a fight last night in the pub?' Mrs Murphy said. 'It was a really nasty fight – or so they was all telling me. Some fellow had too many whiskies and he punched one of the locals. He was a stranger and it seems like he was a man with a streak that was really dangerous and vicious. But they soon got him out because all the boys from the neighbourhood sided against him. There was still quite a lot of smashed glass on the floor this morning.'

'I'm very sorry to hear that,' Mrs Blunt replied in the conciliatory tones with which she invariably greeted this kind of information. 'Speaking of glasses, Mrs Murphy, I wonder if you could get me a couple and could you open the champagne for Mr Corrigan. Do remember that champagne corks can be very treacherous and dangerous,' she added. 'They often surprise you. They can come out like bullets. They are a major cause of blindness. They can hurt you very badly if they hit you. So perhaps you could please try not to point the bottle at Corrigan as you open it.'

Images from 'The Lament for Art O'Leary' were still running through her head and she had little wish to go into her drawing-room and find Corrigan slumped in his chair having been inadvertently murdered by Mrs Murphy.

Corrigan seemed extremely happy once the champagne had been safely opened for him. Mrs Blunt served him the goose-liver pâté followed by her steak and salad. Her mood then changed and she was glad that he had stayed for lunch and her previous desire to be left alone with her past and the lament that he'd brought to her completely vanished.

'What a joy it is to be sitting here drinking the magnificent vintage fruit of the vine in front of your roaring fire,' he said. 'Virginia Woolf believed that "Moments of Being" were all that counted in life. I worship her phrase . . . I agree with her most profoundly . . . She felt the rest of one's experience was nothing more than cotton wool. Obviously we can only capture such "Moments" occasionally. But they still remain the only little nuggets of magic that make it all seem worth it.'

'Didn't Virginia Woolf kill herself?' Mrs Blunt asked. She was relieved that she knew something about a writer whom Corrigan seemed to admire.

'She did. Indeed, she did . . . And maybe at that point she found that her all-important "Moments" were no longer available to her. I've thought about her death quite a lot. You know I was telling you about the eye of the emotional hurricane that we've all got raging inside us? Maybe towards the end she lost all ability to make essential contact with that eye . . . That's just my suggestion.'

'I don't know how people dare to kill themselves,' Mrs Blunt said. 'I don't think I'd ever manage to get up the courage.'

She had started to drink some of the champagne in order to keep pace with Corrigan.

Colonel Blunt had been a connoisseur of wine and brandy and he'd laid down a cellar which she'd been told was valuable. After he died, his cellar had saddened her. She'd felt that drinking, like going to church, was an activity that should be shared and she'd decided that she'd find it a desolating, rather than an exhilarating experience, to drink any of the Colonel's cleverly chosen wines on her own. She'd insisted that Nadine take over her father's cellar, telling her that since she'd now become a teetotaller all the exquisite clarets and burgundies that she owned were of little use to her. Nadine had seemed curiously reluctant to accept her mother's gift and appeared to be disapproving rather than pleased when she was told of Mrs Blunt's plan for complete future alcoholic abstention. However, Justin, who purported to be a wine connoisseur, had been all too keen to take up his mother-in-law's offer. He had supervised the removal of all the bottles and arranged that they be transported to his house in London. Mrs Blunt had felt only relief when a van had arrived to take her late husband's wine away from her. She'd hoped that Nadine would eventually be glad to be able to serve these rare vintages when she entertained Justin's friends.

The bottle of claret that she'd retained until she shared it with Corrigan had been precious to her because it had been part of a little trick she'd liked to play on the Colonel.

Mrs Blunt had never known very much about wines or brandies, although in the past she'd loved to drink them with her husband. Recognising him to be the true authority on that subject, she had still found a way of delighting him. She sometimes used to go off alone to Salisbury in a taxi, for she'd never learnt to drive and usually she was driven everywhere by the Colonel. She therefore found these clandestine taxi expeditions very enjoyable and daring. Once she got to Salisbury, she used to go to the best wine store in the town and select a bottle of the most expensive claret they could offer. She was always shocked and also in some way thrilled by the price of the wine that they were glad to sell her. She would vaguely add it to the cost of the cab fares she'd run up as she travelled the long journey from her home – a cost that was magnified by the fact that she always kept her taxi waiting while she shopped for her husband. She'd recognised that the sum she'd expended on making a surprise gift to the Colonel was exorbitant. But she'd never cared about that at all. The Colonel never failed to be amazed and delighted by the quality of the wine she brought back to him as a present. He was always wildly generous in praising her powers of selection, and Mrs Blunt would look smilingly mysterious, never explaining how she'd acquired her expert wine knowledge. She'd found it very gratifying that the purchase of good wine turned out to be such a simple procedure. If she bought the most expensive claret it seemed to be the one that was the most appreciated by the Colonel, and she'd loved to see the childish pleasure with which he drank the absurdly costly wine that she was offering him.

As the Colonel paid all their household bills, she'd sometimes wondered if he noticed that his bill from the wine shop in Salisbury was an astonishingly high one. If he did notice, he never mentioned it, for he'd seemed to be amused rather than dismayed by her little acts of extravagance, and she had suspected that he felt that any sum she expended on bringing him surprise and joy was worth it, because he so enjoyed her pleasure in delighting and spoiling him.

Now, as Mrs Blunt drank champagne with Corrigan, having refrained from all alcohol for several years, she could feel it rising to her head in a very pleasant fashion.

'When you say you'd never dare to kill yourself, is that quite true?' Corrigan asked. He was scrutinising her again and he had a mystical expression that frightened her. She'd seen it in the eye of a female clairvoyant she had once visited in India.

'It's quite true,' she insisted. 'I'm a coward.'

'The human being has many ways of annihilating himself. He can do it with an act of bravura. He can jump off the Eiffel Tower, he can throw himself under a train. Those kinds of acts have panache, but they are not essential to the suicidal intention. There are more subtle modes of self-destruction ... There are other ways that are quieter and in a sense more deceitful. But eventually they are just as effective.'

Mrs Blunt drank more champagne. She disliked the course the conversation was taking. 'Can we not talk about suicide,' she said. 'I know so little about it. Can't we choose a more cheerful subject?'

She poured out more champagne for Corrigan.

'We can choose any subject you like,' he said. 'But when I'm gone, I'd like you to ponder the things I've just put to you and take them as a warning. And I don't want you to take them as the warning of an impudent stranger, for I'm no stranger to you and I think you know it.'

Mrs Blunt went very red. Corrigan's tone had become so ardent she felt he was making her a declaration of love. This made her feel unnerved because she was certain she must have imagined this.

'I'm unable to use my hands for the while,' Corrigan said. 'But that's all temporary – it's superficial. I can still offer you the metaphorical hand that can pull you back from the bridge.'

'I'm all right,' Mrs Blunt said defensively. 'I lead a quiet life – but I find it a pleasant one.'

'I don't think you are telling me the truth,' Corrigan said to her. 'If you try to obfuscate the truth, you give me no way of helping you.'

'I don't really need any help,' Mrs Blunt persisted stubbornly. 'But it's very kind of you to offer to give me some.'

'You offend me when you say that. You were more honest when you wrote to Rupert Sinclair than you are now being with me. I have to resent that.'

'I can't really remember what I said in my letter to Sinclair.' Mrs Blunt was starting to look a little trapped and frantic. 'I just dashed Sinclair off a note because you asked me to. Quite honestly I regretted having sent him such a letter. But once I'd posted it, it was too late. My letter was a very silly one and he probably thought it came from a mad woman. But I found it quite a difficult task to write to a man I've never met . . .'

'Sinclair never thought your letter came from a mad woman,' Corrigan said. 'I've already told you how much pleasure it gave him. He read me your letter. He read it to me aloud . . . I hope you don't mind that. When he received it, I think he felt you were already his friend because I'd talked so much about you.'

Mrs Blunt was slightly perturbed by the idea of these two crippled men perusing her letter in St Crispins and then endlessly discussing her. She would have very much liked to have known what Corrigan had said to Sinclair in the course of these discussions, but she feared he might think that vanity was making her fish for compliments and prudence prevented her from asking him.

'Of course, Sinclair was distressed by your letter – just as I was,' Corrigan said.

'Distressed? But you just said that he was pleased.'

'He was distressed by the pain that he read in it – he read it as a plea for help, but as the poor man has no mobility he could see no way that he could aid you.'

Mrs Blunt looked horrified. 'Well, I certainly didn't intend Mr Sinclair to think that I was asking him for help of any kind.'

She felt that this was one of the conversations with Corrigan that started to go circling round and round. She'd thought she was helping Rupert Sinclair by writing to him, but instead, as it had turned out, he'd thought she was asking him for help of some sort.

'There's been a great misunderstanding,' Mrs Blunt said. 'I find it all really very embarrassing.'

'You shouldn't be embarrassed. I think Sinclair was quite flattered that you had turned to him.'

'But I didn't turn to him!'

Mrs Blunt was now suddenly indignant. She simply couldn't bear the way that both Corrigan and Sinclair seemed determined to present her as a figure who had asked an immobilised invalid stranger for some kind of favour.

She wished that Corrigan would move his chair so that it was a little less close to her. She was finding his solicitude intrusive and she felt a need to reject it because it presupposed a knowledge of her situation to which she really couldn't see that he was entitled. She'd broken down and she'd wept in front of him, but now she wanted to retreat and establish control again, for the intimacy of Corrigan's approach was starting to threaten her.

. 'I know why you won't admit you are in any danger,' he said. 'You feel guilty because you know that the course you are pursuing is a criminal one – that it's leading you to murder.'

'Murder? What do you mean?' The word was too strong for Mrs Blunt.

'It's a slow murder that you are committing. It's also a hidden one. You think that if you commit your murder in secret you are absolved of all responsibility. But there you deceive yourself. I've gathered from your letter to Rupert Sinclair that you have a child . . .'

'Well, my daughter's not exactly a child. Nadine is a married woman and she has two little boys of her own.'

'She's your child, none the less. A woman's child never ceases to be her child.'

Corrigan's tone had become aggressive. It suddenly occurred to her that he might have a very violent temper. She couldn't quite understand why he seemed to be getting angry with her, but she poured him more champagne in order to placate him.

'I've witnessed slow self-murder before,' Corrigan said. 'It's not a very beautiful thing to watch. There were extenuating circumstances in her case, to be sure. But all such cases can be excused on similar grounds. I'm afraid that the crime remains. It can never be absolved.'

Mrs Blunt wondered if he was talking about the death of his mother. A look of resentment and anguish had contorted his handsome face. She was suddenly terrified of the dark emotional territory through which he now seemed to be trying to drag her, and feeling unable to deal with it, she decided to try to change the whole trend of a conversation which was becoming increasingly disturbing to her.

'When you talk of murder,' she said, 'I'm afraid you must have noticed the terrible condition of my garden.'

'I have indeed.' Corrigan still looked disapproving and angry. 'To be perfectly truthful, I'm not over-fond of the appearance of your garden.'

'I know that it looks as if it's been murdered by weeds and neglect – but quite recently I've decided that I'm going to bring it to life again. It will need quite a lot of work. But it will be an exciting project . . .'

Corrigan's expression changed. Her decision to improve her garden clearly delighted him.

'I've had an idea,' Mrs Blunt continued. 'I'd like to ask you what you think of it. I remember that you told me that the food they give you at St Crispins is pretty disgusting.'

'It's the sad truth that the food at St Crispins tastes like cardboard and glue. It's not the fault of the staff – the fault, I'm afraid, is economic.'

Mrs Blunt's face had lost its customary woebegone and apathetic expression and become quite flushed and animated for she enjoyed telling Corrigan her plan. 'I know a lot about gardening,' she said. 'Cooking and gardening used to be my main hobbies – actually they were more than hobbies for they were the only two subjects in which I really became quite a professional.'

'I detected the hand of the hard-core professional when I tasted the splendid lunch that you've just served me.'

'Well, that meal certainly wasn't the best I can do. You see, I didn't expect you. If I'd known you were coming I'd have prepared something a little more elaborate.'

'I think you did expect me . . . I refuse to believe that you didn't know that I'd be coming. But I'll let you get away with that little lie. I'll grant you that you didn't know the precise day or the hour when I'd be arriving – but I think you really knew that I'd soon be coming back to see you, just the same.'

Corrigan's aggressive tone had completely vanished and although Mrs Blunt was relieved that she had pleased him by her plan to restore her garden, there was now something bantering and flirtatious in his manner which she found almost as difficult to respond to as his criticism.

'Let me tell you what I intend to do with my garden.' Mrs Blunt refused to concede that when she'd heard his wheels approaching she had not been very surprised to hear them. 'My garden is quite a large one, I don't know if you have taken that in. It stretches out to the back of the house and it covers many acres. There is also an orchard attached to it. Many of the trees will need a lot of attention and some will have to be cut down and replaced – but if some time and money was spent on it, I think it would yield quite a lot of fruit . . .'

'Since my boyhood I've had a romantic love of orchards,' Corrigan said. 'I think that there are few things more lovely on earth than to see wild flowers and lush green grass growing round the gnarled trunks of trees that are heavy with fruit.'

'My late husband had a passion for wild flowers,' Mrs Blunt said.

'So did my mother. She used to pick them from the hedgerows and bring them to me when I was in the ward.'

Mrs Blunt felt this exchange was getting too charged and the past was intruding itself when they should have both been concentrating on the future. She therefore started to outline her ideas for replanning her garden.

Whereas previously it had been predominantly an ornamental one, she told Corrigan that she'd decided she now wanted to put its acres to more practical use and grow fruit and vegetables, rather than flowers and shrubs. 'I was thinking that the patients at St Crispins would probably adore to have some really lovely fresh salads and raspberries and things like that. You see, I'm here all on my own . . . I eat so little when I'm by myself that all the delicious things that I could grow would be of no use to me. That's why I'd love to give them away to people who'd properly appreciate them.'

Mrs Blunt had not expected Corrigan to get quite so excited by her idea.

'You've hit on a notion of total genius! But are you serious about this project? It's inspired, you know! It comes straight from the heavens! You see, when you are in hospital, you've got almost nothing to look forward to except your food. You toss around and you often feel bored and lonely and frightened and you start to count the minutes, looking at your watch, hoping some meal will arrive. But then when it comes, the disappointment is always a very cruel one. Most of the fare you are given is so foul and unappetising – you wouldn't care to serve it to a dog.'

'Oh, I know,' Mrs Blunt agreed. 'And apart from the fact that the taste of the food is usually unspeakable, I always feel that the junk that patients are given must be very bad for their health. It's nearly always frozen, or it comes straight out of a tin. It doesn't have a vitamin. It has no nutritional value at all.'

'You are so right,' Corrigan said. 'I'm afraid that malnutrition is the curse of the patient in the modern hospital. I've the awful suspicion that many may have died from it.'

'Once I get my garden going, you'll be astonished how much fruit and vegetables I'll be able to produce,' Mrs Blunt said. 'I think I'll be able to grow enough crops to keep the kitchens of St Crispins very well supplied indeed. I've decided that I'll be adventurous and I won't only plant the basics, such as carrots, leeks and things like that. I love your idea that people who are ill need luxuries . . . I'm going to enjoy growing them more exciting things such as artichokes, mange-touts, and asparagus. I'll plant a lot of tarragon and basil and rosemary, so the food at St Crispins will have some flavour. I think it would also be exciting to install some hot-houses and have a try at growing peaches, figs, and muscat grapes. Just think of the beautiful exotic flowers and plants I could grow once I had the equipment to help them survive our climate. But I think it would be a mistake to devote the entire garden to foodstuffs. I'm sure the patients would also like some wonderful rare flowers to brighten their wards. Do you agree with me?'

Mrs Blunt looked happier than she had for years. Her garden had started to bloom in her mind and she could see the magnificence of the damsons and nectarines, and red and black-currants, the Comice pears and the Cox's Orange Pippins, with which she'd soon be supplying the hospital.

'I more than agree.' Corrigan looked just as happy as she did. 'I find your plan to create this fabulous garden more intoxicating than the champagne you've been generous enough to serve me.'

Mrs Blunt noticed that as they'd been talking they'd finished their bottle of champagne and she went off to get another one from the refrigerator.

'You and the cripple seem to be enjoying yourselves,' Mrs Murphy remarked. 'It's good for you. It's good for you to have something to get you out of yourself.'

The obsessive interest that Mrs Murphy took in all her actions, and her compulsion to comment on them, was usually jarring to Mrs Blunt, although she knew the interest to be a protective and well-intentioned one. However, today, she suddenly had no wish to contradict Mrs Murphy. Her future garden was still flowering in her head and producing an abundance of beautiful shrubs and luscious fruit and delicate fresh vegetables.

She took the bottle of champagne back to Corrigan. But as she started to open it, he waved his bandaged hand with a courtly gesture of refusal.

'Although I'd be happy to go on drinking in your company till this lovely day turns to dusk, I must try to sober my senses and get off back to London. And as I've already sampled so much of your beautiful hospitality, I'd feel easier in my heart if you allowed me to take this bottle with me. I'd like to give it to Rupert Sinclair.'

Mrs Blunt felt she had been rebuked by Corrigan. 'I've got another bottle that I was hoping you'd take to him,' she said defensively. She didn't want Corrigan to think she was selfish, that while she was enjoying herself drinking by the fire, she had completely forgotten the unfortunate Sinclair.

'I've also got some pâté that I'd like you to give him as a present. And maybe it would be nice if I wrote him a little line to go with it.'

'A little line from you would certainly delight Sinclair just as much as the champagne and the pâté. He'll take both to be tokens of your love.'

Mrs Blunt was uncertain whether she wanted Sinclair to take her gifts and her letter as tokens of such strong feeling. But just as long as Sinclair didn't take them to be signs that she was asking him for anything she felt she had to shrug and accept it.

She went over to her little Queen-Anne walnut desk and got out some paper.

'You have beautiful furniture,' Corrigan said. 'I've been admiring it. I know quite a lot about good furniture. I'm interested by all the craft that has gone into it. You have excellent taste. Everything in your house is superbly well-chosen.'

'I don't really look at it any more,' Mrs Blunt said. 'I think it is quite good. But somehow I don't treasure it for that. I only like it because it's part of my past and if furniture could see, it would have seen a lot of my life.'

Mrs Blunt started concentrating on her letter.

'Dear Rupert Sinclair,
   'I am here in the country with Corrigan. We've had a very nice day together and we've been thinking of you. We've made some exciting plans which he will tell you about – I hope they will improve life at St Crispins. Corrigan is bringing you a few little things from me. Some of them are against doctor's orders, but I don't think you'll mind that. I trust Corrigan to smuggle them in to you.

                                        Yours sincerely,
                                        Devina Blunt.'

'Can I read what you've written to Sinclair?' Corrigan asked her.

'Why do you want to read it? It doesn't say very much. It's just a polite little note.' She was surprised by his request.

'I'm curious,' Corrigan smiled at her. Once again she thought that his manner seemed flirtatious, but she decided that she must have imagined it.

'I'm curious about everything about you. I'm curious to know how you have described this day which has been a very important one to me. And then maybe I'm a little jealous of you and Rupert. You'll find that an odd admission, considering the fact that I was the one who first brought you together with him.'

Mrs Blunt was even more astonished by Corrigan's statement. She wished he wouldn't say she was 'together' with Sinclair. She was unable to see why he was so keen to pretend that her relationship with this disabled soldier was an intimate one. She found the concept absurd and unpalatable.

'I told you before that I felt you were willing to show more of yourself to Rupert than you seem to wish to show to me,' Corrigan said to her. 'I'd be inhuman if I didn't feel a few pangs of envy on that score. But having confessed to my unworthy emotions, I can assure you that I'll never allow them to influence my actions and I'll take your champagne and your letter to Rupert in London – and I'll do everything in my power to see that your relationship with him flourishes.'

Mrs Blunt suddenly wondered if Corrigan was completely sane. She felt that he sometimes started to lose all touch with reality. Maybe this was the result of living his life in a chair. It could also be the result of his accident. She would never have dared to question him about this, but she was curious as to the nature of it. There was always the possibility that when he'd injured his spine, he'd also sustained serious head injuries.

She put her letter to Sinclair in an envelope and defiantly sealed it. There was something provocative in the way she did this. If Corrigan was becoming childishly jealous of her nebulous pen-friendship with Rupert Sinclair, she now found it entertaining to fan that jealousy. She was determined not to allow Corrigan to see what she had written.

She suspected that when he arrived at the hospital and gave her letter to his friend, he'd immediately ask to be shown it. She wondered if there was some ruse by which she could prevent this from happening. It occurred to her that she could write 'For your eyes alone' on the envelope. But when Mrs Blunt thought how deranged that would make her look to Sinclair, she quickly dismissed this idea as too undignified to be worth further consideration.

'I'll be on my way,' Corrigan said to her.

She went over and handed him the sealed letter she'd just written to Sinclair and her face had the mysterious expression it had worn when it used to amuse her to refuse to tell the Colonel how she'd acquired her expertise in choosing excellent wine.

'So you won't reveal the contents,' Corrigan said.

'I told you it doesn't say very much. I can't understand why you feel you have to see it?'

'Even the things that your letter omits to say might interest me. They might tell me something about *you*.'

'Well, if you really want to learn about me, I don't think that reading my letters is the best way to do it. I hope you'll come back one of these days. I'd like to discuss our plans for the garden.'

'I'll be back, sure enough. You know that quite well, I think.' Corrigan was staring at her with his eyes half-closed. She had the feeling he was trying to mesmerise her.

'Well, I know you are very busy and I know that your work takes you very far afield.'

'I'll continue with my work, of course – but I'm going to see that it never takes me all that far. The bee returns to the blossom . . .'

'I'll just get that other bottle of champagne for Sinclair. I think it would be nice if I gave him two bottles. I hope he doesn't get so tipsy that the doctors will discover he's been drinking.'

Mrs Blunt knew that Corrigan was fencing with her and she was surprised to find herself entering his game. As she made her ripostes, she was aware that her manner had become coquettish. She felt she was tempting him like Eve, but unlike Adam, Corrigan was not being offered an apple, he was being offered the garden.

'How would I get all the flowers and fruit and vegetables up to the hospital if I really got my idea under way?' she asked him.

'That would present very few problems,' Corrigan said quickly. 'I have a friend who has a truck. He's always wanted to do voluntary work for the disabled. He'd be quite prepared to come down here at least three times a week and collect it.'

'How resourceful you are, Corrigan.' It was the first time she'd used his name and she was surprised how intimate it sounded.

'I can't afford to be anything else,' he smiled, showing his very white teeth.

'We should pool our resources, Corrigan. We might then accomplish something very worthwhile.' Once having dared to call him by his name, Mrs Blunt kept repeating it.

'I can't think of a more attractive project. What should I call you? Mrs Blunt seems a little formal.'

'My name is Devina, I suppose you can call me that if you want to.'

'Devina!' He gave a little whistle. 'Although I claim to be

116

psychic, I confess that my powers have failed me badly. My intuition should have told me that your name could only be Devina.'

'I've never really liked it very much. I've always felt it sounds a little affected. I don't know why my mother chose it. My husband never thought it suited me. He never called me Devina. But then he always liked to call me silly nicknames.'

'I disagree with your late husband, although I'm sure he was a very remarkable man and I would have respected his opinions on every other given subject. I understand completely why your mother chose you such a name.'

After Mrs Murphy had helped him down the steps, Mrs Blunt stood and waved as he went off, his chair loaded with the champagne she was sending to Sinclair.

'I feel like one of the Magi,' Corrigan said. 'I am bringing priceless gifts to the Messiah. My only regret is that my role is only the one of the humble bearer!'

'But the humble still enter the Kingdom of Heaven, Corrigan.' Mrs Blunt was enjoying the familiarity of their oblique badinage.

'*Au revoir!*' he said.

'*Au revoir!*' she answered. She watched him until he turned out of her drive and disappeared from view.

7

The day after Corrigan set off for London, taking her champagne and pâté to Rupert Sinclair, Mrs Blunt ordered herself a taxi and went to Salisbury where she'd made an appointment to see her solicitor, Mr Hicks. She had not gone into Salisbury ever since the day that she'd bought her last bottle of expensive claret for her husband. As she drove through the countryside she was saddened by memories of that last trip and she wished that her pretext for making this excursion was as frivolous and pleasant as when she'd made her old forays to get pointlessly special wine for the Colonel.

But as she was driven through the pretty villages and the rolling countryside, whose beautiful colours seemed to shine like exotic Indian jewels in the rays of the autumn sun, she also felt a thrill of release. She saw this journey to see her solicitor as a hazardous one. She was still stimulated by its challenges. She was glad to be in motion, and she was curiously aware of the wheels of the taxi as they bore her towards the town. She imagined that Corrigan must get a similar sense of freedom as he went speeding down the lanes and the highways.

Once she got to her solicitor's office, she told Mr Hicks that she wanted him to send a personal cheque to St Crispins. She explained to him that it was a hospital for the disabled. She asked him to enclose a letter which said that he had become very interested in all the valuable work their ex-patient Corrigan was now doing – that he was a great admirer of such enterprises and he hoped that Corrigan would put the money he was offering to any purpose that he thought fit.

After Mrs Blunt had given the matter quite a lot of thought she'd finally decided that she wanted Mr Hicks to send Corrigan a cheque for two thousand pounds. If she gave him less she was frightened that he would be loath to spend it on himself, feeling that other patients in the hospital were in greater need and should therefore be given priority. If she gave him more than two thousand, she was frightened he might be so astonished by the largeness of the sum that there'd be a danger he would try to track down the unknown figure from whom the gift had originated.

Mrs Blunt felt that the sum she had decided to give Corrigan was a subtle one. It allowed him to acquire a new chair, while at the same time giving him extra money that could be put at the disposal of the other patients. She hoped this would prevent him from feeling any guilt that he was betraying them by taking too large a slice of her charitable offering.

Mr Hicks looked bemused and shocked when Mrs Blunt explained what she wanted him to do. He obviously couldn't understand why she wanted so much secrecy to surround her gift. Mrs Blunt insisted that when he enclosed a letter to the secretary of St Crispins he must on no account use formal notepaper from his office. She was adamant that the hospital must never be allowed to know the true address of the donor. He must therefore invent one.

Mr Hicks also looked very startled when he was told the size of the sum she planned to donate to charity. Mrs Blunt became defensive as she saw perturbation in his bland and waxy face.

'My late husband was always very interested in helping the disabled,' she said defiantly. 'I feel that he would have liked me to contribute towards this cause. I am his heir, so that's why I feel it is only right that I should spend his money in the way that he would most have approved of.'

She wondered why she felt she had to lie to Mr Hicks. The Colonel, as it happened, had never been particularly involved with the disabled. He had gone through life without their plight having been brought to his notice. She was ashamed that she found it necessary to excuse her gift by shifting its responsibility on to her late husband.

'I wish Mr Hicks wouldn't behave as if I'm giving away money that belongs to him,' Mrs Blunt thought. 'I suppose that these men who have to advise other people on their finances soon start to feel that the funds they manage are their own. But he still has no right to make me feel that I'm being irresponsible and robbing his own wife and children. I shall spend my own trust funds as I choose to.'

She felt inadequate and exposed in his office with all its typists and its neon lighting and its atmosphere of legal solemnity. However, when she left it, she did so with a sense that she'd triumphed over something very difficult. She had overcome her tendency to behave with a cautious inertia. She had assailed the dreaded office of Mr Hicks with all the courage of a Hannibal. She had been shaken, but not defeated by the fierce antagonism he had shown towards her project. She'd made him bow to her wishes. Her mission had been successfully completed. The most unwilling Mr Hicks had sent off the cheque according to her instructions.

Mrs Blunt went off to her favourite wine shop and asked them to tell her what claret they recommended. They produced a bottle with such a vast castle on its label that it gave it the look of the most expensive and august superiority. She ordered a case of this wine and had it carried out to her taxi. She wondered who she was buying it for, and then realised it had to be Corrigan.

As she drove home she felt elated, knowing that for once she'd accomplished something of value. By mobilising herself, she had done everything in her power to restore mobility to a disabled human being.

'Could you open the window?' she asked the driver of her taxi. She wanted to feel the wind blowing on her face.

8

Nadine was making breakfast for the twins when she next received a letter from her mother. She opened it with her usual sense of dread, expecting one more understated little declaration of Mrs Blunt's general sense of hopelessness. All such plaintive communications from her mother left her feeling depressed for the rest of the day, and for this reason they were far from welcome to her.

'How are you? How are the children?' Mrs Blunt had written. This was a familiar start and to her daughter, it seemed like one of her customary accusations. She laid aside the letter and it was not until the twins had gone to school that she managed to force herself to go on reading it.

'I have met a very impressive man called Corrigan,' her mother wrote. 'He is disabled, but he is very brave and he refuses to be got down by his disability and he devotes himself to helping others.'

Nadine wondered how her mother had managed to get to know this courageous and crippled person. As far as she knew, Mrs Blunt hardly ever left her house except when she went off to visit the graveyard. She found her mother's new acquaintanceship a very startling one.

'My state of mind has been completely changed by meeting him,' the letter continued. 'He has made me realise how selfish my life has been ever since your father died. I am now taking all sorts of energetic steps to change all that. I am going to throw myself into charitable works. You have always advised me to do that and you were right. But I think I wasn't really ready before. Now I am suddenly feeling very much stronger and I am planning to work full-time for the disabled. There is so much to be done for them. Corrigan has persuaded me of that.

'Another thing you will be glad to hear is that I intend to overhaul and restore my garden. I've already got this project in motion and I'm getting enormous pleasure from it. I'm going to make the garden quite different from the one that your father and I created. At this point, I want to concentrate on market produce and I mean to run the whole thing as a commercial enterprise. I intend to sell all the vegetables and fruit that I grow, and I will send the proceeds to various charitable institutions. A wonderful thing has happened to me. I can hardly believe my good luck. Fifteen acres of very fertile land that directly adjoins my property came up for sale last week. I went into Salisbury and saw Mr Hicks, and I've arranged for him to bid for them on my behalf. These new acres, in combination with those that I already own, will give me a very sizeable amount of land with which to work and I'm certain I can do something exciting with them.

'Do you remember Mr Peebles, the dear old boy who runs the big market garden in Coombe Abbot? He has a son named William who is a brilliant gardener and is highly experienced in the growing of fruit and vegetables. I hired him yesterday and he is now working for me as my estate agent and he will oversee the men that I'm going to employ to get the garden into shape. I think my idea to hire him was an excellent one because it's so important to have the advice of experts.

'Anyway, I'm very thrilled by it all and hope you will come down to see the new garden once it gets really underway.

'All my love to the twins and love to yourself.

Mummy.'

Nadine found this letter astonishing. It had a new confidence in its tone and it lacked any of the woefulness that was usually so oppressive to her. She was amazed that her mother had dared to go into Salisbury in order to consult her solicitor. Yet the whole idea of Mrs Blunt charging round the countryside buying up land as she vigorously embarked on her large-scale commercial enterprise was a very unwelcome one.

Justin came into the kitchen while Nadine was trying to absorb the unexpected contents of her mother's letter. He sat down at the pine breakfast table and started to read the papers with the nonchalance of a man in a restaurant waiting to be brought a meal.

Nadine made him some coffee and fried him some eggs.

'I hope you haven't forgotten, darling,' he said. 'I've asked the Crickstones to dine tonight.'

Nadine had not forgotten. She had already decided she was going to serve them avocado mousse, then chicken casserole with fennel, wine and cream. She had not yet planned the dessert, but she would decide what the Crickstones would be given for dessert later. 'How pointless it is to cook for these rich, young, well-fed couples,' she thought.

She had no desire to tell Justin about her mother's letter. She was frightened that he'd see nothing surprising about it. He'd probably make some heavy point about how he'd always known that his mother-in-law had great resources.

Nadine cleared up the breakfast cups and plates and kept thinking about the letter. Mrs Blunt had admitted that in recent years her life had become selfish. 'My life is not exactly selfish,' Nadine thought. 'I behave unselfishly to a selfish person – that is probably almost worse.'

She went to tidy the twins' bedroom. Their room was the only spot in the house she now liked. She still felt there was a magic in all their childish paraphernalia. The bright posters on their walls pleased her. She was cheered by the sight of all their books on football, their tanks and machine guns and their robots.

Her sense of order was always jarred by the careless way

123

they treated their possessions, but she could excuse it because they always managed to make their floor look like a battlefield and she enjoyed feeling like a Florence Nightingale as she picked her way through the miniature carnage of strewn military figures with their sadly ruined vehicles and their trampled high technology armaments.

In the mornings Nadine would sometimes get into one of her sons' beds and just lie there. She would feel warm and illicitly protected as she snuggled under their Swiss feather duvets. She liked the smell of their pillows and their crumpled pyjamas. Lying there as though hiding from all the pressures of her life in their beds and surrounded by toys, she had the feeling she had dressed herself up in the trappings of their childhood, and by so doing, she managed to recapture something pleasant from her own.

Today Nadine resented the temptation to snuggle down and bask under the blanket-like illusion of safety that the beds of the twins could give her. She felt very threatened by the letter she had just received from her mother and she knew she ought to think about its implications rather than play games in which she made a temporary retreat from adult responsibility.

Nadine's perfectionism often made her procrastinate, and she tended to put off taking certain necessary actions because she was waiting for the ideal moment to take them. When she looked at her own face in the mirror, she could never quite accept the reflection in front of her as the real one. In her mind she automatically improved it so that she managed to see herself as she hoped she would be in an imaginary future when her hair would have been better cut or washed, when she'd have become either thinner or fatter, or gone on some diet that improved the condition of her skin.

In the same way that she avoided seeing the reality of her current image in the mirror and automatically replaced it with a superior one that she hoped would exist later, she had persuaded herself that it was not yet the right time to approach Mrs Blunt for help; still she had continued to entertain the belief that her whole relationship with her mother would eventually magically improve, and one day they would establish a closeness and understanding which would make her feelings that it was humiliating and corrupt to accept money from her mother seem futile and foolish.

The Colonel had not left Nadine anything in his will. He'd left everything he owned to his wife. He had not done this out of any hostility towards his daughter. He'd always had such perfect trust in his wife's generosity that he had taken it for granted that she would arrange to see that Nadine was adequately provided for.

Although it had not been her father's intention to disinherit her, Nadine had been very wounded by the provisions of his will and emotionally she saw herself as having been disinherited. There was a childish element of pique in her fierce disinclination to take money from her mother. If her father had not had sufficient respect for her individuality to leave her some money of her own, she preferred to penalise herself rather than be put in the demeaning position of accepting financial help that came from him only indirectly. The idea of accepting any of her father's money as a gift from her mother was abhorrent to her because she felt she would be taking the very symbol of his rejection.

After the Colonel had died, Mrs Blunt had asked her daughter if she needed any financial assistance and Nadine had reminded her in prickly tones that Justin earned a good salary – that he had adequate trust funds of his own. She had advised her mother to keep the Colonel's inheritance to meet her own personal requirements. Mrs Blunt was vague about the state of her own finances and those of others and she had meekly accepted that Nadine had no need for any economic aid. She had been puzzled as to why her daughter seemed so obviously displeased by her offer. From childhood, Mrs Blunt had been brought up to believe that discussions about money were vulgar. In her simplicity, she had decided that her daughter was trying to rebuke her for crassly raising an unsavoury topic. At that time, Mrs Blunt had been feeling so overwhelmed by the loss of the Colonel that if Nadine had asked for her entire fortune she would very probably have given it to her. But as her daughter didn't seem to want any help, she'd simply accepted this fact, with an equal lack of emotional involvement.

In the weeks that immediately followed the Colonel's death, Mrs Blunt had been convinced she'd been left penniless and had gone into a state of panic, but Nadine had misunderstood the reasons for her mother's agitation. She had never been terrified that her material way of life was threatened. She had suffered from an emotional pennilessness which then became transmuted into a terror of poverty. In some perverse way she had wanted to feel she was economically ruined. At that point, if Mrs Blunt had found herself forced to sleep like a vagrant in a ditch, she would have almost welcomed the misery of her predicament. She would then have been able to reconcile her external situation with her inner sense that she'd been stripped of everything that had any value.

As Nadine tidied the bedroom of the twins, she realised that it was now urgent that she examine the reasons why she felt so threatened by her mother's letter. When she'd first married, she had been content to be supported by Justin and it had been a psychological luxury to refuse to take money from her mother. But now that Nadine had received this letter with the news that her mother had developed this unexpected passion for charitable causes, she had to ask herself why she found the information so ominous and disturbing.

Recently, since her marriage had started to seem like a prison to her, Nadine had been sustained by her dream that she would one day be able to escape from it.

Mrs Blunt's letter had jolted that dream because she immediately inferred from its contents that it was one which she might very soon have to abandon. She suddenly realised she had been most foolish when she'd been proud and haughty and refused her mother's offer of economic aid at the time that Mrs Blunt had originally made it.

Now that her mother had apparently found many alternative ways in which to spend her money, Nadine could hardly feel it was the perfect moment to start reaching out for her mother's purse strings. She'd left that all too late. She felt her role could now only seem disgusting if she was to put herself into greedy competition with a lot of deserving figures in wheelchairs. The more she thought about it, the more she knew that now the disabled had become her chief economic rivals, her own conscience would force her to retire and suffer defeat.

'I must try to remember that I'm lucky that I have Justin to support me,' she thought to herself. 'I'm not forced to beg money from my mother. Her money's only available to her because she got it from her husband. I've got my own husband . . .' She recognised that she was putting on her usual proud brave face, and that face could not impress her since she was putting it on only for herself.

When she looked out of the window, the London sky looked overcast and grey as concrete and it seemed very like her future. She felt depressed that the Crickstones were coming to dinner. There was nothing wrong with them. But she didn't like them particularly, and they didn't particularly like her. None of Justin's friends liked her very much. She was so eager to please them that she somehow failed to do so. Tommy Crickstone was a legal government adviser and Justin found him amusing because he enjoyed hearing all the current political gossip. His wife, Valerie, was a fashion designer. Justin liked her because she always flirted with him in a harmless, but flattering way. 'Justin's friends all see me as a "dumb waiter",' Nadine thought. 'I'm afraid they're right. I'm just like those bits of furniture that you put on dining-room tables. You twirl them around and they bring you your salt, your pepper, your sugar. Americans call them "Lazy Susans".'

She wished she could feel her life had the promise that her mother suddenly seemed to believe that hers had. Nadine felt she was in an unhealthy see-saw situation with her mother. As Mrs Blunt went up, she could only go plunging down. She knew that she must try not to resent Mrs Blunt's new happiness – she must try to be glad that her mother was getting such great pleasure from lavishing her money on the disabled.

Having made the resolution that she would try and fight any of the petty-minded thoughts that sprung into her mind, Nadine went off to put some avocado in the blender for the Crickstones.

9

A week after Corrigan went off to London bearing her gifts, Mrs Blunt received a letter of thanks from St Crispins. Rupert Sinclair wrote to say that he found it difficult to express the pleasure that he'd felt when he had received the two bottles of champagne and the pâté. Corrigan had smuggled them into the hospital with his usual panache and both of them had drunk to her health in plastic mugs behind the backs of the nurses, and the whole occasion had taken on the delightful and furtive feeling of the midnight feast at boarding-school. The champagne had seemed like nectar and the pâté had been pure ambrosia. He had to confess that after he had consumed the second bottle he had felt a little drunk, but afterwards he had suffered no ill-effects. In fact, he had found his drinking spree extremely restorative.

Rupert Sinclair was glad to be able to tell her that he was feeling physically much better and that all the discomfort he had gone through in the last weeks was beginning to seem like a receding nightmare.

He told her that he was now able to start reading again and Corrigan was keeping him well supplied with books from the local London library. 'The library here at St Crispins is an intellectual desert,' he wrote. 'Corrigan does his best to ensure that those of us at St Crispins whom he has taught to love literature are supplied with serious books from the outside. But he is one man working alone and recently, since my descent into the abyss, I have accused myself of abusing his infinite willingness to put his time at my disposal. I have noticed that he often looks quite exhausted lately and then I hate myself for allowing him to go scurrying backwards and forwards bringing me books which are unobtainable here. You see, it was Corrigan who taught me that reading was the great way out. It was Corrigan who made me understand that human beings find it unendurable to dwell all the time in the quagmire of reality – that they have to have moments when they can flee to the beautiful palaces of imagination and intellect. Recently I've had the feeling I've learnt Corrigan's lesson too well and it has made me over-demanding and it is my poor friend who is paying the price . . .'

Mrs Blunt read this part of Sinclair's letter with dismay. She found it disturbing to think of Corrigan going backwards and forwards bringing Sinclair books from a library outside the hospital. She hated to hear that he was looking exhausted. She felt it ought to be quite easy to arrange for the patients in St Crispins to have serious books to read. She was starting to understand why Corrigan felt that it was so vital to establish a good library on the premises.

In the old days, Mrs Blunt had used to enjoy going to local antique furniture auctions with the Colonel. She now remembered that when the contents of various old country houses came up for sale, the books were often sold off in separate lots and they usually went for very little. She wondered if this might not be a clever way of starting a very good library at St Crispins. She decided to suggest it to Corrigan. He could always weed out the uninteresting volumes that she would inevitably acquire if she went around the local antique auctions buying up these books at random. She still believed she might well get hold of some valuable editions if she was to pursue this idea. This thought was very exciting to her.

As Mrs Blunt went on reading Sinclair's letter, she suddenly gave a little smile. It informed her that a miraculous thing had just happened to Corrigan. As she must know, he had been desperately worried because his chair had been destroyed. He'd been dreading having to endure a period when he would be bed-ridden. 'You know what a mentally active man

Corrigan is,' Sinclair wrote. 'He sets himself so many goals. The prospect of a period of enforced idleness was therefore anathema to him.'

Rupert Sinclair said that some unknown man had suddenly sent an amazingly generous gift to the hospital. 'If I could go down on my knees to this unknown person, I would most certainly do so,' Sinclair wrote.

He went on to say that this astonishing bequest had enabled Corrigan to acquire a new chair. When it had arrived, the hospital committee had asked all the patients who were currently being treated there to take a vote as to how they felt these funds would best be employed. The vote had been unanimous. They had all felt a large portion of the money should be spent on a new chair for Corrigan, and they'd felt the remains of the bequest should be spent on Sony earphones and cassettes.

Mrs Blunt had a childish streak in her character which had always enjoyed both giving and receiving the Father Christmas-like surprise. In the last years she had felt that all her powers of giving or receiving joy had perished with the Colonel. But now she was astonished that she could get so much pleasure from hearing about the stir that her anonymous gift had apparently created in the hospital.

Sinclair's letter went on to tell her that he'd heard of her brilliant plan to grow fruit and vegetables for the patients at St Crispins. He hoped she wouldn't find him greedy when he confessed that he found her project thrilling. 'The food in this hospital is unspeakable,' he wrote.

Mrs Blunt felt some kind of shame as she read this. It was so easy for her to grow fruit and vegetables and they would obviously mean so much to those who were imprisoned in the hospital. She was ashamed she had never before thought of the simple things she could do to make life a little more endurable for people like Sinclair. She went to the telephone and rang William Peebles, asking him to come round to see her so that they could discuss what could be done to create a thriving market garden.

10

The next time that Corrigan arrived at her door, Mrs Blunt felt no surprise when she heard the crunch of his approaching wheels. She knew that he would soon be coming back to see her, although he had never telephoned or given her any warning as to when she might expect a visit. He seemed to enjoy making the unexpected arrival. She wondered if this was his way of asserting some kind of independence.

It was possible that as his physical movements were very constricted by his chair, he felt a need to shroud his whereabouts in mystery and enjoyed the feeling that his comings and goings were completely unpredictable.

'So he's back,' Mrs Murphy muttered sullenly when she heard Corrigan tapping with his umbrella on the stone steps that led up to the front door. 'Now I suppose he'll be expecting me to do all that terrible struggling to get him in.'

Mrs Murphy rarely showed any ill-humour and Mrs Blunt was quite shocked by the surliness with which she reacted to Corrigan's appeal for help. As Mrs Murphy was such an immensely strong woman, she felt that it was unbecoming that she seemed reluctant to employ her unusual strength in order to give a crippled man some help in getting up the steps.

'Mrs Murphy doesn't like Corrigan,' Mrs Blunt thought. She had sensed this during his last visit, but something had prevented her from properly facing up to the truth of it. She couldn't understand how Corrigan had managed to antagonise

Mrs Murphy. He had treated her with much more gallantry and courtesy than she usually received from Mrs Blunt's other visitors. Nadine was often really downright cold and rude to her, and although to many people Mrs Murphy seemed larger than life, Justin always treated her as if she was invisible. Mrs Blunt had always been puzzled by the fact that when Mrs Murphy was with her son-in-law, even her unique noisiness seemed to fall on deaf ears.

Yet poor Corrigan had put himself out to be pleasant to Mrs Murphy. The last time he'd come to lunch he had thanked her with a fervent eloquence for the wonderful meal that she'd served him, although he'd known just as well as Mrs Blunt that she hadn't really cooked it.

She wondered if some complicated racial clash was going on between the two of them. She knew that Irish people seemed to find it hard to get on with each other. They always seemed to be blowing each other up, and shooting each other in the knee-cap. She could never understand their reasons for committing such atrocities, but she knew that they existed for she continually read about them in the papers.

'Well, aren't you going to give Corrigan a hand with his chair?' she asked.

Mrs Murphy just kept standing there. She had a funny defiant expression on her face and she was deliberately making no move to go to the front door although the unfortunate Corrigan was now starting to tap on the steps quite frantically with his umbrella, being unable to reach the bell.

Mrs Blunt was suddenly terrified that Mrs Murphy was planning to go on strike, that she was going to refuse to give Corrigan any assistance. She didn't know what on earth she would do if this disturbing thing was to happen. She knew that she couldn't possibly get him into the house herself. She suddenly loathed herself for her own frailty. She wondered if she could ring the local police and ask them to send an officer to get Corrigan up her steps. But the idea was too embarrassing to her. It wasn't really an affair for the police. Her request would seem too odd to them.

Mrs Blunt realised with despondency that if Mrs Murphy

chose to go on strike Corrigan would have to go on pathetically tapping until he realised he had no way of entering the house and then finally he'd have to give up and she'd never see him again, for he would have to accept the snub and go wheeling away.

Mrs Murphy was still making no move to give him any help. Her expression was surly and intransigent and Mrs Blunt trembled before the unexpected and stubborn force of this show of rebelliousness.

Mrs Blunt had a lot of food in the house. Not knowing when Corrigan would be arriving, she had stocked up her larder so that she could produce any amount of delicious emergency meals whenever they were required of her. Her kitchen no longer had the barren and desolate atmosphere of a disused unit. Her refrigerator was now bulging with pleasant things to eat, and when she opened it she had ceased to feel that she was opening a freezing and empty white coffin.

If Mrs Murphy was to go into open rebellion as was suggested by her current stance, Mrs Blunt wondered if she ought to cook Corrigan a meal before he was forced to depart. Or would he find it ignominious if it was brought to him as he sat there outside on her gravel? He was very proud and he might well see his situation as extremely demeaning. Mrs Blunt had to admit that she could see that it would not be very dignified for him to accept food under such conditions, even though she would cook him something extremely tasty and he could always drink some of the lovely new expensive wine that she'd just ordered from Salisbury. However well she was to feed him, she couldn't see how she could avoid giving him the feeling that she was treating him like a stray dog – that any nourishment she produced would seem like old bones tossed to him with contempt.

Mrs Blunt found her position intolerable. She now had this cripple tapping with true desperation on her steps. When she looked out of the window she saw that it was just about to rain. Somehow it always seemed to start to rain when Corrigan came to her house. Soon the whole situation would become even more appalling – she would have a drenched invalid beating on her steps while she was powerless to give him shelter.

'Please, Mrs Murphy,' she begged, 'please help Corrigan get in.'

Like a child she resorted to saying 'please'. It was the word she'd been trained to believe got the only solid responses.

Mrs Murphy looked at Mrs Blunt, and her expression was still defiant.

'It's my back,' she muttered stubbornly. 'I can't help him into the house. All this week, my back has been playing me up something powerful.'

Mrs Blunt realised immediately that Mrs Murphy was lying to her. She knew all about Mrs Murphy's health for every day she was given a running commentary on the subject. Mrs Blunt knew that Mrs Murphy had ankle-swelling, that this was due to water retention. She knew about all the pills that Mrs Murphy had been given to combat this condition. She also knew that she had thyroid trouble and that this explained why her eyes protruded from her head. But Mrs Murphy did not have a bad back. That was obviously the purest fabrication. If she had trouble with her back, Mrs Blunt knew that she would have become very well acquainted with every detail of her sufferings. If it was hurting her, she would certainly not have been able to keep feeding the drawing-room fire by carrying in endless baskets that were stacked high with heavy logs.

'Please,' she repeated plaintively, 'Please, give Corrigan a hand and help him in.'

Mrs Murphy had all the power. Mrs Blunt was close to tears. She couldn't even bear to go out to talk to Corrigan. If she went outside to speak to him she was certain he would find it all the more insulting. She would have to warn him that she couldn't possibly get him up the steps and however polite and friendly she was, he would still feel rejected and eventually she would have to tell him he might as well go away.

Mrs Murphy saw that Mrs Blunt was shaking with agitation and misery. She looked so tiny in her little dove-grey dress. Her childish round blue eyes were brimming with tears. Mrs Murphy weakened and her face took on the affectionate and

134

maternal expression that it acquired whenever she saw that Mrs Blunt was in distress.

'Well, I'll have a try at bumping him up,' she said. 'But my back is very bad. So I'm not giving any promises that I'll be able to make him make it.'

Mrs Blunt slipped away and she went to sit by her fire in the drawing-room. She didn't have the courage to watch Mrs Murphy getting Corrigan into the house. Now she'd realised how much Mrs Murphy disliked him, she felt that the whole enterprise was hazardous.

However, Mrs Murphy was merciful and she didn't take advantage of Corrigan as he entrusted himself to her powerful arms and she got him into the house and he wheeled himself into the drawing-room. Mrs Blunt anxiously searched his face, looking for the signs of exhaustion that Sinclair had described, but he looked surprisingly healthy and he gave the impression of being rather pleased with himself.

Mrs Blunt saw that he had a brand-new shiny chair, and, whereas his last one had been backed with shabby blue leather, this one was backed with red uncracked material and it matched his scarlet shirt.

Mrs Blunt wondered if she ought to compliment him on his chair, but feared this could seem tactless. He might be embarrassed to admit that he had accepted it as a gift from charity and think she was patronising him as if he was a child being complimented on his new toy.

'What do you think of my glorious new chariot?' he asked. It seemed that he didn't mind bringing it to her attention, and he wanted her to comment on it.

'I like the red leather,' she said. She then felt this remark was inadequate.

'It goes twice the speed of my last one,' he said. 'It's much better designed. When I go down the roads in this one, I have the feeling that I'm racing the wind.'

Mrs Blunt couldn't really see that its design was very different from his last one, but then she was not an expert on wheelchairs and she accepted that it had subtle points which were an improvement. She was glad that he seemed so happy with it. It pleased her to know that he was sitting in her chair without having any idea of it.

'Is it borrowed from the hospital?' she asked with fake innocence.

'No, it's my very own property and if an Englishman's house is his castle, I feel this chair is my own splendid castle and it came to me from the most beautiful and bountiful queen.'

Corrigan was looking at Mrs Blunt through his long dark eyelashes.

'I think he knows,' she thought and a blush spread over her forehead. 'Why should he say it comes from a queen when he ought to think it came from an unknown man?'

'Let me get you some champagne,' she said. 'I've got a bottle on ice.' She wanted no further mention of the chair. She was terrified by the idea that he might start expressing his indebtedness to her. When he'd first arrived she had liked to feel that he was in her chair but now that he knew it too, she was frightened to have such enormous power over him – in a sense his whole life had been saved by her.

'What are we celebrating?' Mrs Murphy asked, when Mrs Blunt went to get the champagne from the kitchen.

She found the question a good one. But she didn't know how to answer it. Was she celebrating the fact that she'd restored mobility to Corrigan? She remembered that William Peebles had arranged for some men to come over to plough up her garden. They would be starting work tomorrow and that seemed something worth drinking to. Or was she only celebrating her feeling that it was going to be very pleasant to open a bottle of champagne and share it with Corrigan? She couldn't really tell and she knew that she was certainly not going to try to give any explanations to Mrs Murphy, because as she took the bottle out of the refrigerator she noticed that her protruding eyes were staring at her with anxiety and disapproval.

'Why does Mrs Murphy think that she is the only person who should ever be allowed a drink?' she wondered. 'And why does Mr Hicks think he is the only person who knows how I should spend my trust funds?'

She recognised that she aroused a protective attitude in other people which she found patronising and onerous. It made her feel rebellious.

'I read the "Lament" that you brought me,' she said to Corrigan when she returned to the drawing-room. 'I've read it so many times that I almost know it by heart.'

' "My love and my delight," ' Corrigan answered. ' "The day I saw you first . . ." '

' "Beside the market house," ' continued Mrs Blunt. ' "I had eyes for nothing else. And love for none but you." ' She faltered and once again she blushed. The words made her feel shy.

'It's a beautiful poem,' Corrigan said. 'I'd have found it devastating if you'd had no response to it.'

'I found it very sad,' she whispered.

'I would imagine you did. It's the tale of a tragedy after all, and I suspect that your own experience has not been too dissimilar. But there's one great difference between you and the widowed Eileen O'Leary. She can ask for revenge on the English and towards the end of the poem she does this. But when you look for vengeance, who can you take it on? All your vengeance is going inwards and you are taking it on yourself.'

Mrs Blunt fidgeted. She found it disquieting when he started to make this kind of personal analysis of her situation. She thought he was being presumptuous, for he really knew very little about her. She didn't feel that his assessment of her predicament was correct, but when he started fiercely scrutinising her face with his strange blue-green eyes, she reminded herself that he had psychic powers, and she started to wonder if he could perceive truths to which she had blinded herself.

In order to change a conversation that was making her uneasy, she told him that some men were coming to work on her garden tomorrow. This news obviously pleased him. She also told him about her idea of going round the country houses that would be coming up for sale in the neighbourhood, and described how she hoped to buy up some of the books from their disbanded libraries.

Corrigan became frenetically enthusiastic about this idea. It had obviously never occurred to him before.

'You could get yourself some really magnificent books by doing that,' he said. 'You might even get yourself some of those lovely old leather sets of the classics. You could even pick up some valuable rare editions.'

'But I wouldn't be picking them for myself.' It surprised Mrs Blunt that he seemed unable to understand her intentions. 'The whole point would be that I'd be buying them for the patients at St Crispins. They need them much more than I do.'

'Well, this whole idea overwhelms me,' Corrigan said. 'The patients would die of gratitude if you were to do this for them. But I think that you should keep some books for yourself. I see none in this house. And I'll confess that it saddens me. It gives a touch of impoverishment that I don't care to associate with you.'

Mrs Blunt did have some books, but they were all upstairs in her bedroom and Corrigan had therefore never seen them. They were mostly books on gardening and wild flowers. She also had some volumes on military history and tactics that had belonged to the Colonel, and she had a few thrillers which he'd enjoyed reading in the evenings. But she knew that Corrigan would have small respect for her little library, so she was meek and she made no mention of it when he reproved her.

'Yes, I must get more books,' she whispered.

'If you were to go round the country house sales you might spot some lovely antiques that no one has recognised the worth of, and you could make a daring bid for them,' Corrigan said to her.

'I've already got a lot of antiques.' Mrs Blunt waved her hand at the furniture in her drawing-room. 'I don't think this house could take much more.'

'You have very lovely furniture,' Corrigan said. 'I've already praised it. I can see that every single item has been selected with the eye of someone who appreciated the beautiful. I worship that imperishable eye, for I have a healthy horror of those who surround themselves with ugly objects. I go into many houses when I'm going round the country fund-raising. And though many of the people that I encounter have a sweetness and generosity that gives them a beauty, none of that is reflected in the hideous interiors they inhabit. Oh, what venomous sofas they choose to sit on! What damnable lights they choose to light their rooms! And the pictures that adorn their walls – they are mostly excrement. I find it a melancholy thing to see what they are content with.'

Corrigan made a gesture to express his disgust and Mrs Blunt suddenly noticed that he was no longer wearing bandages. She saw that his knuckles were badly scarred and clotted with dark dry blood and they looked very painful. He had a deep and nasty cut running down one of his thumbs.

'Now you can say these people lack the money to create an interior with any charm or harmony,' Corrigan continued, 'but you'd be lying if you said that – for the most part it's impossible to pretend that poverty excuses them. I've often gone to the houses of people who have cars spilling out of their garages, and servants teeming in their cellars, and the sky reflected in their swimming-pools – but the way their houses are furnished – it makes goose-pimples rise on your skin.'

Mrs Blunt looked round her drawing-room as if she'd never really examined it before. Now that Corrigan had shown that he was so critical of the way that people furnished their houses, she looked to see if she owned anything to which he could take exception. Her Queen-Anne walnut writing-desk was quite a good little piece. It was perfectly authentic. She didn't think he could object to her Regency chairs or her buttoned velvet eighteenth-century sofa. The pictures on her walls were all quite valuable, although they were only the work of minor Victorian artists. There were horse and flower paintings and they were nicely framed in maple. But none of them was a copy, and she hoped Corrigan didn't see them as excrement.

'I've always been very affected by my surroundings,' Corrigan told her. 'My little flat in London is very simple, but it has a congenial atmosphere and when I take a look around it, everything pleases me. When I was a patient at St Crispins, the ugliness of the way that the building is furnished used to really cause me great suffering. If you are confined in hideous surroundings and your eye never alights on anything that it can approve of, the ugliness eats into your brain like acid and you feel it is making holes in your heart.'

'I didn't realise that St Crispins was so ugly inside. But I suppose most hospitals are furnished in awful taste. Everyone is so busy concentrating on the medical side of things they don't care what anything looks like.'

'Well, that's the tragedy,' Corrigan said, 'and as St Crispins is very ill-equipped with funds, the furnishings are a little more terrible than most. You ought to see the "recreation room". That's the godforsaken room where the days of most of the patients are spent. That's the room where Sinclair's condemned to spend the greater part of the life that is left to him. It has this repulsive neon lighting that makes everyone feel bilious and every time you go in there you are turned to the colour of a string bean.'

'I hate neon lighting,' Mrs Blunt said. She looked at her own Victorian china lamps which gave out a comforting rose-coloured glow through their waxy shades.

'The lighting in that room is the least of its horrors,' Corrigan said. 'It has a carpet with a bold and whirling pattern, and you feel there's a devilish design behind that horrible floor covering. It's as if it's only been woven in order to cause the maximum offence to the aesthetic sense of the unfortunate patients.'

'Poor Sinclair,' Mrs Blunt said. She had a vivid impression of that loathsome carpet and she hated the idea that at this very moment, he was being forced to put up with it.

'Yes, it's men like Sinclair who feel especially assaulted by that vile carpet. As you have gathered, he is a man of extraordinary taste and refinement . . . But the other patients suffer as well. You'd have to be inhuman not to be affected by the decor of the recreation room at St Crispins. I tell you that the design of that benighted carpet used to enter my sleep. I saw it every time that I shut my eyes. It became like the fibre of my bad dreams.'

'It would be so easy to get a nice carpet for that room,' Mrs Blunt said.

Corrigan shrugged and he made a helpless gesture. 'It's easy if you have the means, and it's difficult if they are lacking. But once I've built up the library, I intend to devote all the proceeds that I receive from my fund-raising to improving the "recreation room". I've pledged my whole life to that. I'm going to get all the foul and peeling mustard paint stripped off the walls of that room. I'm going to burn the dirty dish-rag curtains and replace them with curtains made of decent material. I'm going to throw out all the rotten old chairs and tables and get some furniture that doesn't make you reel with nausea every time you look at it.' Corrigan smiled. 'But that's my dream. It will take time before it turns to reality.'

Mrs Blunt felt very sorry for Corrigan. It would certainly take him a long time to realise his dream, wheeling round the countryside in all weathers picking up tiny sums of cash in exchange for his sad little flags.

She asked him if he felt that Wiltshire was a good area for fund-raising. Corrigan's dream was starting to infect her. It was becoming her own dream. She, too, wanted the horrible mustard paint stripped off the walls of the recreation room at St Crispins. She wanted to take up its offensive carpet and lay down Persian rugs or perhaps an Aubusson. She longed to transform this horrible room and give it elegance and beauty, and see that it was furnished with eighteenth-century antiques and lovely pictures.

Corrigan said that he believed that Wiltshire could be an excellent area for fund-raising. 'To seem a little crass,' he said, 'there's money around in this county. I believe they call it the cocktail belt of England.'

'If you ever want to fund-raise in these parts, I'd love you to stay with me,' she said. 'I'd be delighted if you would use my house as if it was a hotel. If you were to stay with me, you could do a lot of work in the neighbourhood and you wouldn't have the inconvenience of having to return to London every night.'

A curious look came over Corrigan's handsome face. He looked upset and embarrassed. His embarrassment communicated itself to Mrs Blunt, for she realised that she had blundered. She'd forgotten that the man was crippled. She found it easy to do this when she was drinking champagne by the fire with him. He was so energetic and lively that his infirmity seemed to lack importance. But now it seemed to rise up like a dark monster and the gloom of its shadow spread over her drawing-room. She realised that a crippled man obviously had very special requirements. He couldn't be asked to stay, just like that. She ought to have first established what medical equipment was necessary for him. Yet it would be mortifyingly difficult to ask him.

For a start, if he was to become her guest, she realised that he would obviously need some kind of ramp so that he could get up and down the stone steps in front of her house. It would be unthinkable if he was to be permanently subjected to the capricious moods of Mrs Murphy.

'Your invitation is a most enticing one,' he said. 'But unfortunately there are certain factors that mar the possibility of me ever being able to accept it.'

She saw that his face had the same look of pain and humiliation that it had worn when he'd described the loss of his chair. He obviously hated to discuss the details of his physical limitations and was reluctant to admit the extent to which his life was circumscribed by them.

'I told you that I sometimes stay with people when I go deep into the country – that I sometimes put myself up at an inn. But I didn't make it plain that whenever I've done this, I've always been accompanied by an attendant. A male nurse from the hospital always comes with me whenever I spend the night in a house without equipment. He's a fine strapping young man with the strength of an ox, and a very jovial companion to add to his merits. He's someone who likes to crack open a bottle of wine and talk the night away. He's so well used to dealing with the needs of the disabled that I feel no shame when I have to call on him.'

'But if you'd like to make use of my house, please bring this young man. I'd be very pleased to have him as my guest.'

Mrs Blunt rather liked the idea of this robust and entertaining young man and she felt she would enjoy spending her evenings drinking wine with him and Corrigan. However, she was told that he was no longer available as an attendant. It appeared that just this week, he'd been transferred to some hospital in the United States.

'Is there no one else you could bring with you?' she asked.

'No one.' Corrigan suddenly looked tired and helpless and she was aware how isolated and lonely he must often feel.

'Is it very difficult to install the equipment you need?'

'Well, there's no particular difficulty. But you'd have to have the advice of an expert.'

'I'd be delighted to have such advice.'

'But I can't ask you to do this for me,' Corrigan said. 'I can't ask you to turn your lovely house into a home for the handicapped.'

'But you don't understand,' Mrs Blunt said. 'I don't care very much about my house. I hardly live in it any more. Well, of course I live in it.' She stuttered because she thought she must sound stupid. 'I'm not explaining myself very well,' she continued. 'I'm trying to say that I'd really like to feel my house was of use to someone else.'

She could see that he was moved by her suggestion, but he seemed uncertain whether to accept.

'I'll tell you why I might take you up on this,' he said. 'I would like to have the opportunity to get to know you better. Together, I feel we could share many glorious "Moments of Being". You are just as confined to a chair as I am. You are tied to the chair of your grief. But I would like to get you in motion once again so that you can feel the wind rushing against your cheeks . . .'

Mrs Blunt could feel the champagne fizzing in her brain. Corrigan's voice was mellifluous. She was mesmerised by the intensity of the stare of his blue-green eyes. She somehow knew that he was going to accept her offer, that all this talk was just a preamble.

Eventually he did accept. He told her that he'd arrange for an expert from the hospital to come down and advise her on the equipment he would need if he was to stay with her.

She cooked him lunch and he praised it extravagantly. He

told her that he wanted to write and that was one of the reasons he'd like to spend some time in the country.

'Before I depart this life,' he said, 'I'd like to feel I've said my say.'

He then told her that he found it difficult to write in London. 'I was brought up by the lake and the brook,' he explained, 'and my wealth was always the gold of the furze-bush. When I'm divorced from the tranquillity of nature I feel denuded. My talents are fed through the eye. I need to see the magical green of the sycamore and the maple. My eye needs to rest on the sumptuous copper of the beech.'

'There are lovely trees round here,' Mrs Blunt said to him.

'So I've remarked. I bow to the beauty of the English trees. They are the pride of this country and they almost excuse the abuses of her Empire.'

'The Empire wasn't entirely bad,' Mrs Blunt said. 'The British built a lot of roads in India. I know that because I spent so many years there with my late husband. They built a lot of schools and hospitals. They made the country much more hygienic.'

As they were finishing lunch, Corrigan suddenly said something that frightened Mrs Blunt.

He had gone back to his theme that the human eye had to be able to alight on something beautiful. He once again started praising the taste with which she had furnished her house. 'You are a primitive,' he said, 'but you have a natural instinct for selecting the beautiful.'

She was not all that pleased to be called a primitive. The word had pejorative associations from her years in India.

Corrigan then went on to say that it surprised him that someone with such an innate ability to create a uniquely harmonious environment would allow all this valuable harmony to be desecrated by a figure as jarring as Mrs Murphy.

'She may have a good hand for slapping on the rashers and the sausages,' Corrigan said, 'but I don't find her appearance very aesthetically appealing, and I don't think she does much honour to your house.'

'Corrigan detests Mrs Murphy,' Mrs Blunt thought. There

was a menacing glint of malevolence in his eyes as he started to denounce her, his lips curled, and the angry scorn with which he spoke of her seemed disproportionate and she was repelled by it.

'He is going to try to make me get rid of Mrs Murphy,' she thought. Suddenly she regretted having asked him to be her guest. She had a premonition that Corrigan, with all his passion and his energy, was going to try to come wheeling into her life and smash down every little edifice of safety that she had constructed for herself.

'No one has ever pretended that Mrs Murphy is a great beauty,' she said, 'but she has many qualities and she is very hard-working.'

It was the first time that Mrs Blunt had spoken quite sharply to Corrigan. He obviously didn't like her rebuke. His eyes looked anxious and angry.

'I shouldn't have spoken such rough words about your good lady,' he said. She noticed that he was doing his best to placate her; his tone had changed. It was now honeyed and beguiling.

'No, I really don't think you should be nasty about her,' she said. 'Mrs Murphy has been very kind the way she has helped you up the steps. She's not a young woman. There are not many women of her age who would be willing to put themselves out for you like she does.'

'I don't know how willing she is,' Corrigan said. 'My last entrance into your house was certainly not the smooth and balmy passage that I received when she gave me my first exhilarating ride. My experience today was one of extreme peril. I can only give thanks to God that I survived it. I felt she was putting me in a cement mixer. Even when I went out of control on that hill, I don't believe I was nearly so endangered. I really had the feeling that great rhinoceros of a woman was trying to break my neck!'

'Well, I know she's a little clumsy,' Mrs Blunt agreed. She wondered if she had been too severe with Corrigan. It was quite possible that he'd had a very bad time when he'd been lugged into the house by Mrs Murphy. As her attitude towards him was extremely hostile, there had probably been a certain deliberate callousness in the way she'd handled him.

In order to escape from the whole insoluble issue of the mutual dislike of Corrigan and Mrs Murphy, she suddenly produced a hamper of delicacies that she had packed up for him to take to Rupert Sinclair. The hamper contained a couple of bottles of her good claret, one bottle of champagne, a jar of taramasalata, some fresh smoked salmon, and smoked turkey, and some crisp French bread and an avocado pear with a dressing in a cardboard carton.

Corrigan was thrilled and astonished when she showed him her gift for Sinclair. 'I've rarely seen such a delectable selection of foodstuffs,' he said. 'It elicits the evil gluttony in my nature. Sinclair will be fortunate if he receives it intact. I'll have to muster all the force of the will of the tempted saint, in order not to pillage your hamper as I carry it to him on the train!'

'I hope it won't be too heavy for you,' Mrs Blunt said.

'I can perch it on my knee, and when I get to the station someone will give me a hand with it.'

When he went off, Mrs Blunt felt no regret at his departure. She was planning to have another conference with William Peebles, for she kept getting more and more ideas for the expansion of her garden, and the challenge of the project was extremely stimulating to her. She also planned to write to the main auctioneers in Salisbury and ask them to send her a catalogue of any sales of furniture and books that were coming up in the near future. She stood on her stone steps and she waved goodbye to Corrigan as he went off down the drive with her hamper. She had no feeling their parting would be a long one. She was confident that he would very soon come back.

II

Soon after Mrs Blunt acquired the idea of refurnishing and transforming the recreation room at Corrigan's old hospital, Nadine received a postcard from her which she read with bemusement and a certain dismay. Her mother told her that she was taking up driving lessons, that at the beginning her instructor had seemed to be deeply alarmed when he had to be in a car with her, but she thought that he was now pleased with her progress.

Nadine could well understand why her mother's driving instructor had felt such trepidation when he had to entrust his life to Mrs Blunt's shaky skills on the road. She found it difficult to visualise an experience more hazardous and frightening than being taken out on a main road in any vehicle driven by her mother.

Nadine felt that Mrs Blunt's general vagueness and hesitancy would constitute a serious threat to herself and others. She couldn't believe that she would ever master the road signs.

'I have so much more confidence since I've met Corrigan,' her mother wrote. 'Cross your fingers and think of me in two weeks' time. That's when I'll be taking my test.'

'Who is this crippled person, Corrigan, and why does he have such an influence over her?' Nadine thought. 'I can't understand why he is making her drive. Some people are constitutionally unfit to be in charge of a car. My mother is obviously one of these characters. So why is this Corrigan persuading her to get behind the wheel? Does he want her to have a fatal accident? The whole thing seems most irresponsible.'

*

Nadine was mistaken when she assumed that Corrigan was encouraging her mother to take up driving lessons. He had no idea that she was taking them and the possibility that she might learn to drive had never occurred to him. As Mrs Blunt sped along the lanes with her instructor and practised her jerky stops and starts and her U-turns, she got pleasure from thinking how much her new accomplishment would surprise him. She was relieved that her sight was still so good. As she grew older she had retained excellent vision and she only needed spectacles for reading. She wished she could tell the Colonel what she was doing. He would be as amazed as Corrigan by the way she was learning to master this new skill. She wished the Colonel was in the car and that she was driving him. She could imagine how astonished his face would look. He would be so very proud of her.

12

Sabrina had promised Nadine that she would go down to Wiltshire in order to see how Mrs Blunt was faring, but she was unable to do this as soon as she had intended because Coco, her lover, made an attempt at suicide. He was taken into hospital, and she felt she had to devote her time and energies to visiting him.

Sabrina explained this to Nadine when they met for one of their usual Monday lunches in the Italian restaurant. Nadine's face immediately took on the look of childish dismay that it always acquired whenever she was told of behaviour and situations that were jagged and savage.

'I thought you'd got rid of Coco, Sabrina. I thought you'd got him out of your flat.'

'I did get Coco out of my flat. In fact, for days I didn't hear a squeak from Coco. Then I heard he'd landed up in the hospital.'

'But you don't feel it was your fault? I hope you don't feel that you've got to keep on taking care of this creature because you see yourself as responsible for the state he has got himself into.'

'Oh no, I don't feel that at all,' Sabrina said. 'Even Coco's hardly responsible for his own awful state at this very moment. I suppose somebody has to be blamed. But I certainly don't feel it's me.'

'But surely you don't intend to go on seeing him. When Coco gets out of the hospital, surely you're not going to let him move back into your flat?'

Sabrina's beautiful face had the faraway expression that was so effective when she was photographed. 'Oh, I'll have to let Coco come back for a bit. Can't you see Nadine, he'll have nowhere else to go to. The poor little creature doesn't have a soul in the world who cares if he lives or dies.'

Sabrina couldn't explain to Nadine that Coco's dismal predicament affected her more than Coco did. When she'd first visited him in hospital, she'd found him slumped like some old man in a chair. He appeared to be enclosed in the black shell of his own depression. At the beginning he'd hardly seemed to know that she was there. Later he'd become weepy and made various childish complaints accusing his doctors of brutality. Sabrina had been able to understand his sense of grievance for when they'd 'dried out' Coco, they appeared to have dried out all the small energies he'd once possessed. His whole sexuality seemed to have been dried out along with the drugs to which he'd been addicted. He had lost the nihilistic humour which had been the quality she'd once liked in him. When she visited him in the hospital, she felt that he had all the limpness of the despondent-looking ducks that she'd seen hanging hooked upside-down in the windows of cheap Chinese restaurants.

'I think it boosts Coco's morale when I visit him,' Sabrina said. 'There are not many top fashion models who go to see anyone who is locked up in that ghastly hospital. When I make my appearance I think it gives him a tiny bit of status with his fellow-patients and his doctors.'

Nadine looked with bemusement at her lovely friend and wondered why she saw her good looks as so fraudulent that she felt she ought to scatter them like wedding confetti on the hopeless Coco.

'I'm going down to see your mother next week,' Sabrina told her. 'Coco's okay. Well, he's not a bit okay. But I think he can survive a couple of days without a visit from me. This weekend I'll go down and find out what's happening to your mother. I'm quite inventive and I'll tell you what I think should best be done for her. I'll make a full report . . .'

'But this is awful – you mustn't do this for me,' Nadine

protested. 'I'm the one who should be going down to see her. You've got enough with Coco. You shouldn't have to think about my mother.'

'But it's no skin off my back,' Sabrina said. 'I'm all too delighted to go and see your mother. She's always been very kind to me. My visit will have no emotional overtones. You see – unlike you, Nadine, I really rather like her.'

'Sabrina is a saint,' Nadine thought. She found it strange when her friend presented none of the conventional images she connected with saints. She could only gaze at Sabrina with wonderment.

*

When Sabrina came back from visiting Mrs Blunt, she once again lunched with Nadine. She had the exuberance of those who feel they are the bearers of good tidings. She reported that Mrs Blunt seemed extremely well.

'The most extraordinary things are going on in your mother's house,' Sabrina said.

'How do you mean?' Nadine's voice had the nervously rapid, almost irritable tone that came into it whenever she discussed her mother.

'I don't know if you've taken it in,' Sabrina said. 'But Corrigan is now living with her.'

Nadine's face went so white she looked suddenly very ill.

'What on earth do you mean?' she repeated. Her voice had become shrill.

'But surely you know about Corrigan,' Sabrina said. 'She said that she had written to tell you how much he had changed her life. But you hadn't answered.'

'It's true she did mention him. I know that the man is a cripple. Beyond that I know nothing about him at all.'

Sabrina then explained that when she had arrived at Mrs Blunt's house she had been amazed to find it full of workmen.

'But what were all these workmen doing?'

'They were knocking down the wall of her downstairs lavatory.'

'Knocking down the wall of the downstairs lavatory?'

Nadine was so horrified she could only parrot the unwelcome piece of information.

Sabrina explained that Mrs Blunt was knocking down the wall in order to install a bathroom which would extend into her hallway.

'But surely that will completely wreck her hallway?' Nadine asked. 'What on earth is she doing that for?'

Sabrina agreed that the hallway was going to be badly disfigured by the new bathroom, that it was a pity because it used to have such pretty original panelling and mouldings, but she felt that as Mrs Blunt seemed so pleased with her plan for the new bathroom, and the wall had already been demolished, there was little point in moaning about it.

'But the whole value of the house will be affected if my mother builds some hideous bathroom that juts out into the entrance hall. I've never heard of such an awful idea. You can't start knocking down walls in a lovely period house like that. It's a criminal thing to do.'

'Look, please, Nadine, I didn't knock down your mother's wall. So don't start attacking me. I'm really not to blame for the whole thing.'

Nadine apologised. She had not realised that she'd been speaking to Sabrina with such accusatory anger. Having apologised, she insisted that she still couldn't understand why her mother wanted to build a ground-floor bathroom. She had a perfectly good one upstairs next to her bedroom.

'How did my mother really seem to you?' she asked. Sabrina had told her that she seemed well. But she now wondered if she'd only said this out of kindness. She was suddenly frightened that loneliness, grief and neglect had affected Mrs Blunt's mind.

'Did my mother seem peculiar in any way?' she persisted.

Sabrina did her best to reassure her. Mrs Blunt had seemed extremely balanced and energetic and excited by various projects. Sabrina had gone to see her expecting to find a miserable little paralysed shadow of a woman. Mrs Blunt had not seemed like that at all. She had cooked a delicious lunch for Corrigan and herself, even though most of her house was in a shambles.

The workmen had made the entrance look rather like a bomb-site. It was in the most horrible confusion of dust and planks and bricks and tangled electric wires, and various articles of plumbing. Mrs Blunt had not seemed at all dismayed by the current condition of her house. She had been talkative and animated and she had obviously taken great care with her appearance. She'd had her hair restyled and it suited her very well. She'd been wearing quite a lot of make-up and she'd been looking as charming and pretty as Sabrina remembered she'd once used to look in the old days when the Colonel was alive.

'But why is she suddenly knocking down her own walls? I think that sounds terrifying. I've never heard of anything quite so sinister and destructive.'

Sabrina was shocked that Nadine didn't seem pleased to be told that her mother's state of mind had miraculously improved. Nadine only appeared to be obsessed by the news that she was making alterations in her house.

She tried to explain to her friend that she didn't see there was anything demented or sinister in Mrs Blunt's decision to build a bathroom on her ground floor. There was a logic to the whole plan.

'Don't you understand, Nadine, she needs a downstairs bathroom because she is turning her drawing-room into a bedroom for Corrigan.'

'A bedroom for Corrigan!' Nadine's reaction was one of total horror.

Sabrina still found it difficult to grasp that Nadine was emotionally incapable of accepting the importance that Corrigan had assumed in her mother's life – that the idea that he was going to sleep in her drawing-room rocked her to the very essence of her being.

Nadine had so many memories of her parents talking and laughing in that drawing-room. Sitting with Sabrina in the Italian restaurant, she suddenly remembered it as it had once been before her mother had let the garden revert to a waste-land. In the summer, her parents liked to leave the glass windows at the end of the drawing-room open. The Italian restaurant smelt of cheap cooking oils and garlic, but for a moment Nadine could only smell the scent of roses and wistaria and all the other flowers that had once wafted through that door.

The idea that any drawing-room should be turned into a bedroom was extremely offensive to her sense of formal propriety. The news that this particular one, where she still retained an image of her tall and handsome father standing by the marble fireplace, was now going to become the sleeping place of a strange cripple was such threatening information that it made Nadine feel like weeping.

'I really don't understand what my mother thinks she's doing,' she said. 'What on earth is she up to – letting this man move in with her? You know what a frail little creature she is. How does she think she is going to take care of him? A cripple must have all sorts of requirements. Presumably he has to be nursed round the clock. I imagine that he has to be waited on hand and foot. My mother will never be able to do that. Her health isn't nearly good enough. It all sounds like total insanity. I can hardly bear to hear about it.'

Sabrina once again tried to reassure her by explaining that Mrs Blunt was being very sensible in her approach to this whole problem. She'd consulted an expert on the technical needs of the disabled. She had arranged for some man to come down from London. She had taken his advice on what medical equipment should be installed in her house so that Corrigan would be able to manage to take care of himself without requiring too much assistance.

Sabrina had gathered that the new bathroom was going to be similar to any in a hospital for the disabled. It would have all sorts of handrails and pulleys, and the bath and the lavatory were being constructed to the specifications of the expert advice Mrs Blunt had received.

'But surely she's not going to put a lot of hideous medical equipment in that lovely drawing-room,' Nadine said.

'Well, I'm afraid she is,' Sabrina said. 'Corrigan will need various things installed. At least that's what I gathered.'

'Does that mean the workmen will have to break into all that beautiful panelling?'

'I would imagine they will,' Sabrina said. 'It just can't be helped. I know it's a shame to ruin the panelling, but I can't see how your mother can do anything else. You see, Corrigan can't get up the stairs so it's quite a clever idea to turn the whole ground floor of the house into a self-contained suite where he can function with dignity. This way he will be very little burden on either your mother or Mrs Murphy.'

Sabrina felt that her friend was laying far too much emphasis on the destruction of the beautiful period panelling in her mother's house. Nadine had painted such a grim picture of Mrs Blunt's desolate condition that she had dreaded going to see her. She had been so relieved to find her looking well and happy that she'd felt her damaged panelling was very unimportant.

'How is Corrigan going to get in and out of the house?' Nadine asked. 'Those stone steps in front of the house are quite steep. I don't see that it would be easy to get a wheelchair up them. I hope to God the man doesn't expect my poor mother to lift him in and out. I suppose that awful hefty Mrs Murphy might manage to do it. But then she's not there all the time.'

'Oh, your mother has dealt with that problem. That was one of the things she seemed so proud of. She has constructed the most enormous ramp for Corrigan. She's designed it herself. She didn't even need the advice of any medical expert. She was rather touching about it. She told me that when she was a girl she always felt that she might have a little bit of talent as a designer – but somehow she never pursued it . . .'

Nadine found it unbelievable that her mother had known how to design a ramp. Her voice became shaky with disapproval and anxiety as she asked Sabrina what it looked like.

Sabrina admitted that the ramp looked rather strange the first time you saw it. But then you soon got used to it. Originally, she'd been rather astonished by the size of it. It was such a vast edifice that it completely covered the front steps. It looked rather like the raised gangway of a ship and it had banisters so that Corrigan could pull himself up it. The whole construction was made of steel and Mrs Blunt had designed a large flat enclosed area at the very top of the steps so that he could rest in his chair after he had run up the ramp. He could then pause there while he looked for the key to the front door.

Mrs Blunt had explained to Sabrina that she had deliberately made this flat enclosed area so large because she thought that when summer came it would be pleasant if she could sit out there and have a drink with Corrigan. It would provide a good vantage point from which they could both view all the improvements which by then would have taken place in her extended garden.

Although Sabrina described Mrs Blunt's ramp with such admiration and enthusiasm, her description seemed to disgust Nadine rather than delight her.

'A huge steel construction in front of the house – surely it must look perfectly ghastly,' she said. 'The facade of that house was always one of its loveliest features. Those wonderful old grey stone steps covered with lichen, I used to love them too. I really hate to hear that you can't see them any more. It seems barbaric.'

Sabrina admitted that she couldn't pretend that the ramp added very much to the aesthetic aspects of Mrs Blunt's facade. But she insisted that the ramp had been designed with such ingenuity that once you accustomed yourself to the look of it, you could pretend that all the gleaming steel set against the slate-coloured stone of the house made an interesting contrast. The whole effect could be seen as the most daring combination of the ancient and the new.

'I can't understand how my mother has turned into such a vandal,' Nadine said. 'She used to have so much respect for beautiful old things. I always thought she had so much natural taste.'

Sabrina asked her friend to give some serious thought to the life that her mother had been leading in recent years. 'How much time did she spend sitting out in her gravel driveway and gazing at the beauty of her stone facade? Can't you see, Nadine, the ugliness of the ramp doesn't really affect her . . .'

She tried to explain that Mrs Blunt liked the idea of sitting on top of it and surveying all her new fields because that was where all her new enthusiasms and her hopes for the future lay.

Nadine admitted that she couldn't feel very excited by her mother's new plans for her garden. Mrs Blunt had been content to allow it to go to pieces, even though the Colonel had once been so proud of it. It had never seemed to occur to her that Nadine had desperately wanted her to preserve it so that it could exist as a beautiful memorial to her father. She resented the way that her mother liked tending her late husband's grave when it would have been much more valuable if she had continued to tend the garden into which he'd put so much work after his retirement. Recently her mother had informed her that she planned to enlarge it in order to grow vegetables for the disabled. Nadine thought this whole enterprise sounded half-baked. If Mrs Blunt wanted to buy vegetables for the disabled, why didn't she simply open an account with some vegetable shop in London and arrange to have vegetables delivered to them? That would probably turn out much cheaper and less time-consuming.

Sabrina told her that she understood that Mrs Blunt was already supplying St Crispins with fruit and vegetables from some shop in London and she then explained all about Corrigan's old hospital, and informed her of some of the plans that Corrigan and her mother had got for improving the lives of the inmates.

'I think your mother is trying to create much more than a garden,' Sabrina said. 'She now seems to be going into farming and in quite a large-scale and serious way. You simply couldn't believe all the activity that's going on in the fields that surround her house. When I visited her, they were swarming with men who were all ploughing and cutting down trees and hedges. They were crashing around in a sea of mud with scythes, and tractors and bulldozers – and God knows what else. Your mother seems to have even more men working in her fields than she has in her house. The whole thing made me feel totally lazy and inadequate. I don't often find myself in such a hive of constructive activity.'

'It must be costing her a fortune to employ all these men,' Nadine said. 'The whole thing sounds as if it has got completely out of control. I can't believe she knows what she's doing. My mother was always quite good at growing roses – but she knows nothing about large-scale farming. And even if she makes a profit – and I feel that to be a very unlikely prospect – she's still going to ruin herself, since she plans to give away the proceeds to charity . . .'

Her voice trailed once again until it became a whisper. Once again she looked very close to tears.

Sabrina found it disturbing that although Nadine seemed to take a horrified interest in hearing about all the work that her mother was doing to her house and her farm, she had hardly asked a single question about Corrigan.

She'd assumed Nadine would be intensely curious to know what he was like. After all, it was Corrigan who had inspired and galvanised Mrs Blunt so that Sabrina had been astonished to find her a transformed character. She decided that she would force Nadine to listen to her personal impressions of this man for her friend might then take a less negative view of all the projects that now seemed to be engaging her mother.

'I think it's very good for your mother that Corrigan is going to live with her,' Sabrina said.

Nadine's narrow little face puckered, and she gave a shiver. 'When you keep saying that Corrigan is going to live with my mother, could you explain more precisely what you mean by that? Surely you are not saying that he's having some kind of an affair with her. Are you telling me that my mother is having a sexual relationship with a man in a wheelchair? That would be one of the most creepy things I've ever heard.'

Sabrina realised that the possibility that her mother was having an affair with Corrigan was devastating to Nadine and once again she did her best to reassure her. She told her that she felt certain that their relationship was completely platonic although Corrigan treated Mrs Blunt with a flirtatious gallantry and she thought that he was rather obsessed by her.

'I can't help hating the idea of Corrigan,' Nadine said. 'I can't help hating the idea of a flirtatious cripple.'

Sabrina said that his flirtatiousness was not at all offensive. 'I think Corrigan probably used to have quite a keen eye for the ladies before the poor man had his accident,' she said. 'I suppose that once you start to operate in a certain way, you simply go on doing it.'

'Did Corrigan flirt with you?' Nadine asked.

'Well, yes, he did a bit. He flirted with me in a very light-hearted way. He cast his eye over me, and he made me realise that I met with his approval. But I didn't interest Corrigan at all. You know how you can feel these things. He's only really interested in your mother.'

'But why should Corrigan be so very interested in my mother?' Nadine asked.

'It's as if Corrigan feels she belongs to him,' Sabrina answered. 'It's as if he thinks like Pygmalion, he has somehow created her. It's rather hard to explain it.'

'But that's such rubbish,' Nadine said. 'My mother was created quite a long time ago. She's certainly been around as long as I can remember!'

Sabrina ate some spaghetti and Nadine admired the deft elegance with which she twirled spaghetti round her fork with an ivory textured wrist that could make eating seem erotic rather than mundane and animal.

'Your mother is being very kind to Corrigan,' Sabrina said. 'Corrigan has probably never met with much kindness. He's been living in institutions for years. Institutions are not very kind to the individual. They can't afford to be. I've seen that when I go to visit Coco. I know Coco is a different case, but Coco and Corrigan are both crippled in a different way. I think that kindness seems rather magical to them.'

'Well, it's nice to hear that my mother is being so kind to Corrigan – but is he being kind to her, that's the only thing that matters.'

'Yes, he's being very kind to your mother. At least he was very kind to her while I was there. He's very fond of poetry and he's made her love it too. He reads poetry aloud to her in the evenings and she told me that she adored being read to.'

'But how much time is Corrigan spending with my mother? Surely he hasn't moved in yet?'

Sabrina said that he hadn't quite moved in yet. He was still living in his flat in London. But he came down to see Mrs Blunt very often and he then took the train back to the city after dinner. He couldn't move in until the house had been properly equipped for him.

'He's quite possessive about your mother,' Sabrina said. 'It's really rather funny. He doesn't seem to like her speaking to any other man. She went out into the garden to talk to some young man called Peebles – apparently he's helping her grow all her vegetables. I was left in the drawing-room with Corrigan. He started to get very restless and peculiar. He has rather strange eyes and they looked so angry that I found them almost frightening . . . Corrigan kept saying that he couldn't see why your mother was taking so long speaking to Peebles – that he didn't believe all these endless discussions about the garden were necessary.'

'But that's outrageous,' Nadine said. 'How dare he become jealous if she speaks to her market-gardener.'

'I'm not defending Corrigan,' Sabrina said. 'I'm just telling you that he was most certainly jealous. He kept asking me what I thought she could be talking about with William Peebles. I told him that I assumed they were talking about all the crops they were planning to grow – but Corrigan wouldn't really accept it. He kept frowning and tapping on his wheelchair with his hand. He was obviously working himself into quite a neurotic state. I had the feeling he might have a very violent temper.'

'The more I hear about Corrigan, the more awful you make him sound,' Nadine said.

'No, he's not really awful. He's really rather charming. He's a very good-looking man. He could have been a film star if he hadn't had his ghastly accident. Even now he could easily be a male model. I kept wondering if I should suggest that to him. He could make a lot of money and he needs money – not for himself but for his charity. Corrigan could easily do ads for silk ties and hats and shaving lotions and cigars. He'd be wonderful for what they call "quality" shots. But don't worry, Nadine, I wasn't so tasteless as to suggest it to him.'

Nadine was indeed relieved to hear this. She found it

extremely tasteless that Sabrina should think of trying to make a cripple take up high-fashion modelling.

'Corrigan has rather an odd and flowery way of speaking,' Sabrina said. 'But then he's Irish – so I suppose that's natural.'

'How does Mrs Murphy get on with him?' Nadine asked her.

'I had the impression that they detest each other,' Sabrina said. 'Corrigan is always asking Mrs Murphy to do things for him. He's quite tyrannical in the way he treats her. He keeps making her fetch him this and that. I could see that she hates lifting a finger for him – that she would go on strike and tell him to fuck off, if she didn't think it would upset your mother.'

'But why has my mother allowed Corrigan to have so much power over her? It's all happened so quickly. I find the whole thing too extraordinary.'

'Corrigan's really done quite a lot for her. He's got quite a talent for making one realise how little one is doing with one's life. I've never thought that I led a very worthwhile existence. But Corrigan made me feel like such an idle insect that I decided I had to do something – if only to appease my own conscience. I think I'm going to put on some kind of fashion show and give the proceeds to his hospital.'

Nadine was almost more shaken to hear that Sabrina was going to throw herself into charitable causes than she was disturbed by all the altruistic ventures of her mother. Yet she knew that Sabrina would go ahead with the fashion show and arrange it very efficiently. She would get the best London designers to show their dresses for free and convince them they could only benefit from the publicity. Sabrina would take over the dining-room of one of the big hotels and a lot of fat rich ladies would buy wildly expensive tickets in order to have a table from which they could watch a team of tall, slim beauties pirouette on a platform as they displayed the beauties of their costumes to the sound of romantic music and the flashing of cameras. Nadine knew that Sabrina would know how to whip up a general excitement about her fashion show, that she'd made the whole occasion seem very recherché, and the tickets would sell out because they would be paper passports to an evening which would celebrate the marriage of clothes with charity.

Nadine found it difficult to explain to herself why this worthy enterprise chilled her. The results would probably be admirable and benefit those who were in need. She wondered if her negative approach to Sabrina's project came out of a hidden feeling of envy. If her friend managed to raise a lot of money for the disabled by using all her professional know-how in order to put on this fashion show, Nadine knew that it should not be sneered at. It would be a much more valuable and constructive act than making a salmon mousse for Justin and most of the other activities that *she* engaged herself with.

Nadine had always had a rather ill-defined conviction that everyone's life should have a purpose. Now she was ashamed that it could jar her to hear that her mother and her frivolous friend had suddenly found a much higher moral motivation than she had.

'I think I'm going back to school,' Sabrina said.

'Back to school!' Nadine could hardly believe her friend was being serious. She was feeling very oppressed by school at the moment. Having been so miserable at her own, she felt overwhelmed by the way the twins were dragging her back to it. Sometimes she felt she had never really been allowed to leave school – because every evening she still found herself struggling through dreary brown satchels of unintelligible home-work, and infected by the anxiety of her sons, she suffered from it more than they did. There also seemed to be so many school meetings which she was meant to attend. She'd sit there feeling frozen in a draughty hall with hard, wood benches. She would glumly listen to laborious discussions as to whether the boys should put their gym-shoes in their lockers before assembly or afterwards. Debates on what was stimulating reading-matter for the under-twelves, then more discussions about which mothers should control which cake stalls in the school Christmas fair.

Nadine could only feel Sabrina was very misguided when she wanted to go back to school. She thought she must have forgotten what it was like to listen to recorder concerts and

nativity plays, to watch football matches on freezing after-
noons, to sit trembling in the headmaster's office while he
scolded you for your son's poor performance in mathematics,
or his reprehensible behaviour in class.

'I think I'm going to say farewell to modelling before it says
farewell to me,' Sabrina said. 'I'm going to put on a fantastic
fashion show for Corrigan and that can be my swan-song. I've
decided that I made a mistake when I thought I was too
attractive to need to take exams.'

She told Nadine that she was going to take her A-levels, and
then she was going to apply to various colleges. Eventually she
hoped to study psychology.

'But why psychology?' Nadine asked. 'I never knew you
were interested in that sort of thing.'

'I think I'm quite good with people as long as I never sleep
with them,' Sabrina said.

Nadine wanted to know why her friend had suddenly
decided to make such drastic changes in her life.

'I think it was meeting Corrigan,' Sabrina said. 'You see,
apparently he educated himself while he was in the hospital.
Corrigan's achievements can make you feel guilty on quite a
few levels.'

She said she'd been interested to see the way that poor Mrs
Blunt was so obviously embarrassed by her own illiteracy
when she was with Corrigan. 'She longs to be able to discuss
the use of symbolism and myth in the modern novel – but she
finds it so difficult.'

Apparently Corrigan was supplying Mrs Blunt with a lot of
books and she was doing her best to plough through Joyce and
Kafka, and Melville.

'But she really seems to love poetry,' Sabrina said. 'She has a
real feeling for it. It's quite impressive how much she has learnt
by heart. She likes to play a little game with Corrigan. He'll
quote a couple of lines from some poem and then your mother
will chime in and she'll recite the next two lines. I never
expected her to be so good at it. I didn't recognise half the
quotations that he was testing her with. I was quite jealous of
how much she knew.'

'I don't think I'd like to hear my mother spouting a lot of poetry. I think I'd find it rather affected. I wouldn't believe she really liked it. I'd think she was just pretending in order to please Corrigan,' Nadine said.

'You are so hard on her, Nadine. I didn't find it affected. Corrigan and your mother were enjoying their little literary game so much, it was really touching to watch them.'

'If she doesn't really like poetry, it all seems rather silly to me,' Nadine said stubbornly.

'But of course she likes it. Otherwise she wouldn't have been able to learn so much.'

Sabrina blew a smoke ring and she watched it thoughtfully as it went spiralling into the air. 'Your mother may well have pretended to like it at the beginning,' she said, 'but I think it's possible that if you pretend to like things for long enough, you end up genuinely liking them.'

Nadine shrugged. She obviously didn't agree.

'You really ought to go down and see your mother,' Sabrina said. 'She won't depress you like she used to. She's very busy and excited by all the things she's doing. Did you know that she has passed her driving test? I think that is really quite a feat.'

Nadine started waving her hand at the waiter. She suddenly wanted the lunch to be over. She longed to get out of the hot and noisy Italian restaurant. She had no wish to receive any more disturbing information about her mother's recent accomplishments.

'She's bought herself this huge van,' Sabrina said. 'It's extraordinary to see such an enormous vehicle sitting outside her house.'

'Huge van?' Nadine repeated numbly. The waiters were refusing to bring her the bill and she was forced to listen to yet another item of information that filled her with the deepest dismay.

'Why has my mother bought herself a huge van?' she asked. 'That is one of the maddest things I've ever heard! A tiny little creature like her – how can she possibly drive a heavy thing like that?'

Sabrina shrugged. She told Nadine that Mrs Blunt managed it very well. She assumed it had power steering. 'Anyway, she is whizzing round the countryside and she certainly hasn't had an accident yet.'

'But what's the point of my mother buying herself a huge van?' Nadine asked. 'It all sounds as if she's suffering from senile dementia.'

Sabrina explained that Mrs Blunt planned to go to auctions of antique furniture whenever they were held in the neighbourhood. She was going to buy various pictures and pieces of old furniture and donate them to St Crispins. She was going to use the van in order to transport the antiques.

'But why on earth should disabled people need antiques?' Nadine waved her hand so frantically that she finally attracted the attention of a waiter. Sabrina's account of her mother's energetic exploits had exhausted her. She had an appointment with Roland's French master at his school. She had to discuss Roland's poor mastery of verbs. She felt so drained she only wanted to go to bed.

13

Mrs Blunt was sitting in her bedroom and writing a letter to Sinclair. She no longer went into her drawing-room now that Corrigan was using it as his bedroom. She suspected that he wanted to feel that he had complete privacy in that room. She assumed that he would hate to have her stare at the medical equipment that had been installed there. As far as was possible she tried to make him feel she had forgotten his infirmity.

Now when they ate meals together they used her small dining-room. She had moved out the table and she and Corrigan both ate on trays in front of a fire and she liked this new arrangement because it was informal and cosy.

She had moved her Queen-Anne writing table up to her bedroom as it was not suitable for Corrigan's use when he wrote his novel. He had a special typewriter holder which he could draw in close to his wheelchair.

> 'Dear Rupert,' she wrote. 'I am so glad that the last assignment of champagne reached you safely. Whenever Corrigan and I open a bottle down here in the country, we always drink a toast to you. I'm also glad that the food at St Crispins has improved now that the kitchen is receiving the fresh fruit and vegetables that I've laid on. Once my farm gets underway, I intend to see that it improves even more. I plan to grow much more exciting things than one can usually obtain in the shops.

'A wonderful thing has happened to me. A small farm came on the market recently. It's only about half a mile away from my house. I decided to buy it because I thought it would be nice to keep a few cows. Nothing is so wonderful as fresh butter and cream.

'I feel my whole life has been revolutionised since I passed my driving test though I did have quite a lot of trouble passing it. Oh, please, I beg you, oh, please, don't tell Corrigan. I failed it three times. I can't bear him to know that. He thinks that I just went sailing in and passed with flying colours. I very much want him to think that – but I'm afraid it wasn't true. At the beginning, when I first started my lessons, I couldn't understand the brakes. I got them muddled with the accelerator. I did something really awful. There was an old gentleman with a walking stick. The poor man seemed to be very lame and he was going across a pedestrian crossing. I saw the poor fellow very clearly – but I made this dreadful mistake. I tried to stop, but the car seemed to go faster and faster. I didn't know what to do. I thought that the worst had happened – I really thought we were going to mow him down. But I was so lucky that I had the instructor in the car with me. He had another set of brakes. It's so clever what they do nowadays. It was miraculous. He slammed his foot down on the double brakes and our car stopped just within an inch of the old gentleman. Oh, my God, what an escape we all had! The instructor was very angry with me. I could see he didn't like me having such a near miss . . . He really made me feel ashamed of myself. I didn't dare go back for more lessons with the same driving instruction firm. I changed and I went to learn with another firm. They seemed to teach me better. Or maybe I got better. These things are so hard to say. Now I feel my driving has improved so much that I feel I'm safe on the roads, and I never want Corrigan or Nadine to know that it was all quite difficult at the beginning. Corrigan has always told me that it was only by perseverance that any snails reached the ark. If one thinks about it seriously, I don't think anything can be more true. I'm more of a snail than I want Corrigan to know. So please don't tell him that I had difficulty with my tests.

'Now that I've got my licence, I can't believe that I ever had any problems. It is such a marvellous thing to have this new freedom. I can go into Salisbury whenever I feel like it. I can drive round my farm and supervise all the new developments.

'I have also just started going round the furniture auctions whenever they are held in the neighbourhood. I've always loved antiques and there is always the feeling that one might discover an old masterpiece amongst all the junk that comes out of country house attics. I enjoy all the excitement of the bidding and I like competing against the dealers who come from London although I must say they are rather greedy, unpleasant men and it's very hard not to hate them.

'I picked up the most lovely little Regency, inlaid rosewood table a few days ago. I think I was very lucky. I really got it quite cheap. Whenever I buy any furniture, I've decided to keep it in storage in my house just for the moment. I don't see there is much point in moving it up to St Crispins until the building has been painted. Corrigan is arranging for a very good firm to start decorating in the next few weeks.

'As you know, Corrigan is staying here at the moment. He is not in the house right now. He has gone off fund-raising. But he will be back for dinner and I very much enjoy having him here. He is such good company. I find him the perfect guest.

'The only sadness in my life at the moment is that I almost never hear from my daughter, Nadine. I so long for her to meet Corrigan. I'm sure they would get on very well.

'Nadine has a friend called Sabrina. She very sweetly came to visit me recently. She is a ravishing-looking girl and I've always been very fond of her. She liked Corrigan very much and she seemed quite impressed with all his projects. She even offered to do some door-to-door fund-raising in London. I think Corrigan was astonished that such a sophisticated and sought-after creature was prepared to go trudging round the houses. He's going to get her a box of St Crispins flags and I have the funny feeling she will do very well for him. If I opened my door and found such a lovely blonde vision standing on my doorstep, I think I'd open my purse very quickly!

'I've been doing quite a lot of fund-raising myself, of course. My van comes in very handy for that. It enables me to reach parts of the county that I could never have reached on foot. I've been amazed by the sums I have raised every time that I've knocked on the door of various country houses. Corrigan teases me and says that I'm a natural saleswoman. I wouldn't quite agree with that. But I am beginning to see that fund-raising really is an art.

'It is also pleasant to discover that most people are not at all heartless, or mean-minded. I've received a few snubs and slammed doors, of course, but I'm getting much tougher and Corrigan has taught me to take that as part of the game.

'I think I've really learnt quite a lot from Corrigan. Sometimes it makes me rather unhappy that I've learnt certain things so late. I wish that Tom, my late husband, could return to earth and see me driving that van. It would make him laugh – but I think he would be quite proud of me.

'I sometimes get upset that Nadine takes so little interest in my life. Corrigan always tells me that I have no right to expect much attention from her now that she is happily married. Married couples get so involved with each other that they hardly have any time for anyone else. I suppose that Corrigan is right when he says I ought to understand that this is natural. If I think back on it, I don't think I was very nice to my own mother. I was so very involved with my husband . . .'

Mrs Blunt paused before finishing her letter. She realised that once again she seemed to be writing only about herself. Why should this stranger want to know about her various doings – and her feelings? Yet it still seemed insensitive to enquire about the life of a man who probably had very little life. She decided that she ought to pay a visit to St Crispins. If she got to know Rupert Sinclair properly – if she got to know the other patients – she would then find it much easier to write to him, for she'd understand more about his world.

'After my husband died, I didn't really want to leave this house,' Mrs Blunt wrote. 'It may seem rather silly, but I felt that Tom might come back. If he was to come back, I knew that he'd make a bee-line for this house. I didn't really think he'd ever come back. Yet sometimes I did . . . It's very hard to explain it. But I hated to leave the house. I thought it would be awful if I was out when he arrived.

'Oh, I know this must seem very mad to you. It seems mad to me when I see it written down. It used to make Nadine angry when I refused to leave the house. Corrigan also thinks it's something I should get over, and I'm doing so more and more. In fact, now that I've got the van, I am thinking of driving up to London. I'd really love to pay you a visit. I'm dying to see all the new decorations, and if I was to see the interior of St Crispins I'd have a better idea of how to furnish it. Anyway, that is my new, most adventurous project and I look forward to it very much. When Corrigan comes back this evening, I intend to discuss it with him. I thought it would be nice if we were all to meet up together in the hospital and drink a wicked glass with "beady bubbles winking at the brim". I love that line.
Yours sincerely,
Devina Blunt.'

As she finished her letter she heard the grinding sound of Corrigan's chair crashing up her ramp. She hurried downstairs to welcome him. She found it miraculous that the ramp had turned out to be so functional, and it amused her that Corrigan took such a childish pleasure in speeding up it. It was as if he liked to pretend that he was in a jet taking off on a runway.

'How did it go?' she asked him. 'You look tired. I think you need some champagne.'

Sometimes she wished that Corrigan didn't feel obliged to continue with all this arduous fund-raising. He would go out all day and he often came back with dark rings round his eyes, looking very haggard. She'd have preferred him to stay in the drawing-room and work on his novel. Now that she had bought the van, she felt that she could raise more for the hospital than he could. She was able to cover ground so much more quickly, whereas poor Corrigan wasted a lot of time wheeling laboriously down the lanes.

She knew it would be very cruel to point this out to him. He took such a feverish pride in every penny that he managed to collect. He should not be allowed to see that his activities were becoming redundant. At the end of the day they both enjoyed showing each other the fruits of all their efforts. They held them out like a hunter holds out his rabbits – they boasted about them as a fisherman boasts about his catch.

Corrigan had apparently raised thirty pounds since the morning. Mrs Blunt showed delight. She took him into the dining-room and she opened some champagne.

She told him she'd had some good ideas while he'd been out. She'd been thinking that the patients at St Crispins might love to have a screen projector. They could then hire the most recent films. They would probably find it quite a welcome change from television.

Corrigan was thrilled by this idea. He found it an idea of genius. If they had a proper projector they could hire educational films as well as trivial Hollywood movies. That would be a godsend to the intelligent patients like Sinclair.

'I am thinking of driving up to London to see Sinclair,' Mrs Blunt said. 'I've written to tell him that I'll soon be coming up in my van!'

'Now that I'll never permit,' Corrigan banged his hand on the arm of his chair. 'I'll never allow myself to be the indirect cause of your destruction. You've achieved an estimable mastery of that cumbersome great monster of a vehicle. But I didn't pull you from a death from indolence, in order to let you end up as one more statistic of a carcass on the highway. You are still a learner, Devina. You may have discarded your L-plates, but you are none the less a learner. You do very well on the country roads, but for the most part they are sleepy. Remember that there is no speed limit on the main roads, Devina, and most of the drivers that make use of them display all the symptoms of psychotics. I refuse to allow you to play the lemming. All the things you are doing now are valuable and you have a duty to them. You have a duty to me as well. I like to think you do. But maybe you don't feel that . . .'

Mrs Blunt felt slightly hurt that he had so little trust in her driving. But she was glad that he'd said she was valuable to him and she was touched by his fiercely protective attitude. She had to admit that the idea of taking that heavy van into high-speed traffic was frightening to her.

'I don't have to take the van if I go to see Sinclair,' she said. 'I could always go to London by train. We could even travel together.'

Corrigan was silent. He stared into the fire and she saw his cheek was twitching slightly as it did when anything upset him.

'I'll be frank with you,' he said. 'You may not like to hear it. But Rupert Sinclair doesn't want to see you.'

Mrs Blunt looked dismayed.

'Put yourself in the man's position,' Corrigan said. 'He greatly appreciates receiving your letters – but he never wants you to visit him. You are *not* a member of his family. You may not seem like strangers when you write to each other – but you are still *total* strangers.'

Mrs Blunt thought about the letter she had written to

Sinclair that very day. She was glad she had never posted it, and was relieved she could still tear it up. Corrigan was right that Sinclair hardly seemed like a stranger to her any more.

'Sinclair is a man who has little desire to elicit the dubious emotion of pity,' Corrigan said. 'He knows that his appearance is unsightly and he has no wish to thrust it before the eyes of strangers. I don't think you've understood. Sinclair's accident has left him very badly mangled.'

'But I wouldn't mind . . .' Mrs Blunt protested.

'It's Rupert Sinclair who would mind.' Corrigan spoke quite harshly. 'I think that on this issue, your own feelings are immaterial.'

Mrs Blunt was crushed. But she realised she ought to have checked with Corrigan before she suggested visiting Sinclair. Corrigan understood all the delicate codes of the disabled.

She realised with horror that if she'd posted her letter to Sinclair, she would have put the unfortunate man in the embarrassing position of having to write and tell her directly that he had no desire to see her. Sinclair seemed such a courteous man and he would probably find this the most painful thing to have to do.

'There is a new fellow who has just been admitted to St Crispins,' Corrigan said. 'He has lost both his legs. He has a wife and three sons. He's never going to see them again. He won't allow anyone to contact them. He doesn't want them even to know what's happened to him. His family have no idea where he is. And they are never going to know – not if this fellow has his way.'

'But that's terrible for his family,' Mrs Blunt said. 'They must be worried stiff.'

Corrigan shrugged. 'It depends on your point of view. I certainly agree that it's going to be murder for his family. But then he's not exactly floating through life on a cushion of feather-down. Any feelings that he has, I believe that they have to be respected.'

'I'd love to send this man some champagne,' Mrs Blunt said. She wanted to make amends for her insensitivity.

'I would imagine he could do with the occasional bottle,'

Corrigan said, 'but you can't expect to keep the entire hospital supplied with magnums of Moët et Chandon. Although I know that with your good heart, you'd be all too glad to do this. If you could just keep on with the fund-raising, and I'll continue with it too. Between us, I believe we can raise enough money to make life for the inmates of St Crispins substantially more tolerable . . .'

'Oh, of course I will continue,' Mrs Blunt said with fervour. 'And I have the feeling that if we put our heads together we could think of many other ways of producing even larger sums to benefit people like Sinclair.'

'You really seem to dote on Sinclair.' Corrigan's eyes suddenly had a rather strange expression. She thought they had a certain resentment. She then decided she must have imagined this.

'How do you visualise Sinclair?' Corrigan asked her.

'I see him as much the same type of man as my late husband. I see him as very gentle, and English and considerate.'

She thought it wiser not to tell Corrigan that she persisted in seeing Rupert Sinclair as a very handsome man, that she somehow rejected the information that he was 'mangled'.

'Gentle, English and considerate, that's hardly a description that could be easily applied to myself,' Corrigan spoke with bitterness.

'Corrigan is jealous,' Mrs Blunt thought. 'How strange of him to be jealous of a man I'm never going to meet.'

'Those aren't the only qualities that I admire,' she said.

'What qualities do you admire?'

She gave Corrigan a list of admirable qualities that he could apply to himself. She smiled as she did this and she knew she must seem beneficent. She was beginning to treat him like a child, a child that she could flirt with. As the flirtation could come to nothing, she felt no inhibitions.

'How do you see me?' Corrigan asked her.

' "Shall I compare thee to a summer's day?" ' Mrs Blunt was quite pleased by her quotation.

'If you find the comparison apt, I see no harm in it.'

'I don't think it is very apt. Not when I come to think of it. I don't really see you as summery. There's something wintery about you. There's something stormy . . .'

'Any port in a storm,' Corrigan said. Mrs Blunt felt he was trying to tell her something important. She continued to smile because she had no idea what it was.

14

Several months passed before Nadine had her meeting with Corrigan. Her life continued to be uneventful, and superficially it was well ordered. Her days were spent in performing small domestic chores. She still executed them with frenetic efficiency as though driven on by some relentless inner task master whose high standards she would always fail to meet.

Justin continued to criticise her efforts in the same manner he'd always adopted.

'Oh, darling,' he'd say as he made every fresh demand. 'Oh, darling, we don't seem to have enough towels . . .'

'Have you looked in the linen closet?' Nadine would ask with her voice crackling with the strain of appearing unflaggingly patient.

'But darling, towels are not much use in the linen closet. Why don't you see that they get to the bathroom. That's really where towels belong . . .'

Justin's perfectionist view of how his household should be run was even loftier than his wife's. It was like a golden far-off ideal. She sometimes felt bewildered as to where he had ever acquired it.

She still couldn't believe that it was Justin's inevitable and terrible disappointment with all her domestic arrangements that goaded her into pouring such energy into the trivia of their everyday existence. It was a need to feel she could create some kind of paradise situation for the twins which would compensate them for the fact that their parents were like two would-be warring nations who cohabited peacefully without firing a shot because any outbreak of hostilities could damage their mutual interests.

Justin had accepted that his wife had moved permanently into the guest room. Nadine felt a little piqued that he accepted his physical rejection with such ease and equanimity. It was as if he was grateful to be relieved of a tiresome and onerous nightly duty. He had been invited to appear on a television panel chat show and this engrossed him, for it gave him a platform from which he could impose his opinions on the entire nation. He seemed to find the gratification that he received from this new outlet of power a perfectly satisfactory channel for his thwarted sexuality.

As Nadine rubbed their furniture with beeswax polish until it shone so brightly she felt it was blinding her, she only wished that she could feel that her own existence had a similar shine.

The twins were doing very badly at school. Nadine hid their abysmal reports from Justin. The unruliness of her sons, and their general ineptitude was yet another secret she wished to keep from her husband.

She lived in disguised terror that Felix and Roland were going to be expelled. In order to placate the school staff, she volunteered to be a member of more and more school committees, and with hypocritical zeal she threw herself into more and more school activities. At Christmas, she gave the form master of the twins, and also the headmaster, extremely expensive presents and felt ashamed of her own corruption.

Justin had no idea that his sons were on the verge of expulsion. He never asked to see the reports that described them as 'unmanageable'. He assumed their progress was excellent. On one level, he seemed to see the twins as extensions of himself. This allowed him to assume they were bound to perform with excellence.

At the dinner parties they attended, Nadine would listen with quivering astonishment as her husband told the guests he was still uncertain whether to send his sons to Westminster or Eton. He then pontificated and gravely weighed up the merits and demerits of these two institutions. The arrogance of Justin's dilemma left his wife feeling aghast. It never occurred to him that the twins had little chance of attending either of these schools since they were incapable of passing the entrance exams.

At home, the twins were becoming increasingly obstreperous and disobedient. They treated Nadine with rudeness and resentment, and they fought so viciously that she was often frightened one of them would die like Abel. Justin was unaware that Nadine no longer felt she could control them, for he had laid down house rules that forbade them from entering the rooms that he used. Felix and Roland had their meals separate from their parents, down in the playroom Nadine had created for them in the basement and their most vicious fights took place there. Justin often complained to his wife of the noise that his sons made, but as their brawls were rarely enacted in his presence, he was unaware of their severity and the twins tended to be uncharacteristically subdued when they were with him for they were intimidated by the great height of their father, and his indifference threatened them like a raised wooden truncheon.

Nadine sometimes wondered if her own unvoiced discontent was communicating itself to her sons, if it was manifesting itself in their angry and rebellious behaviour. She did her best to placate them and she treated them with the same unflagging patience and superficial cheerfulness with which she reacted to the censorious demands of their father. She never showed how much she suffered from her children's contemptuous, hostile attitude towards her. Her feeling that her life was a failure on every possible level was aggravated by the ebullient postcards she kept receiving from her mother.

Whereas she had once dreaded receiving Mrs Blunt's stilted formal messages because they had seemed to her like little screams of abbreviated misery, she no longer felt she had to search between the brief, scrawled words for the unwritten, cruel reproach.

Mrs Blunt's postcards now came flopping through her daughter's mail-box and every sentence was lively: 'So much is going on here . . .'; 'It is all so exciting . . .'; 'A thrilling thing has happened . . .'; 'Corrigan feels . . .'

Nadine would read these exuberant postcards with listless eyes as she drank her morning coffee and her day stretched before her, busy, tiring, and pointless.

She found that she couldn't bring herself to answer them, and she made no arrangements to go down to see Mrs Blunt. Whereas Nadine had once hated to be a helpless witness to her mother's seemingly incurable misery, she was now ashamed to realise that she felt just as unwilling to be a depressed witness to Mrs Blunt's new happiness.

She tried to assuage her guilt that she no longer contacted her at all by claiming that her mother had become so involved in all her charitable activities and was so taken up with her new cripple that she no longer had to worry about her.

But she knew this excuse to be a poor one. 'I so long for you to meet Corrigan', was the recurring theme that went threading through her mother's postcards, and as the months went by, and Mrs Blunt heard not a word from her daughter, Nadine finally received a letter containing a paragraph that she found ominous.

> Corrigan says that I must have done something to make you angry. I really long to see you in order to find out if he is right. Corrigan thinks that I should break off with you completely as you seem to want that. But I'd so hate to do that, Nadine, and I don't think it would be right – not until we've made an attempt to thrash things out. *Please*, darling Nadine, *do* come down for the weekend. I'm not gloomy like I used to be and I think I could make it fun for you. I hope you won't find this rude, but I'd prefer it if you didn't bring the twins. Of course I'd love to see them soon, but they make it so hard to talk and just now I feel we have lots of things to discuss . . .'

Nadine read her mother's appeal and it saddened her. She realised that Mrs Blunt was very proud, that it must have been difficult for her to make it. She felt that it would be inhuman to ignore her plea and she decided to go down to Wiltshire immediately. She made this decision not only because she was moved by the affectionate, yet wounded, tone of the letter, but also because she was very threatened by the information that this unknown cripple, Corrigan, had taken it upon himself to interfere in her relationship with her mother.

She telephoned her mother to tell her that she could expect her the following Friday. A man with an Irish accent answered the telephone. His voice sounded very deep and pleasant, but it gave her a jolt that a stranger could sound so at ease in her mother's household. He told her that Mrs Blunt had gone off to attend a sale of heifers.

'Your mother's gone off in her shining loveliness to increase her herds,' he said.

Nadine asked him if he could inform Mrs Blunt of her impending visit.

'The messenger who was the bearer of bad tidings was always executed in ancient times,' Corrigan said. 'I'll be all too entranced to purvey your message, Nadine, for I'll be in a very different position. Your mother will be so overjoyed by the tidings that I'm bringing her she'll have to do the opposite of executing me. What do you think the opposite of an execution can be?'

'I really wouldn't know,' Nadine said dryly. She was dumbfounded by her first little exchange with Corrigan.

*

Justin was extremely annoyed to hear that his wife intended to go down to the country in order to spend the night with Mrs Blunt.

She only broke the news to him early Friday morning because she had expected that her project would arouse his opposition.

'Who's going to look after the twins?' he asked. 'I hope you're not counting on me. I've got two articles I have to finish by Tuesday.'

Seemingly unruffled and reasonable, Nadine explained that she had made arrangements for them to go to the house of one of their friends from school.

'But what about the Wilmot Browns?' Justin asked.

'What about them?' Nadine asked.

'They're coming to dinner tonight. Oh God, darling, don't tell me you've forgotten that. You'd better tell your mother you can't make it, Nadine. Tell her we'll all go down and see her once the weather gets a bit better.'

Nadine explained that she'd made a lamb casserole for the Wilmot Browns. Justin would only have to put it in the oven and heat it. The dinner could start with smoked salmon. As the first course was cold, all that Justin had to do was serve it. She could lay it out on plates on the dining-room table before she left if that would make it easier for him.

He was still not pleased. 'I don't understand about ovens,' he said. 'I know I'll burn the damn casserole. I don't understand how long one's meant to leave the bloody thing in.'

Nadine suggested that he should ask Joan Wilmot Brown to help him.

'I don't think one can really invite guests to the house and treat them as if they're the cook,' Justin said.

Nadine was determined to override all her husband's quibbling objections. Her decision to visit her mother had been such a difficult one to take that the problem of Justin's casserole could not sway her from her chosen course.

'The numbers will be uneven,' Justin grumbled.

'Can't you invite another lady?'

'Don't be so stupid. Really, darling, it's much too late to invite anyone else. It would seem so horribly rude. I don't understand why you've sprung this on me. I must say that I think you really should have warned me. I don't see why you've suddenly developed such a sense of filial duty. In the past it hasn't been your strongest virtue, *if* I may say so . . .'

Having done everything in her power to ensure that Justin's dinner party would be a success, Nadine still felt like a delinquent as she set off for the country in a well-cut tweed suit and driving her buttercup-yellow shiny Cortina. She drove with cool assurance and she rested her elbow with nonchalance on the window-edge of her car, but as she went spinning along the roads, she felt frightened, as if she was driving into a situation of fog and danger, and when she analysed this unreasonable sense of threat, she realised she had a great terror of meeting Corrigan.

15

When Nadine arrived at Mrs Blunt's house, she received two shocks. The first was the sight of her mother's huge brown van which was parked outside on the gravel patio. Although she had been prepared for it, she was still astonished by the size of this cumbersome vehicle and found it incredible that her mother was able to drive it.

Her second shock was the sight of the ramp, which was uglier than she could ever have imagined possible. She had thought about it with so much aversion that she'd hoped that the ramp of her imagination would prove to be much more horrible than the reality. This did not prove to be true.

It was a clumsy and monstrous contraption. It completely enveloped the lichen-covered steps of the house and rendered them invisible. She felt there was something repulsive about its surgical gleam as it rose up like a scaffolding against the weathered grey stone of the old walls.

Nadine adamantly refused to enter the front door by way of the ramp. She was wearing high-heeled shoes and she feared she would break an ankle if she tried to pull herself up into the house. Even if she held on to its railings she was certain that her feet would still go slipping out of control on its highly polished surface, which sloped like a children's slide.

She went round to the back door that led into the kitchen and there she found Mrs Murphy.

'It's been a long time since we've seen you, Nadine. You'll

find many changes.' Mrs Murphy was making Irish bread and her hands were sticky with dough.

'Where is my mother?'

'Ach, you'll find her somewhere. She's somewhere about the house. Maybe she's in the dining-room. Maybe she's drinking with Corrigan.'

'Isn't it a little early to be drinking!' Nadine looked at her watch and saw that it was only half-past eleven.

Mrs Murphy shrugged. She said that Mrs Blunt probably needed 'a little fortification'. Apparently she had got up early. She'd attended some furniture sale that had taken place in the neighbourhood.

'Is she buying a lot of furniture?' Nadine asked.

'She never stops.'

'But what does she do with it? Surely she's furnished Corrigan's hospital by now.'

'She buys up all these old antiques. She buys them in loads, like. And then she sends them up to London and she puts them in a sale up there and it seems she often gets double the price.'

'Surely she doesn't drive all that furniture up to London herself!'

'Ach, no, she doesn't take it up herself. Corrigan is very strict with her. He won't let her drive her van on the big roads. But she'd like to, mind you.'

'Well, thank goodness for that. At least Corrigan seems to have a bit of sense.'

'Your mother looks great,' Mrs Murphy said. She made a hole in the dough that she was making in a china bowl and she filled it with milk so that it formed a small white pond. 'Your mother looks great, Nadine. She looks great. You'll see the change in her when you see her . . .'

'That's wonderful,' Nadine said.

'Corrigan's got her eating again. You remember how she was starving herself. You didn't really see it like I did. But it was desperate . . . Her bones were poking right through her skin.'

'It sounds as if Corrigan has got her drinking as well.'

'Sure, your mother enjoys a jar or two. But you wouldn't grudge her that.'

'I hope she doesn't drive that massive juggernaut of a truck when she's drunk,' Nadine said.

'Oh no, Corrigan is very fussy about that. He makes her be very sensible.'

Sabrina had told Nadine that she'd got the impression that Mrs Murphy disliked Corrigan. It therefore surprised her that she seemed to regard him with approval.

'Have you seen all the changes she's made in the garden?' Mrs Murphy asked.

Nadine looked out of the kitchen window. She still hadn't really noticed the garden. Her whole attention had been riveted on Corrigan's ramp and her mother's truck.

The changes in the garden were certainly extraordinary. The desolate wilderness of briars and nettles that had once distressed her had completely vanished. The old picket fence on which her father had once trained his rambling roses had been removed and the fields that surrounded her mother's house stretched out in an unbroken expanse of well-ordered chocolate acres of plough.

'But what's happened to all those lovely old gnarled apple trees?' Nadine asked.

Mrs Murphy said that Mrs Blunt had decided to have them cut down.

'But they were so pretty and they had such beautiful blossom in the spring.'

Mrs Murphy shrugged again. She was holding her Marlboro cigarette between her lips as she kneaded her bread. Nadine noticed that a large grey glob of ash had fallen from its tip and landed in the wet dough. She hoped Mrs Murphy would try and extricate it, but with a few brisk movements of her powerful hands she made it vanish by swirling it in with all the other ingredients within her bowl.

'The old trees had lovely blossom, but they were no good for bearing fruit,' she said. 'They were past it. They'd been neglected something desperate. So your mother decided to chop them. And she's replanting with good young trees. She's making a new orchard up near the new farm. You haven't seen the farm?'

'No, I haven't seen the new farm.'

'It's great, the new farm. It's going to be really great when she finishes with it. She's modernising it. She's putting in all this new equipment. Your mother's got so much land now that you'd never believe it. She's got this passion for buying fields. Whenever she hears a farmer is selling, she's right in there – she just snaps it up. It's too soon for you to see what the estate's going to look like – but you come back in a year, Nadine, and you'll see it's going to be thriving.'

'But the price of land is exorbitant at the moment. It doesn't seem at all a good time to be buying fields. I really hope she knows what she's doing.'

Mrs Murphy shrugged again. 'William Peebles and Corrigan, they both give advice to her. They don't see eye to eye. But between them they give her loads of advice and now she's more confident, like, your mother makes up her mind herself.'

Nadine was not pleased to hear that Corrigan was advising Mrs Blunt. As the man had spent a large part of his life in an institution, she couldn't see how he could be expected to have acquired a very expert knowledge of land values.

'Your mother loves that farm,' Mrs Murphy said. 'She gets up early and she's always out now. By the time I get to the house in the mornings, your mother's nowhere to be seen. If she's not driving round the countryside buying up furniture, she's out on the farm seeing that the men don't get lazy. She goes out in her big rubber wellingtons in all weathers.'

'How many men does she employ?'

'Quite a few. She couldn't keep a farm like hers running – not if she didn't employ quite a few men.'

'How much time does Corrigan spend here?'

'Corrigan is here quite a bit. He likes the way she's got the whole place fixed up for him. Corrigan goes away, but before you can turn round, Corrigan's always back. He's like Ginger, my cat – I never have an idea where Ginger's gone. But he always comes back. He knows where it's warm and comfortable, and the cream's always sitting in a bowl for him. I never trouble my head about Ginger. I know he'll always be back.'

Nadine was disturbed by the crippled Corrigan being compared to Mrs Murphy's cat. The comparison stirred up unattractive images of stray tom-cats mewing and mating in alleyways.

'I must go and find my mother,' she said. 'I don't think she knows that I've arrived.'

As she left the kitchen she received yet another shock. Her mother's entrance hall, which had once been so well proportioned and elegant, was now blocked by the addition of the new bathroom. It took up so much space that there was only a narrow passage separating it from the staircase with the delicate old carved banisters. The door of the drawing-room where Corrigan now slept was closed and she was very glad she couldn't see any of the functional changes that had been made in it.

She heard her mother's voice coming from the dining-room and when she entered she found her sitting by a fire in an armchair and Corrigan was sitting in his wheelchair very close beside her. They were sharing a bottle of champagne.

Corrigan lifted his glass to Nadine with a courtly gesture. 'I drink to the returning prodigal,' he said. 'I drink to a prodigal we are both very glad to roast the fattened calf for . . .'

Nadine was violently irritated by his toast. She found it accusatory, also insufferably impertinent.

'We are having a little celebration,' Mrs Blunt said. 'You must get yourself a glass and sit down and join us.'

'I think it's a bit early for me.' Nadine looked at her watch and then regretted having made such a governessy and ungracious response.

She noticed that, just as Mrs Murphy had told her, her mother was looking very well. Her cheeks were pink and they had filled out so that her skin no longer had the unhealthy and transparent texture that it had had when they'd last met. Her blue eyes had lost the dead and glazed expression that her daughter had once hated to see. They were now bright and clear. She looked so much younger that Nadine could once again see traces of the pretty girl who had posed with her soldier husband for the family photograph.

'What are you both celebrating?' Nadine asked.

'Your mother had a small triumph this morning,' Corrigan said.

'Oh, did she? How lovely . . . What kind of triumph?'

'Your mother picked up this little beauty of a Dutch cabinet, and she picked it up for almost nothing.'

'It really is rather an exquisite little piece, Nadine,' Mrs Blunt started to stutter apologetically. She was hurt by her daughter's polite hostility. 'I was really very lucky this morning,' she said. 'None of the nasty tough London dealers turned up at the sale. There were just a lot of country housewives looking for second-hand refrigerators. I'll show you the catalogue, darling.'

Nadine stared blankly at the pamphlet that Mrs Blunt handed her. The item of furniture that had caught her mother's attention had been pencilled in brackets. ' "Antwerp ebony cabinet with giltwood mounts. Interior lined with tortoiseshell," ' she read. 'It sounds charming.'

'I was so lucky that no one else seemed to go for it.' Mrs Blunt's round blue eyes were fixed on her daughter's face. They implored a little approbation. 'I must say that it's a beautifully made piece,' she went on. 'It's got all these little drawers. They're all tortoiseshell inside. Those eighteenth-century Dutch craftsmen were just as fine as the English ones, but somehow they never got so well known.'

'What are you going to do with the cabinet?' Nadine asked.

'It's a piece that will be very easy to dispose of.' Mrs Blunt nervously sipped her champagne. 'It would be perfect for some London drawing-room. Someone could make it their centre-piece if they wanted to. They could keep all their paper-clips, their pens and pencils and engagement books, all their odds and ends in the little drawers . . .'

'How clever of you to find it,' Nadine remarked drily.

'Your mother possesses that rare quality, expertise. If you let your mother loose in a saleroom of antiques, she has the eye of

the eagle for picking out the only item worth bidding for,'
Corrigan interrupted.

'I didn't know you were so mad about antiques.' Nadine
ignored Corrigan and only addressed her mother, as if she
hoped he could be erased with his champagne and his wheelchair if she paid him no attention. When she'd first come into
the room she'd noticed that he was a very good-looking man.
He reminded her of nineteenth-century musicians whom
she'd seen in old prints. His face was sensitive, gaunt and
tortured. She could imagine him in a black tail-coat with his
baton raised and his dark hair turned white and springing up
from his head in a wild pale mane. She'd also noticed that
Corrigan ceased to look attractive the moment that he smiled.
She found there was something unpleasant in the way that his
carved pink lips curled away from his teeth whenever he was
amused. His teeth were too pointed and they had a faintly
canine look.

'I first got interested in antiques when your father was alive,'
Mrs Blunt said. 'But I've got to know much more about them
recently. I've bought lots of books which have helped me learn
a lot and then I find that with every sale that I attend I learn
more. I can spot the fakes quite easily now . . .'

'It seems a pity to sell this Dutch cabinet if it's as beautiful as
you say,' Nadine said.

'You see, darling, I've got nowhere to put it.'

Mrs Blunt waved her hand helplessly round the dining-
room. Nadine had to admit that she had made it very pleasant
now that she was using it as a living-room. There were two
comfortable velvet-covered George III armchairs in front of
the fireplace which had a pretty ornamental brass fender. She
had acquired some new pictures, presumably at some auction.
They were nineteenth-century oil-paintings of horses and
jockeys and Nadine assumed they were very good ones. She
had also got a brand new hi-fi set and a lot of records. This
irritated Nadine, for she knew that her mother had never liked
music. She also regretted the fact that when summer came it
would not be like using the drawing-room, for this room had
no doors leading out into the garden.

'I started to get so over-furnished that I've already had to sell all the furniture that used to be in the hall,' Mrs Blunt said. 'There was really no room for it once we made the bathroom. And Corrigan has everything he requires in the drawing-room, so I think I may as well sell the Antwerp cabinet and give the proceeds to those who really need it.'

'What's happened to the dining-room table that used to be in here?' Nadine asked.

'We sold that quite a long time ago, when we were making all the changes. Corrigan and I find it cosier to eat on trays in front of the fire. The dining-room table was just cluttering up the room and we never used it, so finally I sent it up to London with another shipment of furniture that I was selling.'

'I remember it as rather a fine table,' Nadine said. 'Didn't it originally belong to Daddy's family? And what did you do with your set of chairs? I thought they were Regency and really very valuable.'

'They were very nice chairs. I always liked them. But you can't have a lot of chairs without a table.'

'But when people come down to visit, what on earth are they going to eat on?'

'Well, people don't come down very much, if the truth be told. And there's always the kitchen . . .'

Corrigan was silent, but Nadine was very aware of him sitting there like an umpire at a tennis match chalking up every point that she lost.

She noticed that there was a large silver-framed photograph of her father in this room that her mother had created for Corrigan. His eyes stared out of it with a resolute yet melancholy expression. Nadine was glad to see that he still had a place in the house, that he'd not been disposed of like the dining-room table. Yet she felt faintly embarrassed for him as if his pose of authority had become a charade and even his old-fashioned military cap suddenly looked unauthentic, like an actor's theatrical prop.

'Your mother and I were having an interesting discussion just before you arrived,' Corrigan said.

'Oh, really,' Nadine murmured coldly.

'We were discussing a subject of limitless fascination. We were discussing the nature of pleasure.'

Nadine hoped that Corrigan didn't want to pursue this topic. She felt it would be extremely delicate and disturbing to have any such unsuitable discussion with a cripple.

'The moralists insist that the majority of humankind live entirely for pleasure, and they deplore it, Corrigan said. 'I don't believe it to be true. I feel that most people have a tremendous fear of pleasure, the cursed puritan ethic has eaten into their psyches and many of our social ills are the result of this lost art of pure sensual enjoyment.'

'I wonder what kind of pleasure Corrigan is talking about?' Nadine wondered. She was determined not to ask him.

Mrs Blunt was sitting there with a mild and contented expression on her face as Corrigan talked. Her daughter thought she looked a little imbecilic.

'Pleasure is fleeting. You mustn't forget that, Corrigan,' her mother said. 'But then I'm afraid that happiness is fleeting too . . .'

'Of course it's fleeting, Devina,' Corrigan remarked cheerfully. 'Don't you see that if it ever ceased to be fleeting it would instantly cease to be pleasure. Any pleasurable sensation that lasted for infinity would become unendurable. The human mind can only tolerate any state – be it one of pain, be it one of ecstasy – if it can see the possibility that there will eventually be an end to it. That's why the whole concept of heaven can seem every bit as terrifying as that of hell.'

'What a silly conversation this is,' Nadine thought.

'Pleasure is still one of the great gifts that mankind has been offered and those who reject it do so at great cost.' Corrigan's eyes searched Nadine. 'You can see the evidence if you look at the faces in the crowds in any busy city street. You see the anger, the hunger, the frustration, the depression. You realise that most of the people in those crowds have abandoned all hope of experiencing pleasure, they've kicked the very expectation into the gutter and they've chosen to walk past it.'

'Oh, what is Corrigan talking about?' Nadine thought. He made her feel impatient. She had the suspicion that this whole conversation was his subtle way of needling her, and she wondered if she was becoming paranoid. She noticed that whenever he spoke his eyes never left her mother's face.

The champagne was finished and Mrs Blunt went off to get another bottle from the kitchen.

'You don't resemble your mother,' Corrigan said to Nadine. 'I see nothing of her in you.'

'I'm more like my father.' Nadine fidgeted defiantly as if she felt she had been insulted.

'I liked your friend when she came down here, Nadine. What an enchantress! She reminded me of a magnolia blossom. There is something so transient about that kind of beauty. It breaks your heart. Where will it all go? What will Sabrina do with her own delicacy and bloom?'

'She's taking her A-levels,' Nadine said.

'She'll have to retake everything,' Corrigan said. 'Sabrina is a creature that could have wrung great verses out of Yeats. He created her before she existed. "A girl arose that had red mournful lips, and seemed the greatness of the world in tears . . ." '

'I'm very fond of Sabrina,' Nadine said. She felt she was losing her friend as Corrigan seized her and tried to make her his own by turning her into an unrecognisable goddess.

'Don't you fear for your friend?' Corrigan asked her. 'Don't you ever fear for that lovely flower, doomed like Odysseus and the labouring ships, proud as Priam murdered with his peers?'

'Sabrina is quite tough in her way,' Nadine said.

'She is highly intelligent,' Corrigan said. 'She's in danger of being doomed by her own intelligence. Such great physical beauty and such beauty of intelligence . . . It's sad to say it, but it's a rare thing to find two such important qualities in such a flowering combination. But there is danger there for Sabrina. The gods have over-endowed her. I am psychic . . . I see things that I wish I hadn't seen. We can only pray that Sabrina will find some way of harnessing that lovely and fine intelligence to something more substantial than her own narcissism . . .'

Usually Nadine was pleased when people liked her friend

192

and praised her beauty, but she felt Corrigan's extravagant praise of Sabrina had a malicious intention. She had the suspicion that it amused him to try to make her feel inadequate and stir up her jealousy.

'Sabrina seems to have a lovely character, too,' he said. 'Your mother was very moved that she took the trouble to come to see her.'

Nadine longed for Corrigan to stop extolling the virtues of her friend. 'Corrigan hates me,' she thought. 'We've only just met, but he already hates me.' The realisation terrified her. She was not accustomed to arousing hatred. She placated much too quickly. Her only armour was her incessant ability to placate. But she felt naked in her armour in front of Corrigan. His hatred drilled into her nerves. She could feel it shooting like a jet of poison from his blue-green eyes, which had such beautiful long lashes, they made her own seem pathetically short and brittle.

Mrs Blunt returned with more champagne. 'Corrigan's really encouraging her to drink,' Nadine thought. 'She already seems keen to start on a second bottle and it's not even lunch-time.'

She still decided that she would no longer refuse to have a drink herself for she felt that Corrigan would sneer if she kept up her role of the priggish abstainer.

'Let's no longer waste our breath discussing pleasure – let's just partake of it,' Corrigan said. Mrs Blunt was filling up his glass. He stared up into her face and he smiled. Nadine noticed that her mother looked down at him and she smiled beneficently back.

He made another toast to Mrs Blunt and suddenly broke into an Irish ballad. Nadine was deeply embarrassed by his singing, but she still had to admit that he had a beautiful tenor voice.

> 'I'm drunk today,' Corrigan sang,
> 'And I'm seldom so-o-ber
> A handsome ro-o-ver
> From town to town . . .'

To Nadine's horror Mrs Blunt also suddenly burst into song and she completed the lines of the ballad.

> 'But I am sick now,' she sang,
> 'My days are numbered
> Come all ye young men
> And I'll lay me down . . .'

Nadine had the uneasy suspicion that Corrigan and her mother had performed very similar duets many times in the past, as they sat by the fireside, drinking their champagne. Mrs Blunt's voice was surprisingly strong and melodious, and when she sang it sounded professional rather than amateurish. Nadine tried to persuade herself that there was no harm in these infantile, campfire sing-songs. Corrigan and her mother both obviously very much enjoyed them and she felt there was something ungenerous in her nature that made her react to them with such secret but stormy disapproval. She couldn't help finding it unseemly in the extreme that her mother was prepared to break into song like the inebriated old crones who blare out mournful Irish songs in pubs on New Year's Eve.

Corrigan noticed that Nadine had suffered during his last rendition, and this made him mischievous. He became increasingly rowdy and flushed, consumed more and more champagne and very soon he broke into another song.

> 'On the gallows . . .
> Friday morning
> hanging high
> upon a tree . . .
> Kevin Barry
> gave his brave
> young life
> so that
> Ireland
> could be free . . .'

As Corrigan's deep melodious voice resounded through the house, Nadine sat there frozen with her Adam's apple throbbing as her agitation mounted.

> 'Just before . . .
> he faced
> the hangman
> in his dreary
> prison cell . . .'

Corrigan sang louder and with much more throb and emotion. Mrs Blunt, who was also flushed, then joined in.

> 'British soldiers . . .
> tortured Barry
> *just* because
> he wouldn't tell . . .'

'Is anything being done about lunch?' Nadine interrupted without allowing them to finish the lyric. 'Can I do anything in the kitchen? I'm really rather starved after my long drive.'

Mrs Blunt looked flustered. Nadine felt a little sorry for her. She still felt she had been right to try to bring her to her senses. She was aware of her father's eyes gazing out of his silver frame. She was certain that they had acquired an expression of even deeper melancholy. She found it obscene that Corrigan should dare to sing anti-English songs in the house of a dead British officer. She found it an even greater obscenity that the Colonel's widow seemed all too happy to join in with him.

Her mother reminded her of a bear in the circus, waving its pathetic paws and dancing for its master. Nadine wondered how many other vile Sinn Fein songs Corrigan had taught her mother. She assumed that innocent little Mrs Blunt had no proper grasp of the incendiary political content of the material he was feeding her, but she still felt that her mother had degraded herself. She had adopted a spurious Irish accent as she sang and her daughter found this to be one of the most objectionable parts of her demeaning behaviour. Nadine saw it as important that her mother be made to realise that she was very angry with the way she had just comported herself.

'Is Mrs Murphy preparing the lunch?' Nadine asked. 'If so, I'm off to help her.'

'It seems a pity that we all have to bow to the tedious clock of

the stomach just when we are all starting to enjoy ourselves,'
Corrigan said.

'You probably had a late breakfast.' Nadine's reply was acid.
It still gave no hint of her true anger.

'Why isn't that bloody Corrigan out somewhere collecting
for the disabled?' she thought. 'Why isn't that horrible cripple
being disinterested and noble, like my mother always makes
him sound in her postcards?'

Nadine got up from her chair and she went flouncing
towards the door. As she walked out, she was painfully aware
that her disdainful flounce was a dramatic failure. It should
have had the sweep of the empress. It should have been
intensely regal, intensely dignified, and final. But with Corrigan watching her she was unable to make the grandiose and
reproving exit that she'd hoped to make.

This large, broad-shouldered man was so static as he sat
there watching her from his chair. His inability to be anything
other than static made her feel that every movement she made
was trite and superfluous. He had only one role that was left to
him. He could be the most severe and critical observer. And
she felt this as she left the room with this crippled man sitting
motionless as a statue, while his contemptuous eyes followed
every step that she took. As she made her would-be reproving
and disgusted exit, Corrigan managed to give her the feeling
that her tweed skirt had risen above her head displaying sadly
unclean underwear.

The imperial sweeping exit that she'd hoped to make was also
not improved by the high-heeled shoes that she was wearing.
Her choice of footwear had been wildly unsuitable for a visit to
the English countryside in March, and it had been deliberate.
She had hoped that the dainty stylish shoes she'd chosen would
make it impossible for her to be taken on any extensive tours of
her mother's new land and her new farms. She had developed a
dread of being made to admire any of her mother's new
agricultural acquisitions. She feared that they were very ill-
advised, but as there was little she could do to prevent Mrs Blunt
buying them, the last thing she wanted was to be driven to see
them in her mother's van, and had worn these shoes so she could

not be made to walk through the mud and the manure of endless fields and the courtyards of various farm buildings.

She very much regretted having worn these shoes as Corrigan watched her leaving the room in high dudgeon. Her gesture of protest against Mrs Blunt's Sinn Fein song was ruined because the shoes were brand-new and she'd not yet learnt to balance on them. She could feel her ankles wobbling pitifully and her whole body gave a lurch that she knew must look quite drunken. This was particularly unfortunate as she'd hoped to show Corrigan and her mother that she found their early morning drinking reprehensible.

After Nadine had slammed the dining-room door as she'd made her undignified exit, Corrigan looked at Mrs Blunt and he smiled. 'The poor little creature,' he said. 'She's just eating herself up. It's a pitiful thing to watch her . . .'

'I think Nadine has quite a difficult life.' Mrs Blunt immediately became loyal to her daughter. 'The twins are really rather a handful and I'm afraid that they've been very spoilt and now it's difficult for poor Nadine to manage them. I promise you that the twins are very exhausting. I'm really extremely glad that she didn't bring them with her today . . .'

'The twins may well be holy terrors,' Corrigan said. 'I'm all too prepared to accept your view of that lethal couple. I still find it hard to believe that the twins constitute your daughter's major problem . . .'

'What is the matter with Nadine?' Mrs Blunt asked him. 'She always seems so cross with me and I never really know why . . .'

'I tell you that your daughter is eaten up with jealousy, Devina . . . Now jealousy may be the most painful of human emotions, but it's the emotion that evokes the least human sympathy . . .'

'Oh, that's really ridiculous, Corrigan. Nadine has nothing in the world to be jealous of . . .'

'I wouldn't say that.' Corrigan gave Mrs Blunt such an intense and admiring look that she became quite bashful. 'That girl has to live in the shadow of her mother – I don't think that's a position that Nadine much enjoys.'

'But Nadine doesn't live in my shadow, Corrigan. I hardly ever see her. I only wish that I saw her more.'

'I think that the less that you see of that girl, the better it will be for both of you.'

'How can you say that, Corrigan? I really don't think that's very nice . . .'

'I'm not trying to be nice, Devina. I'm trying to be honest. I tell you that Nadine is eaten up by the green-eyed monster, and I warn you that such a monster makes a very dangerous household pet.'

'I think I'd better go and get lunch for Nadine.' Mrs Blunt got up and she showed Corrigan that she didn't wish to continue with this conversation.

While it had been going on, Nadine had walked through her mother's hall which had been made so ugly by the great new wall of Corrigan's bathroom, and she'd felt close to tears. She'd been tempted to get into her shiny yellow Cortina to go back to London immediately. But she knew that Mrs Blunt would be desperately upset if she was to do this, and she feared that if she was to make such a cruel and aggressive gesture, Corrigan would rather enjoy Mrs Blunt's discomfiture.

'I've come to give you a hand with lunch,' she said to Mrs Murphy as she entered the kitchen.

'Sure, there's nothing to be done, Nadine. Your mother did most of the preparations yesterday. She seemed to spend the whole day at it. She was in a holy funk about your coming down here. "We've got to make it nice for Nadine," your mother kept saying to me. She kept repeating it over and over.'

Nadine, who was already feeling close to tears, was made to feel even more distressed when she was told that her visit had meant so much to her mother. 'It's all Corrigan's fault that it's going so wrong,' she thought. 'If that odious cripple would just leave us alone we might have quite a pleasant time together. He has no tact at all. He shouldn't be here. I can't talk to my mother while he's sitting there listening. We don't want all his champagne and his awful singing. We just want to be left alone so that we can talk in peace.'

Nadine decided that when lunch was over, she would tell Mrs Blunt that she wanted to pay a visit to her father's grave. That seemed a good way of getting her mother away from Corrigan. Insensitive as the man appeared to be, he would surely realise that he couldn't accompany them to the cemetery.

Nadine still felt guilty that she'd been so unkind to Mrs Blunt when she'd refused to go with her to the churchyard the last time that she'd come down to the country. She was now also very anxious to make amends for that cruelty.

Nadine heard the sound of Corrigan's wheelchair rolling through the hall as he accompanied Mrs Blunt to the kitchen. 'Why can't he stay in the dining-room and wait there for us to bring him lunch?' Nadine thought. 'Why does Corrigan have to follow my mother into the kitchen? He can't be any help. He can only be a nuisance. Why does he have to go everywhere that my mother goes?'

Nadine was wrong to assume that Corrigan would be useless in the kitchen. He proved to be very helpful to Mrs Blunt. He stirred the sauces, he heated up the vegetables and buttered them, and he made a very expert salad. He helped her get the food out on to serving dishes which he placed on a great tray on his knee and transported to the dining-room. He wouldn't let her mother carry anything heavy. It astonished Nadine that Corrigan and Mrs Blunt made such a deft and efficient culinary team.

They all finally ate their luncheon on little wicker tables in front of the fire. They started with scallops *au gratin*. Nadine, who cooked so well herself, was all too aware of the time and trouble that her mother had taken when she prepared this meal. She must have had to wash each scallop separately before she simmered it in wine and butter and parsley. After she'd put the scallops back on their pretty individual shells, it had probably taken her half the morning to make their cheese sauce, to then surround them with such delicate fluted potatoes.

Nadine exaggerated the time and effort that her mother had put into this lunch because she felt so ungrateful for the gastronomic preparations that had been made on her behalf.

She'd have much preferred to have eaten alone with Mrs Blunt in the local pub. They could have had some greasy shepherd's pie and if they'd found it inedible they could have left it. She felt that they might have been able to talk if they'd gone to eat in the village. If they'd been left alone they might have enjoyed themselves. In the pub they would not have had all their conversation monitored by an intrusive cripple.

When they had finished the scallops, Corrigan wheeled off to the kitchen and he came back with pheasant, which Mrs Blunt had stuffed with a prune purée. He then proceeded to carve it. He was a very good carver; the pheasant slices he produced were paper-thin. Mrs Blunt then served them with a bread sauce and a rich port-flavoured gravy.

'Corrigan was really an angel,' Mrs Blunt said to her daughter. 'He plucked this pheasant for me. I couldn't have done it myself – I can't bear to touch dead birds. I like the end product, but I can't face the dirty work. Corrigan is right to scold me for being so squeamish and hypocritical . . . But I don't seem to be able to change myself. He spent ages pulling the feathers out of its horrible old rotting corpse. The trouble with pheasants is that they are meant to be "high" which really means they have to be ancient. Anyway, I think we ought to drink to Corrigan, Nadine.'

' "They say that *even* up in heaven, the rich lie late and snore," ' Corrigan said, ' "While the poor man rises at seven, to do the celestial chore . . ." '

'Oh, don't put it like that,' Mrs Blunt laughed. 'But I like the lines. Where do they come from?'

'They were written by one of America's best black writers,' he told her. 'They'd have to be written by a black poet. They are black in every sense.'

'I don't understand why you made Corrigan pluck the pheasant,' Nadine said to her mother. 'Why couldn't you have got your butcher to pluck it for you?'

'It didn't come from the butcher,' Mrs Blunt said. 'William Peebles shot it. It was on our land. We get quite a lot of pheasants on our land now. Apparently it's quite all right to shoot them, although I know that it seems rather immoral.'

'I didn't much enjoy plucking the bird,' Corrigan said. 'Your mother had kept it in her larder and it was high as a kite when the task was handed to me. I just kept trying to convince myself that ripeness was all.'

'I wonder if ripeness really is all?' Mrs Blunt's question was pensive.

Nadine was feeling sick. From the very start of the meal she'd felt unhungry. Now all this talk about the plucking of the pheasant was turning her stomach.

'I think that ripeness is certainly all,' Corrigan said. 'I agree with Joubert. He said that life is a country that the old have seen and lived in. Those who still have to travel through it can only learn from them.'

'Corrigan is really unbelievably tactless,' Nadine thought. 'Why does he have to talk about old age with my poor mother?' She looked at Mrs Blunt's face to see if the trend of the conversation had upset her. But her mother was drinking wine and smiling blandly.

'Don't they also say that old age is when you know all the answers – and nobody asks you the questions?' Mrs Blunt enquired.

'Albert Camus said that to grow old is to pass from passion to compassion,' Corrigan answered. 'I think that transition is very worthwhile – I think it's one that's well worth making.'

'But then Disraeli said that youth was a blunder, manhood a struggle, and old age a regret,' Mrs Blunt murmured.

'Where has she read all these things?' Nadine wondered. She excused herself and said she was going to the bathroom. She felt she had to get out of the room. She went upstairs because she refused to use the one that took up so much space in the hall. She was frightened by the idea that it might have a special low lavatory with handrails.

As she returned to the dining-room she heard Mrs Murphy's voice booming from the kitchen.

> 'And the cow kicked
> Nelly, in the belly,
> In the barn.

And the old woman said,
It won't do her any harm . . .

'First verse,
Same as the first.'

'This whole household is going insane,' Nadine thought. 'Why do they all sing so much? What have they got to sing about? It's really quite unbearable . . .' She was still forced to admit that Corrigan and her mother's singing was less painful to listen to than Mrs Murphy's. She had not liked the songs they'd sang, but at least they'd been in tune.

Once she was back in the dining-room, Corrigan served her with apple pie and cream and he poured them all a glass of port and he laced the port with brandy.

'In Ireland, they believe that port mixed with brandy is the remedy for all human ills,' he said. 'They use it to cure everything from meningitis to a simple hangover.'

Nadine found the mixture lethal and refused to drink it. Her mother seemed to enjoy it very much. She'd already drunk quite a lot of red wine and her daughter studied her anxiously. Mrs Blunt was still a little flushed, but otherwise she seemed in perfect control of herself. The claret that she'd served had been excellent and Nadine wondered how much it had cost her.

'Dr Johnson said that if any man aspires to be a hero, he must first drink brandy,' Corrigan said. 'If his saying is a true one, you will prove to be a very great heroine, Devina, and I hope that I'll make a passable hero.'

Nadine found Dr Johnson's statement a very fatuous one. Now that she had abstained from drinking she felt more and more excluded by the heightened mood the brandy had induced in her mother and Corrigan. With this couple, she felt as she'd often felt as a child that once again she was the odd one out.

'I hear you have two charming sons,' Corrigan said to Nadine. 'Your mother is always talking about them. They sound delightful.'

Even though he seemed to be trying to be nice, she suspected that he was teasing her. Could he have heard from Mrs Blunt that the twins were quite difficult and belligerent?

'I'm very fond of children,' Corrigan said. 'I'd have loved to be able to have some.'

'He really knows how to embarrass one,' Nadine thought. She looked at her mother to see if she'd also found his announcement disturbing, but she was sitting there happily drinking her port, apparently undismayed.

'Did you know that Corrigan is writing a novel?' Mrs Blunt asked her daughter.

'No, I didn't know,' Nadine said.

'I've chosen to write a novel because I find the whole glory of fiction lies in the fact that it forces one out of oneself and into the lives of other people,' Corrigan said.

'What is your novel about?' Nadine asked. She hoped he wasn't writing about her mother.

'I don't think any writer likes to disclose his material before his book is completed. And my humble effort is very far from completion. It's going quite slowly because naturally I am not giving up my work for the disabled. But I try to do a few hours of writing every day. This morning I got nothing done. All the preparations we had to make for your arrival proved quite a distraction.'

'He's really got a nerve,' Nadine thought. 'He never stops trying to put me in the wrong. Now he's trying to blame me for interrupting his blinking novel.'

'I would rather like to go down to Daddy's grave,' she whispered to her mother as Corrigan started taking out the dishes.

Mrs Blunt looked surprised but quite pleased and she went to get her coat. Nadine went to find her handbag which she'd left in the kitchen. She opened it, looking for her compact for she wanted to powder her nose. She always kept her handbag very neat and she noticed immediately that there was a ten pound note missing.

She wondered whether to tell her mother. It would certainly upset her, because it looked as if the thief really had to be Mrs Murphy, and her mother seemed so strangely attached to her. After some indecision she decided she simply had to let Mrs

Blunt know about the stolen money. If Mrs Murphy had the audacity to pinch a ten pound note from a guest's handbag, goodness knows what she was pilfering daily from her poor vague mother.

'I had a ten pound note in my bag,' Nadine said when she joined Mrs Blunt and Corrigan in the dining-room. Mrs Blunt had put on her coat and she was ready to go off to her late husband's grave.

'Oh, did you, darling?'

'Yes, I did, and I'm afraid it's gone.'

'Oh, how awful,' Mrs Blunt said. 'Please don't tell Mrs Murphy. She'll think you are accusing her and it will hurt her feelings dreadfully.'

'Well, I can't see who else could have taken it except Mrs Murphy. If the woman is a thief I don't see why I have to be so careful about her feelings.'

'Mrs Murphy would never steal. It couldn't possibly have been her.' Mrs Blunt was looking quite agitated.

'I'm not so sure,' Corrigan said. 'I've always felt that those huge purple hands might have very slippery fingers.'

'Oh, nonsense, Corrigan!' Mrs Blunt suddenly seemed very annoyed and it was the first time Nadine had heard her mother speak to him sharply.

'I think you and Corrigan are both being horrible about Mrs Murphy. It will really upset me if either of you accuse her. Maybe you never had a ten pound note in your bag, Nadine. It's a very easy mistake to make. One intends to put some money in one's bag and then one forgets to put it in. I do that all the time.'

'You are rather a vague character, Devina. Your daughter is not at all like you. She gives me the impression that she never makes such mistakes.'

Nadine noticed that he seemed to be taking her side against Mrs Murphy. As he was so protective of her mother he'd probably felt for a long time that it would be much wiser if Mrs Blunt ceased to employ her. It was quite possible that he knew of other things that had mysteriously vanished from the household.

She still refused to put herself in a position where she sided with Corrigan on any issue. Her mother was getting very upset and she had not come down to visit with the intention of making her miserable. Ten pounds was not a large enough sum to be worth creating a great fuss about.

'I think you must be right,' Nadine said. 'I suppose that I never put that ten pound note in my bag. One can be so silly about these things.'

She then remembered that she'd checked to see if she had some money just before leaving her house. She'd thought she might need ten pounds for petrol.

Mrs Blunt looked very relieved that the matter had been cleared up and set off with Nadine towards the cemetery. They walked there in silence. Nadine had hoped they would be able to talk if they were left alone together, but neither of them seemed to be able to think of anything to say. She knew that her mother was hoping that she'd say how much she liked Corrigan, but she couldn't bring herself to do this. The stolen money also rankled, although the subject was not referred to.

Once they got to the Colonel's grave, Mrs Blunt shut her eyes and she seemed to be praying. As Nadine stood there feeling rather awkward beside her, she suddenly heard the sound of wheels and she realised that Corrigan had followed them. She turned round feeling very angry. She thought it would be outrageous if he were to come into the cemetery. But Corrigan remained outside the gate and he sat there in his chair watching them and he had such a savage and unpleasant expression on his face that it made Nadine feel frightened. She assumed that the hatred that she saw in his eyes was directed at herself for she knew it couldn't be aimed at her mother.

'Corrigan is watching us,' she whispered to Mrs Blunt. 'How dare he sit there watching us. I think it's really awful.'

Mrs Blunt opened her eyes. She looked dazed, as if she'd just come out of a trance. 'Oh, he often does that,' she said benignly and she gave an amused little smile. 'He often watches, but he never comes in. I won't allow him to.'

'How strange she is,' Nadine thought. 'Why doesn't she hate being watched? Most people like a little privacy when they visit a grave. My mother doesn't seem to mind being watched at all.'

'Did you have a good wallow?' Corrigan asked them as they came out of the cemetery gates.

Nadine found his question inexcusably tasteless and she examined her mother's face to see if he had offended her.

Mrs Blunt did not yet seem to have come out of the state she'd been in when she stood by the Colonel's grave and it was as if she hardly registered his gibe. As they all went back to her house she walked like a somnambulist. Neither Corrigan nor her daughter seemed to exist for her.

Nadine noticed that the cripple's hands were turning the wheels of his chair with irritable jerky slaps and he was glowering. He clearly resented the withdrawal of Mrs Blunt's attention and it was making him very sullen. Nadine had not realised that her mother was still so emotionally involved with her dead father. She'd assumed that Corrigan had replaced him in her affections and that with the energetic new turn that her mother's life seemed to have taken, the Colonel would have ceased to have much importance to her.

Nadine was disturbed to see that her mother could easily slip back into the state of dumb inarticulate misery from which she'd appeared to have emerged. She viewed Mrs Blunt's regression with ambivalence. She was relieved that her mother was not fickle to the memory of her father. But when Mrs Blunt entered into a sorrowful and solitary communication with the Colonel as she'd done at the graveside, or when she became boisterous and drunk with Corrigan, Nadine was made to feel equally rejected. She remained the unwanted bystander. The two contradictory roles that Mrs Blunt now seemed able to assume baffled Nadine, and as she had no part in either of them she could only view them with equal hostility.

When they got back to the house, Mrs Blunt vanished upstairs to her bedroom and Nadine was left alone with Corrigan.

'Your mother makes me feel impotent,' he said. 'I'll confess to you that it sometimes angers me.'

Nadine looked at him with horror. She was very aware of the lower part of his torso, hidden from sight by his tartan rug.

'All her doting on past losses – it's very unhealthy. Or at least I find it so.'

Nadine agreed with him, and yet she was still unwilling to concede that she shared any of his opinions.

'I see your mother as a patient who has only made a partial recovery from a fatal disease,' he said. 'When bouts of her old illness recur, it's a dispiriting thing to witness. I sometimes feel that I'm your mother's physician, I offer her medicine in the spoon, but she's stubborn and she often rejects it. All her wreath-carrying – I despise it, and she's quite aware of my position. I understand that your father was a very remarkable man – but she'll never recapture him by making obeisance to his bones. She must learn to incorporate all his virtues within herself – that's the only way she can keep him alive and confer on him some temporary immortality.'

Nadine felt that Corrigan was making very great sense and she was suddenly ashamed that she'd been so wilfully blind to the positive aspects of his relationship with her mother.

'I'm not a member of her family,' Corrigan said. 'I am only a lodger. When I try to convert her to my way of thinking, she resents it and finds it presumptuous. But you are her flesh and blood, Nadine. You have influence over her and I beg you to exert it. I implore you to support me when I try to convince her that she must look forward to the future. If she keeps looking back over her shoulder, she'll become like Lot's wife, she'll only turn into a pillar of sorrow and salt.'

Nadine found herself feeling increasingly in agreement with Corrigan. His appeal moved her. He seemed so humane and disinterested, and yet she was still unable to reconcile herself to the position that he'd taken in her mother's household and the ambivalence of her own emotions made her feel that she'd like to break down and start to weep. Corrigan's little speech had made her realise that she had no influence over her mother at all. Mrs Blunt hadn't even cared when her money had been stolen by Mrs Murphy. She still resented this very deeply. When Mrs Blunt had been forced to choose between her daughter and that uncouth, dishonest creature who ruled her kitchen, she'd instantly sided with that awful woman.

'My mother won't listen to me,' she said plaintively. 'I don't think I've ever meant very much to her.'

She was amazed to find herself making such a painful and personal confession to Corrigan. But when she looked at his handsome tortured face and he was no longer smiling in the way that she disliked, she suddenly felt that he looked rather like a priest, his whole expression could take on the luminous purity that she'd have hoped to find in the face of a father confessor. He made her feel that she could blurt out the feelings of childish grievance that she usually attempted to repress and she trusted him to listen to them without mockery, and believed that he would respond with a compassion and wisdom that might help her to get them in proportion.

'When you say that your mother cares nothing for you, Nadine, you malign her,' Corrigan said in grave soft tones. 'I speak only as an outsider, but my role gives me a certain detachment. I know that she cares for you very deeply indeed. But she has received little evidence that you have much affection for her.'

'But I love her,' Nadine protested. As she stared at Corrigan, her eyes had the desperate expression of the little girl in the family photograph. They were fixed on his handsome features as they'd once stared at the camera. They implored a little approbation.

'Love is, of course, a very admirable emotion,' he said. 'But it's not one that should remain abstract. It needs a few concrete manifestations. I'll tell you something, Nadine. You may not like what I'm going to say. But I'm going to take the risk of offending you.'

Nadine was frightened of what he was going to say. He no longer reminded her of an Irish priest. Now, as he stared at her, his eyes had a penetrating and accusatory glitter.

'If you care for your mother as much as you protest, how could you leave her in the rapacious clutches of a she-devil like Mrs Murphy? Answer me that – and be filled with shame . . .'

Nadine's narrow little oval face went scarlet. 'I've never much cared for Mrs Murphy,' she stuttered, 'but if my mother chooses to employ her, it's not really my business to interfere.

Mrs Murphy seems quite devoted to her in a rough and ready way.'

'Devoted!' Corrigan gave a sarcastic laugh and his lips curled away from his teeth.

'But I've never had any proof that she was dishonest or anything.' Nadine sounded increasingly plaintive as she tried to justify her shaky position. She quailed before the contempt in Corrigan's eyes. She remembered the money that had vanished from the kitchen.

'When I first agreed to accept the hospitality that your mother has been great-hearted enough to offer me, I accepted not only because it gave me a rare opportunity to pursue the only work I feel to be of value, but because I felt I might be able to do something to save her from the fangs of this great vampire bat that I found flitting round her house.'

Mrs Blunt suddenly came into the room and Corrigan broke off. She seemed to have shaken herself out of the melancholy state to which her visit to the cemetery had reduced her.

'Shall we have tea now?' she asked. 'Or shall we be bolder and more debauched and celebrate Nadine's visit with another bottle of champagne?'

'It's your choice, Devina,' Corrigan said. 'The decision must rest with you.'

Mrs Blunt laughed and she chose to open some more champagne.

'If a woman drives one to drink,' Corrigan said, 'at least one should have the courtesy to thank her.'

As Mrs Blunt filled his glass he looked up into her face with the caressing expression that Nadine had originally found objectionable. She'd started to like him when he'd confided that he was troubled by the way that her mother still refused to relinquish her morbid and pathological obsession with her dead husband. He'd appealed for her to support his position and she'd been flattered by his request. While he'd treated her as his confidante, she'd been able to respect him for his intelligent concern.

But once Mrs Blunt came back into the room, all his interest in Nadine immediately vanished, and his attention became entirely focused on her mother.

'Devina is a minefield of unsuspected, untapped talents,' he said. 'Did you know, Nadine, that your mother is very good at French?'

'Oh, I'm not really all that good,' Mrs Blunt said modestly. 'I used to spend holidays in France when I was a girl and I once spoke quite well. Now I'm afraid it's very rusty.'

'Your mother has now started to read Pascal with pleasure. So I don't think her French is as rusty as she'd like to claim. In my opinion, Pascal is one of the greatest writers that ever lived. He was a very sickly man. He was very nearly deformed. Maybe I identify with him because he, too, had an unenviable physique. When he wrote "*Notre nature est dans le mouvement*", it's proof that he transcended his afflictions. Finish the lines for me, Devina.'

' "*Le repos entier est la mort*," ' Mrs Blunt recited bashfully. Nadine was surprised that her accent sounded very good.

'I keep telling your mother she must keep those lines in her head forever. They could have been written for her personally, and she'll only fare badly if she forgets them!'

Nadine was piqued by the way that Corrigan hardly seemed conscious that she was still in the room. If he included her in the conversation he now only used her as a convenient ally who could join in with him whenever he paid an admiring tribute to her mother.

She'd never heard of Pascal and she found the literary exchanges that Mrs Blunt now enjoyed with Corrigan very difficult to appreciate. His accusation that she'd done nothing to protect her innocent mother from the exploitation of Mrs Murphy continued to rankle.

In one last competitive bid to regain Corrigan's approval and attention, she decided to bring up the subject of the missing ten pound note. 'I've been thinking about that money that was taken from my bag,' she said to Mrs Blunt. 'There's no question that I forgot to put it in. Corrigan is right. I never make mistakes like that.'

Mrs Blunt quivered with dismay. She'd been enjoying listening to Corrigan talking about Pascal. She'd held her own.

She'd been hoping that he'd ask her for more quotations for she'd read so much Pascal on Corrigan's instructions that she'd memorised a lot of his work by heart.

' "*Tout le malheur des hommes vient d'une seule chose, qui est de ne savoir pas demeurer en repos dans une chambre.*" ' As Mrs Blunt remembered these lines, she found it unbearable to be asked to think about her daughter's tiny sum of missing money. Nadine's timing as she made her protest could hardly have been worse.

'I'll pay you back, darling,' Mrs Blunt said. She raised her hand and gave a dismissive little wave. 'Corrigan and I have filled a huge cooking-pot with money that we've collected for the disabled. You'll find it in the larder, Nadine. If you've lost a ten pound note, why don't you go and take another one from there.'

Her bland remark infuriated Nadine. She felt she had been humiliated by her mother. 'I'm not asking for you to pay me back!' she snapped. 'And I think it's outrageous that you suggest that I take money that belongs to the disabled. I'm asking you to find out what happened to the ten pound note that was in my handbag.'

Mrs Blunt looked abashed. Her daughter's anger always made her feel childishly afraid. 'I thought we'd settled all that,' she said. 'I thought we'd all agreed that you must have made some kind of a mistake.'

'But I didn't make any mistake. That's the whole point of what I'm trying to tell you. I think it's horrible that you don't mind when your servants take my money. Why do you have to protect that dishonest Mrs Murphy? I think it would be nicer if you tried to protect me.'

Sitting serenely in his chair on the sidelines, Corrigan watched mother and daughter with the cool eye of the spectator at a bantam fight.

'I don't think it's very nice of you to come to my house and start accusing my servants of theft, Nadine.' Mrs Blunt's cheeks were burning with agitation.

Nadine was hoping that Corrigan would side with her. She'd only reintroduced the unpleasant topic of the money because he'd goaded her on to do so. She felt that he'd forced her to try and make Mrs Blunt face up to the fact that she was employing a thief. If she took the easier course and dropped the whole matter, she was frightened that Corrigan would think she had very little concern for the welfare of her mother.

He was oddly passive as the dispute became more heated. Nadine couldn't understand why he chose to remain silent as he seemed to mistrust Mrs Murphy much more than she did.

'Mrs Murphy was very kind to me after your father died,' Mrs Blunt said. 'I think you should remember that, Nadine. I'll never forget her kindness until the day that I die.'

'But I was very kind to you too!' Nadine's voice had risen and become as plaintive as that of an offended child. 'Well, I certainly tried to be kind to you . . . But you wouldn't let me be kind, Mummy. You just seemed to want to shut yourself away. I really don't think you ought to take Mrs Murphy's side against me.'

'I know you were very kind to me, Nadine. And I'll always be grateful for everything you did for me. But that's not the point. I'm not taking Mrs Murphy's side. Remember that no one is accusing you of stealing, Nadine, and I certainly wouldn't allow anyone to make any such nasty accusations against you. I'd defend you with my last breath.'

'I don't need to be defended with your last breath!' Nadine no longer sounded plaintive. She had become too angry. 'I don't go helping myself to the money that I find in other people's handbags!'

'If Mrs Murphy was dishonest,' Mrs Blunt was stubborn, 'she'd have taken things before now. I told you there's a big kitchen pot in the larder and it's always full of money. Corrigan and I use that pot as our safe. But I can tell you that it's certainly not at all a safe place to store large sums of cash. All Mrs Murphy has to do is lift the lid and help herself. But I always count the money before Corrigan takes it up to the hospital. There's never once been a penny missing.'

'Mrs Murphy's sons seem to go in and out of detention centres,' Nadine said. 'I think the whole family is as crooked as corkscrews. I think they are all rotten to the quick.'

'Hold it, Nadine,' Corrigan suddenly interrupted. 'You should never judge a woman by her children.'

She found his remark very barbed. When she'd talked to him alone, she'd thought he was starting to like her, and she'd been prepared to tell him that she suffered from the impenetrable emotional wall that had always seemed to separate her from her mother. Now she felt bitter that she'd trusted him and she wished she'd never confided in him. He seemed to be trying to exacerbate the tensions between herself and Mrs Blunt rather than attempting to heal them. He'd betrayed her by making her feel it was her duty to challenge the honesty of Mrs Murphy and then he'd become wise and judicial and withdrawn and he'd listened disapprovingly to every point she made, as if he felt she was being cruel and unfair.

'When I suggested you take ten pounds from the pot in the larder, Nadine, I don't like you thinking that I was suggesting that you take money that has been raised for the handicapped.' Mrs Blunt spoke with great fervour. 'That would certainly be very wrong indeed. Naturally, I intended to replace any money you took from there. Of course I always intended to replace it from my own purse.'

Nadine suddenly had a seizure of hysterical anger which exploded with all the more force because her whole pent-up personality was accustomed to exerting self-control.

'I don't want anything from your purse!' she said. 'I'm not one of your cripples and I don't need any of your donations.'

Having uttered these unforgivable words in front of the paralysed Corrigan, Nadine felt that she only wanted to get out of her mother's house and never return.

This time she made no attempt to make a dignified sweeping exit. She went scuttling out of the dining-room feeling like a hen that was being chased by a broom. In her hysteria, she ran to the front door and she flung it open. She'd completely forgotten the ramp and she cursed it for being an ugly steel obstacle that seemed to have been deliberately erected to prevent her from making an escape.

She retraced her steps and went running through the kitchen where Mrs Murphy watched her with a quizzical and bulbous eye as she went rushing into the garden through the door that led out on the side.

> 'And the cow kicked
> Nelly, in the belly,
> In the barn,'

Mrs Murphy softly crooned as she watched Nadine through the kitchen window and saw her drive off in her yellow Cortina.

> 'And the old woman said,
> It won't do her any harm . . .

> 'Second verse,
> Same as the first . . .'

She went off to get the Irish bread that Mrs Blunt had asked her to bake that morning so there would be something special for Nadine's tea. She put it on a tray with some butter and raspberry jam and prepared to take it to the dining-room where Mrs Blunt was still sitting with Corrigan. 'She'll not touch a crumb,' Mrs Murphy thought. 'Not with Nadine going off like that, not with Corrigan having started her off drinking . . .'

When she carried the tray into the dining-room, she found Mrs Blunt in tears. Corrigan had drawn up his chair so that he was very close to her and he was trying to comfort her by stroking her hair.

'It's so awful that Nadine's gone,' Mrs Blunt was saying to him in choking tones. 'I always do something that upsets her and I never really know what I've done.'

'You shouldn't take your daughter's dramatic little exit too seriously,' he said. 'Dorothy Parker said that the only way you can keep your children at home is to let the air out of their tyres.'

Corrigan told Mrs Murphy that Mrs Blunt didn't feel like having any tea, that he thought she'd do better if she had another glass of champagne.

16

Months went by after Nadine's disagreement with her mother over the issue of Mrs Murphy's probity, and she made no effort to contact her and heal the rift.

She knew that she ought to apologise to Mrs Blunt for reminding her that she was not one of her cripples, but she was very loath to do so until Mrs Blunt herself apologised for having taken the theft of her money so blithely in her stride.

The only news that Nadine received about her mother in that period came from Sabrina. Her friend had laid on the fashion show for Corrigan and as Nadine had predicted, it had been a great success. Sabrina had been a little disappointed that neither Mrs Blunt nor Corrigan had been able to attend, for it had been a glittering occasion with many celebrities present, and she thought they might have enjoyed it. Such an event was not one that they would normally attend in the routine of their quiet, hard-working lives.

It appeared that Corrigan had not been well on the night that the fashion show had taken place, and Mrs Blunt had sent her apologies to Sabrina and expressed her disappointment that they were both unable to be present.

'What's wrong with Corrigan?' Nadine asked Sabrina.

But Sabrina didn't really know. She thought he'd been suffering from some chest infection.

Nadine found this information disquieting. She'd found it a solace to convince herself that it was pointless to feel any guilt about her mother now that she was so well cared for by

Corrigan, but if the man was to become gravely ill, she realised her mother would be in an appalling situation. She would never be able to cope with the needs of a seriously ailing cripple. And if Corrigan was to die . . . Nadine refused to think about this eventuality for she hardly dared to contemplate the effects it would have on her mother.

Sabrina was reassuring. She didn't believe his infection had been a serious one. Mrs Blunt had telephoned her to thank her for organising the show and she'd said that Corrigan was well enough to have resumed his fund-raising. Apparently she had just bought him a little car.

'A little car?' Nadine asked.

'Yes, it seems your mother has got him one of those little cars for invalids and now he's scooting all over the countryside like Toad of Toad Hall.'

'I wonder if they make special little helicopters for invalids.' Nadine's tone was sarcastic. 'If they do, you can be sure my mother will soon buy him one and then he can do all his fund-raising from the air.'

Sabrina said that Mrs Blunt sounded in very good form. Her farm was thriving and she was longing for the first crops. It seemed that St Crispins had now been furnished like an old country home and had an excellent library and many other recreational facilities. Rupert Sinclair had written to her to say that never in her wildest dreams could she estimate what beneficial effects all her improvements had made on the lives and morale of the inmates. Now that Mrs Blunt felt confident that she'd done all that was in her power to transform St Crispins, and make it as luxurious as possible, she now planned to devote her time and energies to raising money to help complete a similar transformation in various institutions around the country.

'My mother sounds well occupied,' Nadine remarked dryly.

Sabrina said that she thought this was true, but Mrs Blunt had given her a message that she'd very much like to hear from Nadine.

'She gets letters from Rupert Sinclair.' Nadine's response

was very childish. 'She gets endless letters from that man telling her what a great-hearted soul she is. That really ought to be enough for her. Why does she need to hear from me?'

*

Soon after Sabrina had laid on the fashion show, she withdrew from her modelling agency and enrolled in a tutorial college where she started studying for university. She told Nadine that she enjoyed the work and found it a relief that her body was no longer being 'colonised' by fashion photographers.

'I've bitten my nails to the quick,' she said. 'I never wash my hair any more. If I stay out late and get "bags", I rub ink under my eyes and make them much worse! It's really wonderful!'

Nadine felt that her life was becoming increasingly static with every day that passed. The twins were getting older, but she couldn't chalk that up as her personal achievement. She sometimes found herself thinking of the lines that Corrigan had quoted when she'd paid her last ill-fated visit to her mother. She couldn't remember them at all precisely, but the sense of them still remained in her brain. Without movement you might as well be dead. She felt everyone was moving except her. Sabrina was studying and hoping to pass her exams, Mrs Blunt was gallivanting around in her van, and Corrigan was speeding down the roads in his invalid car.

Only Justin and herself now seemed to lead a frozen existence. The articles that he kept writing appeared to be very much the same as the ones he'd written in the past. When he made appearances on his chat shows, he presented much the same spectacle as when he'd appeared on them before.

' "*Plus ça change, plus c'est la même.*" ' Her French was not good, so she found it strange that this phrase had remained in her mind. 'I am competing with my mother,' she thought. 'Oh, my God, I am becoming pathetic. I'm trying to outdo my mother in order to impress Corrigan!'

*

Nadine was making breakfast for the twins when the news

217

came. She answered the telephone and heard the voice of Mrs Murphy, who sounded hysterical and inarticulate. Mrs Blunt had been found lying dead in her bed. The doctor said she'd suffered from a heart attack. 'God bless her!' Mrs Murphy started sobbing noisily.

Nadine reacted with the serenity of those who have gone into shock. She started staring at various objects in her kitchen as if it was of the utmost importance that she made a precise mental record of every detail of their appearance. She looked at the red enamel-painted coffee pot that she'd once bought when she went with Justin to Holland. In her mind, she photographed its redness and the curves of its handle and its spout. She precisely recorded the band of small black leaves that encircled it. They were a belt of tiny shamrocks or maybe they were four-leaf clovers.

Nadine looked at her electric kettle and concentrated on the silvery gleam of its surface and the contrasting darkness of its cord. She felt like a moth, she was so attracted by the central highlight which shone out from its plump side like a tiny brilliant moon. She stared at three tomatoes which she'd put to ripen on the windowsill of her kitchen. Their redness matched her coffee pot and they too had highlights like the kettle. It all matched – it all made some kind of sense. As Nadine paid such careful attention to the appearance of all these familiar objects, she managed to wipe out any image of her mother lying chalk-faced in her bed. She avoided seeing her being roughly shaken by Mrs Murphy.

'Does Corrigan know?' Nadine asked. She found her own calm unnatural and wondered why she felt that he ought to be the first to be informed as if he was the most important member of the family.

Mrs Murphy said that Corrigan had dined with Mrs Blunt yesterday evening. They had eaten game pie in front of the fire and they had both drunk quite a lot of claret. Mrs Murphy had found all the bottles.

'Where is Corrigan now?' Nadine asked.

Mrs Murphy didn't know. He'd not been there when she arrived at the house in the morning. She assumed that he'd gone off to London yesterday evening. Mrs Murphy had noticed that he'd taken two of Mrs Blunt's paintings.

'Paintings? What paintings?' Nadine asked sharply.

Mrs Murphy explained that in the last few months Corrigan had persuaded Mrs Blunt to take up painting. He'd shown her work to some art gallery in London and they had been very excited by it.

'The first time she sold a picture she was like a child,' Mrs Murphy said. 'She was never a one for boasting. But I could see that she was over the moon.'

'She never told me that she had started painting,' Nadine said.

'Corrigan told her not to tell you.'

'Why on earth did he want it kept a secret?'

Mrs Murphy didn't quite know. She thought that Corrigan had made Mrs Blunt believe that it would upset Nadine.

'Why would it upset me? I'd have been very proud if I'd known that she was selling her paintings.'

'I think that Corrigan was after telling her you wouldn't like her to be getting professional – that it would make you jealous. You see, Corrigan didn't really want her to start giving away any of her pictures to you. When he sold them up in London it seems they were very popular and they were fetching very big prices.'

'How dare Corrigan tell her that I'd be jealous!' Nadine felt very indignant. She hated to hear that he'd been trying to poison her mother against her.

'Corrigan is Corrigan,' Mrs Murphy said.

'What sort of paintings did my mother do?' Nadine wondered why she kept talking about her mother's paintings rather than her death. She was so stunned by the news that all she could experience was a violent hurt that her mother had not told her about her most important achievement. She knew that Mrs Blunt would have certainly been 'over the moon' when she discovered that a London gallery was able to sell her work for very big prices. Nadine would have liked to have shared her pride in her accomplishment. Now she realised she would never be able to do so.

'Your mother did pictures of flowers. She did beautiful pictures with beautiful colours. You wouldn't have thought she'd have been able to paint them. But she'd work at them all day when she wasn't running round doing her bits and pieces for Corrigan.' Mrs Murphy started crying again and Nadine waited uncomfortably for her noisy bout of sobbing to subside.

'Do we know what time she died?' Nadine asked.

'The doctor said her heart attack must have struck her about midnight,' Mrs Murphy said. 'God bless her! She looked very peaceful when I found her. She was lying there in her bed and she had the look of a sleeping baby. She had a bottle of champagne on the table beside her.'

Nadine was quite shocked to hear this. She couldn't bear to think that her mother had become a solitary drinker. She'd known she was drinking a lot with Corrigan but she found it strange and disturbing to think of Mrs Blunt going up alone to her bed with a bottle of champagne. She wondered if her mother had become much more of an alcoholic than she'd ever realised, and if this had been the cause of her heart attack.

'She's better off where she is,' Mrs Murphy said.

Nadine had the suspicion that Mrs Murphy was going to bombard her with Irish sentiment and she didn't feel strong enough to listen to it. She told her that Justin would make all the arrangements for Mrs Blunt's funeral, that she would ask him to drive down to the country in the afternoon.

'Corrigan is going to be desperately upset,' Nadine said. Although she disliked Corrigan, she felt a little sorry for him. Presumably her mother had seemed in perfect health last night when he'd dined with her, otherwise he would surely never have left her. When he next came cheerfully wheeling down the drive to Mrs Blunt's house, he was going to be devastated to hear what had happened. He had lost the human being who very probably meant more to him than anyone else in the world. Nadine hoped that someone else would break the news to him. As the man had already had to put up with so much, she felt it would be extremely unpleasant to be the one to tell him that he'd suffered yet another tragedy.

'Yes, Corrigan is going to miss her,' Mrs Murphy said. 'It was a good thing she was with him for her very last night on earth.'

Nadine was wounded by this statement. She felt that she, herself, should have been with her mother yesterday evening and Mrs Murphy should also have wished this. As Mrs Murphy had never appeared to like Corrigan, she couldn't understand why she felt it was such a good thing that he'd been the last person to see Mrs Blunt alive.

'I offered to cook a dinner for her, Nadine. I offered to stay late. But she wanted to make the pie herself. She was funny that way. I'd have liked to have cooked her last meal for her.'

'I must go and tell my husband this awful news,' Nadine said.

But when she went to look for Justin, he handed her a list of the people that he'd asked to come to dine that night and she nodded blankly and he never noticed how strained and white she looked. She felt no desire to tell him the news that she'd just received from Mrs Murphy. Eventually he would have to be told, but she didn't want to do it yet. He would be pious and philosophical and remind her how quick and painless her mother's death had been and she knew that his clumsy consolations would offend her. She only wanted to tell Sabrina that her mother was dead. She knew that her friend would get into a taxi and come round to see her immediately. She felt that the fact that she dreaded telling Justin about an event that had such importance to her was final proof that her relationship with him was rotten beyond repair.

'If I didn't have Sabrina,' Nadine thought, 'I wonder what I'd do?'

Sabrina broke the news to Justin. She came round to see her friend as quickly as Nadine had known she would. She put Nadine to bed, because she was worried by the way she seemed so unnaturally serene and almost elated.

Sabrina arranged for the twins to be picked up from school and telephoned a domestic agency who sent round a temporary nanny so that Nadine could rest until the funeral was over.

Justin drove off down to the country to make all the

arrangements and Nadine was very glad when he left the house and she could be alone with Sabrina. Nadine didn't speak to her friend very much, but she was grateful when she brought her cups of tea.

Justin telephoned Nadine once he got to her mother's house. He boasted about the efficiency of the arrangements that he had made. He told her there would have to be an autopsy – but that was routine. Nadine listened with a look of dazed incomprehension on her face. Sabrina could see that she was not really taking any of this in.

Justin told Nadine that while he had been talking to the undertaker, Corrigan had suddenly arrived at the house. He'd come rolling up in his usual happy-go-lucky fashion and Justin had broken the news about Mrs Blunt's heart attack.

'I'm afraid, darling, that the poor chap was dreadfully cut up,' Justin said. 'I've never seen a man cry like that. He became quite hysterical.'

Nadine realised that Corrigan's reaction must have been very extreme for Justin to have noticed his distress. She envied Corrigan for being able to give vent to his feelings. Her own still seemed anaesthetised.

'Mrs Murphy gave Corrigan some whisky and now he's gone back to London,' Justin said. 'We told him the date of the funeral and he seems anxious to come to it.'

Nadine wondered if she was glad that Corrigan was coming to the funeral, or whether she resented it. As she seemed to have lost all feeling about anything, she couldn't really tell.

17

Corrigan arrived late for the funeral service. Mrs Blunt's coffin was being lowered into a grave beside that of the Colonel as he came wheeling down the cemetery path dressed in a black suit and a black tie.

Nadine hardly noticed his arrival for she seemed in a trance. As she stood there mute and frozen, she found that she mourned her imperfect relationship with her mother which could never now be improved.

Mrs Murphy, whose face was made to look as plump and circular as a pudding by the black headscarf that she'd wrapped around it, was crying so loudly that she didn't seem to hear his wheels approaching. But Sabrina felt that this black-haired cripple, dressed in such heavy mourning, looked like Death himself arriving with a rush of cold wind to the graveside. As the vicar finished the service, Corrigan bent over in his chair and held his head in his hands and Sabrina saw that tears were streaming down his cheeks. His posture of grief haunted her. She hoped that Nadine would overcome her dislike of him and invite him back to Mrs Blunt's house after the service. But Nadine did not do this. Whether she intended to snub him, or whether she was too dazed to remember to ask him, Sabrina was unable to decide. After the service, Corrigan went spinning out of the cemetery alone and vanished through the gateway that was flanked by two cypress trees. Sabrina saw him as a pitiful figure. She wondered what this lonely cripple's future was going to be.

A few days after Mrs Blunt's funeral, Nadine spoke to Sabrina on the telephone. She told her that she was starting to feel guilty about the way she had treated Corrigan. She now realised she'd been very cruel in not inviting him to come back to her mother's house after the burial service. Mrs Blunt would certainly not have wanted him snubbed like that. For her sake, she suddenly now wanted to apologise to him.

Sabrina was glad to hear this, for she thought that Nadine had been extremely unkind in not inviting him back to the house with the other mourners. Corrigan had come all the way down from London in order to attend the service. He was obviously grief-stricken, and Sabrina felt he should not have been allowed to go back to the city without anyone addressing a word to him.

Nadine found it difficult to explain that the alterations which Mrs Blunt had made to her house seemed more offensive since her death. When they'd gone back there to have tea after the funeral, Nadine had insisted that they should all go up to have it in her mother's bedroom. She'd found that everything still seemed peaceful and pleasant there, with the pale lilac walls, the dove-grey curtains, and all the flower prints. The Colonel was still gazing with mild authority out of innumerable silver-framed photographs. There was order and tranquillity in that room, with its bed with the snowy white quilt. There was no steel ramp, there was no sinister surgical equipment. Nadine felt that Corrigan had mutilated the rest of the house and she was thankful that his ravages had not extended to her mother's bedroom.

At the time, Nadine had felt very glad that she'd not invited Corrigan to come back with them, that she'd let him go wheeling off alone like a pariah in his suit of coal black mourning. At that moment, so soon after her mother's burial, she would have found it intolerable to have Corrigan as her guest in a house which she felt he'd despoiled.

But now, as she talked to her friend, she admitted that her callous treatment of this cripple was starting to weigh on her conscience.

'I think I ought to find Corrigan,' she said. 'I think I ought to see what's become of him.'

Sabrina told her that she knew the address of his hospital. Corrigan had given it to her when she'd put on the fashion show for his charity.

'My mother would have wanted me to see that Corrigan is all right,' Nadine said. 'I think I'll drive up to the hospital and they'll tell me where I can reach him.'

Sabrina found it peculiar that Nadine had not yet made any attempt to get hold of Mrs Blunt's will. She seemed to take it for granted that she was her mother's sole heir. In view of Mrs Blunt's unusual attachment to Corrigan, Sabrina felt this was most unlikely. After the funeral, when they had gone back to Mrs Blunt's house, Nadine had behaved as if she was its proprietor. Sabrina couldn't help thinking that her friend was being cocksure and unrealistic in automatically assuming that the house had been left to her.

She felt that there was a serious possibility that Mrs Blunt had bequeathed most of her property to Corrigan. When Nadine had refused to invite him back to the house, Sabrina thought that it would be ironic if she had excluded him from a house which would eventually turn out to be his own. She suspected that the idea that her mother might have left most of her fortune to Corrigan was so threatening to Nadine that she refused to allow it to enter her mind.

Sabrina was much too tactful to encourage Nadine to find out the contents of her mother's will, but she urged her to go and see Corrigan. She felt that the animosity and the rivalry that had existed between the two of them might be diminished by Mrs Blunt's demise. Sabrina knew that her friend was much more upset by her mother's death than she chose to show, and she felt that at this unhappy period of her life she might be quite glad to see Corrigan. He'd been so fond of Mrs Blunt and Nadine might find it a relief to talk to someone who could share her grief.

Sabrina saw that Justin was quite unaware of how badly affected his wife had been by the loss of her mother. He kept reminding her that she'd not seemed keen to visit Mrs Blunt in the last months of her life. His cruelty was none the less distressing to Nadine for being unconscious. Sabrina felt that Corrigan would be more understanding, for his disability seemed to have made him sensitive to the complexities and ironies of human relationships. She could see that her friend was suffering from her inability to make any reparation for the many hurts she now felt she'd inflicted on her mother. If Nadine was to treat Corrigan with sympathy and generosity, Sabrina thought it might help to assuage some of her guilt and they might form a relationship that would turn out to be rewarding to both of them.

Encouraged by her friend, Nadine set off in her car, hoping to discover Corrigan's whereabouts from the doctors at the hospital. She was wearing a neat little black suit with a nipped-in waist and her shiny brown hair had been set so that it curled inwards like that of a medieval page.

When she consulted her road-map, she saw that the street where St Crispins was situated was to be found in an area of grim and sprawling urban development that lay behind Paddington Station.

As she drove, she listened to music on the car radio in order to calm herself. She kept wondering what she was going to say to Corrigan when she found him. She would obviously have to apologise for her rude behaviour after the funeral and try and persuade him that it had not been intentional. She also wondered if she could bring herself to offer him the use of her mother's house even though the idea was not appealing to her. If it gave him a useful base from which to continue with his fund-raising, she saw no reason why he shouldn't be allowed to stay there for at least a few weeks. The house was equipped for his needs and no one else would be occupying it for a while. Eventually Nadine knew that she would have to rip out the hideous bathroom and all the surgical equipment which at present disfigured it, and she would have to do her best to repair the damage her mother had inflicted on it, for whether Nadine decided to make it her home and move there permanently with the twins, or whether she decided to place it on the market, she felt it was imperative that she should try to see that it regained some of its old period charm and beauty. For the moment, Nadine still felt too dazed and stunned by the shock of Mrs Blunt's death to make any clear plans for her own future.

She still recognised that she had reached a crucial point in her life, that her mother's fortune would enable her to leave Justin and set up her own *ménage* with the twins. Unlike Sabrina, she was not, in fact, at all worried that her mother might have disinherited her in favour of Corrigan. She believed that her mother had been much too responsible a character to allow her fondness for Corrigan to take precedence over her duty to her only child.

It took Nadine some time to find the street where St Crispins was situated. The area struck her as very seedy. The streets were dirty, the houses were grimy and dilapidated and many of them had their windows boarded up as if they were only waiting for demolition.

Eventually, after much circling she came to Billington Road where she'd been told that she would find the hospital. It was a particularly dismal, narrow little street. Two ill-fed-looking boys were kicking a ball in the centre. Rows of black plastic bags were stacked against the walls of the grimy houses. They were like decorations, like dark shining balloons, swelling with filthy foodscraps and rusty beer cans.

Nadine drove from one end of this unpromising street to the other. She soon realised that she must have been misdirected. There was not a sign of any building large and imposing enough to suggest that it was a medical institution. All the houses and shops were small and old and rickety, and the paint was peeling from their façades. She picked out a betting shop. She passed a laundromat and a little store that sold radios and plugs.

She wondered how Sabrina could have given her the name of this awful little road. Sabrina had obviously made a mistake when she'd got the address from Corrigan. Nadine rechecked the number of the street that her friend had given her. 'St Crispins, 15 Billington Road.' She decided she might as well find number fifteen, even though Sabrina seemed to have made some kind of error. Once she'd found the correct number Nadine decided she might as well give up and go home.

She finally found number fifteen. It looked like some kind of sleazy coffee bar. It had a yellow sign above it. Nadine read this sign with disbelief, 'St Crispins Pancake House'. Beside the door of number fifteen there was another huge painted wooden sign. It had a picture of a smiling monk. He was wearing brown robes and round his head there was a golden halo. 'Saint Crispin invites you to a tasty snack,' Nadine read. 'Come to Saint Crispins, Patron Saint of the Crispy Pancake.'

Nadine parked her car. She took a long time parking it because her knees were shaking and she wanted to park perfectly, but she seemed unable to get her wheels in a totally ideal relationship to the kerb.

When she finally entered the pancake house, she felt as dazed and numb as she'd felt at her mother's funeral. The interior was lit by fluorescent tubes of neon lighting which shed a bilious glow on the orange plastic tables and chairs which were dotted around. At the far end there was a steel counter with a formica top and behind it there was a hatch which opened into an evil-looking kitchen where a dark-haired woman was frying up greasy pancakes. Smoke came pouring out of this recess, filling St Crispins with the odour of ancient fat.

Nadine went over to the counter. Her thin legs in their high-heeled shoes were trembling so much that she was frightened she was going to collapse. As she approached, the woman stuck her head through the square hatch that led to the kitchen so that she was framed by it. She looked about sixty, but she was clearly making an effort to look younger. She had a cloud of gypsy-like hair which was dyed such an artificial black that it made a most unflattering contrast with her pale and raddled skin. She was wearing scarlet lipstick and a crumpled low-cut satin dress. When she smiled, her glossy lips parted to show she had gaps in her teeth and also a lot of gold. In her youth she had probably been quite handsome. Nadine thought she now looked like an ageing prostitute who was still making a bold play for clients. Something about her seemed familiar and she found this puzzling. She couldn't think where she could have seen this woman before.

'What flavour do you want, sweetheart?' the woman asked Nadine. Her accent was Irish. She pointed at a menu that was lying on the counter. On its cover there was another picture of the cheery St Crispin with his halo. This time he was depicted against a turquoise background. He was holding a frying pan and giving a holy smile as he tossed a golden pancake.

'Sweet or savoury?' the woman asked. Nadine picked up the menu. It was very sticky. Someone seemed to have covered it with maple syrup.

Nadine felt so weak and despairing she decided to order herself a pancake. She read through the menu with scrupulous attention as if she felt it to be of vital importance that she make the truly perfect selection.

'I'd like a chicken and onion savoury.' She hoped that wouldn't be quite as sickly as the pancakes that had fillings of raspberry and strawberry jam.

'Why don't you sit yourself down at a table. You might be more comfortable,' the woman said. 'Jimmy will bring you your pancake once I've fried it.'

Nadine felt quite grateful to the woman. She wondered if she'd made this kind suggestion because she'd realised that she was feeling giddy and was swaying dangerously on her stool.

She went and sat at one of the spindly orange plastic tables. There were other customers sitting around in this pancake house and she sensed that they were staring at her with great hostility as if they felt she had no right to be there wearing her expensive little tailored suit of mourning and her spotless white blouse with a frill.

Nadine hated the atmosphere in this rundown eating house. In the corner she noticed that there was a bunch of youths with shaven heads and weak vicious faces. They were all wearing ear-rings and this reminded her of the pirates she'd read about in the gaily illustrated books of her childhood. But whereas she'd always accepted that pirates would slit your throat with a cutlass, she'd still managed to see them as glamorous. This group of unpleasant adolescent pirates had no glamour for Nadine. She felt they would be quite prepared to slit her throat in order to grab her patent-leather handbag that was hanging on a strap from her shoulder, and they would use switch-blades which had none of the romance of cutlasses.

She was puzzled by a peculiar scented smell that was drifting through St Crispins. It mingled strangely with the fumes of rancid fat floating out of the kitchen. She wondered why it evoked ill-defined memories of religious occasions that she'd attended as a child with her parents. The bazaars of India came back to her. They wafted insidiously in that mysterious perfumed scent. It made her remember high Anglican church services and choirboys and the inspirational chords of organ music. Death and marriages seemed to float together in that smell. They seemed identical, yet different. Nadine felt she could no longer tell one thing from another.

She slowly realised that she'd only tried to give the smell some holy and elevated associations because the whole atmosphere in this pancake house exuded evil and she was terrified. When she tracked down its source, it was not at all exotic. It was coming from the little group of thuggish boys. As they stared with greed at her handbag they were passing each other joints of pot.

'I am ill,' Nadine thought. She waited for Jimmy to bring her a pancake. Feeling so ill she began to wonder if it mattered whether Corrigan ever came from a hospital for the disabled.

Jimmy slapped down a chicken savoury pancake on the unwiped plastic table where she was sitting. 'Coffee or chocolate?' he asked her. Jimmy seemed real to Nadine in the sense that when he claimed that he was producing a pancake, you soon saw it lying there on a plate in front of you. He was a little squirt of a boy whose whole energies seemed to have gone into cultivating a crop of acne boils. They bloomed on his face like little red- and creamy-topped roses. He was dressed like a chef. He wore a classical white chef's uniform, a classical tall white hat. But there was something ludicrous about his culinary uniform. It didn't fit him and it was very dirty. The fluorescent lighting of this pancake house allowed every stain to show up.

As Nadine looked at his jacket, she was reminded of Joseph's coat of many colours.

'Chocolate or coffee?' he repeated.

'Chocolate – no coffee,' she said. Her pancake lay on its plate in front of her. She thought it looked as desolate as an expiring bullet-ridden soldier in a khaki army greatcoat.

In the corner of St Crispins the little gang of cruel-mouthed boys wearing ear-rings continued to retain their interest in her gleaming patent-leather shoulder bag. Their eyes X-rayed it as if they could see through its shiny surface and detect the wealth of credit cards, all the cash, and the car keys that it contained.

'I am in danger here,' Nadine thought. 'I should leave at once.'

She felt too weak to leave. She needed time to absorb the shock of her discovery. She remembered Mrs Blunt's childish excitement about her farm, her house-to-house fund-raising, all her plans for improving the hospital. She would never become aware of the extent of her humiliation, but her daughter now experienced it. When she saw the gang of boys laughing as they whispered and discussed her, she felt they had every right to laugh.

There were other people sitting at the orange plastic tables. Feeling sea-sick with humiliation, Nadine saw there were some older men wearing tweed caps. They had grey stubble on their chins. They were smoking pipes and, like the boys, they conversed in conspiratorial whispers. They looked just as ruthless as the youths, but Nadine felt that whatever nefarious pursuits they engaged in would be carried out with much more skill and sense of purpose.

At one table very close to Nadine's, there was a very old man who seemed to be using St Crispins as a warm place to sleep. In front of him he had an empty vodka bottle which he'd presumably brought in from outside. His hands and his clothes looked filthy and his boots had great holes that showed his grimy, pink-black toes. He was slumped over the table and his head was resting on a plate holding a pancake so that the top of his snowy hair was stained with a streak of raspberry jam.

Nadine found herself envying this ancient man. He was

untroubled by any loss of dignity. He could sleep soundly. In his dreams, he had very probably left St Crispins.

The youths put some coins in a juke-box in the corner. The music blared 'You said – that – I – was the only one . . .'

Nadine wondered if she ought to ask the dark woman in the kitchen if she'd ever heard of Corrigan. A very frightening thought then occurred to her. Supposing he was to suddenly come in? What would he do to her if he found her snooping round his headquarters? What would he get all those youths, all those men with grey stubble, to do to her?

She rose unsteadily to her feet and once again approached the formica counter. The dark woman's face appeared through the hatch. She seemed to think that Nadine wanted another pancake.

'Do you know of someone called Corrigan?' Nadine asked. 'I think he comes here sometimes.'

The woman looked at her suspiciously. Her eyelashes were clogged with a paste of black mascara.

'Corrigan?' she said. 'Why do you ask me that?'

'I am trying to get in touch with him,' Nadine stuttered. The woman was scrutinising her clothes as if they could give her some clue as to the reasons why such a conventional-looking girl was asking to see Corrigan.

'So many people come in and out of this place – I hardly knows the names of any of them,' she said evasively. 'I don't remember any fellow called Corrigan.'

She still seemed extremely interested in Nadine's clothes and she continued to examine them with a shrewd eye as if she was trying to estimate the cost of every single item. 'Are you a friend of his?' she asked.

'What a liar this woman is,' Nadine thought. 'She pretends she's never heard of him and then she asks me if I'm his friend.'

'Yes, I'm a very good friend.' She'd suddenly decided that she was also going to lie.

'Are you one of his girlfriends?' the dark woman asked. 'He's always somewhere in the country with a girlfriend. He won't ever tell me where he is. He won't ever tell me who he's with. He turns up, when he turns up. Ever since he was a child, he's always been like that. Very secretive . . . He uses this place when it suits him. I get on with my own business. I never expect anything from him. He does very well for himself. But I'd be the fool of all time if I was ever to rely on Corrigan.'

'So you do know him,' Nadine said quickly. 'Have you any idea where I can reach him?'

'I'll ask the boys,' the dark woman said. 'One of the boys might know where you could reach him. They keep track of him more than I do.'

She leaned out of her hatch and shouted across the room to the group of men with grey stubble on their chins who were smoking pipes and talking in soft whispers.

'Robinson!' she shouted. 'There's a girl here looking for Corrigan.'

'Oh, my God!' Nadine thought. 'Sabrina wrote the cheque for the fashion show to someone called Robinson.'

The group of men looked up and they all stared at Nadine with the same sullen suspicion she'd seen on the face of the dark woman when she'd first made her inquiry.

'Why does she want to reach Corrigan?' one of the men asked. Nadine assumed that he must be Robinson. He was a massive fellow with a puce complexion that suggested he drank a lot. He was more flashily dressed than his companions, and was wearing a tweed jacket with a gaudy yellow and mustard design. He had a scarlet kerchief round his neck and his shoes looked very shiny and new. He had the self-indulgent arrogance of a successful and dishonest bookie.

'Corrigan could be anywhere,' he said. 'None of us have seen him for quite a while.'

'You see how it is,' the dark woman said to Nadine, 'he turns up when he turns up, and there's no future in your hanging around here waiting for him.'

Nadine paid for her pancake and her coffee.

'T'is a pity we couldn't be more help to you,' the dark woman said. 'Is there any message you want to leave for him? I'll give it to him the next time that he comes in.'

'There's no message,' Nadine said. As she walked unsteadily towards the door, she received yet another shock. She noticed that standing against one of the walls in isolated splendour, and looking extremely out of place in the general décor of St Crispins with all its orange plastic and its bright gleam of formica, there was an imposing Louis-Seize varnished commode. It had very fine and intricate ormulu handles.

18

When Nadine got back to her house after visiting the pancake house, her first impulse was to telephone Mrs Murphy. She had to tell someone about her horrible discovery and she thought that she might know something about Corrigan.

She rang her at her home and one of Mrs Murphy's sons told her that his mother had gone over to Mrs Blunt's house in order to sort out her clothes.

When Nadine finally reached her there, Mrs Murphy was in a very charged and emotional state, for her task had upset her.

'It broke my heart to see your mother's shoes lying there all ready for her in the cupboard,' she said. 'I've been packing them up in boxes.'

Nadine thanked her for doing this and then told her that she'd just been up to Corrigan's hospital and she'd discovered that it didn't exist.

'Now that's no surprise to me,' Mrs Murphy said.

'You mean you always knew!'

'Oh, sure, I knew from quite early on – I knew that Corrigan was never a cripple.'

Nadine was so shocked that she found it hard to speak. 'But Mrs Murphy! Why on earth didn't you tell my mother? Why didn't you say anything to me?'

Mrs Murphy said that she hadn't wanted to worry Nadine. 'I felt you had enough on your plate, taking care of the twins.'

Nadine suddenly felt like crying. 'I really think that the way that you have behaved is quite unforgivable. I simply don't understand how you could have allowed my mother to be fooled by that dreadful creature.'

'Corrigan did a lot that was good for her,' Mrs Murphy said stubbornly.

Nadine was infuriated by Mrs Murphy's unruffled attitude.

'Oh, yes, Corrigan certainly did a lot that was good for her! He wrecked her house, he took thousands of pounds from her under false pretences!'

'Oh, yes, I know that he did all that. But Corrigan loved her, none the less.'

'What do you mean, Mrs Murphy? How can you say that he loved her? I've never heard anything so ridiculous.'

'Corrigan loved your mother, Nadine. I saw that when he came down that day to the house when your husband was here arranging the funeral. That day I did some kind of a test on him. I only did it to tease him. But it made him start weeping like a baby, and it was the way that he started weeping that made me know that he loved her.'

'Corrigan has turned out to be a complete crook and a fraud, Mrs Murphy. I don't find his tears very moving. I only long to have him reported to the police. I'm determined to have him tracked down.'

'Ach, sure, you can track him down, Nadine. But I wonder if you'd be well advised to do that.'

'Of course I'm going to track him down, Mrs Murphy. Corrigan is the most revolting confidence man, he is the most disgusting fraud and trickster.'

'Oh, I know that Corrigan did his best to get all that he could from her, but Corrigan was no different from most men. They all try to get the most that they can squeeze out of a woman. But he gave her a lot.'

Nadine found Mrs Murphy exasperating. She was maddened by her sentimental and forgiving attitude towards Corrigan. Yet she suspected that Mrs Murphy knew more about this diabolical man than she did, and she wanted to ask her a few more questions before she put down the telephone with a hysterical and hectic slam.

236

'When you say you tested Corrigan, Mrs Murphy, could you tell me what kind of test you made?'

Mrs Murphy said that she'd been in Mrs Blunt's kitchen, cooking, when Corrigan had rolled up in his chair.

'Your mother was lying there like an angel upstairs in her bedroom. Your husband had told me that he was hungry. He'd been complaining that he'd missed his lunch because he'd had to drive down all the way from the city to meet with the undertaker. So I started frying up the bits and pieces that I found in your mother's refrigerator.'

'Yes, yes,' Nadine said. She could hardly bear to hear Mrs Murphy's account. She could all too easily imagine Justin behaving in a bossy and authoritative fashion as he arrived at the house of her dead mother. Justin had the sensitivity of a telephone pole. Nadine could understand that his first and dominating impulse would be to make Mrs Murphy cook him a meal.

'I lit your husband a fire,' Mrs Murphy said. 'I tried to make it warm for Justin so that he could do his business with the undertaker. They were both in the dining-room together eating the mutton chops that I'd fried up for them, when Corrigan arrived.'

Nadine could visualise the scene. It was not one that she cared to dwell on.

'Bang! Bang! Corrigan came smashing up the ramp that your mother had made for him,' Mrs Murphy said. 'He was still using his chair. He couldn't have come to her house without it.'

'I'm going to track down that awful man, Corrigan,' Nadine said. 'I promise you that I'm going to see that Corrigan is prosecuted if it's the very last thing on earth that I do.'

'Prosecutions are prosecutions. Seamus and Patrick are always being prosecuted. It never does them too much good, in my frank opinion.'

'I want Corrigan put in jail, Mrs Murphy.'

'But that won't help your mother.'

'Nothing can help my mother now. But if I can get Corrigan put in jail, it will stop him playing the same tricks on any other unfortunate people.'

'But your mother wouldn't want you to do that to Corrigan, Nadine. Your mother wouldn't want you to go persecuting a cripple.'

'But Corrigan isn't a cripple, Mrs Murphy. You know that perfectly well. I don't understand why you are suddenly calling that odious man a cripple!'

'Sure, I think that Corrigan must be some kind of cripple, Nadine. It's only a cripple that would enjoy pulling the wings off a poor little dove of a creature like your mother.'

'You don't seem to be very consistent, Mrs Murphy. One moment you tell me that you think that Corrigan did so much for my mother. The next moment you say that he was pulling off her wings.'

'He was doing both.'

Nadine said that she couldn't see there was much evidence that Corrigan had done anything very positive for Mrs Blunt. He'd made a complete fool of her. She refused to believe that his feelings towards her mother had not been entirely malevolent.

'Now, that's not true,' Mrs Murphy said. 'I told you that I tested Corrigan when he came to the house.'

'How did you test him?'

'Well, you know that Corrigan always hated the Colonel?'

'But that's complete nonsense. Corrigan never even met my father. How could he hate him?'

'I know that he never met him, but he hated the Colonel all the same. He didn't like seeing the Colonel's photographs all over the place. He didn't like her going to the grave. You see, the Colonel took her attention away from him, and Corrigan was a man who couldn't stand for that. He was the same with the other cripple that he'd invented. Your mother was always writing to Rupert Sinclair. She was always sending him gifts and cigars and champagne. At the beginning, Corrigan liked her doing that. But after a while he didn't care for it at all. He didn't like Rupert Sinclair being so much in her thoughts. It made Corrigan angry when she wrote to him because he felt that her attention was wandering away from him.'

'Corrigan sounds completely unbalanced. How could he be jealous of a man who he'd invented himself? I've never heard of anything more absurd.'

'Corrigan was like that.'

Nadine wished that Mrs Murphy wouldn't sound so philosophical.

'When I teased Corrigan, I said to him that your mother was now where she'd always really wanted to be – that she'd joined the Colonel. And Corrigan's face went all dark and he got this savage miserable look in his eyes and then he burst out with this terrible fit of crying and I knew that he wasn't only crying because he'd lost her – he was crying because he couldn't abide the idea that she'd gone to join the Colonel!'

'I don't trust Corrigan's tears, Mrs Murphy.'

'I believed they were real, Nadine. If he hadn't had some feeling for your mother, he'd never have cared if she'd gone off and left him to join the Colonel.'

Nadine felt it was useless to argue with Mrs Murphy. She asked her why she thought Corrigan had gone down to her mother's house, why he had bothered to go to the funeral. Once Mrs Blunt was dead and he couldn't get much out of her any more, she'd have expected Corrigan to vanish.

Mrs Murphy thought that he must have decided that it would look suspicious if he disappeared too abruptly. 'I don't think Corrigan wanted you poking into his background, Nadine – not till her will was read.'

'I don't see how my mother's will comes into it.' Nadine suddenly sounded very agitated. She couldn't bear to think about the will. She felt there was something immoral in seizing a dead person's possessions – it seemed too heartless and final an act. Scavengers robbed dead soldiers of their watches when they were lying on the battlefield, and Nadine felt that if she was to take all her mother's money and belongings, in some way she would be profiting corruptly from her decease. She found that she had much the same resistance to accepting bounty from her mother in death that she'd always had in life. Yet her feelings on this subject were ambivalent. She hoped to be Mrs Blunt's sole beneficiary for she needed some comforting symbolic proof that her jagged relationship with her mother, at the end, had finally been repaired.

Also the idea that the snake-like Corrigan might take one penny from her mother's estate was too horrifying to her, and she preferred to cast all thoughts of the will from her mind, and blithely assume that Mrs Blunt would have had far too much honour and good sense to deprive her only living relatives of their rightful inheritance.

She was still shattered by Mrs Murphy's assumption that Corrigan was counting on the contents of the will. She found it terrifying to think that he'd appeared at her mother's funeral in order to appear in the role of staunch and grieving friend, so that when he received whatever he assumed she'd bequeathed him, no one would question his right to receive it.

Mrs Murphy then told Nadine that she felt certain there had been several reasons why Corrigan had chosen to go down to Mrs Blunt's house, the day after her death. He wanted to see her for the last time.

'Corrigan kept telling me that he wished that he could go upstairs to pay her a last visit, and he looked all white and twitching. And I was thinking that if the man would just stop fooling and get out of his chair, there was nothing to stop him from going up to say goodbye to her. But poor Corrigan never got to pay his last respects to your mother because he couldn't go bounding up the stairs on his legs – not with Justin and the undertaker and myself all staring at him. So he had to go on playing the cripple and he had to stay down on the ground floor.'

'Poor Corrigan. I pity him,' Nadine said with sarcasm.

'But he minded, Nadine. That's what you won't believe.'

'What were Corrigan's other reasons for going down to the house? He wanted to say his romantic farewell to my poor mother. What else did he want to do?'

'I think he wanted to pretend that your mother's death came as a big surprise to him. He put on quite a show when Justin told him about it. He kept saying "Oh, no! Oh, no!" and he acted very shocked and he held his head in his hands.'

'But to be fair to Corrigan, Mrs Murphy, it must have been quite a shock to him.'

'It couldn't have come as all that much of a shock to him,' Mrs Murphy said. 'He didn't want any of you to know it – but Corrigan was with her at the moment that she died.'

'But, Mrs Murphy! Why on earth didn't you tell me this? You said he'd gone off to London – that he'd gone off taking her paintings!'

'I only said that when I got over to the house in the morning there was no sign of Corrigan.'

'But this is awful, Mrs Murphy! If Corrigan was with my mother when she had her heart attack, why didn't he call the doctor? Why was a doctor not called until the next morning?'

'There's no point in your getting yourself all upset about it, Nadine. There's nothing you can do about it. There's nothing any of us can do. Your mother is out of all harm now.'

Nadine suddenly found it intolerable to continue this conversation with Mrs Murphy. The woman's whole attitude towards Corrigan was unintelligible to her. Nadine couldn't understand how she could have so few illusions about Corrigan and yet also seem to condone his behaviour. She still found it utterly sickening that Mrs Murphy had never warned her mother that she was the victim of this unscrupulous creature. She wondered if there could be some kind of sinister collusion between Mrs Murphy and Corrigan. Why didn't Mrs Murphy seem troubled by the fact that he had allowed her mother to die without making any effort to save her? How did Mrs Murphy know that Corrigan had been with Mrs Blunt at the very last moments of her life? Had Mrs Murphy also been there that evening with Corrigan, and not, as she pretended, cooking dinner for her sons? Could Corrigan have done something awful to Mrs Blunt? Could he have done something that had caused her death?

All these questions were so disturbing to Nadine that she decided it was wiser not to put them to Mrs Murphy. She felt too battered by recent events and she had reached a point when she hardly trusted anyone. She thanked Mrs Murphy for all the information she'd given her. As usual, whenever she was distraught, Nadine only wanted to speak to Sabrina.

That evening Nadine fell ill and began to run one of the same shivering fevers that had often plagued her when she'd been separated from her parents and felt desperate and helpless in her grim, unfamiliar English boarding school.

She tried to reach Sabrina, but failed to do so because her friend was visiting Coco in his hospital. Nadine retired to her bed. Justin came to see what she was doing about dinner and was annoyed rather than sympathetic when he saw the shivering, agitated state that his wife was in.

'Why don't you take an aspirin, darling?' he said. 'If you took an aspirin and had a bath, I'm sure you'd feel well enough to run up something for us to eat. You can cook in your dressing gown if you want to. I promise you, I don't mind. You don't have to dress up at all. Once we've eaten you can go right back to bed.'

'I'm really too weak to cook, Justin. And I don't think aspirin can help me,' Nadine said.

She felt her fever rising. She had a headache that made it seem as if two hypodermic needles were injecting poisons into her brain. One moment she felt burning hot, the next moment she was shivering with cold. She would shut her eyes and just lie there. She'd then open them with a little start of terror. Justin couldn't think what was wrong with his wife. He found her behaviour alarmingly out of character. When Nadine felt unwell, she normally refused to admit it. Usually she was very plucky and she became almost more active and efficient around the house than when she felt well. It was as if she had a knack of drawing additional nervous energy from any malady.

'Oh, please don't leave me,' she suddenly said to Justin. She never usually made such requests and he found it disturbing.

He could see no point in staying with her. He'd suggested she take an aspirin and she'd stupidly refused. If she was unable to cook dinner he was going to eat out in a local restaurant. Nadine might not be hungry, but he was very hungry. He couldn't see why she wanted him to hang around. He could be of little use to someone who kept lying there with her eyes shut and then, just when he thought she was asleep, would open them with a little scream as if she'd woken from a nightmare. He couldn't understand that she only wanted him to remain, disapproving and impatient, by her bed, because she was frightened to be left alone.

Her husband knew nothing about her visit to St Crispins Pancake House, he knew nothing about her disquieting conversation with Mrs Murphy. He couldn't understand that every time she closed her eyes her brain teemed with terrifying questions and images. Had Corrigan really murdered her mother? Could he have poisoned her? Could he have pushed her down the stairs? The doctor who'd been sent for by Mrs Murphy had apparently found no evidence of foul play. But then he was only a simple country fellow and it wouldn't occur to him to look for it.

If Mrs Blunt's death had been a natural one, why had Corrigan been so afraid to let anyone know that he'd been with her when she died? Nadine found that sinister in the extreme. Even if he hadn't directly caused her death, he'd deprived her of any chance of recovery by his refusal to summon any medical assistance. Nadine found this tantamount to murder.

'Is there anything in the kitchen that I could heat up?' Justin asked.

There was nothing. There was no casserole. After she returned from the pancake house, she'd felt too shaken and demented to prepare anything for dinner. After speaking to Mrs Murphy, she'd found herself unable to bear the idea of handling any meat. Meat had too much blood in it. Meat reminded her of murder.

'Could you get me a doctor, Justin?' she suddenly asked him. 'I think I may be dangerously ill.'

He looked alarmed, for he'd hardly ever known her ask for a doctor. She'd regularly attended a gynaecologist for check-ups when she was pregnant with the twins. But otherwise she used her own remedies to cure herself whenever she felt ill. She would gargle with salt, drink hot lemon and whisky, take massive doses of vitamin C.

Justin saw that she certainly looked very flushed and that her hair was damp with perspiration. He decided she might well be as dangerously ill as she claimed. He went off and called a doctor and he never realised that his wife was secretly disappointed when the man arrived. Justin had no way of knowing that she was playing out one of the most terrifying of the images that kept haunting her. She was trying to relive what she saw as the last agonising experience of her unfortunate mother. Whenever Nadine closed her eyes, she kept seeing Mrs Blunt lying moaning and writhing on the floor. She was reaching out her arms and imploring Corrigan to get her a doctor who might relieve her terrible pain. But he just sat there watching her. He never moved from his invalid chair. He had a little smile on his carved lips and his eyes were glittery and very cold. Once Nadine reached the end of this sequence, she would open her eyes with that odd little scream that made Justin wonder if she was losing her sanity. She always opened her eyes because she couldn't bear to see it all through until the end.

The doctor said that Nadine was suffering from glandular fever. She lay as weak as a dying sparrow on her pillows and listened to his diagnosis with such a deep lack of interest, she might have been listening to his report on the medical condition of someone she'd never met.

This very same doctor had attended the twins throughout all their childish diseases. She had a vague memory that he'd always said they had glandular fever whenever their varied symptoms were beyond his powers of diagnosis.

He prescribed some antibiotics and some medicine to make her sleep. Justin became rather hushed and awed as he heard the gravity of his wife's condition. He stood there listening, very tall, nodding very seriously. He did his best to be nice to Nadine and offered to fetch her prescriptions and take the twins round the corner to eat a hamburger. Nadine felt so hazy and fevered that she hardly knew what was happening all round her. But she still vaguely wondered if their meal together would be a success. It occurred to her with wonderment that it would be the first time since their birth that Roland and Felix would have eaten with their father alone.

The meal was a catastrophe. When Justin came back, he told his wife that the table manners of the twins were abominable, that they'd never stopped squabbling.

She found it really rather astonishing that this had come as such a shock to him. He told Nadine that when she felt better, she'd really got to do something to discipline them. As she felt no better, and felt quite a bit worse, she lay back and once again closed her eyes. Even if Justin's meal with the twins had not been what he'd hoped for, his surprise should not have been so great. They'd all eaten – no one was hungry. Beyond that she couldn't care.

Despite the doctor's sleeping medicine, she slept very badly. All through the night she was plagued by haunting images of her dead mother. She remembered Mrs Blunt going off alone to the graveyard in her pale cream raincoat while she'd stayed behind to play Monopoly. She remembered the contorted savage expression she'd seen on Corrigan's face when he'd stared at her mother and herself through the iron gates of the cemetery. Later, he had become jaunty and debonair and charming, and she'd chosen to forget that she'd ever seen that menacing expression. But now the buried memory rose again whenever she closed her eyes.

Nadine couldn't believe that she deserved to sleep, knowing that she'd allowed her frail little gentle mother to be left all alone in a deserted country house with a pseudo-crippled criminal.

*

The next day Nadine made a valiant effort to recover and managed to get out of bed. She was still very weak, and her head still felt as if it was being pierced by very fine needles. But she organised the future household meals, she cleaned all the bathrooms, vacuumed the carpets and sorted out the children's sports outfits so that the twins would be prepared for their important forthcoming school football match.

As her fake energy started to fail, she felt resentful that Justin refused to employ a cleaner to help her with the housework. This had originally been her own fault, although today she would not admit it. When she'd first got married to Justin, she'd been so eager to parade her prodigious domestic efficiency that she'd successfully persuaded him that to employ any outside help would be a ludicrous waste of money.

Although, recently, Justin had seemed increasingly displeased with all the work that she did in his household, he seemed to be expressing a generalised dissatisfaction rather than a precise one. Whenever she suggested that he ought to employ a professional housekeeper who'd do a better job than she could, her husband's attitude changed immediately. He became instantly appreciative of her efforts. No one, he claimed, could run the house better than she did. He seemed to forget that a few weeks ago he'd come into her immaculate kitchen, and finding little to reproach her for, had squeezed his hand down the back of the refrigerator where he'd discovered the tiniest ball of congealed fluff. He had become incensed and obsessed by his findings and had warned her that it was highly dangerous to create such unhygienic conditions, and claimed that her lazy, slovenly habits were jeopardising the health of himself and the twins.

Nadine had smarted under this unjust criticism, but she had made no protest and, compressing her lips, she'd gone off to wash her hair. She always washed her hair whenever she was criticised. It was as if she was trying to purge it of the imaginary dandruff with which any lack of approbation seemed to sprinkle it.

Today as she felt her fever returning and was still tackling all the chores like a robot, she saw her own patience as an illness. She felt it would consume her if she didn't get out of the house. She had to tell someone that she could think of nothing else except her mother's possible murder. She made several frantic telephone calls to Sabrina and finally she reached her.

They met in the Italian restaurant. The waiters, the Chianti, and the pasta were much the same as usual, but her friend soon realised that Nadine was in a far more unstable condition than she'd ever seen her in before. Sabrina had spent a lot of time in Coco's hospital in the last weeks, and Nadine's eyes had much the same glazed and tormented expression that she'd seen in the eyes of the female patients who were being treated there for nervous depressive illness.

'Oh, my God! Corrigan really is a bastard!' Sabrina exclaimed once she'd listened to Nadine's description of her visit to St Crispins.

'Can you imagine what a fool I feel when I think of all the time and effort I put into arranging that bloody fashion show! We managed to raise really rather a spectacular sum for his hospital. I wonder what he did with it?'

'I wonder what he did with any of our money.' Nadine's voice sounded low and very bleak.

'I suppose we ought to try to see it as a joke. There's not much else we can do. If we were all such idiots, I suppose that in a way we deserved it.'

'I don't see it as much of a joke, Sabrina. Nor do I think that my mother deserved it.'

'I'm sorry, Nadine. I should never have said that. Of course she didn't deserve it. But she had much more excuse for being fooled by Corrigan than we did. She was such an over-protected and unworldly figure. She wasn't very young. She was also not very happy.'

'I was never really fooled by Corrigan, Sabrina. I know that you rather liked him. I never liked him at all.'

'I know that you never liked him. But you couldn't have really known what he was up to. Otherwise you'd have surely done something to expose him.'

Nadine couldn't answer this. Her friend's sensible comment had triggered off her deepest feelings of guilt. If she'd only gone down to see her mother more often she could have studied Corrigan more closely. If she'd only gone down to the country more often, he might never have gained such ascendancy over her mother. If . . . If . . . If . . .

'Do you realise that Corrigan not only pocketed all the proceeds from the fashion show, Nadine, but it was worse than that. I gave him quite a tidy little sum that I raised myself by trailing round all the other flats in my building and knocking on the doors. Do you know I nearly reduced the wretched occupants to tears, I became so emotional as I described the plight of Rupert Sinclair and his fellow sufferers. Bloody hell! I'd like to put Corrigan in his wheelchair and roll him off a cliff!'

'You can't imagine what I'd like to do to him, Sabrina.'

'Well, I can, Nadine. I promise you that I really can. Do you know that Corrigan nearly got me on to the streets. I was all prepared to go. He'd armed me with his confounded white paper flags. It was only the decadence and inertia of my nature that saved me from a fate worse than death!'

'Where did you send all the money you raised for him?' Nadine asked.

'I sent my money to the same place that your mother always sent her money. I made out my cheques to a Mr Robinson who I was told was the secretary of St Crispins, and I suppose that Corrigan used them as a filling for one of his pancakes!'

'The whole thing is really ghastly.' Nadine wished that Sabrina would seem less amused and gleeful. Sabrina appeared to view Corrigan's corrupt conduct with a fascinated delight as if she almost found it admirable. She was hurt and astonished by her friend's insensitive reaction. But then she reminded herself that she'd not yet told her that there was a very serious possibility that Corrigan might have killed her mother.

'I just adore the way that the man was so high-minded Nadine. Has there ever been a person with such delicate scruples – such serious and thought-provoking principles? He filled me with shame. But then I suspect that the ability to evoke shame was one of the "specialities" of Corrigan's particular "*maison*".'

'I don't find it amusing, Sabrina. I'm afraid that all Corrigan's lies and poses weren't nearly as harmless as you think.'

'I don't see them as harmless. But I still find them interesting to examine. I'm trying to reconstruct my only meeting with Corrigan. In the light of your discovery of the pancake house, every detail of his behaviour seems worth remembering.'

'I think they are only worth remembering if they can be of use to the police,' Nadine said. 'Otherwise they are just sickening and I'd prefer not to hear them.'

'I have an image of Corrigan that still remains with me and it's still very vivid,' Sabrina said. 'It may not be of much use to the police, but it's certainly of interest to me. Your mother had just cooked us all lunch. She'd made us roast lamb with all sorts of vegetables and garnishes. I was astonished when Corrigan went off to the kitchen. He came wheeling back, carrying a huge butler's tray with this great massive roast on it and all the plates and cutlery. He was holding it in one hand balanced high above his head, while with his other hand he propelled himself along. The strength of the man was amazing and so was his sense of balance. It was really a feat. I should have known there was something strange about it. But I was as innocent as your mother. I was just as impressed by the expertise of his balancing trick as I was impressed by his beautiful delicate carving.'

'I remember Corrigan's carving,' Nadine said. 'He was very good at that. He really carved my mother up in little pieces.'

'But let's analyse some of his techniques, Nadine. I'm sure it would be worth our while.'

Sabrina was trying to persuade her friend that it was futile to take Corrigan's perfidious exploits too seriously. She felt that the whole thing should be viewed with fatalism. Mrs Blunt had been taken for a ride. But the poor woman was dead now and Corrigan could no longer continue to exploit her. The money that he'd taken from her could never be recovered so there seemed little point in grieving about it. The only thing that Sabrina found seriously disturbing were the undisclosed contents of Mrs Blunt's will.

'When I was first introduced to Corrigan,' Sabrina said, 'he treated me like some exotic flower with a perfume so subtle that only he could appreciate its true fragrance.'

'It's disgusting,' Nadine said.

'Of course it's disgusting. But it's still interesting because it worked with me. I have to admit that. Do you remember how charming I found him?'

'My mother found him charming, too.' Nadine's voice had sunk to a mournful whisper. She was thinking about Mrs Blunt's end.

'It's one's inner beauty that Corrigan detects. It's one's inner beauty that he wants to nurture – that's what sets him apart from other men.'

'Please, stop talking about him, Sabrina. The whole subject is making me feel ill.'

'But if you don't examine his techniques, Nadine, you will never be able to understand what happened to your mother. I don't believe that Corrigan is psychic like he claims. But I think he has quite a cunning flare for nosing out all one's most vulnerable little areas of self-blame and guilt. He finds these areas in every single person that he tackles. Corrigan goes straight for the soft underbelly.'

Sabrina was wearing none of the high-fashion make-up she once used to wear. She'd scraped her blonde hair behind her ears and she was wearing shabby denim overalls. She was enjoying her new role as student and Nadine noticed there was something self-conscious in the way she obviously enjoyed being dressed for the part. Yet, she still made her conventional student's attire seem like some new stylish and deliberately simplistic fashion.

'Once Corrigan has found the soft underbelly,' Sabrina continued, 'that's where Corrigan mounts the full force of his attack. Once he'd built me up, Nadine, he then proceeded to smash me down. At first, I was made to feel so rare, so gifted, but then it turned out that I was just frittering all my talents away. Once he'd made me face this nasty truth, very humbly, very reasonably, Corrigan started to clobber me with his own example. He really started to kick me with his crippled legs. And down I went in front of him. He soon had me writhing on the ground. And once Corrigan had got me down, Nadine, that's when he kicked me the hardest. He kicked me with his infirmity, his love of literature, his devotion to the disabled, in particular his Christ-like loyalty to his friend, Rupert Sinclair. Do you know that Corrigan made me feel such an ignoble and ignorant slug of a person, that I only wanted to go chasing after his wheelchair – I only wanted to shower him with every penny of my earnings!'

'Oh, can't you stop this, Sabrina. I told you I can't bear it.'

'But I'm doing it for your sake, Nadine. If you refuse to examine any of his tactics, I think you'll be devastated when you read your mother's will.'

'You think my mother has left everything to Corrigan, don't you, Sabrina?'

'I'm afraid that I think it's highly probable. But it won't be such a tragedy. Under the circumstances I'm sure you can contest it. But I think it may still be a great shock to you if you find out that she has made him her sole beneficiary. I'm only telling you my impressions of the way he operated because I want you to understand that if the worst has happened, the money was never really left to Corrigan. She really only intended it to go to the disabled.'

Sabrina ordered herself a spaghetti bolognese.

'*La signorina?*' the waiter asked, looking at Nadine.

'*La signorina non fa bene,*' Sabrina announced firmly in her bad Italian. '*La signorina*, non well. *La signorina*, non eat today . . . *Comprende?*'

The waiter seemed bemused. He looked at Nadine suspiciously. Sabrina eventually managed to make him go away.

'Did you know that Corrigan was with my mother when she died?' Nadine asked her friend in choked emotional tones.

'No. I certainly didn't know that. I thought he'd gone back to London.'

'That's what he wanted us all to think. But Mrs Murphy says that he was with her. He never got her a doctor . . .'

Nadine suddenly started to cry and Sabrina felt she'd been cruel to take such a flippant approach to all Corrigan's chicaneries.

'How does Mrs Murphy know that he was with her? Was she there with him too?'

'I don't know how she knows. I don't know anything. Mrs Murphy may be in league with Corrigan – that's what I find so terrifying. I don't know what I ought to do, Sabrina. Should I go straight to the police? If I find out that Corrigan killed her, I don't think I'll be able to survive it. All last night, I kept having these horrible images. I kept seeing my poor mother . . .' Nadine buried her face in her napkin. She knew that all the other people in the restaurant were staring at her.

'But your mother may have died of natural causes,' Sabrina said.

'But why didn't Corrigan call a doctor?'

'How do we know he never called a doctor?'

'She had an autopsy you know, and it seems that she died at midnight. Mrs Murphy only called a doctor when she found her in the morning.'

'That doesn't sound too promising. Did you get the autopsy report from the doctor?'

'No, I didn't.' Nadine looked ashamed. 'I let Justin deal with all that. I felt in such a strange, stunned mood, I couldn't face all the gruesome details.'

'But was there any need for an autopsy? That seems sinister in itself. Surely that must mean there was some suspicion of foul play?'

Sabrina was starting to get as agitated as her friend. She could accept that Mrs Blunt had been defrauded, but she found the idea that she might have been murdered insufferable.

'No, I think that the autopsy was routine. If someone's found dead on their own, they often hold one. But she wasn't alone, and only you and I and Mrs Murphy know that.'

'All the same, the autopsy report must have been satisfactory – otherwise the coroner would not have accepted it,' Sabrina said.

'I suppose so,' Nadine said. Her fever had returned and she felt unable to think very clearly. Sabrina saw that her friend was starting to crack under all the strain of the revelations that had followed the death of her mother. She decided that Nadine should go home and try and rest. She didn't feel that she ought to go to the police and tell them her suspicions until she had first acquainted herself with more of the facts. She realised that Nadine was much too ill to do this. Sabrina decided to go down to the country and try and get more of the truth from Mrs

Murphy. She would also speak to the doctor who'd attended Mrs Blunt and she'd ask him for a detailed account of the findings of the autopsy. Once she'd armed herself with more information, Sabrina felt she would be in a much better position to advise Nadine what her next move should be.

The next day she went down to the country to see Mrs Murphy.

Nadine stayed in bed, and before Sabrina left she spoke to her on the telephone.

'I really shouldn't let you miss your classes. I feel so awful. I'm just lying here in bed worrying. I've got nothing important to do. It's me who should be talking to Mrs Murphy.'

'You're not very well, Nadine. Don't put on one of your brave faces with me. You can keep them for Justin.'

'Do you think I'm going mad, Sabrina? I can't face seeing Mrs Murphy. She's always despised me because she thought I was nasty to my mother. And then I don't know how much one ought to trust her. Do you think she's related to Corrigan? Since I went to that pancake house, I feel suspicious of everybody. I keep thinking about that awful old prostitute who was frying pancakes in that stinking kitchen. You don't think she could be Corrigan's mother?'

'She may well be Corrigan's mother, Nadine. I don't know why it's taken you so long to grasp that.'

'But do you think that Mrs Murphy is Corrigan's great-aunt or something? I don't trust anyone any more. My mother was such a clean, good person. I can't bear the idea that she got mixed up with people like that. Do you think she was killed by Corrigan, Sabrina? When I shut my eyes, I see Corrigan. He's sitting there in his chair. He's very urbane, and he's quoting Pascal or something. Then he gets out of his chair and he goes for her. Are you sure I'm not going mad, Sabrina?'

'I really can't believe that Corrigan would do a thing to hurt your mother, Nadine. When I saw them together, I felt that his attitude towards her was extremely protective.'

'But then you fell for Corrigan, Sabrina. You were very impressed by the noble cripple. He made her redecorate a hospital that didn't exist. He ruined her house by installing medical equipment that he didn't need. Do you call that very protective, Sabrina?'

Sabrina found it difficult to argue with Nadine. She wanted to calm her friend, rather than fan her hysteria, but secretly she was starting to wonder what Corrigan was capable of.

'I'm so interested in Corrigan,' she said. 'I'm so interested by his intense high-mindedness. I've noticed that high moral fervour often seems to go hand-in-hand with extreme corruption. Even Coco sees himself as a very spiritual person. He feels he has a purer vision of life than anyone else does.'

'Oh, surely Coco can't feel that,' Nadine said.

'But I assure you that Coco has a very elevated vision of his own sensibilities. He's always had leanings towards the mystical. In the hospital he became very thick with a very mentally disturbed patient who was a mystic. When I met this man, I thought he was a real creep – but Coco was very impressed by him. This lunatic told Coco that reality was an illusion – that you had to shatter it to find a greater meaning. He made all Coco's mystical leanings much worse.'

'Where is Coco now?' Nadine asked.

'Coco is back in my flat. Unfortunately that's not an illusion, although I very much wish it was.'

'But how long is he going to stay with you?'

'I've told him that he can only stay for a couple of weeks. He's trying to blackmail me, of course. He says he'll make another suicide attempt if I kick him out. But I've reached a point when I feel that I'll have to take the risk of that. He's immensely time-consuming, like all people who have nothing to do. He hates me going to my classes. He says I'm embracing corrupt Western values, that I ought to be looking inwards, that I ought to be trying to find myself. But that's exactly what I don't want to do. If I was to find myself, I know I'd get a very nasty shock . . .'

'You've got to get out of Coco's clutches, Sabrina. He sounds nearly as bad as Corrigan.'

'Oh, Coco is much worse than Corrigan. He's certainly much more destructive. All Corrigan's lofty exhortations were really rather beneficial in their effects. And then Coco isn't at all handy around the house like Corrigan. If one takes a superficial view of Corrigan's behaviour without looking too closely at his motivations, he seems rather a paragon.'

Sabrina was again starting to sound flippant and Nadine tried to make her be serious. 'You won't forget to speak to my mother's doctor, Sabrina. I feel so ashamed that I never asked to see the autopsy report. I wouldn't even go to the coroner's hearing. I made Justin go. I simply couldn't bear the whole thing. I hated the idea that she'd had an autopsy. I found it sickening. I wanted to pretend that none of it had happened.'

'I think that's quite natural, Nadine.'

Sabrina promised Nadine that she would contact the doctor. She would cross-question Mrs Murphy and try and find out if she had any more information about Mrs Blunt's death which she was withholding. And while she was in the country, she wanted Nadine to speak to her mother's solicitor and find out the contents of the will.

'I think we've got to know the worst,' she said 'Otherwise we don't know how to proceed.'

Nadine agreed to speak to Mr Hicks, although she still dreaded doing so. She assumed that she could contest the will if she'd been disinherited by her mother. Her dread of hearing its contents did not spring from mercenary considerations. It was the symbolic significance of the will that threatened her. She was terrified that she would be given proof in cold and final legal language that her mother had loved only Corrigan.

19

When Sabrina got back from the country, as usual she met her friend in the restaurant. She found Nadine sitting alone at her table and she had a strange, stunned expression on her face.

'I spoke to Mr Hicks while you were away,' she said. 'He read me my mother's will.'

'And what did it say?' Sabrina hastily ordered herself some wine. She was very frightened of hearing the answer.

'My mother has left all her money and her property to be divided between myself and Mrs Murphy. She hasn't left a penny to Corrigan.'

Sabrina whistled. Nadine continued to sit there looking stunned. The information was so unexpected that for a moment neither of them could think of anything to say.

'It all fits,' Sabrina said. 'It's all rather like a jigsaw. But now all the pieces I've learnt from Mrs Murphy are starting to fit.'

'I cried after I'd finished speaking to Mr Hicks,' Nadine told her.

'But why did you cry? Surely you don't mind Mrs Murphy being included in the will? Aren't you relieved that your mother left nothing to Corrigan?'

'Of course, that's why I cried. I cried with relief. But I don't understand the whole thing. I don't think I've ever felt more confused.'

Sabrina asked to be allowed to describe her visit to Mrs Murphy. If Nadine would just listen to what she had to tell her, she thought everything would become more clear. She'd gone to see Mrs Murphy in her council house. Her sons, Seamus and Patrick, had both been there.

'The whole atmosphere in Mrs Murphy's home was really very strange,' Sabrina said. 'They'd got all the blinds down and they'd turned the place into a house of mourning. I can't tell you how muted they'd made it. Her sons were tiptoeing around, bringing Mrs Murphy cups of tea. "She's still taking it very hard," one of them whispered to me as I came through the door. Both her boys seemed very worried about her.'

Sabrina said that Mrs Murphy had been sitting in a chair beside her stove with a huge black shawl over her head. 'You've never seen such a desolate Mother McCree. Mrs Murphy looked like a statue of grief incarnate. She embarrassed me when I first arrived. I felt myself to be an intruder. But her sons seemed glad to see me. "The shock's just hit her," one of them said. They seemed to feel it would be good for her to talk to someone. I liked her sons. I found them rather attractive.'

'Oh, really, Sabrina,' Nadine said quite sharply. 'Don't tell me you are planning to move Mrs Murphy's sons into your flat. I really wouldn't put it past you.'

'I'd rather have Mrs Murphy's sons than Coco. By the way, he's leaving, Nadine. I really can't believe my good luck. He's suddenly decided he wants to go back to Algeria to live with his mother. The poor woman . . . But I can't feel sorry for her. She produced Coco, so I feel she's got to live with him.'

'What did Mrs Murphy tell you?' Nadine asked. She was very relieved to hear that Coco was leaving, but at that moment she only wanted information that pertained to Corrigan and her mother.

Sabrina said that she'd told Mrs Murphy that Nadine suspected that Corrigan might somehow have been responsible for Mrs Blunt's death. Mrs Murphy had seemed really outraged by the suggestion.

'How dare Mrs Murphy seem outraged? She always knew that Corrigan was a complete impostor and she kept very quiet about it. Maybe she's doing the same thing about my mother's death.'

Sabrina didn't think this was true. Mrs Murphy had only seemed outraged by the suggestion because it implied that she'd not protected Mrs Blunt sufficiently.

'I don't think Mrs Murphy protected her at all,' Nadine said. 'She certainly ought to feel guilty. How dare she dress up in a black shawl and pull down her blinds. It's really nauseating.'

'Mrs Murphy felt she was protecting your mother by allowing Corrigan to move into the house. She was convinced she was going to die of loneliness and grief. So when Corrigan came rolling along and she saw how much happier he seemed to be able to make her, Mrs Murphy decided that it could only be to your mother's advantage if Corrigan was always around. As Mrs Murphy loathed Corrigan, it was quite unselfish that she didn't try and expose him.'

'As things have turned out, it wasn't to my mother's advantage at all.'

Sabrina said that she couldn't agree with her. She thought Mrs Murphy had been absolutely right. Corrigan had given Mrs Blunt's life a purpose. He might very well have even prolonged it. Her last days had certainly been much happier than they would have been without him. She'd squandered a lot of money on him, but Sabrina took the same view as Mrs Murphy, that the money was of very little importance as compared with her well-being.

'But what if Corrigan was always planning to bump her off so that he could inherit her fortune? I refuse to believe that Corrigan was very concerned with her well-being.'

'Mrs Murphy insists that he had no such plans. She maintains that he became very fond of your mother. "Corrigan was a man that got caught in his own web", that's how she described it.'

'But Mrs Murphy is just a sentimental old peasant. We've got no evidence at all that Corrigan was particularly fond of my mother.'

Sabrina said that Mrs Murphy realised that he'd become very attached to Mrs Blunt when she noticed that he was starting to become insanely jealous of the Colonel.

'But that's such a crazy idea of Mrs Murphy's. How can anyone be jealous of a dead person?'

'Oh, I'm sure it's quite common, Nadine. From what I gather from Mrs Murphy, Corrigan was very childish. Apparently he would often throw a tantrum when she went off to the graveyard. He was always trying to get her to take down your father's photographs. He used to pretend that he was doing it for her sake. He'd give her lectures explaining that he felt it was unhealthy that she still lived in the past. But Mrs Murphy insists he was really wildly jealous of the Colonel.'

Nadine remembered the savage expression that she'd seen on his face when she'd gone down to the grave with her mother.

'Don't you understand, Nadine, Corrigan would have liked to feel that he had total power over her. But he was never going to have that. He could never compete with the Colonel. You almost have to feel sorry for him. He couldn't have had a more threatening and powerful rival. There isn't a man on earth who could really compete with the Colonel – not as he was seen through the eyes of your mother.'

Nadine had to agree that this was true.

'Mrs Murphy says that your mother never took the slightest notice when Corrigan tried to prevent her from going down to the grave. He'd follow her and he'd watch her, and do his best to make her feel foolish and self-conscious, but it never had the slightest effect on her. Corrigan could take her money and her furniture, but he could never take the Colonel away from her. Apparently he knew this quite well and he didn't like it at all.'

'But she seemed obsessed with Corrigan,' Nadine said.

'I think she had a very happy relationship with him. You should be grateful for that, Nadine. Mrs Murphy was describing their life together and she made it sound rather idyllic with all the champagne and the poetry readings by the fireside. But I don't think that your mother ever felt that Corrigan came up to the Colonel.'

'But what about all the lies that he was telling her, what about the money he was taking? I don't see anything so idyllic about that.'

'But don't you see that he repaid her, Nadine? What he gave her was priceless. Does it really matter that he never really had a hospital, just as long as she got such great pleasure from working for it?'

'But that's so cynical.'

'I think it's the truth.' Sabrina shrugged.

'I see her end as very sad and humiliating,' Nadine said.

Sabrina insisted that she didn't see it like that at all. Mrs Blunt's situation would have been very much sadder if Corrigan hadn't come along. She told Nadine that she'd been thinking about her mother's life and she'd come to the conclusion that, in a sense, Mrs Blunt had also always pretended to be crippled, she'd put on an act of helplessness in order to please the Colonel.

'Mrs Murphy was very frightened of Corrigan at the beginning,' Sabrina said. 'She very soon found out that he wasn't really disabled. Her sons had seen him around in the local pubs and bars and they'd also seen him driving around.'

'In the little invalid car that my mother gave him?'

'Not in his invalid car – I don't think he made much use of that once he was out of sight of your mother. He always had a regular estate car and he used to park it in the village.'

'It gets worse and worse,' Nadine said.

'Corrigan was banned from a lot of bars and pubs because he used to get into such vicious fights,' Sabrina said. 'He was obviously quite a dangerous character, but once Mrs Murphy realised he'd never do a thing to harm your mother, she wasn't worried about him at all.'

'What made her so sure that he'd never harm her? I think that stupid woman was taking quite a risk.'

'You'll laugh when you hear this, but once Mrs Murphy saw that Corrigan was becoming wildly jealous of the Colonel, she felt your mother was quite safe with Corrigan. You see, it seems that he always had a terror that she might suddenly die and go off and join the Colonel. Corrigan started to become very dependent on her. That's what you've got to understand, Nadine. When he kept exploiting her, he was testing her to see how much she cared for him. He was always trying to find out

260

how much she'd be prepared to do for him. Apparently he used to get her to take him out for walks, Nadine, and she'd push his chair down the lanes, and he'd let her wheel him along while he ate chocolates from a paper bag. He wasn't getting any money from making her do that.'

'It's so awful to think that she was prepared to do almost anything that Corrigan wanted.'

'That's not true, Nadine. She was prepared to do what Corrigan wanted – but only if it suited her. He could throw his childish tantrums, but he couldn't stop her going to the graveyard. And remember that she wasn't at all prepared to leave Corrigan one penny in her will.'

'Her will is certainly very peculiar. I don't understand it at all.'

Sabrina agreed that she'd have found it hard to understand Mrs Blunt's intentions if she hadn't spoken to Mrs Murphy. 'She doesn't believe that Corrigan ever really wanted to inherit your mother's fortune. Maybe he did at the beginning, but once he got to know her, apparently he started to enjoy their relationship just as much as she did. He only wanted it to continue. After all, he had everything that he wanted. He could disappear whenever he liked on the pretext that he was fund-raising. He lived in luxury and he also had total freedom.'

'But I'm convinced he'd have preferred my mother to die. If she was dead, he could get her house – he could get her trust funds. I'm sure that Corrigan thought he was going to get them.'

'But Nadine, he already had your mother's house. He already had unlimited use of her trusts. Corrigan didn't want an empty house. I think he only really liked her house because she made it so pleasant for him when he came there. Mrs Murphy insists that he never wanted her to die, Nadine. If she died, he thought she'd join the Colonel and he'd lose her to your father for eternity.'

'I'm sure that's absolute rubbish. I don't believe that Corrigan would have minded one little bit if she joined my father – not if she left him her fortune.'

Sabrina looked at her friend with her quizzical eyebrows raised. Her expression was mildly exasperated. 'But it was much more complicated than that, Nadine. Mrs Murphy thinks that he was rather in love with her.'

'I know Mrs Murphy thinks that. But remember that Mrs Murphy seems almost half-witted.'

'I didn't find her half-witted, Nadine. On the subject of Corrigan, I found her rather shrewd. You know that she listened to every word that passed between Corrigan and your mother. She felt that it was her duty to eavesdrop so that she could keep abreast of all the games that he was playing.'

'It doesn't surprise me that Mrs Murphy is an eavesdropper. It's all part of her general dishonesty.'

'But she overheard some interesting things that throw some light on Corrigan's relationship with your mother. Apparently your mother was perfectly aware that he had a pathological terror that she might die and go off to a longed-for reunion with the Colonel. She used to play on this little power that she had over him. "When I join darling Tom," she would say. She'd make these remarks sound very innocent. But she obviously knew Corrigan hated her talking like that. It apparently made him very angry. Your mother seems to have been quite a tease.'

'I don't believe any of this, Sabrina. I don't believe she had any power over him. I think she was his pathetic victim.'

'I don't see that she was his victim. I think she got as much from Corrigan as he got from her. Remember that he could have left her alone for months. He could have told her he was in Scotland fund-raising. She'd have quietly accepted it. She'd have still sent him all the money that he demanded. But he must have liked being with her. Apparently he spent more and more time with her. Towards the end he hardly left her side.'

'Corrigan may have hastened her end – that's what I find so terrifying. You are getting so sentimental about him, Sabrina. You are getting just as bad as Mrs Murphy. If he loved her so much, why did he feed her such a pack of lies?'

'Lots of men lie to women they love. It's quite often been known, Nadine.'

'But, Sabrina, the point you're making is ridiculous. Most

men are not sitting around in wheelchairs pretending that they're crippled.'

'I think a lot of men are just as crippled as Corrigan and pretending that they're not. They can do much more harm than he did.'

'But we still don't know what harm he may have done her, Sabrina. Did you get the autopsy report from the doctor?'

Sabrina had got the report. It established that Mrs Blunt had suffered two heart attacks. The first one had been mild and it had occurred about two hours before she'd had the massive coronary that had killed her. She had almost certainly recovered consciousness after her first attack.

'Oh, my God!' Nadine said. 'I'm afraid I see the hand of Corrigan.'

'No, it's all right, Nadine. You mustn't get upset. Just let me explain.'

Apparently Mrs Murphy had the theory that Mrs Blunt had suffered her first heart attack in the dining-room. She'd found her reading spectacles and a wine glass lying in the middle of the floor and she found it peculiar that she'd dropped them there. She was certain she must have fallen down. Corrigan had presumably been in the room with her. They'd finished their game pie. The remnants were lying on their plates. They'd obviously both drunk a lot of claret.

'He killed her by making her drink like that,' Nadine said bitterly.

Sabrina went on to tell her that Mrs Murphy believed that Mrs Blunt had suddenly dropped down on the floor – that Corrigan had got out of his chair and picked her up and carried her up to bed.

'But that's awful, Sabrina!' Nadine gave a little gasp of horror. 'If Corrigan picked her up and carried her up the stairs and she'd recovered consciousness, she must have realised that he wasn't crippled. I'm sure the shock would have been quite enough to bring on her second coronary.'

'No, it's much stranger than that, Nadine. Mrs Murphy thinks that your mother had known for quite a while that Corrigan was only pretending to be crippled. Obviously she didn't realise at the beginning, but once she found out she never let him know that she'd discovered his trick.'

'But my mother must have been out of her mind, Sabrina! If she knew, why on earth did she let him stay on in her house? Why did she go on growing vegetables for the disabled? Why did she go on buying them furniture? She couldn't have known. I refuse to believe it.'

'Mrs Murphy is convinced that towards the end she knew about Corrigan and she didn't mind a bit.'

'But she would have to be insane not to mind.'

'Well, not really, Nadine. I think she probably realised that she didn't have very long. She enjoyed her farming. She enjoyed going to furniture auctions. I think she enjoyed the idea of lavishing her money on Corrigan.'

'But that makes her worse than a sucker. It makes her a masochist!'

'No, it doesn't, Nadine. If she'd let Corrigan know she'd discovered he was a fraud, she'd have had to have thrown him out. She'd have had to have tried to prosecute him for fraud, or something. She obviously didn't want to do any of that. She'd have lost Corrigan if she'd admitted that she knew he was a bogus cripple. Mrs Murphy saw no sign that she suffered at all from her discovery. But I think she'd have suffered if she'd lost Corrigan, Nadine. You can't deny that's true.'

Nadine wanted to know Mrs Murphy's reasons for thinking that her mother had seen through Corrigan's fraudulent infirmity.

'She would say funny things to Mrs Murphy. She'd say, "I heard footsteps on the gravel last night. Do you think we had a marauder?" And then she'd give a little smile. I imagine she was trying to stop Mrs Murphy worrying about her relationship with Corrigan and she was too shy to bring the whole thing out in the open. So she'd only give her oblique little hints. It sounds as if she wanted Mrs Murphy to know that she was in control of the situation and there was no need for her to be concerned.

'But her little hints don't sound very convincing. They don't really prove that she knew what Corrigan was up to.'

'But Mrs Murphy tested your mother one day. She seems to love doing tests. They seem to give her the greatest satisfaction.'

'What was her test?'

'You know how Mrs Murphy always floods the kitchen whenever she cleans the floor? Apparently she worked late one evening and just before she left she washed it down. I imagine it must have been like one of those disaster areas that have to receive relief funds from the nation. Anyway, it seems that it took hours for the linoleum to dry out. Corrigan must have got hungry in the night and he must have tiptoed out of the drawing-room. In the morning, Mrs Murphy found footprints on the kitchen floor. They were going towards the refrigerator. They were quite distinct. She decided to show them to your mother to see how she'd react.'

'How did she react?'

'She looked at the footprints, and she was cool as a cucumber. She didn't seem alarmed by them. She didn't seem at all surprised. "Oh, we must have had a prowler, Mrs Murphy," she said. "How lucky he hasn't taken anything." '

'Was that all she said?'

'That was all she said.'

'Maybe my mother thought there'd really been a prowler.'

'I very much doubt it, Nadine. I don't think prowlers usually prowl in bare feet.'

Nadine could think of no reply. She looked even more stunned, as if she was unable to assimilate all this startling information.

'I'm going to be like Corrigan,' Sabrina said to her. 'I'm going to insist you drink something. I don't care if you eat, but I insist you have some wine.'

Nadine nodded. She'd become very passive, childishly eager to carry out the wishes of her dominant friend.

'But what about my mother's death?' she said after she'd gulped down a glass of Chianti. 'Corrigan saw her fall down on the dining-room floor. Corrigan picked her up and carried her up to the bedroom, but he never thought of making a telephone call to me – he never thought of getting a doctor. He must have known my mother was gravely ill. She should have been rushed to a hospital in Salisbury. You seem to have been seduced by that ghastly Mrs Murphy, Sabrina. Neither of you want to admit that Corrigan was a cold-blooded murderer.'

'Corrigan was not at all cold-blooded, Nadine. Not at the end – not when he saw your mother was dying.'

'How do you know?'

'Well, I'll admit that I don't know for certain. But I've got a lot of evidence from Mrs Murphy. All of it fits with my own intuition.'

'But how can you trust the evidence of a peculiar creature like Mrs Murphy?'

'I trust her evidence because she hated Corrigan so much, Nadine.'

'But maybe she didn't really hate him – maybe she was in collusion with him. Have you ever thought of that?'

'You're being paranoid about Mrs Murphy, Nadine. I really believe that she loathed him. Apparently he was always trying to poison your mother against her. He was always trying to make her get rid of her. He thought she might get wise to his game. He saw Mrs Murphy as a very serious threat.'

Nadine remembered how Corrigan had tried to persuade her that it was her duty to try and get Mrs Murphy fired. If it had really been Corrigan who had taken the ten pound note from her handbag, she felt she'd have been cruel and despicable when she'd upset her mother by insisting that Mrs Murphy was a thief.

'Corrigan seems to have given Mrs Murphy a very bad time. I think she was astonishingly patient with him. Not only did he hate her because he was frightened she might expose him, but he was jealous of her as well. He knew that your mother was very attached to her. He didn't want her to be fond of anyone but him.'

'Do you think that's why Corrigan was so nasty to me?'

Sabrina found this question childishly plaintive. 'Naturally Corrigan would have hated you,' she said quickly.

Nadine looked very relieved as if she saw it as an honour to be hated by this man.

'Mrs Murphy was only patient with him because she thought he was doing your mother so much good,' Sabrina said. 'And then I think she also knew that your mother was much stronger than she appeared, that she was much too loyal to get rid of her just to please Corrigan.'

'I really don't understand Corrigan,' Nadine said. 'How can he be so evil? He doesn't need to lead the corrupt life that he does. He's extremely good-looking. As you said, he could be a model or a movie star. He seems to be very intelligent. My mother thought he was a genius. Why does he want to make his living by battening on to a defenceless little person like my mother?'

'I've been thinking about Corrigan,' Sabrina said. 'I think he must be a character who wants to try and beat the system. He enjoys his own act. I don't think he'd be very keen to act out a script that was given him by anyone else. I'm certain that half the time that Corrigan was with your mother, he almost believed that he did very valuable work for the disabled. I think he must have half-believed it or he'd never have been so persuasive. And I'm sure he loved your mother admiring him for being so courageous and selfless and all that. I imagine that the more she admired him for having all the virtues he didn't have, the more he could start to feel he had them.'

'Corrigan may want to beat the system. But I'm going to do my best to see that the system beats him! I'm going to try and see that it beats him into a pulp!' Nadine spoke with such violence that it shocked Sabrina. She thought her friend sounded like an angry Colonel's daughter.

'I don't see there's any point in your trying to see that Corrigan gets his just deserts, Nadine. In the end, he did very little harm to anyone. You must only think of all the good he did your mother. I even think he did quite a lot of good to me.'

'But he didn't try and save her when she was dying. I still find that unforgivable. He was present at her death and he never reported it. I'm quite certain that's illegal. I'm really determined to get the police on to him. If they catch him, I want him put away for a very long time.'

'I feel that's rather futile, Nadine, and so does Mrs Murphy.

I don't think your mother would have wanted Corrigan prosecuted. You can't even say that he stole from her – not if she was happy to allow him to take whatever he wished.'

'But what about her death?'

'Corrigan's behaviour the night she died wasn't nearly as sinister as you imagine. He seems to have done everything he could for her – everything that she wanted.'

'How do we know she wanted to die without the chance of seeing a doctor?'

'She wrote Rupert Sinclair a letter, Nadine. She posted it only a few days before she died. Corrigan must have picked it up at the pancake house. He must have carried it back to the country. After your mother died, Mrs Murphy found it in her drawing-room – in the room she'd turned into Corrigan's bedroom. I think he must have left it there deliberately. He probably wanted you to see it. It may make you sad, Nadine. But in the end, it will make you feel better about her death.'

Sabrina fumbled in her handbag and she pulled out a letter written on flimsy notepaper.

Nadine took the letter. Her hand was shaking.

'Dear Rupert,' she read. She was chilled by the sight of her dead mother's ornate handwriting.

'I have something important to say to you – something that I want you to pass on to Corrigan. For quite a while, I have known that I am seriously ill. I have been to the doctor and I've been told that I have dangerously high blood pressure – that I am in grave danger of having a stroke. My heart is also in very bad condition. The doctor says that my chances are really very thin.

'I would like you to tell Corrigan that the idea of dying doesn't frighten me at all. I feel ready to go. I've had a very happy life and I would like to thank him for everything he did to make my last days so pleasant. His company meant a lot to me, and I'm also grateful for all the encouragement he gave me in so many directions. He certainly made my life as rich as he could. Please tell Corrigan that he was my wine and my walnuts.

'I have not told Nadine that I'm seriously ill. I have a horror of becoming a burden to her. The idea that I may have a stroke terrifies me. I'd like to go very swiftly. I only pray that my heart goes long before my brain. It would be so horrible to linger on like a vegetable. I can't think of anything worse.

I am particularly anxious that Corrigan should know my feelings on this subject. If I ever fall ill while he's in my house, I really do not want to be resuscitated. I don't want any medical attention. I just want to be allowed to go. I think I'm lucky to feel so resigned. I will just quote you a few lines to explain my state of mind.

'From too much love of living,
From hope and fear set free . . .'

'I won't finish the verse. I'm sure you know how it ends. If you don't know the next lines, Corrigan will tell you them. We've always enjoyed finishing each other's verses.

Yours sincerely,
Devina Blunt.'

'Oh, my God! It's the most pitiful letter,' Nadine said. Her eyes had filled with tears. 'How do those lines go on Sabrina?'

'I got hold of one of my English teachers. He looked them up for me. I knew you'd want to have them, Nadine.' Sabrina handed her another piece of paper and Nadine read the lines aloud.

'We thank with brief thanksgiving'
'Whatever gods there be
That no man lives forever,
That dead men rise up never;
That even the weariest river
Winds somewhere safe to sea.'

'It's pathetic,' Nadine said. 'It also seems quite demented the way that she went on writing to Rupert Sinclair even though she knew he didn't exist.'

269

'It was her little game with Corrigan. And she obviously wanted to play it out to the end. I think she was probably teasing him when she sent off this letter to Sinclair. But she obviously also felt very grateful to him. She could have teased him in a much more cruel way. She could have brought in something about joining the Colonel.'

'I wish that she'd sent a letter to me and not just written to Corrigan by way of Sinclair,' Nadine said.

'I don't think she'd have known what to say to you. There was really nothing you could do for her. There was nothing that she wanted you to do.'

'I suppose that's true. This letter certainly makes her wishes very plain.'

'And Corrigan respected them,' Sabrina said. 'You must be thankful for that. I think she was really very clever the way that she got the best she could out of him. In a way, he was perfect for her. She had a wonderful late-life flirtation with Corrigan, without any complications. Your mother could never have had a proper love affair with anyone. She wouldn't have wanted one. She'd have felt it was much too disloyal to the Colonel. So she must have been very glad of Corrigan's wheelchair. It allowed her to move him into her house without any fear of impropriety. She soon discovered he wasn't really crippled – but that didn't bother her at all. Just as long as he kept up the pretence that he was disabled, she was glad to go along with him.'

'But at the end he didn't keep up the pretence.'

'At the end I shouldn't think the pretence mattered very much to either of them. If your mother suddenly collapsed on the floor, like Mrs Murphy thinks she did, I would imagine that Corrigan was so horrified to see her lying in a little heap that he must have bounded out of his chair without giving a thought to his crippled legs. She aroused a very protective feeling in every one she met. Mrs Murphy certainly insists that she aroused it in Corrigan.'

'Corrigan stole her paintings, Sabrina. They were the last paintings she ever did. I'd have really liked to have had them. Corrigan wouldn't let her tell me that she'd taken up painting. I still don't really understand why.'

'Oh, yes, I heard Corrigan going on about that. He told your mother that you led such a frustrated housewife's existence that you'd get very jealous if you knew that she was having such a professional success.'

'But that was so cruel of Corrigan, Sabrina. I know my life is a boring one – but I'd never have resented her success.'

Sabrina felt that Nadine was wasting her energies by dwelling on old pieces of Corrigan's mischief. Now that it appeared that he'd done nothing to harm Mrs Blunt, she thought that Nadine should forget all about him and use the financial freedom that the will accorded her to improve her domestic situation.

'I'm determined to get the police to track down Corrigan – I really want those paintings back.'

Sabrina made no comment, but she thought that once again Nadine was misdirecting her energies. She was too tactful to tell her that she felt that Corrigan deserved the paintings. In a sense, they were his own creation for they would never have existed without him. Mrs Murphy had told her that Corrigan had noticed Mrs Blunt had a talent when he saw the wild flower illustrations she had done for the Colonel, and he had urged her to pursue it.

Sabrina suspected that he'd only taken the paintings because he wanted them as mementoes. They were certainly not the most valuable objects in Mrs Blunt's house. When he'd vanished that night, he could have taken what he wished.

'I keep begging you not to bother to go to the police,' she said. 'Even if you get Corrigan a life sentence, I can't see that it will make you any happier.' She thought it depressing that Nadine was obsessed with the idea of avenging her mother when there seemed to be nothing that should be avenged.

'When do you think my mother first found out that Corrigan was deceiving her?'

'I would imagine that she found out soon after he moved into the drawing-room,' Sabrina said. 'Once Corrigan started roaming round the house in the night, it couldn't have taken her very long. Those old houses have very delicate, creaky floorboards, and your mother may have been simple – but she wasn't deaf . . .'

'But why did Corrigan start roaming around? It seems such a mistake from his own horrible point of view?'

Sabrina agreed with her and she was silent for a moment while she thought about it. She then made a tentative suggestion. 'Maybe, in certain moods, Corrigan half-hoped your mother would discover that he wasn't the cripple that he was pretending to be. Maybe he sometimes felt a bit frustrated in the night, maybe he felt a bit of an idiot being always confined to his chair . . .'

'I wonder what Corrigan and my mother said to each other after he'd carried her up to her bed?' Nadine said.

'We'll never be certain, Nadine. But it must have been quite a surprise for Corrigan when she wasn't more startled by his legs. We know that he brought her up a bottle of champagne, and I imagine they carried on their usual flirtatious banter. Remember that neither of them knew that she had a very short time to go. The doctor told me that you can have a heart attack and not realise you've had one. Your mother probably felt quite normal once Corrigan had got her something to drink. I think he probably read some poems to her – Mrs Murphy found a book of verse by the bed. Corrigan may have kissed her, you know. It wouldn't surprise me. After all, it was the first time he was freed from his chair.'

'Oh, Sabrina! What an awful thought!' Nadine said.

'I don't find it so awful. After all, Corrigan is a very handsome fellow and we mustn't forget that. I think your mother had a very happy and frivolous end.'

Nadine couldn't understand Sabrina's point of view. She felt it was unserious and a little disrespectful to the memory of her mother. When they'd finished lunch and were getting up to go, she suddenly asked her friend one last question.

'There's something I want to know, Sabrina. If Corrigan gave my mother such a new lease of life – if he gave her so much to live for – why do you think she died?'

'Oh, Nadine,' Sabrina gave a little sigh of exasperation, 'that's really a hopeless question to ask me. I should imagine she was tired – I should imagine she was really very wearied, like the river in the poem she quoted. In the end, she may not have felt that the whole thing was quite enough for her. Remember it was a very strange life that she was leading – growing vegetables for non-existent cripples and drinking champagne with Corrigan.'

It was at six o'clock the very same evening that Justin, lounging in his chair, called to his wife to bring him a whisky and soda. Six o'clock was always his hour of relaxation and it was the time when he liked to make Nadine listen to his articles, which he would read in such awed and emotional tones that he often seemed humbled by his own creativity.

This evening she was spared any articles because Justin started to scold her for not having made any effort to get Corrigan prosecuted.

'You are such a funny, lazy character, darling,' he said. 'I can't believe that you haven't yet gone to the police and given them a report. Every minute that you waste gives Corrigan more of an opportunity to escape. He can change his name. He can go abroad . . .'

Nadine hated Justin knowing that Corrigan was not the cripple he'd pretended to be. She had tried to conceal this painful fact from him, and told him nothing about her visit to the pancake house. She still saw her mother's relationship with Corrigan as a very humiliating one and she continued to experience this humiliation as her own.

Mrs Murphy had let slip the secret. She'd assumed that Nadine would have told her husband about Corrigan's dishonourable activities. Justin had telephoned Mrs Murphy, anxious for details of Mrs Blunt's farm management. Mrs Murphy had blurted out some comment on Corrigan which had aroused his curiosity and he'd managed to pump quite a lot of information out of her. When he'd tried to discuss the matter with Nadine, she'd become extremely tight-lipped and reticent, pretending she felt the whole affair had very little importance.

Nadine had been quietly infuriated by the busybody telephone calls that her husband kept making to Mr Hicks and Mrs Murphy. He'd learnt the contents of the will before she had. He kept trying to acquaint himself with every detail of her mother's financial affairs, and she would have loved to have asked Mr Hicks to refuse to disclose any of the details to him, but shyness and pride prevented her from doing so. She was still hesitant to admit to the world that she felt only animosity and contempt for her husband.

She thought that Justin had been much too quick to track down her mother's Antwerp ebony cabinet. The moment that he'd heard the news of Mrs Blunt's death, he'd become obsessed by the idea that she might have bought some valuable items of furniture which she'd not had the time to dispose of.

Justin had heard of the existence of the cabinet when he'd gone down to the country to make the arrangements for his mother-in-law's funeral.

Mrs Murphy had made some passing reference to it and he'd immediately become sleuth-like in his determination to trace its whereabouts. After making many abortive telephone calls, he'd finally managed to find the address of a storage house in Salisbury where Mrs Blunt kept the antiques that she acquired in the country auctions until she had a sufficiently large load to make it worth her while to hire a furniture van that would transport them to London.

'That Dutch cabinet that your mother picked up – it's really quite a little gem,' Justin had said to his wife. 'Thank God, she never got round to sending it to Corrigan! It's a real collector's piece! What an eye that woman had! And she'd got other stuff in that storage house as well. Every single piece is worth a bomb, but that Dutch cabinet is unique. I don't think we should sell it right away. If we hang on to it, it can only go up in value.'

'I think we ought to keep your mother's house and use it at weekends,' Justin had said to her. 'It will be perfect for giving house parties. I've always thought we needed a place in the country. It will be fun having somewhere to invite all our friends. We can get Mrs Murphy to be the caretaker . . .'

Nadine couldn't bear the way that her husband seemed to feel that he'd automatically inherited Mrs Murphy just as he'd inherited the ebony Antwerp cabinet. He didn't seem to take in that Mrs Murphy was now a wealthy woman and she had no need to be Justin's caretaker.

'Corrigan really did us quite a good turn,' he'd informed Nadine. 'We lost on the roundabouts, but then we gained on the swings. Your mother wasted a tidy sum on his home for cripples and all that . . . But I think we've made it up with all the land she's left us, and those farm buildings are worth a packet . . .'

Nadine had marvelled that her husband seemed incapable of seeing that there was pathos in the reasons why she had acquired all the land that he was so greedily excited by. He only wanted to plunge at her mother's estate and reap the profits that it would accord him.

He looked very supercilious as he sat back in an armchair with his long legs stretched out in front of him and reproached her for not having taken any proceedings against Corrigan. Recently Nadine had wondered if his tallness was responsible for his lack of normal human responses. Maybe he didn't have a sufficient supply of blood in his long body for the necessary amount to reach his brain. She realised this thought was fanciful, but she required some kind of explanation for the way he trampled on her feelings by making it so plain that he regarded her dead mother as a winning lottery ticket.

'You've got to get off your arse, darling,' Justin said. 'You've really got to do something about that crook. I know that we've done quite well out of all Corrigan's trickeries, but that doesn't change the facts. The man is still a criminal and we have to think of his intentions. You can hardly pretend they were very honourable. A man like Corrigan shouldn't be allowed to be at large . . .'

As her husband instructed her to wreak legal vengeance on Corrigan, she had the peculiar feeling that goose pimples were rising on her neck, and with this prickling physical sensation came the realisation that she didn't care if Corrigan remained at large. It simply didn't matter. He'd extorted large sums of

275

money out of Mrs Blunt, but that didn't matter because her mother hadn't cared that they were being extorted. He'd given Mrs Blunt companionship in the last days of her life and Sabrina was right, his contribution had been priceless. He'd also given her mother a sense of her own potential which had given her great satisfaction and if it had come too late in Mrs Blunt's life to replace what she felt she'd lost through the death of the Colonel, that was not the fault of Corrigan.

It was her husband's rough and punitive attitude towards him that made it possible for Nadine to examine his role in a new perspective. As Mrs Blunt hadn't cared when she discovered that Corrigan was tricking her, Nadine couldn't see why she should be made to care. Certainly there was no reason for her husband to get so incensed by his behaviour.

As Nadine reacted against Justin's bossy, self-righteous approach to the whole affair, she was astonished to find herself taking an increasingly lenient view of Corrigan. She had never cared for Mrs Murphy's contention that ever since the Colonel's death, her mother had only one true objective, and that was 'to join him'. But Nadine suddenly felt that she had to accept this and she was therefore forced to admit that he had done everything possible to dissuade Mrs Blunt from her destructive course. He'd tried to make life fun for her, and to a point he had certainly succeeded. If Mrs Blunt's longing for oblivion had finally proved too strong for him, he had definitely fought against it with more resourcefulness than she herself had ever been able to muster. If her mother had seen the end of her life as a long slow journey towards a final reunion with the Colonel, Nadine had to admire her for having seized the opportunity to make that journey as pleasant as possible. Mrs Blunt had whiled away the hours most enjoyably. She had used Corrigan's ill-motivated encouragement to very constructive purposes. She'd grown to love driving, poetry, painting and farming, and in the tea-time of her life, she'd drunk champagne by the fire and flirted with Corrigan.

Now that Nadine admitted that no one could have turned Mrs Blunt from her relentless passage towards the death which she equated with reunion, she wondered whether all the attractions that Corrigan had presented to her mother might not have slightly delayed it. She realised she'd never know, and she felt that it didn't really matter. With a new fatalistic feeling that nothing really mattered, she experienced a lifting of some of her painful guilt that she'd been unable to be nicer to her mother. That, too, didn't seem to matter. Or if it did, it was too late to change the facts and she saw no point in tormenting herself over things which were irreversible.

Corrigan had been much more attuned to her mother's needs than she had been, and now that she had finally come to terms with this, she could see no point in trying to have him prosecuted. Even if some of his motives had been impure, he'd found ways to alleviate her mother's misery so that her last days on earth had been much less painful and lonely than they would have been if he'd not come wheeling up in his chair. Nadine suddenly agreed with Sabrina that she had to be very grateful to him for that. For this reason, she only wanted him to go free.

She suddenly wondered if Mrs Blunt had ever secretly laughed at Corrigan when she'd sat there giving sly little smiles as she wrote her letters to Rupert Sinclair. Had she really been laughing at her dissimulating crippled lodger? Corrigan had been a plaything for Mrs Blunt. It had suited her to have him around and all the time that Corrigan thought he was fooling her, she'd also been fooling him, for, as she played the innocent victim she'd encouraged him to become much more dependent on her naïve kindness than he had ever intended.

It suddenly occurred to Nadine that in the peculiar game that her mother had played with Corrigan, Mrs Blunt had probably always known that she was destined to be the winner. She'd always had the trump up her sleeve. She must have known it would not be very long before she went sailing out of life and left Corrigan crying, and whether he had shed genuine tears of grief as Mrs Murphy claimed, or whether his tears were bogus, Nadine could no longer see that it mattered. All that seemed interesting was the fact that he'd shed them.

'Why are you standing there with that stupid blank expression on your face?' Justin asked Nadine. He had no idea how many thoughts had been going through her head. She had decided that she wanted Corrigan to go free and with this decision had come the realisation that there was nothing to prevent her from freeing herself.

'I'm just going to see if the twins are all right,' she said.

'Of course they're all right. Don't worry about the twins. You ought to be getting on to the police. If they catch that crook, we might be able to get back a lot more of the furniture that your mother gave him – that's if he hasn't already disposed of it.'

'I'm going down to the playroom to see the twins,' she said firmly. She walked out of the door and closed it very quietly. She could have slammed it, but she didn't feel that histrionics befitted the situation. Her exit was as lacking in passion and drama as her marriage.

She went downstairs and told Felix and Roland to put their things in a suitcase, for she was taking them down to the country. As she'd always found it so difficult to talk to Justin, she felt it would be inappropriate to tell him she was leaving him. Her absence would have to speak for itself.

The twins were very well-behaved as she drove down to Wiltshire. Usually they fought in the car and made the journey seem hellish. She wondered if they'd sensed that this was no ordinary trip.

It was dark when she arrived at her mother's house, and her headlights illuminated the dreaded ramp. She found, to her surprise, that it no longer dismayed her as it used to. Even Corrigan's unaesthetic bathroom didn't bother her. Now that she'd accepted that all his effects had been beneficial to her mother, the traces he'd left behind him no longer seemed threatening and sinister.

She went into the house through the back door and entered the kitchen. It was very clean, but she found it cheerless. She suddenly realised what a bustling, lively centre Mrs Murphy had once made it.

The house was cold. She lit a fire in the dining-room and opened a bottle of champagne that she found in the refrigerator. The house seemed too silent. The twins had run outside and were playing somewhere out in the darkness. A dog barked in the distance and she was very glad to hear it. She found it strange but pleasant to feel there was so much land around her. It was very odd to know she owned it. She wondered whether she would enjoy running the farm. She wondered whether she would be very lonely living in the country with the twins spending most of the day at school.

As she sipped her champagne by the fire, she could understand what her mother must have felt when she was alone in this isolated house. Nadine suddenly wondered whether she would really mind should she hear a chair crashing up the ramp, rattling and clanging as it announced the arrival of Corrigan.